When Demons Float

Other books in this series:

Where Drowned Things Live: A Kristin Ginelli Mystery
Wipf and Stock, 2017

Every Wickedness: A Kristin Ginelli Mystery
Wipf and Stock, 2017

When Demons Float

A Kristin Ginelli Mystery

SUSAN THISTLETHWAITE

RESOURCE *Publications* · Eugene, Oregon

WHEN DEMONS FLOAT
A Kristin Ginelli Mystery

Resource Publications
An Imprint of Wipf and Stock Publishers
199 W. 8th Ave., Suite 3
Eugene, OR 97401

www.wipfandstock.com

PAPERBACK ISBN: 978-1-5326-9625-1
HARDCOVER ISBN: 978-1-5326-9626-8
EBOOK ISBN: 978-1-5326-9627-5

Manufactured in the U.S.A.   09/04/19 for my grandchildren

Thus Satan talking to his neerest Mate
With Head up-lift above the wave, and Eyes
That sparkling blaz'd, his other Parts besides
Prone on the Flood, extended long and large
Lay floating many a rood, in bulk as huge
As whom the Fables name of monstrous size . . .
—JOHN MILTON, *PARADISE LOST*, BOOK I (192-197)[1]

1. John Milton, *Paradise Lost*, Book I, 192-197, Thomas H. Luxon, ed., *Milton Reading Room*. Accessed July 23, 2019. https://www.dartmouth.edu/~milton/reading_room/pl/book_1/text.shtml

Contents

Preface

H uman beings do not live in a perfect paradise, a Garden of Eden if you will. Instead, people live between the love that we sometimes name Heaven and the hate that we often call Hell.

Over centuries, human beings have come to make these forces of love and hate into characters, such as Angels who represent love, and Satan and Demons who are the forces of hate. The struggle between love and hate, between our "better angels" and the temptation to sin and evil, can be considered the human story in this world.

I cited a short passage on a previous page from John Milton's *Paradise Lost*, a 17th century epic poem that is loosely based on the beginning of the biblical book of Genesis and the story of how human beings get kicked out of the Garden of Eden (the "Fall").

When Milton begins his classic poem, Satan has already rebelled against God, and he and his minions are cast out of heaven and thrown into an abyss. But, even God can't keep Satan, and the Demons who follow him, down for long. I took the title of this novel from the few lines I quote where both Satan and his "mate," the arch demon Beelzebub, fall into a burning lake. But, instead of drowning, Satan lifts his head above a wave and talks to Beelzebub and they float "prone on the Flood."

Whether this is what Milton intended, or not, my interpretation of this striking scene is that you can't keep a Demon or Satan down for long. Just like Milton shows, they float back up again and go on to create chaos in the world.

One of the main ways Satan sows chaos in the world is by lying to Eve and convincing her to disobey God. This, in my view, is an accurate way to describe how Satan operates for, as the Christian scriptures say, Satan is "a liar and the father of lies." (John 8:44)

Lying is becoming normalized in the United States. Just calling that out doesn't seem to be enough, so I decided to write a work of fiction that could show what happens in a community when hate takes over. This novel explores what happens when some people are so deluded by the falsehood that their race or their religion is superior that they will commit violence and even murder to protect that lie. These people are often called white supremacists or neo-Nazis.

To write this work of fiction, I needed to do research on how white supremacists seduce people into believing the lie of white supremacy. I used public library computers for this research with anonymous login numbers. In the novel, my main character uses identity-masking software for her online probing into the white supremacist communications, but I have been made aware that this software is not foolproof and I do not recommend you use that method. These are dangerous extremists and you really don't want to have them know who you are.

In the novel, I have reproduced chat room dialogue among the white supremacists mirroring some of the exchanges I found in these Internet excursions, but I have coded their language. These extremists use the most crude, even foul words to denigrate and demean those whom they consider inferiors. I made a decision that I would not help them in that awful work, but instead indicate what they say by coding it. For example, these chat room dialogues routinely refer to women by a crass term that means their vaginal area, but I have rendered that C***s. The racism in these chat rooms is hideous and very repetitious. I refuse to reproduce those words, and instead render these references as N*****s or other terms you will recognize despite the codes.

I chose this method of rendering their fictional online communications because I refuse to help them do their dirty, demonic work. You, as the reader, will get the sense of what they are up to without the assault of the full words themselves. As a writer, I know words have power and I believe as writer and reader we should respect that.

I became conscious, as I was researching this novel, how much this online white supremacist rhetoric fed on itself, drawing people in and over lines that they would not have ordinarily crossed unless they were tempted into it.

As a theologian, I came to realize this was the very definition of the demonic, the tempting forces that prey on human beings, drawing them in and down into the depths of depravity. Indeed, I ended up drawing on classical theologians such as Thomas Aquinas more than contemporary ones for mapping how the demonic actually works. I do not agree with Aquinas on demons having an ultimate, divine purpose, but when he is describing how demons go about their business, I felt he was often spot on.

The demonic is very real in our time, and I have given it one of its names, white supremacy. As Jesus knew, if you call a Demon by its right name, you can cast it out. (Mark 5:1-20). Now, one novel is not going to do that, but together, if we call the Demon of white supremacy by its right name, we can greatly reduce its power.

Acknowledgments

The University of Chicago is, of course, a real place, but no people, events, or even structures described in this work of fiction are real, with the exception of Rockefeller Chapel. I do also refer to the well-publicized struggles over "political correctness" at the university. The latter forms the backdrop for one scene.[1]

While the events depicted in this novel are fictional, sadly enough, colleges and universities around the country are being subjected to attacks by white supremacists in various ways. In my view, this is an assault on the very purpose of higher education. One of my main reasons for creating this work of fiction, therefore, and locating it on what could literally be one of dozens of university campuses, was to allow the reader to see the destructive nature of this kind of extremism and realize how difficult it is to counter it.

On a positive note, I would like to acknowledge my husband, Dr. J. Richard Thistlethwaite, Jr. for his unfailing support of all my writing, and for his willingness to put up with being asked numerous questions. I would like to thank my sons James Thistlethwaite, Doug Thistlewolf, and Bill Thistlethwaite, and our extended family, for their love and support. I particularly need to thank Bill and his son Rowan for technical advice on how kids can get around parental controls on electronic devices.

I would like to thank Rev. Nathan Dannison for his insight into how white supremacists recruit young, white males online through the chat rooms of violent video games. I have incorporated that idea into the novel with his permission. In addition, Rev. Dannison, and his work to try to prevent the recruitment of young, white males into white supremacy, and get them out, is the inspiration for a pastor character in the novel.

Thanks need to go out to Rev. Jane Fisler Hoffman, retired United Church of Christ Conference Minister and pastor. Jane reads all drafts of my novels and gives me detailed feedback. She is the inspiration for the University Chaplain character. In addition, I would like to thank Cherry

---

1. Richard Pérez-Peña, Mitch Smith, and Stephanie Saul, "University of Chicago Strikes Back at Campus Political Correctness," *The New York Times* (August 26, 2016).

Gallagher, an experienced book editor and friend. Cherry, as does Jane, gives me the gift of honest feedback, and that kind of intellectual challenge is truly priceless.

There is now a community of people who read my novels and give me encouragement and comments online and in person. Some of these folks have used my novels in book clubs, and I have therefore, once again, included suggestions for book club discussion questions at the end.

Among these readers is Dr. Mary E. Hunt, liberation theologian and co-founder of W.A.T.E.R., the Women's Alliance for Theology, Ethics and Ritual. Mary wrote an article on how three feminist theologians, myself included, have started writing fiction. I highly recommend all the novels she reviews.[2]

Dr. Elisabeth Schüssler Fiorenza, the Krister Stendahl Professor of Divinity at Harvard Divinity School, asked me for copies of the first two mysteries and she wants to include them in a feminist theology courses. I am very honored by this.

Finally, I would like to acknowledge the courage of those who resist the demonic deformations of white supremacy day in and day out. This is a terrible struggle, and it can even be a struggle to death.

We must call white supremacy by its proper name. It is Evil and we must defeat it.

2. Mary E. Hunt, "Feminist Theologians Bring Wisdom to Fiction," *National Catholic Reporter* (May 29, 2019). Accessed July 23, 2019.
https://www.ncronline.org/news/opinion/feminist-theologians-bring-wisdom-fiction.

Prologue

I knocked on the apartment door and it swung open. It was unlatched. I called out once, my words sounding loud in the darkened room, but then I didn't call again. The smell had hit me.

I saw the feet dangling. I forced myself to look up past the slack arms and stretched neck, all the way to the bloated face. It was grotesquely disfigured, pushed up by the choking rope. It was barely recognizable, but I knew who it was.

I had been afraid something like this would happen. And now it had.

I pulled out my cell to call 911 with one hand, while I tried to support the body's weight with the other. I was trembling with rage.

This was one of the rare times when I was sorry I wasn't still a cop. The room looked like the stage set of a suicide, but I doubted it.

I thought it was murder.

Chapter 1

White Pride World Wide

—"Stormfront" logo

Monday of the previous week, 5:30 a.m.

"That's a noose," I said.

"Ya think?" growled Officer Alice Matthews, a campus policewoman and my friend, who had called me out here in the frigid mist of dawn to look at this ugly coil of rope hanging from the branch of a tree on the main quadrangle of the campus.

Yeah. Even though I hadn't had any coffee, I knew a noose when I saw one.

A shadow of the tree branch fell over Alice's grim face as the sun began to rise behind it. A light breeze swung the noose to and fro as it dangled from the limb. Cheap clothesline, inexpertly tied. But it was doing its terrible job quite well. Behind her professional mask, Alice's dark skin seemed stretched over her facial bones, the fear ruthlessly suppressed. But it was there.

I felt my own face flush with rage at whoever had chosen to hang this symbol of hate and outright threat that had put that look on my friend's face. And, I realized, I was also weirdly pissed off at being white. Go figure. Well, I'm as white as white gets, the kind of pale, tall blonde that figures in a lot of guys' fantasy of a Scandinavian goddess. Well, they can stuff their nasty, white illusions. I am of Scandinavian descent, and I know the dangerous toxicity of whiteness, up close and personal. I've known it for quite a while. I had been a Chicago cop before I'd quit the force and decided to escape into what I had thought, incorrectly, would be the low-stress work of being a university faculty member. Because of how I looked, my white cop colleagues had assumed I was as racist as they as they made their vicious remarks and acted on that hate. That, among a lot of other reasons, was why

3

I was no longer a cop, though now I did "consult" part-time for the campus police. And here I was, "consulting" by looking at a noose hanging from a tree at dawn in the middle of the university campus.

"And what's this mess?" Alice asked, the toe of her sturdy, black, Oxford cop shoe pushing at a leaflet on the ground. Hundreds of them were strewn around under the tree. I looked more carefully, and I could see they made a paper trail across the campus. I picked one up. Bold black lettering on white paper jumped off the page.

"White Men Built America Not Africans! We Will Not be Erased!" it shouted. Black swastikas menaced from either side of the text. At the bottom there was a link to a website called "Stormfront."

Oh, crap. The reference to "Africans" was a definite tip off. This wasn't just the general neo-Nazi, Alt-right, "I'm a fascist and I like it" kind of filth that was spreading around American university campuses these days. The wording must mean the hateful rhetoric was directed at my colleague, Dr. Aduba Abubakar, our new hire in Philosophy and Religion, my academic department. As of this semester, he had been appointed as Assistant Professor of African Diaspora and Islamic Studies. He was originally from Nigeria, with a Ph.D. from Oxford and a slew of prominent journal publications. His inaugural lecture, "The African Roots of America," had just been announced in the campus newspaper.

I started to tell all this to Alice, but I saw she had out her cell phone and was photographing the noose and the leaflets littering the ground. And now I saw they were not just on the ground. As the rising sun burned off more of the mist, I could see that the trees around the paths of the central quad, their leaves yellowed and falling in the freshening breeze, had this garbage stapled to the trunks and more were blowing across the grass. I wondered how many more were spread around the campus in addition to this central area. There would be a lot of clean up necessary. Just then I saw two more campus police cars pulling up just beyond the quad at the parking circle.

Well, since this could reasonably be interpreted as an attack on our new colleague, I thought I'd better call my Department Chairperson, Dr. Adelaide Winters, and get her over here. Adelaide was Professor of Women and Religion. Nearly sixty and solid, both in mind and body, she was normally quite unflappable. I knew that for a fact. We'd had plenty of turmoil in our department in the last two years, the kind of turmoil that would flap anybody, including three deaths. Adelaide had held firm. But this hideous stunt might flap anybody.

I took my own cell phone photo of the noose, sent it as part of a text to Adelaide's cell, waited a minute, and then dialed her.

"What the hell?" was her cheery greeting.

I stepped away from where Alice and now three other campus police officers were standing around the tree conferring, and I spoke briskly.

"Adelaide, that's a photo of what's hanging from a tree here on the main quad. That's not all. There's a bunch of white supremacist leaflets scattered around that I think could be targeting Dr. Abubakar and his lecture."

She didn't waste a lot of time.

"I'll be there. Ten minutes tops." And she hung up.

Ten minutes. I looked longingly at the building diagonally across from where we were standing. It had a coffee shop in the basement. I couldn't face any more of this without coffee. The idea that I would suddenly seemed absurd. I gazed at the small knot of campus cops and then trotted over to them.

"Anybody want coffee?" I asked, in as matter-of-fact a voice as I could manage.

Alice looked up at me. The side of her mouth quirked up for only a second, and then it resumed its hard line. If my coffee addiction gave Alice even a moment of wry amusement right now, it was worth it just for that. Well, I mean, no, it wasn't totally worth it just for that. Get serious, I told myself. I needed that coffee.

"Sure, Kristin," she said dryly. The three other cops, guys I had seen but didn't know, just said, "Yeah," and kept up with their own conversation. I knew how Alice liked her coffee. I asked the others what they liked and jogged over to the coffee shop. Thank heavens they were already open. I got six coffees. Adelaide would be upset with or without coffee, but she'd be less upset with coffee.

When I got back with the drinks in a cardboard coffee-carrier, I could see Adelaide in the distance, barreling toward the main quad at quite a clip. She had on her normal garb of dark, flowing dress, and over it, the brilliant, red, wool cape she normally wore instead of a coat. The fabrics billowed out behind her like a parachute, and her grey, grizzled hair blew in all directions, making her look a little like Einstein in his later Princeton years. She held her briefcase to her chest with both arms and was using it kind of like a shield against the rising west wind. I quickly distributed the other coffees and took a couple more big gulps of the dark French Roast in my jumbo cup as I watched her hurried approach.

Then she stopped and stood stock-still as she stared at the noose. That's why they do these stunts, I thought, these miserable white supremacist jerks. To shock and appall and make you ask yourself what century you're living in. To try to put cracks in the veneer of civilization, cracks that can be widened, they hope, and so then they can try to force a farcical "white" re-write into the fissures.

Adelaide came up to me, her normally pale face even paler.

"Jesus, Mary and Joseph," she said, watching now as Alice climbed up on some kind of folding ladder. I handed Adelaide a coffee and she drank almost half in one gulp. Not a bad idea. I swigged some of my own. It helped with the rising gorge.

Maintenance had showed up in one of their small, three-wheeled vehicles while I was watching Adelaide approach. They must have provided the ladder. Alice cut the rope that held the noose and dropped it into the hands of a campus cop I did recognize. Mel Billman, often partnered with Alice, had also arrived. I could only see the back of his tall, muscular frame, and it was rigid. Mel was so tall, he might have been able to cut the noose down without a ladder, but I was sure Alice had insisted on being the one to do it. I was glad they had gotten it down before swarms of students and faculty were about, gaping and photographing the noose. But then, wouldn't the twerps who had hung it have already taken photos and blasted them out? Sure they would have. It was the point. God, we needed to find them and get them expelled. I felt my anger rise again as Alice turned, and I saw her face. She was as grim as I'd ever seen her, and we'd been in a lot of grim situations together before.

Alice walked quickly toward Adelaide and me, taking her notebook out of her back pocket.

"So?" she rasped out, looking angrily at us. But it wasn't us she was angry at.

I turned to Adelaide, who said, "You tell her, Kristin. It's your idea."

"Oh, sure, of course you're the one with the idea," Alice ground out. "So, you have an idea, Kristin. What is it?"

I took the flyer out of my pocket that I'd picked up from the ground and handed it to Adelaide. Alice already knew what it said. Adelaide took it and inhaled sharply, her eyes narrowing in disbelief. I explained to Alice about Dr. Abubakar being hired in African Diaspora and Islamic Studies and especially the title of his inaugural lecture.

I took the flyer back from Adelaide.

"I think it is pretty clear Dr. Abubakar's lecture title has got some of our campus white guys' shorts in a twist. They can't stand the thought that Africans might have contributed anything to building this country."

Alice snorted. I was glad to hear it. Alice had a whole range of snorts she used expressively. This one showed what she thought of these white guys and their shorts. To me it said she was now less shocked now and more her normal, bitchy self.

"What's Diaspora Studies?" she asked Adelaide.

Adelaide frowned. "Well, as I understand it, and believe me I'm learning a lot from Dr. Abubakar's work, diaspora refers to forced migration or slavery. People in this field study why that happened and the influence those who have been forced to migrate have had on the cultures where they end up. So, it's very international."

"Huh," said Alice, writing on her pad.

"You better tell him, this Muslim guy, straight away," she said, without looking up.

Adelaide and I looked at each other with dawning comprehension. Yes, of course we had to, or rather, she had to as his department chair. It would be horrific if he heard about this hateful act from the campus grapevine. What a way for him to get introduced to the university community. But again, that was the point. Make him feel like an outsider and drive him away.

"What?" Alice asked, looking up.

I realized I had been making a kind of growling noise in the back of my throat.

"We need to find them," I said and then paused. Who said drinking jumbo coffees wasn't good for you? My brain was now working. I looked around, especially at the windows of the buildings surrounding the quad.

"They're already here. They must be. They'd have wanted to see what happened with their stunt. Video it."

Alice nodded. Okay, so maybe my brainstorm wasn't such a big deal. She'd already thought of it.

"Yeah. They're here. Bound to be. Several on the force have already fanned out into the quad buildings now, looking for who shouldn't be there at this hour."

Well, good, but there was a lot of space to cover.

I turned to talk to Adelaide, and she was looking at the screen of her cell phone.

"I just wrote an email to Abubakar. I'm asking him to come to my office as soon as he can. I didn't say why." She continued to look down at the phone, re-read what she'd written, I assumed, and pressed send.

A heavy sigh escaped her lips that seemed to rise all the way up from the bottom of the soles of her feet.

"We'll need an emergency faculty meeting, too. Update the others. What a mess." Her large shoulders slumped. She'd fought hard for this new appointment in our department. I had too.

Adelaide said a brisk good-bye and indicated she was heading to the office. Alice turned away and walked toward her colleagues collecting the flyers.

I threw away my empty coffee cup and walked over to the center of the quadrangle. I just stood there alone and then turned slowly and faced each building in turn. I wanted them to see me, their beloved image of the white, Viking goddess. I was silently promising them they would find out what it is like to piss off a Viking goddess.

"What the hell do you think you're doing?" Alice asked from behind me.

"You know exactly what I'm doing, Alice," I said, not stopping my slow turn around the quad.

"This is what happens when you drink a whole jumbo cup of coffee, you know," Alice said, deadpan.

Yeah, well maybe. But right then, I was so incensed I could feel my blood pounding in my ears. If I'd had a sword, I would have waved it over my head.

"I'm coming for you," I vowed, glaring at the dark, staring eyes of the windows on the encircling buildings where I knew they'd be watching. Then I realized I'd spoken aloud.

"Oh crap," said Alice. "Here we go again."

Chat Room of Video Game "Revenge"

Monday, early morning

Demon196: u did great, showed those N****** what the F*** is down white is right white is power

Vampire726: no s***, no s*** shoulda seen those C***s lookin at it the N***** bitch and the white bitch what the F***s up with that she's like Sonja in Mortal Kombat big tits huge

Demon196: betraying her race that white C*** needs to be taught a lesson for damn sure hangin with that N***

Moloch111: damn right what's next, what's next

Demon196: Not here

Chapter 2

Go to university? Modern day propaganda factories

—Nordicheathen@Herrenvolk.com

Monday

After I had finished glaring at the windows of the buildings on the quadrangle, I realized I had time to hurry home and have breakfast with my twin boys, Sam and Mike. Adelaide had already texted that the emergency faculty meeting would start at 8 a.m. I looked at my watch. It was barely seven. As I jogged along the sidewalk, I reflected how much I could get done if I always got up this early. Hah. No chance of that. I am not a morning person.

The boys and I lived a scant three blocks from the campus, the reason, and really the only reason, I'd bought our aging Prairie Victorian house. It needed substantial renovation, and the contractor I'd hired had barely started. He'd taken my deposit check, sent some painters who took months to dab paint on the outside, and I hadn't seen him since. Another problem to address, but not right now.

A live-in couple, Carol and Giles Diop, helped me with the boys and the household chores. Carol, who was from Maine, was finishing a Masters degree at the School of Social Work. Giles, who was from Senegal, was a math Ph.D. candidate. They had a separate apartment on the top floor of the rambling wreck we called home. I'd texted Carol that there was an on-campus emergency before I had dashed off before dawn.

"Mom!" There was a joint chorus from the back of the house where the kitchen was located as soon as I opened the door. Our golden retriever, Molly, woofed a greeting, but stayed where she was. She would never abandon her spot under the kitchen table while the boys were having breakfast. Food rained down for her like mana from heaven when the kids ate. Dog theology is very literal. Why not? It works for them.

I headed back to the kitchen and greeted the boys, who were bouncing around in their seats at the kitchen table, and Giles, who was standing by the stove, stirring a heavy, cast-iron pot. Carol must have been upstairs. Giles did all the cooking and, if your stomach could take the spices, it was marvelous. What I smelled was Senegalese flour porridge. If you didn't stir it, I knew, it became a big lump.

"You have not eaten, yes?" Giles said, not turning his head from the pot. "I have made Bori. It is ready." He lifted the heavy pot and turned, carrying it over to where the boys and Molly were squirming around waiting. Giles was about 5'8" and very thin, but he was also very strong. His wiry arms handled the cast-iron like it was a teacup.

I got my own bowl out of the cupboard and hurried over, holding it out like I was one of the kids. Giles ladled the Bori into our bowls, gave us all his shy smile, and then, seeing Molly's disappointment, went to her bowl on the floor and scooped some of the porridge into it. Giles cannot bear to disappoint anyone.

The boys and Molly started literally inhaling their food. Not a moment was spared by my children to converse with Mom. Usually, at least Mike, my oldest by about 15 minutes, would have quizzed me on where I had gone so early. But now, at seven, it was food first, talk after. They could eat nearly as much as I could. I thought perhaps they were in a growth spurt. I looked across the breakfast table at the two heads bent over their bowls. Their thick, chocolate brown hair was tousled and when they looked up with their dark brown eyes, they were the mirror image of their father, Marco Ginelli. My Marco. A Chicago detective who had been killed in the line of duty when they were less than a year old. I still believed Marco had been murdered, but I'd never been able to prove it. I felt a sharp pang of grief. I shook myself. Of course I was feeling emotional given the way the day had begun. Emotion bleeds from one hurt to another.

"So, guys, backpacks packed and ready to go?"

"Yeah, yeah," Sam said, one hand suspiciously under the table. I could tell he was holding his bowl down for Molly to lick.

"Great, but Sam, don't feed her directly from your bowl, okay?"

Mike got up and made a big show of carrying his bowl over to Molly's and scraping out the leftovers. Not that there was much in the way of leftovers.

"See, Sam?" Mike said over his shoulder, deliberately baiting his brother. "So, whatever," Sam said. He got up, put the licked-clean bowl on the table, gave me a big hug and a kiss on the cheek, and then looked over at Mike with triumph, and ran down the hall. Sam was perfecting his use of charm to get around my instructions. I should have corrected him, but he'd distracted me with the hug and the kiss. And scored off obedient Mike as well.

"Bye, Mom," said Mike, and he too ran down the hall, Molly at his heels.

I could hear Carol in the front hall telling them to zip up their windbreakers. She normally walked them to school as it was right on the way to the building where she had her own classes.

Giles was ladling the rest of the Bori into another bowl. I saw there was coffee, and I got myself a cup. I waited until Giles sat down with his own breakfast and the front door had closed. Then I sat down opposite him. I needed to let him know what had happened on campus. As an African immigrant, the noose and the flyers were, in a very cruel way, directed at him as well as Dr. Abubakar. I cleared my throat.

"Giles, I was called out because there was a very disturbing incident on campus some time during the night."

Silently, Giles put down his spoon, took his cell phone out from his back pocket and tapped the screen. He passed it over.

"*Connards*," he said quietly and then picked up his spoon and resumed eating.

I scrolled through photos attached to a text he had received. Well, yes, they were assholes. All too true in any language.

It was all there, the noose, Alice cutting it down, close-ups of the flyers and what they said, the campus police cleaning them up, and then even my act standing in the middle of the quad. I was starting to feel a little embarrassed by that. Alice was right. I was not entirely rational when I'd taken a big hit of coffee on an empty stomach early in the morning. I squinted at the time on the small screen. These had been sent nearly an hour ago. That fast.

I had read an article about what was now being called the "infopocalypse," or at least I thought that was the term. Basically, the theory was that the end of history, that is, the apocalypse, was being ushered in by the increasing speed and spread of social media used to construct fake realities. This fake "white pride" performance was designed to warp and distort the real nature of what the university was and what it aspired to be. These jerks had gotten their hate out so fast that everything else the administration might say about that would be reaction and most likely ignored in the noise or derisively called "fake news."

"I'm sorry, Giles," I said, looking up from the screen. "This kind of hate is not right, not who I hope we are as a country." Even to my own ears, I thought I sounded like Barack Obama.

"But yes, it is," he said, gesturing at the phone images with his spoon. "That image, the rope, it is American history, right? It is from right after slavery. These kind of white people now, they want to bring that back, no?"

"Well, yes, they do," I admitted. "But we can't let them win," I said and then winced. I looked at his dark visage, now set as if carved in stone. "I know, I know, they won this round with this stunt and then the way they blasted it out. But it must be stopped."

"And how do you plan to stop the next, as you say, 'stunt'?" Giles asked quietly.

"I wish to hell I knew," I said. I looked at his solemn face. "What do you think we should do about it?"

Giles bent his head over his bowl and gazed into the porridge.

"I am contemplating that. Of a certainty, I am contemplating that."

And he resumed eating.

*   *   *

I hustled back to campus and jogged up the three flights of Myerson, the aging building where most of the humanities offices and classrooms were now located. No one ever took the rickety elevator if they could help it.

Even before I reached our floor, I could hear raised voices. I thought it was just about 8, but it sounded like the colleagues were already going at it. I stopped for a moment to throw my backpack and light jacket into the office I now shared with Dr. Abubakar. Yes, we were reduced to sharing offices. Once upon a time, Philosophy and Religion had possessed several more, very large offices down this corridor, but now three of them had been converted into one large classroom/meeting room and a smaller seminar room. We'd had to do that when our second-floor classrooms had been made into small offices and even smaller classrooms for the ever-shrinking Sociology Department. And to think that not long ago, the intellectual reputation of this university had been carried by its extraordinary work in Sociology. Now we were known for the Business School and its ghastly work in trickle-down economics. Sure, why not? Cut the very disciplines like sociology or philosophy that would help you understand why that kind of economics was a fraud.

I hustled down the poorly lit hall, aware that I was already getting irritable, and I didn't even know precisely what my faculty colleagues were arguing about. But I suspected.

As I entered, I saw Adelaide sitting at the head of the very long table that ran down the center of the room. Behind her, faux-medieval, stone tracery held stained glass windows that split the watery Chicago sunlight into shards of color. The colors spilled over the back of Adelaide's head and shoulders, making her look like she was piously sitting in church. Her face, though in shadow, showed narrowed eyes and pursed lips. Adelaide wasn't feeling pious, she was feeling pissed.

I could see why. Dr. Donald Willie, Associate Professor of Psychology of Religion, was standing in front of his chair, pontificating in a raised voice. At least, I thought he was standing. He was so short it was sometimes hard for me to tell. His narrow face was red with rage, and he was blowing out his words under his unfortunate mustache. I disliked him intensely. In incidents nearly a year ago, he had shown himself to be a coward and even a liar, as well as one of those squishy, faux-liberal, white men who are actually deeply racist and sexist. He had been on leave last semester, and I'd hoped he had been using the time to find another job. No such luck. I struggled to listen to his words as they blew out between his thin, pale lips.

"Unacceptable risk, completely unacceptable risk" was what I thought he was now practically shouting. It is actually hard to shout sibilants. He unwisely accompanied this angry hissing by shaking his finger at Adelaide. Now that, Donald, I reflected, is a big mistake.

Adelaide's face turned from merely stern to darkly ferocious in less than a second. I thought, for one scary moment, her head was swelling. Donald took one look and abruptly sat down.

Our newest colleague was sitting very still, maybe because he was stunned. I didn't know how they conducted faculty meetings at Oxford, but I bet it wasn't as ridiculous as this. I had taught summer school at Oxford University for several weeks a few summers ago. I'd drunk sherry in tiny glasses in the Faculty Commons, but I had not been asked to attend meetings. In the Commons, at least, everyone had been civil.

This would be Dr. Abubakar's first American faculty meeting. What an introduction. He was sitting at the table on the opposite side from where Donald had just been standing. In the momentary lull, I pulled out a chair next to him and sat down. He didn't even turn his head. I could only see him in profile. His jaw, with a closely cropped black beard sharply outlining it up to his short black hair, was set, though I could see a muscle working in his dark cheek. He was probably trying to hold in several choice words. Then he took off his glasses, put them on the table and pinched the bridge of his nose.

Adelaide addressed me with what sounded like relief.

"Kristin, glad you're here. I know you were on the quad this morning when the noose and the leaflets were found."

There was a kind of strangled gurgle from Donald, but Adelaide ignored it.

"Now, unfortunately, pictures of that, as well as the work of the campus police to remove those items, are circulating around campus, including photos of what the flyers said. Would you give us a brief update and anything the campus police have learned?"

I hesitated. Then, Adelaide glared at me, and I hurried into speech.

"I assume you've all seen the photos, including what the flyer said, as they have already circulated widely. I don't need to rehearse that. I can tell you that the campus police searched the surrounding buildings, but as far as I know haven't located anyone they thought was involved. But they were there. And more than one."

I took out my own phone from my pocket, put it on the table and just tapped it to make my point.

"The photos I've seen of the active scene were from several different angles, all at approximately the same time. That indicates more than one person is involved. Moreover, I believe this is a hate crime and should be investigated as such. The perpetrators should be found and prosecuted. I also think it is a coordinated effort to stop Dr. Abubakar's announced lecture."

I turned in my chair and addressed him.

"Dr. Abubakar, I think we need most of all to hear your thoughts."

Adelaide nodded, but before Aduba could speak, Donald broke in.

"It is obvious it is too dangerous for him to give this lecture," he puffed. "I don't see why we are even discussing it."

Whitesplaining. Typical. As was the deliberate use of a pronoun rather than a colleague's title and name. And, of course, what Donald really meant is "I think it is too dangerous for those of us who teach in this department, namely Donald Willie," but I didn't say any of it aloud.

Aduba slowly picked up his glasses from the table and put them on.

"I will not be a coward," he said. "I will give the lecture as planned." He folded his arms and looked at Adelaide.

"Well, okay," she said and made to rise.

"It's not about cowardice, it's about common sense," Donald sputtered, rising to his feet again and glaring at Adelaide.

"It's not your call, Donald," I said, not bothering to hide the contempt in my voice. I rose as well and emphasized my words by leaning over the table toward him.

"We're done here," Adelaide said firmly. For a large woman, Adelaide was very quick on her feet. She was up and out the door in a flash. I could hear her office door open and then shut with a bang.

Willie quickly followed her out the door, not glancing at either Aduba or me.

Aduba waited a moment. I was sure he didn't want to encounter Donald in the hall. When he rose to leave, I got up as well and followed him. I was stewing about how to send a more welcoming signal to our new colleague than Willie had. Of course, that wouldn't be hard. Short of tripping him as he walked down the hall, I could hardly do worse than Donald.

"Aduba," I said, as he paused at our common office door to insert his key in the ancient lock. I made a mental note to tell him that all the doors on this floor opened with the same key and to be careful what he left in the office. But right now, I didn't think that was what I needed to blurt out.

"Yes?" he said, finishing unlocking the door and opening it, but not entering. He turned to face me. There was a single line across his forehead. Either he was frowning, or he was squinting in the bad light of our hallway.

"Well," I fumbled. "Well, I was wondering if you and your wife, and your son would like to come to dinner at my house Saturday night."

"Our son is only six," he said slowly.

"Oh, that's okay, my twin sons have just turned seven. It will be informal, believe me."

"I think that should be fine, but I will consult my wife and let you know. Thank you." Then he entered the office, went directly to his desk, sat down and turned on his computer.

I thought for a moment about apologizing for Donald's behavior, but when I looked at his unyielding posture, I decided instead it would be best to give him some time alone, though the divider that separated our two desks and bookcases scarcely provided any privacy. I turned and looked down the hall at the inviting coffee area Adelaide had set up outside her office when she had become department chair. She had installed a De'Longhi espresso machine with all the trimmings. It made quite a change from her predecessor who might have provided free arsenic to both faculty and students if he had thought he could get away with it.

I walked toward the espresso machine like I was on a tractor beam in a Star Trek movie. I really shouldn't have any more coffee, but I kept moving toward it. I was trying to cut down on my coffee consumption. I realized it had become an addiction. I'd already had two cups and the day had barely started. But, I kept walking toward the coffee.

I felt like I had spent the whole morning so far in one of those tilt-a-whirl things at the amusement park the boys loved so much. You were spun around and around and then the floor dropped out. You hoped gravity would hold you up. But today, I was questioning even gravity. God damn these white supremacists. That was their goal, to make you question whether your commitments would just drop away and let you fall.

I caved into temptation and got a double espresso. I stood there and took a few sips. I would have liked to talk this morning over with Adelaide, but I knew she was teaching in the smaller seminar room. I deposited my donation in the jar for coffee purchases, cleaned up my grounds from the machine, and turned to head back down the hall. I saw Aduba heading for the stairs. He was leaving the office.

I unlocked the door and sat down on my own side. I finished my espresso, and really, it was excellent, and then I opened my computer. I checked my email first, by habit, and was surprised to already see a note from Aduba accepting the dinner invitation and asking the time. Good sign? I hoped so. I sat back in my chair and went over a possible guest list in my mind. I would invite Carol and Giles, though talking Giles out of cooking, and permitting a caterer in "his" kitchen, would be a little bit of a struggle. Adelaide would be a good addition, I thought, and then, of course, Tom Grayson, a surgeon at the university hospital.

I had been dating Tom for nearly a year. He had patched me up after a knife-wielding assailant had made a deep cut in my arm, and I had fallen for his blue, twinkly eyes, his sandy hair that was always too long, and his profound compassion. But I had kept him at arm's length for months, feeling disloyal, even after six years, to my Marco. It had actually been Marco's father, Vince Ginelli, who had gruffly told me six years was too a long time to mourn. Tom and I had become lovers this past summer on a delicious trip to Paris. I reminisced about that for a lovely few minutes and then sighed. Since we'd been back, his surgical schedule, and the demands on my time with parenting, teaching, and sporadically working on my dissertation had meant we mostly communed by phone. Less than satisfactory from a romance perspective.

Still, I picked up my cell phone. I hoped Tom was not in surgery. I had a lot to tell him, starting with the noose and ending up with an invitation to dinner.

I dialed his cell. Amazingly enough, he picked up on the first ring.

"Kristin, hold on, I'm just walking out of a patient's room."

I held on. He was probably still on rounds.

"Okay, I can talk. I was expecting to hear from you. Are you okay?" Tom sounded very concerned, and I was a little taken aback.

"Sure, yes, I'm fine. Why wouldn't I be?"

"Well, there are photos that are all over the hospital of that incident on quad this morning, and you're in many of them. I assume you were working with Alice on that? Must have been difficult, that's all I meant." His measured voice was warm, but careful. We'd had some struggles over his desire to protect me.

I realized I had been too prickly about his concern. Concern was warranted. Being prickly was a bad move, I said to myself. I took a calming breath.

"Thanks. I didn't realize you'd seen the photos, that's all. Yes, it was very difficult." I thought for a moment. I knew Tom kept confidences well, and I needed to work on trust with him. I went on.

"I was most upset about how awful it seemed to be for Alice, and you know how she is, she kept it all inside, and just did the job. But I was furious about how the whole fiasco played out." I paused again.

"I still am. And we just had a ghastly faculty meeting about it." Then I realized there were voices in the background, probably a resident trying to get Tom's attention. I tried not to resent it, but I should get off the phone.

"Listen, Tom, I'll tell you about that later, but I'll email you an invitation to dinner Saturday night with my new colleague, Dr. Abubakar and his family."

"A dinner? Sure, should be . . . oh, and just hold on, Kristin." I could hear the buzz of conversation around him.

He came back on the phone.

"Sure. Send me that. And can I bring Kelly if she wants to come?"

Kelly was Tom's fifteen-year-old daughter. He had been divorced, but his ex-wife had died the previous year, and now he had custody of a smoldering tower of teenage girl, who alternately hated me and wanted to be me.

"Well, yes, I guess, if she wants to," I replied slightly less than enthusiastically.

"Great. Good. Let's talk tonight." And Tom hung up.

I looked at the silent cell phone in my hand. Paris seemed a very long time ago.

The cell phone displayed the time. It was only 9:30 a.m. I wondered what the rest of this ghastly day would bring.

Chapter 3

Dark chocolate may not be proof of the existence of a benevolent God, but it's a definite indicator.

—SUSAN THISTLETHWAITE

Monday evening

I walked home in the early evening eddy of the rest of the university community, all of us streaming down the sidewalks away from work or study.

To my surprise, nothing ghastly had happened during the afternoon. Not as far as I knew, anyway. I had managed to remain at my desk undisturbed, working on clearing my incessant email and even starting to revise my plan for class the next day. Aduba never came back to the office.

I had called Alice at about 3 p.m., just to check in and see if there had been any progress in discovering who had hung the noose and the leaflets.

"Nope," she said in response to my query, her voice clipped. "Nothing." She'd paused. "Well, nothing but the yak, yak, yak about those photos and that piece of shit flyer. So God damn stupid. Makes me want to spit."

That was a lot of swear words in a row for Alice. The fact that she still sounded so raw made me keep my own views to myself. I thought the whole thing hadn't been stupid at all. It had been very smart and effective precisely because everybody was yammering about it. Just keep quiet about that, I told myself.

"Yeah, well, keep me posted, will you?" I'd asked instead.

"Sure. Okay. And if you get any bright ideas, call me." Alice hung up.

So at 5 p.m. I'd closed my computer and headed home. We had martial arts class tonight after dinner.

∗　∗　∗

19

The boys had raced upstairs to get into their Tae Kwon Do uniforms and Giles, Carol, and I were finishing up the dishes.

"I wanted to run something by you both," I said as I dried a big platter.

Carol turned her calm brown eyes on me, assessing. I was trying to sound casual and pretty much failing. Giles continued to face the sink, rinsing the dishes and stacking them for Carol to put in the dishwasher. But he hunched his thin shoulders a little.

I labored along.

"Well, I know we've agreed that we'll talk about weekend plans in advance, but, you see, today was so crazy awful that I just went ahead and invited Dr. Abubakar and his wife and child for dinner Saturday night. And, well, some others. You know my colleague Adelaide, and Tom and Kelly, and then, well, the five of us if you can make it. I'd like you both to join us for the whole meal, so Giles I thought I'd get a caterer so you won't get stuck in the kitchen, you know?"

I ground to a halt.

Carol silently stacked the rest of the dishes in the dishwasher while Giles dried his hands and turned. But he looked more at Carol than me.

"I cannot attend. I have an engagement and must be out most of the afternoon and evening." Then he glanced over at me. "I hope it is a good occasion," he said quietly, and he left the kitchen, his flip flops making a rapid staccato beat on the hard tile floor.

"I don't think I can make it either, Kristin, but I'll let you know," Carol said in her quiet way, but she sounded a little strained. Then she bent and hit the start button on the dishwasher. It was so old that the clanking, gushing noise it made would drown out any further conversation.

I hit pause on the elderly machine. It gurgled to a halt.

"Carol, is something wrong, I mean something besides my rushing ahead with a weekend invitation before we'd all discussed it?"

She turned and wiped down the counter again. It was already clean and dry. She didn't turn.

"No, I don't think that's it. But as I said, I'll let you know." She hung up the towel she'd been using to dry an already dry counter and also left the kitchen.

I hit the start button and pondered while the machine labored into the wash cycle again. What was up with Giles and Carol?

Well, it had been a terrible day, I thought. There are bound to be emotional reactions for a while. But was that too simplistic? Was Giles upset that I'd invited the Abubakar family who were Muslim? I knew very little about his life in Senegal, but I did know that his father was a Protestant pastor, and the whole family was very devout. The small Christian population in

Senegal was still persecuted by the Muslim majority, I thought, though I'd never heard Giles say a word about it. I realized I may have blundered more seriously than just asking people to dinner without consulting Carol and Giles first.

The boys came thundering down the back stairs into the kitchen, their uniforms on, though Sam's belt was already coming untied. I retied it properly despite Molly's jumping around from the excitement. I have often thought there should be martial arts classes for dogs, they love jumping around so much.

I told the boys to let Molly out for a few minutes while I got into my own gear.

Just then my cell phone rang. I hurriedly pressed "accept" and ran up the stairs to get changed.

"Kristin, it's Kelly," said Tom's daughter.

"Hey, Kelly. Everything okay?"

"Yeah, sure, fine." The litany every teenager knows. "Yeah, sure, fine," means, "no, not really, not fine."

"Like, I wondered if you could like pick me up on the way to class and give me a ride? Dad was supposed to, but he's not home, and like I thought since you were going anyway . . . " She trailed off. Kelly and I have a complex relationship. She resented her mother dying and her Dad having a relationship with me, but she also was longing for some attention. And she and I had been through a crisis a few months ago, and we had gotten closer. In fact, she'd started Tae Kwon Do after that and was doing really well.

"Yep. I can," I said briskly as I struggled to get my sweater over my head while still talking. "I'll text you when we get to your building. Ten minutes, tops." I hung up before I strangled myself with the sweater and jumped into my uniform.

Kelly was waiting in front of her building when the boys and I pulled up. She really was looking better these days, I reflected. She was about my height, and I knew all too well what it was like to be six feet tall and a teenage girl. When I had met her the previous spring, she had been overweight and had slouched to try to appear smaller. It had just made her look like a huge lump. Now she was slimmer from all the exercise, and she stood up straight. She jumped in the front seat, and we took off.

"Thanks," she said to me. "Hello, dorks," she said to the boys, strapped in their boosters in the back seat.

"Hi, Kelly smelly!" they chorused, clearly having rehearsed it. Then they laughed uproariously at their own wit. Kelly ignored them, already checking her phone. Naturally.

All was normal. Well, except Tom as a no-show again for Kelly. I glanced over at her. Her eyes were riveted on the little screen. I thought Tom left her alone too much. I knew a surgeon's schedule was really demanding, but Kelly needed his attention.

Well, nothing I could do about that right now. I thought we'd all benefit from kicking and punching the blue pads. And we did.

*   *   *

When we got home, the boys were so tired they dragged themselves upstairs without my telling them it was time for bed. When I went to check on them a few minutes later, I found they had flung themselves fully clothed on to their beds and were deeply asleep. I just pulled off their uniforms and covered them with their comforters. Molly settled down between them on the floor and resisted all my efforts to get her to go with me so I could let her out into the yard one more time. I gave up. She could be very stubborn, especially when she'd been separated from the kids. She was letting me know she considered them hers, not mine. I'd ask Carol if she or Giles had let her out recently.

I started down the hall toward the door to their third-floor apartment, and Carol came out. She was carrying something and smiling a little.

"Kristin, this came for you while you and the boys were out," she said, moving closer to me. I could now see she was holding a small FedEx package. She passed it over.

I looked at it for a second uncomprehendingly.

"The return address says 'Dr. Grayson,'" Carol said, her freckled face breaking into an even wider smile.

"Oh," I said, gazing down at the little white box. Then I felt a jolt of pure terror. Little box?

I think Carol took pity on me then.

"The corner says 'Reinhardt's,'" she said, with a soft chuckle. "You know, that expensive Chicago chocolatier?"

Chocolate. I looked down at the small package in my trembling hand. Oh. Phew. It was chocolate.

Then my tired brain kicked in. Hey, Reinhardt's made really good chocolate.

I thanked Carol and turned to go, but then remembered I needed to ask her about the dog. Carol assured me that Molly had already been out, and she went back upstairs.

I walked slowly down the hall, the little box almost burning a hole in my hand.

Open it, you idiot, an inner voice advised me. It's wonderful chocolate.

I went downstairs to the kitchen for some scissors and opened it.

Four perfect, dark, chocolate truffles each sat in a little nest of gold tissue paper. There was a note. "Bonsoir," it read. "Tom." That was it. Actually, I thought it was plenty.

I reached into a high cabinet and pulled out a bottle of excellent red wine I had been saving for a special occasion. I thought this qualified. I poured myself a glass and clutching that, and my precious chocolates, I went upstairs to my bedroom and locked the door.

I got my cell phone, my wine, and my truffles, and climbed into bed. But I didn't call Tom right away. Instead, I took a bite of one of the truffles and let it melt on the back of my tongue. Then I took a sip of the wine and its dense, velvety flavor filled my mouth and throat, blending with the deep chocolate flavor. I shivered.

I leaned back against my pillows, savoring the tastes and smiled. I picked up the phone and opened text messaging.

"Are you home?" I typed and pressed send.

"Yes." Tom's reply came back quickly. "Talk now?"

"Got your chocolate truffles," I typed. "In bed with them & some wine."

"In bed?" he replied. "Relaxed?"

"I'm getting there," I typed.

And then I texted some ways I thought I could get even more relaxed.

He texted back some excellent ideas of his own.

Pretty soon I thought we were both very relaxed.

Chat Room of Video Game "Revenge"

Monday, late evening

Demon196: Need to hit again hit hard

Vampire726: Yeah yeah step out and up

Demon196: Gotta get my white on get going figure out how to get those N****** and THOT

Moloch111: no s*** lots with us

Demon196: watch it

Chapter 4

*The function of the university is not simply to teach breadwin-
ning, or to furnish teachers for the public schools, or to be a
centre of polite society; it is, above all, to be the organ of that
fine adjustment between real life and the growing knowledge of
life, and adjustment which forms the secret of civilization.*

—W. E. B. DU BOIS, *THE SOULS OF BLACK FOLK*

Tuesday morning

I watched as the early morning light slowly illuminated our scruffy
kitchen, piteously picking out the holes in the linoleum floor and the
light sheen of grease on the faded orange walls. "Gotta call that contractor," I thought for about the thousandth time.

I was sipping yet another cup of dark coffee and letting my mind settle.
I had been up for a couple of hours, finishing the revision of my lesson plan
for this morning. This semester I was teaching a class about the American religious reformers that had protested the greed and exploitation that
had been so common from the late 19th into the mid-20th century. This
movement was called the "Social Gospel." These reformers had taken on
the excesses of industrialization, and some of them had even confronted
the outright terrorism visited upon freed African Americans in the same
period. Like lynching.

The reading I had already assigned for today sure fit what had happened on campus yesterday. The students were supposed to have read
W.E.B. Du Bois's classic work, *The Souls of Black Folk*. My original lesson
plan had been to use its penetrating sociological analysis to get into a broad
discussion of the tenor of his times, including, as he put it, "the problem
of the color line." But now, as I had reworked it, I thought I'd first get the
class to focus on what had happened on our campus and then bring up Du

Bois, the African American intellectual who had been so revolted by the weekly reports of lynching when he had been a college student at Fisk. And I hoped I'd help them realize how the merciless repetition of those horrors had shaped his views forever. To do that, I was going to have to literally show lynching as it had been photographed, the white population wanting to make a spectacle of this horror. I had been going over those images, and I could still see them in wavy duplicates in my mind's eye.

Would the students then see the pathetic coil of rope that had briefly hung on a tree on the main quad for the hateful threat it was, or would they tune it out? Probably yes, and no.

Suddenly, my cell phone rang. It startled me. It wasn't even 7 a.m. I picked up my phone and turned it over. It was Adelaide.

My stomach clenched, hoping it was not more bad news. But, as I pressed "accept," I knew Adelaide was unlikely to call me at this hour with some really good news.

"Yes, Adelaide?" I said.

"Ah, yes, Kristin?" Adelaide said tentatively.

"Yes," I said dryly. What was this about?

"Well, I wondered if you would come in a little early this morning. Say about 8:15? I know you have a class at 9, but this shouldn't take too long. No, really, not long."

Her voice dropped and the last words seemed to sink and then stop of their own weight.

What?

"What the heck is the matter, Adelaide?" I asked. I was tired and had looked at too many hideous photographs to be diplomatic.

"Well, we'll go over that when you get here, okay?" Adelaide said, ducking and covering like an administrator.

I was having none of it.

"No. Please just give it to me straight. What's this about?"

"Well, you see, Dr. Abubakar called me last night. He objects to sharing an office because it gives him no privacy for prayer. I'd like to see if you and I can work out an alternative."

Well, she was right. This wasn't something to hash out on the phone at dawn.

"Yeah, alright. I'll be at your office around 8:15. I need to go and get dressed. Good-bye."

Adelaide said a stilted good-bye as well and hung up.

I started to put away my phone, and my eye fell on my texting app. I opened it, and I spent a couple of enjoyable minutes re-reading Tom's and my texts from the previous evening. And then I carefully deleted each one and sent them to the trash icon, so they'd be truly gone. Not a good idea for the boys to see those texts. Then I went upstairs to get dressed, trying not to resent Abubakar. But, I mused, if you go out to deliberately recruit a devout Muslim, you can scarcely expect they'll behave like liberal Protestants. Yet, it seemed like I had. Go figure.

*   *   *

"You can't be serious!" I exploded.

I had gone directly to Adelaide's office when I arrived at our building, and she had just floated the idea to me of sharing an office with Donald Willie instead of Abubakar.

"Well, it's not ideal, I grant you that," said Adelaide, still being tentative. I didn't like the tentative Adelaide at all. Events were taking a toll on her. I could see it in the deepened lines on her face. I struggled with my temper.

"Look, Adelaide, it wouldn't work. Even if Donald agreed, and he won't, I'd certainly end up punching him out before the end of the first week. It's not only unworkable, it's dangerous."

I managed to say this in somewhat of a wry tone of voice so she'd think I was joking. I actually wasn't joking.

I sat and thought for a minute.

"You know, Adelaide, Rockefeller Chapel has private prayer rooms."

"I know that as well, Kristin," Adelaide snapped back. "It's the first thing I suggested. Aduba says the chapel is too far away for him to pray during the day and get back to class or meetings. It is all the way across campus." Then Adelaide gave a deep sigh.

"Well, until we can figure out something permanent, what about giving Abubakar a key to Hercules's office so he can pray in private?" Hercules Abraham, retired Professor of Judaism, was away visiting his family in France for this whole fall semester. He still had an office because he did teach part-time for us despite being over eighty.

Adelaide had a considering look on her face. I knew she was torn by having such a large office still occupied by a retired professor, but he did help out a lot with our diminished teaching staff.

She nodded.

"It's a good idea. Let me email Hercules and ask him if that's okay, and then I'll run it by Aduba."

Adelaide opened her computer as if to put act to word, but I still sat there, thinking.

She looked at me quizzically, her bushy, grey eyebrows raised.

"What are you thinking about now?" she rasped, not seeming at all happy I was still thinking.

"I was thinking we need a more permanent solution," I said. "What about renovating that empty storage room right next to the faculty assistant's office and making it a permanent prayer room? There's nothing in it now that the cleaners bring their own equipment."

Not, in fact, that much cleaning ever did happen on our floor, but two years ago the university had hired an outside firm to do whatever cleaning did get done, and they seemed to bring what they needed each time.

"Well . . . ." Adelaide said, considering. "We do need a permanent solution, but there's no budget for that, Kristin, and we can't just stick someone in a dirty, old closet to pray."

I wrestled with myself and then blurted out, "I'll donate the money to fix it up, but it has to be anonymous, okay?"

Adelaide knew about my inherited wealth, though I hoped she was the only one of my colleagues who did. She also knew I was touchy about it.

Before she could reply, however, I had a genuinely good idea.

"Let's name the prayer room for Ay-seong Kim. We could, you know, do it really well, and dedicate it to her."

Ah-seong was a student who drowned on campus the previous year. She had been a lovely young woman, and she had suffered a lot of abuse in her short life.

"Oh, Kristin, what a lovely thought. Really, really lovely." Adelaide looked down at her veined hands, now clenched on the desk. I knew the reasons that dedication would be very meaningful to Adelaide herself, as well as difficult. She had suffered some abuse as well.

I coughed a little, choking back my own emotion.

"Alright then," I said, trying for a neutral tone. "If you'll get permission from whomever, I'll contact my lawyers. We can have it designed and built this fall and then schedule the dedication. Tell the powers-that-be there's an anonymous donation for it."

I got up to leave.

Adelaide looked up at me, tears behind her thick glasses. She just nodded.

Look at that. Necessity could be the mother of compassion.

* * *

I looked around the seminar table. The students were going through their usual motions of doing one last check of their phones for any breaking text messages, getting out their books, putting laptops on the table, and slurping beverages from to-go cups, but I didn't think I was imagining their tension. Cups were gripped a little too tightly, shoulders were up around their ears, and their eyes were looking everywhere but at me. I hooked up my own computer to the overhead projector, and the screen automatically came down at the far end of the room. The hum it made in descending sounded abnormally loud.

"You'll not need your own computers and not even the book right now," I said. "But you will need your cell phones."

That got a reaction. A few people looked up quizzically. Zhang Mei, a Chinese student, looked up in alarm. I was actually surprised to see her face. Normally her long dark hair hung down on either side of her face, hiding it as she bent over her computer, taking careful notes. I knew from a couple of short book reviews I had already assigned that her written English was excellent, but she had never spoken in class except when I had called on each student to introduce themselves. She was a Christian, and, if she were typical of the Chinese Christian population, likely conservative Protestant. She had said she was a math major. I wondered at that brief look of alarm. Did she know something about what had happened yesterday?

I looked around at the whole class, waiting for them to settle. Before I formally started this class, I wanted to tell them up front what was going to happen and give each one of them the freedom to decide if this was something they could take. I was a big believer in what were called "trigger warnings," that is, letting people know that distressing issues would be brought up and letting them opt out if they wanted. This university was famous for its supposed tough stand against faculty taking care to warn students about troubling topics ahead of time. I personally thought that was idiotic. I knew trauma and what it could do to you. I knew it all too well from times I had been on the receiving end of violence.

It was only natural that today was going to be hard on everybody, including me. My main educational goal in this class was to show lynching for what it really was. It was terrorism of the most brutal kind. And I was not going to let them stay a century or more away. We'd start with our own campus, as I'd planned early this morning.

I took a breath and looked around the table. They were back to hiding from me and perhaps from each other. A few thousand students is actually a pretty small community in the age of social media. I wondered what, if anything, they really knew about who hung yesterday's noose.

I cleared my throat and began.

"You know what happened on campus yesterday. A noose was hung on a tree on the main quadrangle."

I could hear their breathing change, with sighs, small gasps, and one sharp intake of breath.

"Today will be a difficult class, and you know I respect the effect of trauma on people. If you feel at any point this class is becoming too hard for you, you may step out with no questions asked, and you will get full credit for the class."

I looked around. Everyone except Jordan Jameson, a computer major who, for some reason, was taking another religion class with me, was looking down. Jordan was looking right at me, and he actually looked a little bored. Probably because there was nothing in what I was saying he dared make a joke about. "Not yet, anyway," I told myself and sighed inwardly.

I waited, giving them time to take in what I had said. There were a couple of students I was worried about. Emma Olson was a Philosophy and Religion major. She was from Wisconsin, and she'd been in my classes before. She was a Protestant liberal and planning on going to seminary. She had told me privately she was a survivor of sexual assault, and I was concerned that perhaps this campus incident could hook some of her bad memories.

I glanced at Jayden Johnson, a junior. Her African American mother was a faculty member here in the Center for Race, Politics and Culture. Her white father was a lawyer, I thought. In her self-introduction in the first class, she had been very clipped, very clear that she wanted a career as an activist, not an academic. I imagined she knew the history of lynching well, but that was no safeguard against pain.

A couple of the others I thought would be okay, though distressed, with what would be presented. John Vandenberg, also a Philosophy and Religion major, was of Dutch ancestry and had gone to a very religiously conservative undergraduate school in western Michigan. Shouldn't project, though, should I? I told myself. I realized I had no concrete way to know what John's feelings about this class might be.

Two other international students rounded out the group. Vihaan Acharya, a senior, was from India. He was an economics major, and I had assumed he was in the class because he was filling out a humanities distribution requirement. He rarely spoke in class. Nari Kim, from Korea, was pre-med and quite clear she was exploring her traditional Christian beliefs, even questioning them. She actually reminded me a little of Ay-seong Kim in that way.

"Okay, then, but remember, at any point you don't have to stay if you don't want to. Now, please open up your cell phones and bring up any photos you may have received of the events on campus yesterday, especially the noose and various reactions to it."

There was a little rustling while they did that, but since they basically lived through their phones, their dexterity with them was astonishing.

I went to the saved images on my computer where I had transferred them from my phone and projected them.

"Here's the first photo I took when I arrived on campus."

I thought I wouldn't remind them of my consulting status with the campus police, just in case anybody wanted to confess. I doubted it, though.

The resolution on the screen was good. My cell phone camera took a pretty sharp photo. The cheap rope shimmered as the morning dew that had settled on the coil was backlit by the rising sun.

"I also got a lot of images forwarded to me by others, but I won't display those. What did you get, and what did you think when the photos arrived in your inbox?"

"I thought, 'What the hell kind of a sick joke is this?'" Jordan said, jumping in first. As usual. "Then I just deleted it, but my idiot friends just kept sending more and more so I finally gave up with the deleting and grabbed something to eat at the Uni." The Uni was a fast food cafeteria right off the main quadrangle.

So, I thought, Jordan might have been near the quadrangle.

"Well, some of us couldn't eat after we saw the noose, you know?" Jayden said through her teeth. "We were like nauseated."

"Uni food can do that too," Jordan drawled.

Jayden reached into a little purse she had on the table and took out a tissue. She held it out like she was going to give it to Jordan, and then she said dryly, "Here. You can use this to wipe that white privilege off your face." She paused. "Oh, wait. You can't. It's like drawn on with permanent, white marker."

A few people chuckled.

I was ready to step in if that exchange escalated, but Jayden had actually shut Jordan up pretty effectively.

"I thought it was awful, just awful," Emma said with a catch in her throat. "I showed it to my roommate, and we couldn't believe it. It's disgusting, and vile, and I think whoever did it should just quit school, and leave. They don't belong here." Emma got out her own tissue and blew her nose.

"Well, there's another side to this," John said slowly, as he tapped a photo on his phone. I could see it was not of the noose, but of the flyer.

"Another side?" Jayden asked, ice coating each word.

"Yeah. Some people are really upset about this department hiring a Muslim guy and then him boasting about America being African. What's up with that?" John looked challengingly around the room.

"Perhaps," Nari said softly, "if you actually attended the lecture you could find out 'what's up with that' and learn something. I think that's the point of a university education, don't you?"

Well. Nari was stepping up. Her words may have been soft, but the point penetrated, I thought, looking at John's pale face, now flushing with embarrassment, or was it anger?

Jayden smiled at Nari.

"This image of the noose is a reference to the American history of lynching, correct? From the time after the Civil War, I believe," Vihaan contributed.

"Yes," I said. "I think in part it is. But now, as John's remarks show, it is being used against a Muslim professor here, trying to create enough havoc that his lecture might be postponed, or even cancelled."

I paused. Since it was Vihaan who had spoken, I thought this was a good time to bring up how global lynching is, even today.

"Lynching is an American word, but the use of mob violence, including public hanging, happens all around the world. In fact," I looked right at Vihaan, "I believe in India, for example, lynching as a public display of anger has happened and is happening right now, correct? I think there's a phenomenon of 'cow lynching' directed against Muslims, right?"

Vihaan sat back abruptly in his chair. It was a physical display of distancing. He must have thought this whole contentious issue had nothing to do with him as an Indian. Just the feckless Americans going at each other again.

He didn't answer.

"They lynch cows?" Jordan burst out laughing.

Vihaan actually rose slightly in his chair, ready to stand in outrage, I thought.

I made a small hand gesture for him to sit, and I jumped in to prevent any more insult.

"No, Jordan, no. Cows are sacred in India to Hindus. The lynching is directed at those suspected of killing and eating cows, especially Muslims."

I turned to Vihaan.

"But there's more it than that, isn't there?"

I didn't think he was going to answer, but then he spoke slowly.

"Yes. Yes there is. Our Prime Minister has a kind of 'cow-whistle' politics to promote Hindu nationalism, like your American President has a 'dog-whistle politics' about race to promote whites. And yes, it is directed against Muslims. They are accused of being 'cow-eaters' and that justifies killing or injuring them. But it's a way to just say, 'you're not Hindu, and we don't want you here.' It is terrible."

"It is." I gestured at the noose, glistening on the screen at the front of the room.

"Thanks, Vihaan. That was really helpful. All of you. Try to get this. There is a kind of universal vocabulary to lynching. It is a social threat. There is ceremonial shedding of blood. Human blood. The mutilated body is displayed in triumph. The victims are those who are being literally expelled from community by death. And why? So that one group can assert dominance."

"Chinese too," came a whisper from Mei. "In California, Los Angeles. Seventeen Chinese men lynched."

"When was this?" Jayden gasped, looking horrified.

"1871. Every Chinese knows."

"Wow. I didn't. Sorry to hear."

"Yes," I nodded. "In fact, that is one of the largest incidences of lynching in American history and almost totally unknown." I cleared my throat. "There's a lot many of us don't know about lynching, not only in the United States, but globally. But after the break, we'll focus specifically on the U.S. history."

I gave them a generous break. I was sure they needed it, and so did I.

$$* \quad * \quad *$$

I got some coffee from the hall and then came back. I took down the noose photo and connected to the Internet.

Everybody came back except John. Well, I'd said they could leave without penalty.

"Here's how this part of the class will go. I plan to show you a series of actual photos of lynching, while also asking each person in the class to read a couple of lines of a poem by Richard Wright called 'Between the World and Me.'

"I have made copies and I have one for each of you, and I have highlighted the lines I'd like you to read. Your name is on the paper."

Emma raised her hand.

"Yes, Emma?"

"I thought that was by that guy Coates. He like writes for the *New York Times* and stuff?"

"Ta-Nehisi Coates wrote a book by that title, true, but the words are from Wright's poem. Coates's book is worth reading if you have not done so. It is in the form of a letter to his teenage son. The original, the poem, I mean, is much older. The reference is on the paper."

I started to hand out the papers and registered again that John was missing.

"Jordan, would you read John's part as well?"

He had been looking at his phone, but he seemed to hear me and just nodded, not being a smart-ass for once.

I handed the copies to Nari who was closest to me and she started passing them. They were now almost all so tense their arms moved like robots to take a copy and pass it.

"Let me read you part of what Du Bois wrote about hearing about lynching while he was a college student at Fisk when he was basically the same age as you are now." I turned to my notes.

"'Lynching was a continuing and recurrent horror during my college days: from 1885 through 1894, seventeen hundred Negroes were lynched in America. Each death was a scar upon my soul, and led me on to conceive the plight of other minority groups; for in my college days Italians were lynched in New Orleans [and there were] anti-Chinese riots, echoes of Jewish segregation and pogroms in Russia.'"

I looked up.

"See, that's what Mei pointed out. The riots included Chinese lynching. And more groups considered alien others.

"That's more than one per week, week after week, month after month, year after year. And it changed Du Bois. As he says, it scarred him. And it changed his whole career as an intellectual, I believe."

I looked at the class and waited a moment.

"'Seventeen hundred.' Let that sink in. Now, I'm going to start the slide show from this website. These are postcards of actual photos of lynchings, collected by James Allen over twenty-five years. I'll show it twice, once with the narration on and then silently as each of you to read in turn the portion of the Wright poem highlighted on your individual paper."

I pressed "play" and the voice narrated the finding of these nauseating postcard images of burned bodies, tortured sometimes almost beyond recognition as human, with crowds of white spectators, often in their Sunday best, gathered around with evident satisfaction, even pleasure on their faces, taking pride at their role in the ruination of these human beings.

But this time, I didn't watch the film. I watched the students. Jordan's smirk was gone. Emma was crying again. The others mostly stared with expressions ranging from shock to resignation to anger. Jayden's lips were tight, her eyes lasered on the screen.

The video came to its grisly end.

I touched mute and signaled to Nari who had the first line. I started the video again and the photos showed the charred proof of the poet's words.

The students' voices rose and fell, some choking out the words, some reading so softly the sound did not make it around the table, some reading each
word like it had nothing to do with the ones next to it, and a couple reading
with angry hisses, willing the words away. But still they rose and fell, certain words too powerful to be stilled, either with anger or hesitation, words
like "a scorched coil of greasy hemp," or "trousers still with black blood," or
"a drained gin-flask," or "gasoline," and "thirsty voices," with "a thousand
faces," and "a blaze of red."

I had noted each reader and her or his voice. Anger was certainly justified, as was sobbing or whispering. I compared their voices reading the
sections of the poem to their earlier remarks. Did anyone sitting at this table
know or even suspect who had hung our very own coil of rope? I couldn't
tell. I hoped someone would be moved enough to tell me at some point.

I let them go early. They were all looking shell-shocked. I know I felt
like the class had already been going on for days.

Chapter 5

People shouldn't call for demons unless they really mean what they say.

—C. S. Lewis, *The Wisdom of Narnia*

Tuesday afternoon

After class ended, I went to my office and just sat behind my desk. The grey skies kept most of the daylight behind clouds, but I didn't turn on the lights. Aduba wasn't there, and I was glad to be alone. I wondered briefly if he was already using Hercules Abraham's office for prayer. Of course, I had only a vague idea of when Muslim prayer times would be. Again I was just astonished I had given no thought to the practicalities of having a Muslim colleague. Neither, apparently, had Adelaide.

I leaned back and pressed my hands to my eyes. Big mistake. Behind my eyelids I could see again the twisted, charred, but still human forms of the victims of lynching, and the gloating, even glorying, faces of the watching crowds. I shuddered. The white skin and teeth of the watchers had gleamed in the firelight like something summoned up from hell.

A loud knock on the door made me jump in my seat.

"Yes?" I called out sharply. "Who is it?"

"It's Jordan, Professor. May I come in?"

"Sure," I replied in a more civil tone. "The door is unlocked."

Jordan. The class clown. I was so not up for his smartass act right now. His "they lynch cows?" snarky question still rankled with me.

He opened the door, and I immediately saw this was not Jordan the clown coming to see me. His pale, nerd face was even more pasty than usual and his lips were compressed into a solid line of tension.

"Have a seat," I said neutrally.

Jordan dropped his backpack and sat down heavily. He didn't look at me. He looked down at the floor, his narrow shoulders hunched in his worn T-shirt. I waited.

He cleared his throat.

"Well, I just wanted to explain about John, see? And I don't know for sure."

He looked up and peered at me through the thick lenses of his large, dark framed glasses, his eyes magnified like those of an insect. He seemed think this remark might make sense to me. In a peculiar way, it did. Just not in the way he was pretending. Jordan knew something, and he didn't want to admit how much he knew. The trick in this kind of thing is to keep quiet. Cops know that well. Give a witness enough silence, and they'll say more than they planned. I just nodded slightly. He looked back at the floor, his large glasses sliding down his nose a little.

"It's just that this Muslim guy and his lecture got him going, you know?"

"Professor Abubakar, you mean," I said quietly.

Jordan realized he'd made a mistake.

"Yes. Yes. That professor." He paused. "That's why John left the class, you know. He texted me. I think he'll drop. He was already pissed, I mean angry, that the department had hired a Muslim, and then in class you went on and on about that stupid rope. He's a Christian, you know, and since you called the class 'Social Gospel,' he thought it would be about Christians."

"It is about Christians," I said dryly. "Don't worry about it. I'll follow up with John, Jordan."

He didn't reply right away and just picked at holes in the knees of his jeans for a while. They already had large tears in them. If he kept going, he'd turn them into shorts before he left my office. I just watched him.

Finally he looked up again, and spoke.

"I can't really say I know anything, but like people talk online, and well, I mean, John, he was really pissed off, and like he takes this religion stuff so seriously. Not like us in computer sciences. We just write code, you know, and don't pay attention to that stuff so much."

He smiled his lopsided smile, back to being the clown.

"Is that a nerd thing, ignoring reality?" I inquired, playing along.

"At this school, it's more of a geek thing, really. Geeks are the more academically inclined nerds," he said, mimicking a lecturing voice.

"How can you tell the difference?" I asked, continuing the game.

"You have to be dork to tell," Jordan chuckled. Then he grabbed his backpack and stood up. The legs of his jeans remarkably still held together, but jeans shorts were clearly in his immediate future.

"Anyway, I gotta go."

"Okay," I said, mildly. "Thanks for letting me know."

"Sure," he said, by way of farewell, and he slouched out the door. He didn't shut it. Typical.

I went around my desk and walked slowly to the door to shut it, thinking about Jordan's motive for coming in to see me. He thought John had hung the noose. But just John?

I crossed back to my desk and sat. There had certainly been rumblings around the campus for about a year now, maybe even longer, by people arguing about identity, and race, and so forth. We had more than our share of young, white guys who'd be very vulnerable to a "white is right" kind of message.

My phone rang. I looked at the display. It was Rev. Jane Miller-Gershman, the University Chaplain. I liked her a lot. Jane was a "take me or leave me" kind of person. She was married to a woman rabbi at a local synagogue. She had been a great help on an investigation last spring.

I reflected, as I reached for the phone, how much the uproar on campus created by the noose and flyers would have affected the students and their groups she advised.

"Hello, Jane," I said warmly. "Good to hear from you."

"Hello, Kristin," she said in a serious voice, and then she didn't say anything else. I waited. This was my day for waiting people out, apparently.

Finally she went on.

"Listen, Kristin, I just got off the phone with a pastor from Michigan, Rev. Ethan Dunn. He works with parents of white, teenaged boys, mostly, boys who are getting lured into this whole white supremacist ideology. Given what happened with that noose, I thought I'd invite him to come speak on campus."

"Well, good idea, Jane. Do you need me to help with that in some way?"

"No, that's not why I'm calling." She paused again. "The thing is, he said something interesting about how these young, white supremacist guys are recruited, and then how they communicate. I thought you should know and maybe pass it on to campus police colleagues. See somehow if that could be going on here."

I grabbed a pad to take some notes.

"Really? That could be helpful, Jane. What did he say?"

Jane went on.

"Well, he said they use the chat rooms of violent video games. The kids go on the games, and then they go to the chat rooms and there are these guys waiting there, and they lure them in."

Made a horrible kind of sense.

"Jane, did he say which games?"

"Well, the most popular one is called 'Revenge,' but there's another one called 'Hitman,' and he also mentioned one called 'Death Rally.'"

Nice names. I wrote them quickly on my pad.

"Jane, thanks. I'll check this out."

"There's one more thing," she said hurriedly before I could hang up. "He said everybody who plays these games and goes on the chat rooms uses fake names, creepy names, and the creepier the better. So it's not going to be easy to figure out if students here are doing this."

"Well, I'll pass this along to my colleagues in the campus police, and then we'll check it out. Tell Rev. Dunn thanks, and I look forward to meeting him."

"Sure, Kristin. I'll let you know when he can come."

Even as she was saying good-bye, I had my computer open, and I searched "Revenge, video game." Many links appeared. I clicked on the first one. "Revenge" was a first-person shooter game by an international group of designers appropriately called Carnage Inc. From the description, it seemed like there was one guy who wants revenge on everybody, and so he kills indiscriminately, wiping out both civilians and law enforcement. I read further. Ah. The game was designed as a "reaction to video game political correctness." Well, that figured. Can't be politically correct and a lone shooter at the same time, can you? No. Certainly not.

I decided to open the trailer, and I watched the game. A grainy, urban landscape appeared and a scruffy white guy with "sociopath" all but written on his forehead, wearing the trench coat garb so beloved of mass shooters since the Columbine High School mass shooting, started walking toward a group of people. Good gad, he took out a flamethrower and burnt up dozens and dozens of people. I shuddered, thinking about the lascivious, white faces watching African American bodies burn in the lynching photos. Then the weird, white guy (called "the Archenemy," I had read) pulled out his AK-15 (helpfully labeled) and shot at people running away. Then he used his big knife to finish off any survivors by cutting their throats.

After the initial shock, though, the game seemed boring to me, but then again, I was not the target audience. In scenario after scenario, the trailer showed the Archenemy doing the same flamethrower, AK-15, knife thing. The backgrounds changed, but the actions were pretty much the same. He committed mass murder at political rallies, the waterfront, the train station, and he even killed gun dealers. I guessed he really did want revenge on everybody. All through this, there was a creepy, atonal voice that rasped a nihilistic voice-over. I replayed it, listening to the voice again. What did it remind me of? Oh yes, Lord Voldemort in the Harry Potter movies.

There was a teaser in the trailer that you could play in "God mode." Sure. Which "God" was not specified. Probably Anubis, Egyptian god of the dead or something equally appropriate.

I felt like I needed to shower.

I imagined students playing this game and then coming to class. Now I was the one who felt like speaking in a creepy, raspy voice. "Don't be assholes, don't be assholes" would be a good voice-over message for these gamers.

I closed the computer. Time to call Alice. Maybe John Vandenberg was pissed, but Alice was really going to be pissed.

*   *   *

I reached Alice on her cell and just said I'd gotten some information that might lead us to who hung the noose. She didn't even acknowledge that, but just growled that she was on foot patrol on campus and could meet right away.

"The university coffee shop," she specified in a rasping monotone, eerily like the Voldemort voice.

That was Alice's favorite coffee shop as it was centrally located, brightly lit with overhead fixtures that emitted a fake, sunny glow, and kept at a consistent 72 degree temperature year-round. That counted a lot with Alice as she had to be outside so much, enduring the ridiculous Chicago weather extremes, and maybe she liked the pretend sunlight as there was almost never actual sunlight in Chicago. I preferred that basement coffee shop across the quad. It was located near the steam pipes and was usually uncomfortable and dimly lit with fluorescent lights. But the coffee was better, and I didn't feel like I was on the set of Baywatch, getting a fake tan. Alice called the coffee shop I liked "that dump."

When I got to the brightly lit, pleasantly warm, but not too warm, coffee shop, I stopped and got a cup of French Roast. It was the least offensive of their coffee blends. Today's other featured coffees, I saw with horror, were "Maple Bacon" or "Spicy Taco." I slapped a lid on my French Roast before it could get contaminated by bacon or taco flavoring. I looked around for Alice, and I spotted her back through the window. She had abandoned the fake interior and was sitting at an outside table, smoking. Nicotine was her go-to stress response like caffeine was mine. We had each promised the other to cut down on our drugs of choice. We were not succeeding.

I walked up to the table. Like all good cops, she was aware I was behind her, and she just said, "Don't" without looking around.

She got up and took the half-smoked cigarette over to one of those black, outside cigarette disposal units that looked like an upside-down sledge hammer, ground it out and shoved it into the slot. She turned and clumped back toward the table, her sturdy cop shoes crunching the dry leaves littering the flagstones.

She sat back down, took out her notebook, and only then did she look up at me, her deep brown eyes opaque. She was still shut down.

"What you got?"

"Hello, Alice, glad to see you too. How are you? How are Shawna and Jim?"

"Always so damn cute," she muttered, but her heart wasn't really into pushing back at me. Then her shoulders relaxed a little under her dark, uniform jacket, and she softened her tone as I knew she would whenever I brought up her daughter, Shawna, who was six.

"Last spelling test, 100 percent," Alice bragged. "She purely loves school." She glanced at me under her fringe of dark hair. "Must be you rubbing off on her." She paused and then went on more seriously, "And Jim is good too, I mean, now that he's driving that truck and out of the house. Hard to have him gone so much, though." Then she stopped, I assumed not wanting to share too much. But I thought she knew I understood.

Her husband, Jim, had been a firefighter in their south suburban town, but budget cuts had eliminated his job, and he'd been out of work for almost eighteen months. Then he'd gotten a truck driving license and, it seemed, a good job. But I bet it was hard on them, his being on the road. I knew Alice had family around to help with Shawna, as her hours were no picnic either. As a widow now for six years, I knew well what it was like to have to do solo parenting. And Alice knew that I knew.

"Sounds like it's tough," I replied neutrally. "But hey, 100 percent on the spelling is great. The boys do okay in spelling, but they complain that it is so dumb now that there's spellcheck." Yes, at seven they knew spellcheck on the computer.

Alice hmphed, opened her notebook, and clicked her pen. She was done with chit-chat.

I took her cue and just summarized what Jordan had said when he'd come to my office about John Vandenberg. Then I went on to Jane's call with the information from Rev. Dunn about white supremacist wannabe's using the chat rooms of violent video games to recruit and also to communicate. Perhaps they had used a chat room to plan the hanging of the noose. Jordan had implied John Vandenberg had acted alone, angry at the hiring of a Muslim professor in Philosophy and Religion and then at the title of his planned lecture.

"I don't know, though, Alice, if that's right, either that John Vandenberg hung the noose, or if he did, that he did it alone. There's some white guy students here who even tried to get Richard Spencer to come speak. It could be a larger group," I finished.

"Who's he?" Alice said, pausing in her writing and looking up quizzically.

"You know, that neo-Nazi, rich idiot who's always quoting Germans and saying 'Heil Trump' and so forth?"

Alice looked blank for a minute.

"White guy?"

"Yeah. Sort of a professional white guy, really, with rich parents so he doesn't actually have to do anything to support himself. He keeps claiming 'America belongs to the white man,' and tries to get on to college campuses and talk about stuff like that under the banner of 'free speech.'"

"And you think I pay attention to mess like that? Give a little shit like that any space in my brain? Do you think I'd let that filth come near me and mine?" Alice sat up straight and glared at me, her whole body rigid with anger.

"No. Of course not," I said. "I'm just saying we need to know who the enemy is."

Oh, hell. As soon as the words were out of my mouth, I realized I'd made a huge mistake. Alice's face went from anger to blank like someone had pulled the blinds closed. And someone had. Me.

"You think I don't know who the enemy is?" she ground out between clenched teeth, her lips barely moving. "You think I haven't known that all my life, had it shoved in my face every day, on the street, on a bus, in school, in this damn job for this 'oh we're so liberal, white people we don't see you' school? Do you?"

"Yes, you do know that. I shouldn't have said what I did. It was stupid and blind. I'm sorry."

She looked away, taking deep breaths.

I just waited.

"Try to think before you open your damn mouth, okay?" she said, still not looking at me.

"Yeah. Okay." I wanted to say "sorry" and "I feel awful for what I just said," and a bunch of other white, guilt-type phrases, but I figured the least I could do was shut up and not make it worse.

Alice opened the zip on her jacket and took out a little metal case that I knew held her cigarettes and lighter. She tapped the tip of a cigarette on the stone-topped table, put it between her lips, and lit it. She took a big drag, inhaling like this was her first gasp of air after having been choked. Then she took another short pull. She glared up at me, daring me to say anything.

I continued shutting up.

"They use these video games to plan stuff?" Alice said, puffing again while looking down at her notebook.

She was all business.

"That's what Jane told me Rev. Dunn had said," I replied evenly. "Yeah, in short, they go online, play the game, and then use the chat room to communicate. And they all use screen names, weird ones, Jane reported, though God knows what they consider weird. We can't just look at the chat rooms of these games and see that it's students."

I paused, thinking. Alice took another drag.

"But we might be able to tell from what they're saying to each other. I mean if they sound like they're talking about our campus."

She paused, looking at her notebook.

"So what's the name of the student who ratted out the other student?"

"Jordan Jameson is the guy who came to see me, and John Vandenberg is the name of the student Jordan said was all upset about Dr. Abubakar's lecture and so forth."

Alice wrote that down. Then she took another deep drag, got up without comment, and took the half-smoked cigarette to the outdoor container. She ground it out, pushed it in, and came back.

She sat, drumming her fingers on the hard surface of the table. I wondered where she had gone in her mind. I realized I had no clue. I had my own ideas, but knew continuing to shut up was best, at least right now.

"Mel," she said, looking up at me.

"Mel?" She was referring to her colleague and often partner, Mel Billman. Mel had been on the quad when Alice had cut down the noose, I recalled. He was a tall, mixed-race guy who rarely said anything, but when he did it was best to pay close attention.

"Mel's a gamer, is that what you mean?" I asked.

"Yeah. Think so." She tapped her pen on her teeth. "Last year, maybe it was, he went to some convention here in Chicago, think it was about these game things. Excited about it."

She took her pen and jotted something down.

"Mel was excited?" I said, disbelief in my voice.

Alice actually grinned a little.

"For him, yeah. Ten more words than usual." She rooted in her jacket pocket, took out her phone and started scrolling.

"Today's duty roster shows he's on. I'll tell him about what that pastor from Michigan said and the mess they could be making with these crap games. What're the names he gave Jane?"

"Revenge," I said, the word coming out in a grim tone, "as well as 'Hitman,' and 'Death Rally.' 'Revenge' is the most popular, apparently."

Alice looked up from writing.

"Yeah. Right."

She made another note, put the notebook away in another pocket, and stood up.

"Alice," I said.

"Yeah, yeah. I know you sorry as hell, but you gotta think first." She paused. "You know that stunt you pulled yesterday?"

I just nodded.

"Me? If I'd done it, I'd be dead today."

She put her hands on the table surface and leaned over so our faces were closer. I could smell the cigarette smoke on her breath.

"You wanna be brave and hell, you throw yourself at stuff scares the shit out of me. But you brave enough to walk around in a black woman's skin? You brave enough for that? They want us purely dead, Kristin. Every damn day."

I took a breath.

"If I could, Alice, I would."

She stood back up.

"Yeah. That's why I can just about stand to know you. But you can't. You purely can't."

She turned and walked away, head high.

I just sat there and thought. Some popular historian had written a book on our current, what Alice would call "mess" in America, and blathered on about "summoning our better angels." It wasn't the angels we needed to be concerned with. It was the demons that lurked right below the surface, demons created by the kinds of hatred that had festered in our history. And this demonic legacy was bubbling up through the cracks now, cracks opened wider by these white supremacist yahoos. I gazed across the lawn toward the tree on the quad in the distance. How long before we had another noose? Or worse?

I walked slowly back to my office, thinking. When I got there, Abubakar wasn't present. Then I remembered he had a class this afternoon.

I opened my computer and started researching identity-masking software. Maybe I couldn't live in a black woman's skin, but I could become someone else online and get these bastards.

Chapter 6

*Through me you go into a city of weeping; through me you go
into eternal pain; through me you go amongst the lost people.*

—Dante Alighieri, *The Inferno*

Late Tuesday evening to Wednesday

I was terrified. I ran through grey, ruined streets, where charred corpses
were strewn everywhere. There was no color except the blood that ran
like streams in the gutters. I couldn't see a way out. A blast of flame hit
the wall nearest me. I had to move. I had to run. There was no one left
alive to save. Then there was a gun. It was in my hand. I was the killer, not
the prey. My gun moved across the landscape, seeking, seeking. It found
a target. It was pointed at a woman who ran from me into a boarded up
building. I fired and fired and chunks of the building flew in all directions. And then a body shattered a window above me and started to fall.
I was falling. I screamed.

"Mom! Mom!"

The voice seemed far away.

"Mom!" The voice was more frantic. Then there was a loud bark right
in my ear.

My face felt wet and I jolted awake.

"What?" I croaked.

I opened my eyes, and my son Mike's scared face was inches from
mine. He was on the bed with me, holding me by the shoulders. The dog
was on the bed on my other side, panting and, I realized, drooling on me.

"Mom, you okay? You were screaming," Mike said, not letting go of
me.

"Yes," I said shakily. "I'm okay. I just had an awful nightmare."

I struggled to sit up, and Mike released my shoulders, but he didn't
move off the bed.

"Molly, get off!" I said to the dog, and she jumped down, though she whined a little. I moved over so Mike could have more room next to me on the bed. I shoved my computer aside where it was lying beside me. The computer. I must have fallen asleep playing one of those idiot video games, I thought. I was relieved to see the screen had gone dark while I'd been asleep. It would have been horrible if Mike had seen it. I closed it and put it on the end table. Then I put my arms around my trembling child.

"You okay?" I peered into my son's face, still tight with fear. "And where's Sam?"

"Yeah. I'm okay. It's just . . . I heard you scream, and I ran in here, and Molly ran after me, and you wouldn't wake up." He paused, swallowing. "Sam's still asleep. You know him. He could sleep through an earthquake."

He hesitated, then choked out, "What's wrong, what's the matter?"

I try to be honest with the boys, while realizing how young they are. Though Mike acted like he was so mature, he was just a little boy pretending to be the dad they didn't have. My heart hurt. I thought for a second about what to say.

"I was doing some research on the computer, and I saw some scary things. I must have fallen asleep and dreamed a bad dream about them," I said, sticking as close to the truth as I could without further terrifying my son. I felt awful about that.

"Well, you shouldn't do that late at night," said Mike, sitting up. He was starting to feel better, and lecturing always made him feel more in control. Same with me, I thought wryly. That's why I like lecturing too.

"Yes, you're right. Now let's see. Why don't we go downstairs, have some warm milk, and then maybe we can both get some good sleep, huh?"

"Yeah. Good idea. But I want some chocolate syrup in mine. And a cookie."

Mike could tell I was feeling guilty about scaring him, and he would press his advantage. He was going to be a very successful lawyer someday, I thought.

"That could work." I smiled at him.

We went downstairs, and Molly followed, wagging her tail. She didn't know what the new game was, but, when the kitchen was involved, she was always enthusiastic.

I fixed warm milk for us and put one squirt of chocolate syrup in Mike's. I got out an oatmeal cookie from the jar and handed it to him. He finished it in one bite and then took a sip of his chocolate milk. I gave Molly a small dog cookie. She finished hers in one bite too. I poured a little cold milk in her bowl, and she inhaled it.

I could see my son's shoulders start to droop even before he'd drained the mug. I put an arm around him and helped him to bed. Molly settled down on her dog bed located between the boys' twin beds. I checked on Sam, and Mike was right. Sam could sleep through just about anything. He was still snoozing away.

I went into my room and looked at the closed computer like it was an aquarium holding a bunch of writhing snakes. I picked it up gingerly and put it on the top of the wardrobe across the room.

I got into bed but left the lights on and thought about what had happened. After the boys had gone to bed, I'd installed the identity-masking software and downloaded the game "Revenge." I had gone on to the game site and entered the screen name I'd created for myself. I was calling myself "Odin26." There were other Odins, and I had to use a number as well as the name. Odin was the Norse god of war who liked the chaos and violence of war for its own sake, not for any noble purpose, as warmongers today at least pretended. But ancient Odin was also a fairly complex character. He liked poetry, and could, occasionally, assume the more feminine role of Shaman. The Nazis, and I was betting these Nazi wannabes, had revered the furious god of war, ignoring Odin's gender-bending. In fact, they would have been horrified by it had they realized. I'd thought myself so clever in using that name. After I was on the site, I did the game-playing for a while, but then I went to the chat room as Odin26. There was inane chatter about "them" and "claiming our rights" and blah blah, but nothing specific about our campus or any planned actions I could see. There was an extended exchange about THOT. I'd paused and searched that. To my disgust it stood for That Ho Over There. The misogyny was nauseating.

Then I'd checked out the other game, the one called "Hitman." It was another one of those single shooter formats, where I, as the player, was basically just a hand and a gun. As I'd started the play, it quickly had become clear all the women who appeared were targets. They were grotesquely sexualized and were supposed to be prostitutes or strippers. My character was offered extra points and "health" if I killed a prostitute. I couldn't remember any more. Oddly, it seemed I'd fallen asleep about then. I thought about the nightmare, about going from being the one hunted to becoming the killer with the gun. I was not happy with my subconscious.

I glanced at the digital dial of my clock. It was 2 a.m. Still, I needed to think about something else, at least for a few minutes. I didn't want to go back into the nightmare. I picked up a paperback mystery novel I was reading about a detective whose leading characteristic was kindness. Unusual. I opened it, and must have fallen asleep again almost immediately. The next thing I knew it was morning.

Chat Room of Video Game "Revenge"

Wednesday, 3 a.m.

Moloch111: where are you, man? p**** f***** mouthbreathers here totally getting to me talking about protesting hate can you f***** believe it???

Demon196: Stay white fella. Can you do that crap? Fat jelly roll it is. Don't you hump it bro. It's mo crap. Its time alright?

Moloch111: got it

Chapter 7

*You shall not give any of your children to sacrifice them to Moloch,
and so profane the name of your God: I am the LORD.*

—LEVITICUS 18:21

Wednesday

"Where's Giles? We want Bori, not that stuff." I could hear the two, whining voices all the way up at the top of the stairs.

I hurried down and into the kitchen. A tired, and uncharacteristically harassed-looking Carol turned from the counter with two bowls in her hands.

"Hey, guys. That's no way to talk to Carol," I said sternly.

"Sorry, Carol," they said in unison. "But where's Giles?" Mike continued, undeterred. "We don't like that cereal."

"He had to leave early," Carol said quietly, putting down the two bowls of what looked like her homemade granola on the table.

Privately, I agreed with the boys, at least about the granola. Carol's homemade granola tasted like sawdust with some gravel thrown in for variety.

"Mom, can't you make us some Bori?" Sam wheedled.

"You boys know I can't make Bori. Remember what happened last time?"

They both frowned, and I saw they recalled some of what had occurred. I had tried making Bori and it came out so thick it could have been used to fill the numerous potholes on the Chicago streets.

"Oh, yeah," Mike said.

"Let's get the maple syrup Carol's Dad sent instead and put some on the cereal," I countered. I turned to Carol. "Do you know where we put that, Carol?" I asked her.

49

She turned, looked at me, and I was startled to see she was holding back tears. Was it the boys rejecting her granola, or something else? Something to do with Giles leaving early?

"Never mind, Carol. I'll find it. And I had planned to walk the boys to school today, if that's okay. You go ahead and get going."

"Thanks," she said quietly and left the room.

I hunted around for the maple syrup, while the boys watched me in silence. I found it in the pantry. But then I thought I remembered we had a package of frozen waffles in the back of the freezer, hidden from both Carol and Giles. I opened the freezer door and rummaged around. Ah, there it was. I pulled it out of the frost and dusted the package in the sink.

"How about some waffles to go with that syrup?" I asked.

"Yeah. Way!" they chirped.

There were four waffles in the package. I put them in our four-slot toaster and then forked three out on to plates when they popped up. I took Molly's bowl and gave her the last one. She'd had a tough night too, though I had to hold it back from her until it cooled.

With butter and the marvelous syrup, they were pretty good.

I told the boys to go get their backpacks. While they were gone, I rinsed all the dishes, ground up the granola in the disposal and hid the empty waffle package in my own backpack to drop in a recycling can on the way to campus. Best not to leave any evidence. I hadn't been a Chicago police detective all that long, but I knew that.

＊　＊　＊

We only lived three blocks from their school and made it in plenty of time, though avoiding the puddles from last night's rain slowed us down some. Well, it slowed me down as I kept my hands on two backpacks, guiding the boys around the puddles instead of straight through as they loved to do. We got to the school with relatively dry shoes. Sam gave me a fist bump and his cheeky smile, then he ran up the stairs and disappeared inside. Mike looked around, probably to be sure none of his friends were there, and then he leaned in to me for a second for a real hug. Then he broke it off and also ran up the stairs. I still felt awful about scaring him. I just stood there for a minute, contemplating the door of the school.

"Kristin!"

I started out of my reverie and turned around. Jane was hustling across the greenspace that bisected the campus toward me. I waited for her.

"I'm so glad to catch you like this!" she said a little breathlessly. "I was going to call you this morning." She paused, aware that parents and kids were milling around us in front of the school.

"Can we walk together some? I assume you're heading for your office."

"Yes, certainly, Jane." I moved on down the sidewalk with her.

"Thanks for that information you gave me from Rev. Dunn," I said. "We're following up on it through campus police contacts." I decided not to mention my own excursion into that hideous world and my nightmare.

She was silent and I glanced over at her. She looked very tired.

"Jane, how are you? I can only imagine how this turmoil on campus has been difficult for you."

"Oh, I'm okay." She hugged her arms over her raincoat. "I try not to own all the problems myself, but give people support to solve them together."

That sounded good and certainly I had to try to learn to do that, I thought, but I could see from her self-supporting posture that she hadn't been entirely successful in letting others carry their own burdens. Her body, at least, reflected the weight of this past week. And then I thought, "It's only Wednesday."

Jane turned and gave me a wry smile. I realized I'd said "It's only Wednesday" aloud.

"Anyway, Kristin, what I wanted to talk to you about is that a coalition of student groups has gotten permission from the administration to hold a big demonstration this Sunday on campus. They're calling it a 'Rally Against Hate' because of that awful noose, the hateful leaflets, and the horrible social media exchanges people are having because of all that. There is very bad feeling among the students and even some staff and faculty."

I wasn't surprised the campus was in an uproar. I'd seen that myself, but I was surprised the coalition had the okay to go ahead.

"The administration gave permission for a rally? This is the first I've heard of it. It's not like them. Usually they try to minimize any conflict on campus and shove it out of sight." I knew what I was talking about from bitter experience. In fact, I heard my bitterness in my own voice.

Jane put a thin hand on my arm for a second. She knew.

"There's just too many groups going together on this for them to blow it off completely, and it is being well organized, I think." She stopped, and I faced her. She continued, her voice very firm.

"I told the President that we'd have an even bigger mess on our hands if we didn't let the students demonstrate peacefully." So it was Jane who had made the case for the rally. Jane was a very determined person despite her quiet manner. No wonder the President had agreed. The face she was making right now would have fit in on Mount Rushmore.

"Well, good," I replied. "I'm sure I'll hear from the campus police about how we plan to help keep things peaceful during the rally. Where will it be held? On the Quad?"

"No, on the greenspace here." Jane gestured to the central area adjacent to the sidewalk where we were walking. But it wasn't an empty green space now. There was a traveling exhibit of outdoor sculpture right there. And the sculptures were huge. It was a fairly recent installation. I had been planning to take the kids to see it.

Jane saw me looking at the statues and chuckled.

"No. Not right there. Further to the West." She pointed in that direction.

"That's fairly close up on to the park there. I hope the city doesn't have to get involved with permitting too."

The City of Chicago had a permitting system that seemed to be modeled on a labyrinth. With a Minotaur. And no actual exit.

Jane shook her head.

"No, that wouldn't work. We have to stay on campus."

Then she stopped, and I stopped opposite her. The huge university chapel building was right in front of us. It was hardly a chapel, though, since it was the size and design of a medieval cathedral.

"Anyway, here's what I wanted to ask you. The students would like to have Dr. Aduba Abubakar, your new colleague, speak at the rally." She paused and cleared her throat. Jane normally didn't dither.

"Anyway, they wanted me to ask you to ask him to speak."

"Why not just ask him directly, Jane?" I asked bluntly.

"Well, nobody knows him, so they wanted you to ask because you do." Jane was trying for a matter-of-fact voice, but I could tell she too thought they should just ask Aduba directly.

I held in my irritation. This wasn't Jane's fault. I thought for a minute.

"How about this? I'll mention to him that a coalition of student groups wants him to speak at the rally and a representative will be in touch shortly. Do you know who will ask?"

"Ah, no. Not yet."

Well, perhaps the organizing was not as organized as she was saying. But it had to be hard, and I needed to cut her some slack. Her job right now was impossible.

"I'll just say 'someone' will be in touch and leave it at that, okay?"

"Yes, certainly. That will be a help. I'll tell them. Thanks, Kristin. I'm glad I ran into you."

"Me too. Good luck, Jane." Good luck to all of us, I thought.

The shadow of the giant cathedral fell over Jane's face as she turned toward her office.

"We'll need more than luck," she said, looking up at the stained glass window that loomed over us, some angels flitting around.

Well, if she was counting on divine assistance, I wasn't confident we'd get any help. The problem of how God could be good and evil exist in this world never went away for me.

* * *

Aduba wasn't in our shared office when I got there. I did think I shouldn't wait to give him a heads up about the invitation to speak at the rally, so I composed a short email and sent it. Then when I saw him, I'd follow up in person.

Also, I thought I'd better arrange the catering for Saturday night. After all, I smiled wryly to myself, "it's only Wednesday." I called an African vegan restaurant that I'd heard was good, though we'd not eaten there. I knew they did a lot of catering, and vegan food was considered Halal, the Muslim equivalent of Kosher, if there was no alcohol used in cooking. The woman who answered said they'd be delighted, confirmed that they never used alcohol in preparing food, and she took down the number of diners, the time and the address. She told me to go on their website and select the dishes I wanted, and she gave me a code to enter for the catering reservation. I did that and in about ten minutes that was taken care of. Oh, if only everybody were as well organized. Me included.

Since I was already on my computer, I thought it would be a good idea to get some work done. I sighed. Email first. When I opened it, I saw there was an email from the Registrar. I read it. John Vandenberg had, indeed, dropped "The Social Gospel." I'd try to talk to him anyway. I started to write John an email asking him if we could meet and talk, and then I hesitated. Maybe I should talk to Jordan again before I did that. I also thought about talking to Adelaide. I decided I'd wait on that until I'd talked with John.

I was sitting there still pondering John's dropping the class when my cell phone rang. I could see it was Alice.

"Yes, Alice."

"You got time this afternoon for a meeting?" she said. We were back to the no chit-chat Alice.

"Let me check. I think so." I went to my calendar program, and I scrolled through the rest of the day. I had blocked this afternoon out for research. So much for that.

"Yes, I can make a meeting. What's up?"

I was assuming this was a meeting about the rally, but I waited for Alice to fill me in.

"Mel's got a line on those creeps, the ones that talk on that game," Alice said, her voice filled with contempt. And why not? They were contemptible.

She went on before I could comment, her voice stone cold.

"They plannin' something. Writin' in some kind of code, but Mel thinks he knows what it means. We want to catch 'em in the act, so we have to run it by the captain, get him to sign off. The new captain, you've met him, right, Gutierrez? I gave him a heads up, and he wants to meet all of us, you too, he said specific."

Alice snorted.

"Wonder why? Maybe he figures to keep an eye on you?"

I was glad to hear that snort because it meant Alice was more herself, but I didn't joke back.

"What are they planning?" I asked, an edge to my voice.

"Don't get het up. Nothin' big. But we can catch 'em. Since it's students, though, you know, kid gloves and crap."

"Okay. Sure. What time and where?"

"Captain's office. Be there at three." Alice disconnected.

Rats. I'd meant to ask her about what she knew about the rally. Well, I could ask at the meeting. I wondered what Mel had found in the chat room. I hadn't seen anything remotely suspicious when I'd gone on to either game.

My stomach tightened as I remembered the horrible nightmare. And I knew this wouldn't end the waking nightmare either. We might be able to grab a student or two who were part of this particular act, but the hate was spreading, possessing others, tempting them, corrupting them. I sighed and turned back to my email.

✳   ✳   ✳

I'd gone home for lunch. I'd contemplated swinging by the library to fit in some research on my neglected doctoral dissertation on my way to the campus police station, but I just didn't have any enthusiasm for it. And now I hated to go to the library since I'd been attacked there nearly two years ago. I sat in my study at home, munching the cheese sandwich I'd made for myself. Was that the problem, or did I need to change my dissertation topic yet again? I shook my head. No, it wasn't either of those things. I had known for a while what the problem was, but I'd been unwilling to face it. The events of this week were forcing me toward a conclusion I just dreaded. Reasoned, academic work was becoming more and more pointless to me in a society where irrationality and a firehose of lying was sweeping away cherished social norms. Why write? Who read and thought anymore? With that morose thought, I think I must have groaned aloud, as Molly got up from where she had been napping by my desk and put her head on my lap. I petted her. Dogs knew if somebody you loved groaned, you went to them, stood by them.

*   *   *

As I walked up the sidewalk toward the university police station, I had to chuckle a little, despite my gloomy mood about the collapse of western civilization. The whole set-up always struck me as so schizophrenic. The outside of the building itself was charming, with faded brick walls and ivy climbing gracefully up them. It was almost a caricature of classic, academic architecture. The interior, however, was another matter.

I pushed open the carved wooden doors and entered a world I knew better than I knew academia. Inside, the campus police station was exactly like the worst of the Chicago area police stations with cracked linoleum floors, poor fluorescent lighting, and peeling green paint on the walls. I stopped at the desk in front. I wondered if its dirty top had actually been salvaged from some cop shop that had been torn down. I showed my University I.D. without comment and was directed upstairs. I thanked the officer, but I already knew well where to go.

I had a long acquaintance with the office of the Commander of the University of Police. The new hire, Alfonso Gutierrez, who had started in late summer, preferred to be called "Captain." His predecessor had only been temporary, brought in to address some serious problems. He'd been in and out so fast, he'd made no changes to the office décor he'd inherited. As I knocked on the door labeled "Captain A. Gutierrez," I wondered if Gutierrez had.

I heard a sharp "Come in!" and entered. I could see the reception area hadn't been changed a bit. It still looked like a showroom at some kitschy, colonial furniture store, but as I approached the inner office, I could see the wing-back chairs were gone, replaced with a bunch of molded, white plastic chairs, extras of which were stacked along a side wall. Well, well. Gutierrez liked bigger meetings in his office than his predecessors and apparently didn't care that his guests sat in chairs from Ikea. I liked that.

Alice and Mel were already there, seated on two of the plastic chairs. Captain Gutierrez rose from behind his desk.

"Professor Ginelli? I'm Captain Gutierrez," he said, rolling the r's in his name only slightly. His barely accented voice was deep and measured.

"Yes, hello," I replied and I resisted the urge to say we had met before. Better to let him take the lead.

He extended a hand to me without coming out from behind the desk. This forced me to come to him, or not shake his hand. Interesting. I moved forward slowly, deliberately, and I could see his eyes crinkled a little at the corners. He knew I knew what he was doing. His whole face was almost a map of wrinkles, where I could see it anyway. He had a very full, black mustache, sprinkled with grey, as well as black and silvered hair that was slightly too long for regulation. Greying eyebrows shaded his black eyes. He wasn't tall, probably not much over five and a half feet or so, and he hunched forward slightly as we shook hands. He held my gaze for a moment. I was a head taller than he was, but oddly it didn't feel like it. This guy had a lot of presence.

I turned and sat in the empty chair between Mel and Alice. Mel simply nodded at me, but Alice was frowning. "Behave yourself" was the message her eyes were sending to me. I gave her a neutral look and took my seat.

"Lieutenant Billman," Gutierrez said in his deliberate way, "you believe you have found something on a game, something that concerned you that gives an idea of who did our campus prank?"

Prank? Kind of a weak way to describe a hate crime, I though.

"Yes, I think I have," Mel said, opening a tablet he had been holding on his lap. "I took some screen shots. I have them here." He tapped the screen a couple of times, but before he could read out what was there, Gutierrez snapped his fingers and just gestured that Mel should give him the tablet. Mel shrugged and extended it. With his long arms, he didn't even have to rise from his chair.

Gutierrez took it, frowned deeply, and then glared at the screen. He looked up.

"Did they do a mistake? What is this?"

Mel was scarcely intimidated. He just extended his arm again for the tablet. Gutierrez relinquished it, his frown even deeper. Now I knew how those lines came to be so inscribed on his face.

"It's this," Mel said and read from the screen. "*Can you do that crap? Fat jelly roll it is. Don't you hump it bro.*"

"How does this have any meaning?" Gutierrez asked irritably.

"It's a simple, eight-letter acrostic. They're not very good at it, since it is so obviously gibberish, it shouts out that it's supposed to be code. It was quick to decipher. It means that someone who calls himself 'Moloch111' should to go to a copy shop at 4 a.m. Later chat reveals they mean tomorrow. This is likely to be at least one of the students who hung the noose and distributed the previous flyers. I believe they plan to make more flyers about the planned rally."

Gutierrez grimaced. "Yes, that rally." He paused. "You sure it is four in the morning they mean? All campus facilities then are closed, I think."

Alice cleared her throat and spoke.

"There's an all-night copy shop right near the main campus, sir. We think," and here she nodded at Mel, "that's where they mean to go. At that hour, there's less chance of anybody seeing the garbage they are copying."

I realized as I listened to her I was a little miffed Alice had discussed this first with Mel. "Get a grip," I told myself. "This isn't a BFF issue, it's an investigation."

"Supposing you are right, Lieutenant Billman. What do you propose we do?"

Now I was miffed on Alice's behalf. No acknowledgment of Alice's role, Gutierrez? I glanced at Alice, but she had her shuttered face in place, giving nothing away.

"Well, what we think," and here Mel nodded toward Alice, and good on him, I thought, "is that there should be a stake-out at the copy shop starting at about 3 a.m. Someone needs to be in there, pretending to staff it and get a look at what's being copied. If it is like the earlier flyers, they can signal a couple of us hidden outside." He paused. "Should be somebody white, I think."

Gutierrez turned his frown on to me, but Mel interrupted.

"No, no women. This is a guys only kind of operation."

I moved in my chair, preparing to protest, and Alice gave me her major glare, the one that could stop perps in their tracks. "Okay, Alice," I said to her, but only in my head. "Fine." I sat back and just nodded. Besides, I remembered THOT, the acronym the yahoos in the chat room had used meaning "That Ho Over There," and the killing of women getting extra points in their game. I didn't say anything, but I made up my own acronym, WGO. White Guys Only.

"The operation is approved," Gutierrez was saying. I realized he'd been speaking while I was talking to myself. "Coordinate with those you need and write it up. Keep me informed." He nodded and stood. Apparently, we were dismissed. Alice and Mel stood up and walked quickly out. I glanced at Gutierrez before I followed them. He was already seated again, angled toward his computer. But I thought it was an act. A pose. He was nervous about this operation. Well, he should be. The administration wanted a no muss, no fuss approach to students, even ones who committed hate crimes, I reflected as I rose and walked slowly out of the room.

I could see Alice and Mel already far down the hall, conferring. They were heading to Alice's office. I followed. When I got to the door, however, it was already shut. All my resentment that I'd kept inside during the meeting bubbled up. They were shutting me out.

I opened the door and went in. They were seated side-by-side at a small table Alice kept pushed against the wall, a pad of paper already between them. Alice glanced up when I entered, looking surprised.

"Yeah, Kristin, what?" she said.

"I'm in," I replied curtly.

Mel turned, but it was Alice who spoke.

"You heard. You're not in." She turned back.

"I'll be there, down the street, hiding, but I'll be there. You know I will."

Alice's head snapped around, and she gave me the glare again. Too bad. I wasn't budging. But I didn't have two seven-year-old kids for nothing. I thought I'd try wheedling.

"Besides, you need me," I said in that tone Mike and Sam had perfected. "If it's students, and we all think it is, and it goes way south, having a professor there might be helpful." I smiled too.

Alice snorted so hard I thought she'd spray droplets on the pad they were using. Mel's shoulders were shaking a little. I realized he was trying not to laugh.

"Sit down," said Alice wearily, sounding just like I did when I gave in to the kids.

I sat.

Chapter 8

Two things may be considered in the assault of the demons—the assault itself, and the ordering thereof. The assault itself is due to the malice of the demons, who through envy endeavor to hinder man's progress; and through pride usurp a semblance of Divine power.

—THOMAS AQUINAS, QUESTION 114: THE ASSAULTS OF THE DEMONS, *SUMMA THEOLOGICA*

Thursday

I slumped down in the driver's seat of my car, hoping I was well hidden. In dark clothes and a dark watch cap, I should be. I had parked across the street from the copy shop, about a block to the east. At 3 a.m., I'd had my choice of on-street parking. I sipped coffee from my insulated cup while I turned to watch what was happening in the lighted window. It was like viewing a play with no sound.

The copy shop guy was handing his green apron with the COPY 24/7 name and motto, "We're Awake Too," to a campus cop appropriately named Steve White. Steve was a new hire on the campus police force. He was from a southern suburb, Alice had told me. He seemed to be a good substitute for the regular copy guy. They even looked a little alike, medium height, light brown hair, on the thin side. And, of course, white.

The manager of COPY 24/7 had been very cooperative when he'd been contacted by Gutierrez, I'd heard from Alice. He probably didn't want his business to get a reputation as "neo-Nazi central." The plan was to see if anyone came to make copies of more white supremacist flyers and if so identify the person or persons, and that might lead us to who hung the noose. The copy shop already had a security camera in place, and it had been checked to be sure it was working.

I thought of other stake-outs, ones where I'd not been warm and dry with hot coffee handy. I could feel myself tensing, remembering one stake-out in particular when I'd been a cop. It had gone very badly. "Don't go there," I told myself sternly. Instead of thinking about that, I decided to worry about Mel and Alice. I glanced up and down the street to identify where they were hidden. I could see Mel, I thought. He was in an unmarked car parked in the alley that ran next to the copy shop on the side away from campus. I couldn't see Alice. It had been raining lightly for a while, and the drops on the windows made it hard to see. I squinted, and still didn't see Alice. I wondered if she were in the campus police car parked in the alley behind the shop.

I checked my watch, shielding the light with my gloved hand. It was almost four. I looked at the street and realized the rain had stopped. Then I saw a figure in a hoodie hurrying up the street from the direction of the campus. I held my breath. The figure turned in to the copy shop and went up to the desk. The figure passed over some cash to Steve, who was standing behind the counter wearing the green apron. The figure took something from Steve. I assumed it was the copier counter. As the person turned to head toward the copy machines, he pushed the hoodie back. Yes, it was a he. With a jolt, I recognized John Vandenberg, the student who had just dropped my class.

John unzipped his hoodie and took out a paper from inside, where I assumed he'd been protecting it from the rain. He opened the copier lid and the blue light illumined his long face. It had an intent, almost rapt look. He put the paper into the copier and shut the lid. He was concentrating so hard on the task, he did not seem to notice when Steve left the counter and came up next to him. Steve quickly removed one piece of paper from the tray where the copies were piling up and stepped back, examining it. John turned with a jerk and tried to grab the paper from Steve's hand.

Steve was good. I'd give him that. He just stepped back smoothly and said something to John while holding the paper away from him. John recoiled, grabbed the remaining papers from the tray, and just ran out of the shop.

I quickly got out of my car and stood on the sidewalk. John sprinted across the street and cut through two parked cars a little to my right. He then pelted up the sidewalk toward me. I stepped directly into his path.

"John!" I called out, and he nearly slipped and fell on the wet sidewalk. He stood up and started to brush past where I was standing.

"John, wait," I said, more calmly.

"You! You, you race traitor," John turned and yelled at me, nearly spitting with rage. He stood there trembling, and I thought he'd run again in a minute.

"Come on, John," I said, like I was trying to coax a response out of him in class. "This can't be what you really believe."

His normally pale face was splotched with red and his lips were curled in a snarl. God, he was actually baring his teeth at me. I barely recognized him.

"God, you're stupid, you bitch," he practically spit at me. "It's what a lot of us believe. What any decent white person should believe." His narrow chest was heaving. A short sprint had left him winded. The Master Race needed to work on physical conditioning, I thought derisively.

John then looked past me with alarm, and I realized Mel and Alice had come up behind us on the sidewalk. I had already seen Steve approaching from the other direction.

Steve addressed John in a firm voice.

"I already asked you your name. I'll ask again, and you need to answer. Who are you, and who are you making these copies for?"

John looked defiant. He didn't reply, just lifted on to the tips of his toes a little. I thought he'd run right then.

"Come on, son," Mel said calmly, now on John's other side. "There's no point . . . "

Mel didn't get any further.

"Son!" John exploded. "No N***** can call me son! Get the hell away from me." John backed up, trembling and practically in tears. "You ever heard of free speech, you big ape??" he asked in a vicious tone.

"John," I said sternly. "Knock it off." Amazingly, he shut up for a minute. "It's not protected speech when you incite violence, John. Should have checked that out before you decided to put out that piece of paper, with that logo."

I pointed to the one copy Steve was holding. From what I had been able to see just at the top, it was a call to stop the Rally Against Hate and had the skull logo called "The Punisher." That was white supremacist code for "bring weapons." I had researched these idiots and their codes after having seen the game sites.

"You know this jerk?" Alice asked, glaring at him. And maybe glaring a little at me. I chose to ignore that.

"Officers," I said conversationally, "meet John Vandenberg. He's a third-year university student. In fact, he's a Philosophy and Religion major, and he was taking one of my classes until recently. Well, I should say he'll be a student until he's expelled, probably later today. I can send you his student I.D. number and other information for your report."

"You're all doomed," John said, his red face thunderous.

"That was excessively trite, John," I replied. Alice actually tried to hide a smile.

John had had enough. He jerked back from us, turned, and ran toward the campus.

We just watched him go.

"So that's the kid the other kid told you about?" Alice asked, stepping up next to me.

"Yes," I said grimly.

So, the next steps were for me to send his contact information to Mel and Alice and for them to give Captain Gutierrez a written report. That would go to the Dean, whom I hoped would question John about his white supremacist views, who was influencing him, find out who was in this student network, and who hung the noose. And then I really hoped the Dean would, in fact, kick his butt out of school.

And, I realized with dread, I needed to contact Adelaide. She was John's advisor.

"You'll send that information?" Mel asked me.

"Yes, as soon as I get home," I said. Then I turned to Steve. "Could I see the whole flyer, please?"

He handed it over.

We all stood in a circle and looked at it. Big black words in the center of the page read "Separate Is Survival, Not Hate! A White Call to Arms. Stop the Rally!" And there were four symbols, one at each corner: the skull logo of the Punisher, a Confederate flag, a Nazi Iron Cross and a Crusader Cross. I took out my phone and quickly photographed it.

"This thing here," Alice pointed to the Punisher. "That's what you saw made you tell that little jerk this junk is not free speech? That," she stabbed the paper for emphasis. "That means what, exactly?"

"That logo is called the Punisher, and it's white supremacist code for 'bring weapons,'" I told her. "I've been researching their symbols."

"Researching," Alice said dryly. "Course you have." But she said it a little approvingly.

"Well, here's what I hope," I went on. "That symbol, along with the words 'call to arms,' might mean the D. A. could charge this kid and hopefully his collaborators, if he reveals any, with a hate crime."

Alice nodded. "That'd be about right." She glanced at the paper again and let the pain flicker over her face for a second. Then she wiped all expression and looked up, shutters in place.

"Let's get this done," Mel said, his deep voice a little deeper than usual. I looked at his face as well. It was set tight, his lips pulled into a firm line. His attempt to be kind to John had been met with the worst kind of filthy insult. But I'd only embarrass Mel if I said anything about it. I thought all this having to keep shutting up was going to make my head explode soon.

But all I said was "Right," and the others nodded. I moved to my car. As I started the engine, I glanced at the dashboard clock. It read 4:40 a.m., for God's sake. My days were starting to begin at night.

*   *   *

After I'd looked up all John Vandenberg's student information and sent it to Mel and Alice, I took a long, hot shower and drank about a gallon more coffee while sitting at the breakfast table. I could hear the boys just stirring upstairs. I needed to call Adelaide before they came down. I went into my study, shut the door and called her cell. She and I were conversing regularly before 7 a.m. Not good.

"Yes, Kristin?" she answered, I assumed seeing my name on her screen.

"I have something to tell you concerning John Vandenberg," I said.

"John? Is he okay? What's happened?" She sounded alarmed, but for the wrong reasons.

As quickly as I could I filled her in on the decoded chat room message, the stake-out at COPY 24/7, and then John being the one making the copies of the hateful flyers. I described the flyer, both words and symbols.

"John?" Adelaide said disbelievingly. "John was making copies of that? But, but, he plans to go into the ministry for heaven's sake."

Heaven had nothing to do with this, I wanted to say. It was actually an assault on heaven, but again I kept my thoughts to myself. Besides, Adelaide just didn't want her student to be a hate-mongering, white supremacist. I didn't either, though by now I was so angry at John I was having trouble remembering John as a student. My student too.

I just went on as though she hadn't spoken.

"There's a report coming from the campus police that will go to the Dean's office. In fact, it may already be there, for all I know. What I hope is that when the Dean meets with John, he can find out who else is in this white supremacist, student network and who is responsible for hanging the noose."

"Do you think John hung that noose?" Adelaide said hoarsely.

"I don't know, but I think either he did, with some others, or he knows who did."

I paused.

"We'll need another emergency faculty meeting, Adelaide. This afternoon, probably. The rumor mill will get this, and the colleagues should not be blindsided."

She was silent for a minute and then spoke.

"Yes. Yes. You're right. I'll call the Dean's Office in a couple of hours and see what I can find out. We'll need to have our meeting at five. There are two classes this afternoon, and I don't want to cancel them. Too much chaos already. I'll send an email soon setting up that meeting."

Adelaide was breathing hard, and I could hear some scribbling. She was upset, and coping by writing some notes to herself. I did that too, but I no longer felt it gave me any control. We were far from in control. This hate was like wave after wave of assaults, the battering increasing in intensity.

But all I said was "okay," and we hung up.

What I really wanted was to talk with Tom. I looked the time. It was 7:30 a.m., so I thought I might get him before rounds. But the call went to voicemail.

I sent a text.

"Can we talk today? Not an emergency."

But actually, it was an emergency I thought, as I headed to the kitchen to have breakfast with my boys.

I noticed Giles was absent again, and Carol still looked strained. She'd made oatmeal, and we all ate it quietly. Even the boys seemed subdued. They'd picked up on the fact that something was up, something that wasn't good.

They were right. Something was very far from good.

*   *   *

I was waiting in the hospital coffee shop for Tom. He had texted back as I was heading to campus mid-morning.

"What's up?"

"Too long for a text," I wrote. "Can you talk?"

"Hospital coffee shop, noon?"

Now, at 12:30, I had finished my sandwich and was contemplating a chocolate ice cream bar. I was contemplating it so intently, in fact, that I started when Tom sat down opposite me.

"Hi," he said. "Sorry to make you wait."

I pushed over a wrapped sandwich I'd gotten for him, and then I held up my phone.

"Have phone, can work," I said. It was true. I'd cleared my office email.

"I'm so glad to see you," I went on, fervently, putting down the phone.

"Kristin, what's the matter?" Tom said, leaning across the table. He ignored his sandwich and put his hand over one of my hands. His blue eyes lasered on me behind his glasses. He could be so completely present, I thought. I loved that about him.

"Here's what's the matter," I said with relief and laid out the whole thing for him. I spoke rapidly, afraid he'd have to dash away for an emergency any minute, but I thought I got in the main facts. Then I stopped and went on more slowly.

"I've been really angry at John, but in telling you all this, I think I'm also feeling, well, a kind of grief. I'm kicking myself too, because, I don't know, I feel I should have known somehow, should have been able to reach him in class."

"You can't save everybody, Kristin," he said slowly, and I knew, as a surgeon, he'd had to make his own peace with that.

"It sounds like there was a lot in this kid's life you don't know about, and peer pressure especially can pull someone young into terrible things, just step by step."

Tom paused, and I knew he was thinking of his daughter Kelly, and what he'd already been through with her. It's true. The young are so vulnerable it is truly terrifying.

"Yeah, yeah, I know, Tom. But there's Alice and Mel too. The filthy way John talked to them, and how he looked at them, it was like the hate had taken him over. It was all he was. And this crap, these vicious attacks, they've got to be taking a toll on them. I can see it in Alice and in Mel some too. But I know Alice better, and she's pulling in, pulling away. I mean, she has to, right, to survive in this climate?"

I paused.

"And Giles too, I think. There's something up with him, and Carol realizes it. Something with this white supremacy garbage on campus. I don't know though." I paused. "I have started to wonder if he's being hassled, bullied in some way."

Tom was still had his hand over mine, but now my hand had clenched into a fist. I could see Tom felt it, knew what it meant.

"Just be careful," Tom said, squeezing my clenched fist.

"Yes, I will," I said, but thinking of what Alice said, and the risks she runs just by walking around as a black woman. I wanted to get these miserable jerks so badly, I knew I wouldn't be all that careful.

Tom's pager went off. He looked at it, stood up, and muttered, "Gotta go." He kissed the top of my head and was walking quickly out the door before I realized he'd left his sandwich behind.

* * *

I started to walk back toward my office, thinking. Then I realized the rain had started again, in earnest. The cold water trickling down my neck made me pick up my pace. I'd just reached the front doors of Myerson when I heard my text tone. I stepped into the dim foyer and looked at the screen. It was from Alice.

"Vandenberg suspended pending investigation. Not charged hate crime. Security meeting for rally Fri, 9, Holbrook. Be there."

Holbrook was an older building next to the campus police station. It had a large auditorium and was used for bigger meetings. And this one would necessarily be bigger. As it should be. We had a security nightmare on our hands.

I walked slowly up the stairs to my office hearing my wet shoes squeak on the rubber treads, trying not to read too much into the fact that Alice had texted me rather than calling. I unlocked my office door. Aduba wasn't there. I knew he had one of the two classes being taught this afternoon.

I held the phone in my hand and re-read the text. Should I call Alice? No, I thought, give her some space. So I just typed, "Got it. Will be there." My finger hovered over the send button, but then I pressed it.

I leaned forward, my head in my hands. I was exhausted, and I still had the emergency faculty meeting to get through.

I must have actually drifted off for a while. A door slammed somewhere down the hall, waking me. I sat up and realized my neck was horribly stiff.

That's it, I thought. You bastards don't control me.

I checked the time. I still had two hours before the faculty meeting. I grabbed a bag of exercise clothes I kept in the office and sprinted in the rain to the old gym that was two blocks away. There was a cruddy old weight room in the basement and a separate area with a mat and sparring dummy.

I changed, and for an hour, I took out my feelings of rage, grief, and frustration on the dummy.

I don't know how the dummy felt about it, but I thought I won.

* * *

I entered the meeting room with a strong sense of *déjà vu*. Same people, same seats, and largely the same argument seemed to be underway.

"This is ridiculous," Donald was huffing under his mustache. He glanced up as I came in and then huffed out another "Ridiculous!" somewhat defiantly. I was reminded of that Harry Potter banishing spell, "Riddikulus!" Donald wanted to banish anything he didn't like rather than deal with it.

I sat down next to Aduba and looked at Adelaide. She was looking down at a pad in front of her, a frown wrinkling her brow into furrows.

"I have spoken to the Dean. John Vandenberg was observed," and she glanced up at me for a second, her eyebrows now raised, "copying a flyer that seemed to link him to those who hung the noose."

She flipped over a page.

"The Dean has met with John and he was, and I quote, 'very uncooperative.' John has been suspended pending an investigation."

"So the Dean got no other names?" I asked.

"No," Adelaide said flatly. "And I don't know who will be involved in an investigation or what it will involve."

"Well, that's it then," Donald said, trying to sound decisive and largely failing. "Clearly we put out a notice cancelling the lecture, the administration will surely prohibit this rally and things will get back to normal." He rose as if the meeting were ending.

"Sit down, Donald," Adelaide said flatly. "The Dean said the rally is still approved to go forward." She looked with tired eyes at Aduba. "And I have heard, Dr. Abubakar, you are also speaking at the rally?"

Aduba nodded and then added, "That is correct. The student organizers asked me to speak, and I have agreed. They shared their plans with me, and I think they are sound."

I'd read the term "gob smacked," but never had a chance to see what it looked like in reality. Donald was gob smacked. His mouth moved, but he seemed unable to form any words. Interesting.

Adelaide frowned at him for a second, and then spoke to me.

"I assume, Kristin, there are plans for a lot of security for the rally?"

I nodded.

"Yes, there's a big meeting of the campus police tomorrow at 9 a.m. I'll be there, and I'll let you know." I paused, wondering how to put this without being too alarmist.

"The flyer John was copying had a series of symbols on it that I think would also concern the city cops. I'm sure some representatives of the city police will be at this planning meeting as well. There will have to be a lot of coordination."

Adelaide and Aduba nodded. Donald had finally stopped trying to form words and was just sitting there.

"Okay, then," Adelaide said, standing and clearly dismissing us. "Kristin, you follow up with the campus police, and keep me and Dr. Abubakar informed."

"That's it?" Donald managed to get out, disbelief in his voice.

"Yes," Adelaide said firmly, and she swept from the room. She really had that move down pat.

Aduba and I stood up together, leaving Donald sitting at the table.

"Your email alerting me that I would be contacted by the rally organizers was helpful," Aduba said, as we walked together down the hall. "There was time for me to gather my thoughts in preparation for speaking with them."

"Well, I'm glad you agreed, but I will be sure to let you know the security plans," I said.

"Thank you," he replied, rather formally.

We'd reached the office door, but he made no move to enter when I opened the door.

"There are some things I'd like to discuss with you in private," I said, indicating our office interior with my hand.

"I must leave now, but could you call me after the meeting tomorrow?" he said.

"Yes, certainly. And I'll see you and your family Saturday evening. 6 p.m."

"Yes, and again, thank you." He nodded to me and set off for the stairs.

I wondered again if sharing an office with me made him uncomfortable. I shrugged to myself. Well, speaking of uncomfortable, I wondered how he'd feel when I lent him my bulletproof vest and told him to wear it at the rally.

I went home, and after dinner I wanted to just fall into bed and sleep the night away. But I didn't. I set my alarm for midnight and took a nap.

Odin needed to put in an appearance tonight. And it was a good thing he did. At about 1 a.m., an exchange appeared in the chat room of the video game "Revenge" that was very telling. I took a screen shot of it, and sent it to both Alice and Mel with a message, "Let's meet at 8."

I kept checking back into the chat room until 2, and then shut off the light. Even Odin needed to sleep occasionally.

Chat Room of Video Game "Revenge"

Friday 1 a.m.

Vampire726: What the hell what the hell Moloch111 man traitors and N****** what can you expect F*** what else do they know

Demon196: don't F***** freak out there are plans to fix that stay white

Astaroth76: how

Demon196: how many f****** times tell u not here

Chapter 9

God gave angels free will, like God gives people free will.

—Paradox Brown, *A Modern Guide to Demons*
  and Fallen Angels

Friday

"What the hell is with these fools?" Alice demanded, her fingernail stabbing at the screen of her phone. She must have downloaded the screen shot of the chat room I'd sent last night to her and Mel on to her phone.

"This is crazy talk! Vampires, Demons and what all, and what the hell is a Moloch or an Astaroth anyway?" she went on, glaring at her phone and tapping it.

I feared for her phone screen she was hitting it so hard.

I wasn't even technically in her office yet, just in the doorway, and Mel was still out in the hall, but Alice was so angry she was pacing around her office, venting. Alice, Mel, and I had exchanged texts early this morning and had agreed to meet in her office before the big 9 a.m. security meeting down the street.

I scuttled further into the room, Mel skirted around behind me and went to sit at the table. For such a tall, broad-shouldered man, he was certainly agile, and he was such a good cop, he knew to get quickly out of the line of fire. I should have just followed him, but instead, I unwisely answered Alice's question first.

"Moloch is a god of the Canaanites who demanded child sacrifice."

Alice looked up from her phone and frowned deeply at me. Instead of stopping with that, I promptly made it worse.

"Moloch appears a lot in the Bible. He was worshipped by the early people who lived in what is now Palestine and Israel. Astaroth is also in the Bible and he . . . " I stopped speaking when I heard Mel let out a groan.

Alice's frown became a scowl, and she spoke fiercely.

"What you talkin' about, girl? "This," more screen tapping, "is nothin' to do with the holy scripture. Nothin', you get me?" Then she shook the phone at me like she could shake Moloch and Astaroth right out of it on to the floor and, I supposed, stomp on them. Along with any other demonic creatures who happened to be in there as well.

Mel broke in.

"Let's just get started," he said in his deep voice. I looked over at the little table. He had brought his laptop and had the screen shot open.

I went around behind him and sat in the chair opposite. I didn't need to see the screen. I'd memorized it. Alice took a few breaths, but then just came over and sat next to Mel. She took out her little notebook and slapped it down on the table, but she didn't say any more.

When will I learn to just shut up? I thought grimly.

No time for that. Mel got right to business.

"Was there any dialogue before this, Kristin, with any of these three screen names?" he asked me, carefully avoiding actually saying the names. Alice muttered "huh," but otherwise didn't comment.

"Not that I saw," I said, "and I was on the chat room from about midnight on. This popped up and I thought it referred to what happened at the copy shop yesterday morning, so I took the screen shot. I waited around, but no more from these two came up."

"So it's likely John Vandenberg is Moloch111," Mel said slowly, looking intently at the screen. "When I get a chance, I'll check his other posts." He made a note on his own little pad he'd taken from his back pocket.

"Kristin, what screen name are you using?" he asked, not looking up.

"Odin26," I said shortly, a little embarrassed.

Mel looked up and grinned at me.

"Well, that fits," he said, leaning over his pad again.

When he'd finished writing, he turned to Alice.

"What do you think? Take this to Gutierrez this morning after meeting, or wait until I've had a chance to check back and look for 'Moloch111' and the screen names of those who chat with him?"

I liked that Mel consulted Alice.

"Vampire. Demon. Astaroth." Alice growled under her breath. But then, in her regular voice, she answered. "Yeah, let's wait. Get a bunch of names, look for pattern. Maybe Gutierrez can squeeze this Vandenberg then. 'Wanna get off suspension? Give me the names.'" But the whole time she spoke, she wasn't looking at either of us, but out the window opposite. I didn't think she was contemplating the peeling paint and the streaked, dirty glass. What did she see, I wondered, that was triggered by these lines on the screen, these guys and their bland, matter-of-fact racism, and the offhand comment to "stay white"? If it was like a horror show to me, what was it to Alice and Mel? These guys had chosen their names well. I could just about smell the sulphur and hear the panting lust for blood. I gazed at Alice's set profile. Her normally round face with its frame of dark hair seemed narrower, sharper. In my mind, I damned these guys for about the thousandth time.

"Okay, then," said Mel, closing his computer with a snap. "I'll let you know what I get." He went to stand up.

"Hey, Mel," I said, and he paused. "What's your screen name?"

"Shaitan105," he said with a grin.

"Good one," I said. "Arabic for Satan. Excellent choice."

Alice snorted so hard the top page on her notebook fluttered for a second. But then she flattened it with her hand and wrote one word on the page. Shaitan.

Silently, we all departed for the security meeting.

＊ ＊ ＊

Holbrook was right next to the campus police station and looked just like it. Both of these ivy-covered, red brick buildings were formerly part of a now defunct 19th century private school that I assumed had been bought by the university.

The foyer was made of uneven flagstone, worn down by thousands of feet crossing it for more than a century. It was also scuffed and dirty from the muddy shoes of the campus police who had tracked through the puddles still left from yesterday's rain to enter the auditorium on the main floor. I added my own grimy tracks along with Mel and Alice, and we entered the big hall.

It was theater-seating with a stage at the front. The auditorium was large. It held about 200 wooden seats, the kind with the flip down seats and the old retractable arm that had made a writing surface for the long-departed students. The overhead, fluorescent tube lighting was protected by yellowing plastic covers. The sickly light made everyone look slightly waxy, like they'd been recently embalmed.

Mel and Alice moved up the aisle to sit with the campus police, but I hung back. I thought with my marginal "consultant" status, I should sit toward the back.

The big hall already looked packed. There are more than a hundred full-time campus police at the university, and I didn't even know how many part-time. When new students arrive, they and their parents are given brochures on security that brag that the university has the largest private security force in the world, except for the Vatican. I don't know why that is supposed to reassure them, as one might well ask, "Why does the university need this huge security force?"

The university was situated right by Lake Michigan on the south side of Chicago. It is an island of wealth and privilege surrounded by poverty and crime. And it kept encroaching on the poorer and mostly African American areas around the campus, extending into them. People resented it. Why wouldn't they? And now, the giant complex for the Obama Center was being built right on the lake, within walking distance of the campus. What was that going to do to this tenuous security situation? I served on the committee that oversaw the actions of the campus police, and we routinely reviewed complaints of racial profiling, some of which had proved more than justified. More and more "re-training" ensued, but the fact remained that the vast majority of the university community and the surrounding Hyde Park neighborhood, also patrolled by the campus police, wanted security first, and racial justice perhaps a distant second, or perhaps third or fourth after "protect property values" and "economic renewal."

I picked a spot at the back and settled into the uncomfortable wooden seat. My legs were too long for this narrow aisle, and my knees were nearly at my nose. I looked at the stage in front. It was empty now, but there was a podium set up with a mike, some chairs on either side, and one of those old, pull-down screens was at the back of the stage. A big security show was going to take place, I mused. I wondered about who would speak, trying to take my mind off the pain in my knees. Of course, I thought, the main thing would be what would not be said. The university's vested interest was keeping up an appearance of racial tolerance, if not its actuality. And now these neo-Nazis were doing everything they could to say "hip, hip hurray for white guys!" It had the campus in an uproar. But who would be blamed?

There was a stir at the front, and people began to walk out from the right side of the stage toward the chairs. I got such a jolt of surprise, I banged my knees on the wooden chair in front of me. Giles was walking out and across the stage toward a chair on the far side. His thin, narrow shoulders under his customary T-shirt were tense, but his face was set and betrayed no emotion. He did not look at the audience, but walked purposefully to a seat and sat down, his hands on his knees. What was he doing here and on the stage? Was he some kind of student representative? Then I saw Chaplain Jane, but I'd expected to see her. Then a couple of people in campus police uniforms followed her, and behind them I recognized Captain Gutierrez as he came out. He was in uniform as well, interestingly.

A couple of people in Chicago police uniforms followed Gutierrez out. But then I got such a shock I actually levitated a little, and the wooden seat rose with me. Oh, crap. Carl Kaiser, a Chicago detective with whom I had a terrible history, walked out next, his huge stomach proceeding him by at least a foot, his pasty face even more jowly than the last time I'd seen him. I had reported Carl for sexual harassment when I was on the force. Before the case could even go forward, my husband Marco had been killed, shot at a routine traffic stop. His back-up had not even gotten out of the police cruiser. That back-up had been Carl Kaiser. He had sat in the car and watched my husband get killed, and he'd let the killers get away. If that was all he had done, it was bad enough. I had always suspected more, but the private detective and lawyers I'd hired hadn't been able to make any kind of a case. I'd quit the force the day after Marco's murder.

Carl and I had had run-ins since I'd been at the university as well, and his racism, misogyny, and extreme incompetence had all been on display in those cases. I literally felt sick as I sat back down on the wooden seat, my clammy hands clenched in my lap. Talk about a horror show. We had fake vampires and demons and now real monsters.

I glared at that side of the stage, wondering if I recognized any of the other Chicago cops. Of course, there was Al Brown, whom I'd nicknamed "Ichabod" since his bony frame, long neck, and pumpkin head resembled that fictional character. Satan had minions, and so did Carl Kaiser. Brown was always with Kaiser, though two steps behind like a good servant. I wondered briefly how that felt, to always be in someone's shadow, to, in fact, be the shadow.

Gutierrez stepped up to the microphone and after the usual welcome blah blah words, he took out a small device and behind him a map of the campus appeared. He used some kind of zoom function and the portion of the campus where the demonstrators had received permission to hold their event came into sharper relief. Gutierrez then used a laser pointer.

"There will be a small stage here," and he pointed to a spot on the southwest side of the grassy area that bisected the campus. "I understand from Chaplain Miller-Gershman," and he nodded at Jane who nodded pleasantly back, "and the coordinator of all the sponsoring student groups, Mr . . . ," Gutierrez paused to consult a paper on the podium, "Mr. Dop, that there will be singing by the university choir and several speakers. We have also given permission for a balloon with a banner denouncing hate. Is that right?" Gutierrez looked over at where Jane and Giles were sitting next to each other. Jane nodded and smiled. Giles gave a barely perceptible nod.

Well, now I knew why Giles had been gone so much and why Carol was so worried. When Gutierrez had introduced Giles, mispronouncing his name, I turned to watch Kaiser's face. His piggy eyes had narrowed and his mouth pursed like he was holding in several choice words. I just bet he was.

It was stupid, but I was a little hurt that Giles hadn't told me what he was doing about the rally. Oh, shake it off, I told myself. He's entitled to his privacy. Besides, said the small part of me that tried to be self-aware, you'd probably have tried to "help" him, and he wanted to avoid that.

"and the counter-demonstrators . . . " I realized Gutierrez was still speaking and it was important, "will need to be kept to the public sidewalk over here." The red light of his laser pointer traced the sidewalk that ran all the way along the south side of that grassy area. "If they move off of the sidewalk, they will be subject to arrest." Here he nodded at Kaiser and the other Chicago cops. Kaiser looked stony, but a couple of the other guys, and they were all guys, nodded. Kaiser probably wanted to join the counter-demonstrators. He was a big fan of hate.

Gutierrez raised his voice slightly, but he continued in the same measured way.

"No firearms of any kind will be permitted by anyone attending the rally per university policy. Anyone other than campus and city police with a firearm is subject to immediate arrest."

A hand went up somewhere in the front. When Gutierrez nodded, a unformed man stood up and pointed at the screen.

"What about on that sidewalk?"

"No," said Gutierrez firmly. "The university reserves the right to prohibit firearms on sidewalks immediately adjacent to the campus." Another hand went up immediately. When the campus policewoman was acknowledged, she stood almost immediately and turned so she could be heard by the audience as well as those on the stage.

"What about cars and trucks? We don't want another Charlottesville." She was referring to the death that had occurred at a neo-Nazi rally in Charlottesville, Virginia, when a man had driven into a crowd of counter-protestors and killed a young woman. It's true that cars and trucks were becoming the new weapons of mass destruction.

"Yes, yes, very good point. I should have noted that this street will be closed to all vehicles beginning at midnight tomorrow. Any vehicle that remains will be towed, and fire trucks will be parked at each end of the street adjacent to the rally to prevent vehicles entering this area." Again, he used his laser pointer to show the main area.

The campus policewoman's hand shot up again.

"Yes?" Gutierrez said.

"That doesn't mean a vehicle can't cross the grass from the opposite end and drive across to where the demonstration will be," she said sharply.

"Do one of you want to take this one?" Gutierrez asked of the cops sitting to his left.

Oh, please, please don't let Carl volunteer, I thought. But then a tall, red-haired, white guy with sergeant's stripes on his uniform jacket stood up and walked up to the podium. He nodded at Gutierrez and appeared to ask for the pointer. Then he bent to the mike, not bothering to adjust it up. He was a whole lot taller than Gutierrez.

"The Chicago po'lice will be spaced along this area," he said in a deep voice with the lilt of the South in it. He turned to point at the open sides of the grass mall. He turned back and addressed the audience.

"As ya'll know, the regs on firing at a car or truck that is heading toward pedestrians have been, shall we say, relaxed in Chicago." There was a little titter of laughter from some. Great. "So, we see a car going hell bent for leather across that grass toward the demonstrators," and he made the red dot move around the screen, "we'll give a warning, sure, but then we will fire on 'em, that's for damn sure."

Our security choices were either police firing near a crowd or vehicular terrorism? Apparently so. I imagined carnage either way and shuddered.

Gutierrez returned to the podium, and the tall cop sat down.

"We in the campus police will stay at a distance, but, depending on the size of the crowd, be located in a perimeter area around here," and again more red light action made a large semi-circle around the area, inside where the Chicago police would be spaced, but importantly, including the stretch between where the stage would be located and the sidewalk where the counter-demonstrators were allowed to be. "You will each receive individual assignments by email tomorrow. Any more questions?"

A few hands went up, but the questions were mostly about specific assignments, and shortly thereafter we were dismissed.

I stood up on stiff legs and looked at the stage. Giles was talking to Jane and shaking his head no. I pondered going over to them, but decided against it, turned and abruptly left the auditorium, not waiting for Alice or Mel.

The wind from the west had picked up, and the fallen leaves made mini-tornados on the ground. The watery sun disappeared suddenly. I looked up, and dark clouds were massing on the horizon. They were heading for the campus. Well, trite as it seemed, it was a perfect metaphor for our university and even our times. There was a violent storm approaching. I started to hurry after I felt the first drops hit my upturned face.

I hustled toward my office as the rain started to come down in sheets. I had to catch up on student emails, plan a dinner party and then, I thought, Odin needed to show up in a chat room. I blew into Myerson and was soon at my computer. I skimmed and deleted emails for a while, but my mind was elsewhere. I turned and pulled a book off my book shelf on Viking mythology. I leafed through it, and found the "Havamal," the epic poem attributed to Odin from the 9th century. I skimmed many verses, until I got to the part I'd remembered. Odin was feared because he traveled through the human world in a "wily disguise," interfering in human plans and changing the course of battles. Me too, I vowed grimly. Then I closed the book and resumed deleting emails.

Chat Room of Video Game "Revenge"

Saturday 2:00 a.m.

Demon196: red line remember cross red line red line

Odin26: hate is a red line

Demon196: who the f*** r u

Odin26: I am god of gods u know me hate is a red line

Vampire726: r u blue

Demon196: shut the f*** up u stupid f*****

Odin26: hate is a red line red line red line

Demon196: u don't know s***

Odin26: I know hate is a red line red line red line

Chapter 10

The trouble with eating Italian food is that five or six days later you're hungry again.

—GEORGE MILLER

Saturday

I'd taken a screen shot of the most recent chat from the game "Revenge" and sent it to Mel and Alice before I'd shut my computer. I lay awake in the dark, seeing the lines of text like they were written on the ceiling in neon lights. Red line? What did that mean? The police line between the sidewalk and the demonstration would be my first guess. It certainly was Odin's first guess. Odin had messed with them, I thought, at least enough to provoke that question about "blue." I thought I knew what that meant too, and it made me sick to contemplate it.

I looked at the clock. It was 3 a.m. I switched my worrying over to the dinner party. How would that turn out? I couldn't have been too worried about it, because the next thing I knew the ringing of my cell phone was jolting me awake.

I grabbed for it and saw it was after eight, late for me these days. I pressed "accept" and heard Marco's mother, Natalie Ginelli, on the phone.

"Kris-tin-a? Is that you? Are you there?" Natalie had been born in Chicago, but she had a pronounced Italian accent. She always made my name into three syllables, though now she sounded almost rattled.

"Yes, Nonna, I'm here. Is there something the matter?" But I seemed to be talking to dead air. Then Marco's father Vince came on, but he appeared to be talking to his wife.

"I got it Natalie, I got it. Listen, Kristin, you there?" Vince asked, also sounding too tense for just a "how are the grandkids" kind of call. Vince was retired now, but he had been a Chicago cop for decades, and he didn't rattle easily.

"Yes, Vince, yes, I'm here. What's up?" I asked hastily.

"Well, we was heading to Wisconsin, you see, to see Vince Junior and the kids, and well, the RV it like started making noises . . . "

"Tell her about the smoke. It made smoke, Vince," I heard in the background.

"Yeah, yeah, Natalie. So, Kristin, the short of it is the RV was in trouble, and we were damned lucky to get to one of them, you know, truck plazas, on the highway before the whole damn thing blew up," Vince rushed to get that out before Natalie talked over him again.

"No, not blow up, Vince. No, don't scare the child," came Natalie's voice in the background.

"You're both okay, though?" I broke in, raising my voice.

"Yeah, yeah. We slept in the RV last night and all and yeah, we're fine, but the mechanic guy here says the valves are shot. Need to be replaced. He's got 'em, I was damned glad to find out, but we gotta leave the RV here, and let 'em work on it."

"Where are you, Vince?" I broke in again. It was the only way.

"Hang on a second, Kristin. Hey, fella . . . "

I lost the rest as Vince must have handed the phone to Natalie.

"So, Kris-tin-a," the boys are good, yes?" she had just time to ask.

"Talk to her later," Vince said, and came back on the line. "Yeah, we're in Waukegan," and he rattled off the address of the truck plaza.

"Okay, I'll come get you, and you can stay here with the boys and me until the RV is fixed, okay? Have some breakfast, and I'll call you when I know about when I'll get there," I said quickly before I could get interrupted again. "Your room is always ready."

"You a good kid," Vince said. "She's coming?" I heard Natalie say in the background. "Tell her bring the boys."

"I'm coming," I said, and hung up.

✳   ✳   ✳

Amazingly enough, the major highway from Chicago to nearly the Wisconsin border was not jammed. The boys and I were making good time. They sat in the back seat, strapped in their boosters, amiably arguing about the new *Incredibles* movie. I thought about the chat room exchange.

I had checked my email before I'd left, and I'd gotten a reply from Mel, though nothing from Alice. I was only half surprised. These yahoos were making Alice so spitting mad. Mel had speculated on "cross the red line" and the meaning of red line. He'd pointed out a "red line" sometimes meant the fire department. They were called the "red line." I'd emailed him back almost in a panic. Did that mean they were going to try to get a vehicle past the fire emergency trucks blocking the street south of the stage where the rally would be centered? Mel had replied that he was also worried about that, but then how would they know the cops planned to use fire trucks? Then I'd replied about Vampire asking if Odin were "blue." That meant cops to me. "Me too," Mel emailed back right away. I'd told him I had to go, and he said he was going to take the chat room screen shot to Gutierrez.

I drove along, thinking about red and blue. My first thought had been that red line could mean the line between the sidewalk and the mall. Didn't necessarily mean the fire department. But could it be worse? Could it mean using weapons, like the Punisher symbol conveyed, perhaps firing on the demonstrators? Blue almost certainly meant cop. There was a mole in the campus police or Chicago police. Not the first time we'd faced that on campus, I thought miserably.

Then the boys chatter in the back came through to me, as it always did when I heard the word "Mom" or "Dad." They were arguing about whether the mother or the father in the Incredibles family was stronger. "The Dad's the strongest, you dummy," said Sam, clearly convinced he'd settled it.

"Not necessarily," said Mike, practicing his lawyerly argument tactics. "The Mom is more flexible, and she's tricky. The Dad just pushes stuff."

"Man, the Dad has to hold the whole family together and also be stronger than anybody. He's the best," Sam countered.

"Yeah," said Mike, slowly. "A Dad's the best."

Then they were off on how funny it was that the baby could explode.

Not "the Dad," but "a Dad." I felt such a pang of grief it almost made me pull the car over. Marco had been such a great Dad for such a short time. I was so glad they at least had Vince in their life, and Natalie too.

Then I spotted the Waukegan exit, and took it.

*　　*　　*

We got back without a lot of traffic as well. A Chicago miracle. It was just noon, and the Ginellis had retreated to the spare bedroom they always used. I hoped they were napping.

So, I was only about three hours behind schedule.

I fed the boys, and then they took Molly for a walk. This was a new thing they were allowed to do. She was so docile, I thought it was okay. They only went around our block, so they never crossed a street.

I sat down in the library with an iced tea and a granola bar and a pad to make a list. I was back to pretending that writing things down equaled being in control, but with so many things on my mind, I actually did need to make a list. It also kept anxiety at bay. I didn't want to even speculate on an evening with the Abubakar family, Tom and Kelly, Adelaide, and the Ginellis. The dinner party from hell? I hoped not.

"Set the table" was first on my list, and I just got up to do that. Clearly a dinner party would happen if the table were set, right? Then I went around in the front rooms straightening and doing a little surface dusting. Suddenly, I stopped straightening, and sniffed the air. Onions. Oh heavens. Nonna was in the kitchen.

I hustled in and saw Natalie was frying onions. She was so short and rotund that I was always concerned she would set the front of her dress on fire just by standing in front of the stove.

"Nonna," I asked carefully, not wanting her to turn too abruptly from the front burner, "Why are you cooking? We have plenty of fixings for sandwiches. That's what I gave the boys."

"No, we not hungry, and Vincent, he not here anyway. I sent him to that little market down a the block. I make some lasagna for you to have for the guests. Will be plenty." She turned to wave the wooden spoon at me, and the front of her flowered house dress brushed the stove. I held my breath for a second, but the fabric seemed impervious to the flame. She had a lot of these flowered dresses. I had no idea where she would buy them anymore. She must make them herself, I thought, perhaps out of asbestos.

"But Nonna, I have a caterer, I told you."

She turned back to the stove with a sniff.

"You said. Vegetables." Another sniff, with feeling. "How is that enough for all? Nobody get enough to eat."

I caved. But not completely.

"Okay, thanks. But no meat. You hear me?" I asked, since she was still turned away. Nonna could tune you out in a minute if she wanted to. "No meat. The Abubakars are Muslim, and I don't know if any meat we get will be okay for them to eat. So you understand, no meat. Meatless lasagna."

"So, like Jews?"

"Well, yes, pretty much. So, right. No meat?"

She was bent over, crushing garlic with the side of our big knife, but she nodded. I figured I'd better split. Well, I thought, as I went back to dusting and straightening, Tom and Kelly would eat the lasagna. Tom had been noncommittal when I'd shared the dishes I'd ordered with him. I actually thought, having seen him eat, that he paid no attention to what he put in his mouth as long as it was considered edible. I'd enthused to him over the phone about beans on plantain toast, yam canapes, cabbage wraps, chickpea and vegetable stew, a side of fried rice, and a big bowl of fresh berries with both custard and ice cream for toppings. I'd gradually noticed there had been a suspicious silence on the other end of the phone. It could have been he'd been quietly checking his email, though, so I hadn't pushed it.

While I set out glasses in the living room for the various juices I'd bought, I heard Vince come back through the kitchen with the lasagna ingredients. I needed to break it to him that there'd be no alcohol this evening.

*　　*　　*

I managed to get the boys upstairs and into their shower to clean off and change clothes. Then I sent them down to pick out videos to share with the Abubakars's son in the small TV room off of the main living room. I showered and changed in about five minutes and headed back downstairs. I must say the lasagna did smell good.

The kitchen was empty. I checked my watch. It was half past, and I was starting to worry about the caterers showing up when my text tone alerted me. The caterers were parked in the alley. I hurried out the back and opened the gate to the yard to let them in.

Our dining room was large and had a built-in credenza along one side of the room. I had the caterers bring the food in there and set it up in the chafing dishes I'd rented from them on their website. Little flames under the serving dishes would keep the food warm. I'd called the caterers after Nonna had sprung her lasagna on me, and I'd rented two more chafing dishes. Yes, she'd made two whole pans of lasagna. I took them from the oven and put them on the credenza.

The front door bell rang. Show time.

I hurried to the front door and opened it to admit Tom, Kelly, and an African American kid about Kelly's age who looked a lot like Giles, except much taller. Tom had an odd expression on his face. He kind of looked like a stuffed frog. Kelly was wearing a very becoming rose-colored sweater and printed skirt. Her normally stick-straight hair was curled, and held back with a matching rose-colored headband. Wow. She looked terrific, and, I realized, nervous. Her friend was wearing a grey, crew-necked sweater and jeans. His narrow, serious face, complete with wire-rimmed glasses, looked so much like Giles I was a little taken aback. Kelly had had a crush on Giles just last year. I got a little frisson of anxiety. I quickly checked his feet to make sure he wasn't wearing flip flops, Giles's only choice in footwear. No, just sneakers.

I stood back and gestured them to enter.

Kelly spoke in a rush.

"Kristin, sorry, Dad didn't know. This is Zeke Williams, he's my friend, and I asked him if he would like to come, and he said sure, and so we just met up outside, and I hope it's okay."

You had to have young lungs to get out a sentence that long all in one rush.

"Sure it's okay, Kelly, and hi, Zeke, glad you could come." I shook Zeke's hand, and he said, "Hi, thanks." And that was all.

I met Tom's eyes over Kelly's head, and he blinked once, twice, and then I thought he was recovering a little from the shock. Kelly must have presented him with Zeke out on the sidewalk at the front of our house.

Just then the boys ran down the center hall to see who was at the door. Molly was right on their heels.

"Hi, Kelly smelly," they chorused, rushing toward us. Then they saw Zeke and stopped. Molly didn't. She wagged her tail and licked his hand.

"Boys," said Kelly formally, "this is my friend Zeke. Zeke, this is Sam and this is Mike, Kristin's sons. And this is Molly," she said, bending a little to give Molly a pat. Good gad. Kelly could be auditioning for Grace Kelly.

"Hey guys," Zeke said. "Hey Molly," Zeke said and patted Molly as well. Zeke seemed to be a man of few words.

"Hello, Sam, hello, Mike," said Tom.

"Hi," they said shyly. They knew I liked Tom, and they didn't entirely know what to do about that.

I was just about to usher them all into the front room when the Abubakars came up the walk behind them.

Molly started to wag her tail all over again, and the Abubakars's son started to break away from them and run up the walk.

"Dog! A dog! Hello, dog," he said, his whole, little body vibrating with joy as he tried to push past his parents, plainly planning to pet Molly.

There was a piercing scream.

"No! No! Do not touch the animal. Abu, get him, there's a dog, a dog!"

I grabbed for Molly's collar and held her back. Mrs. Abubakar seemed terrified of dogs. Oh, Great Scott. But her son was not. He kept running forward as I pulled Molly back. His mother let out another scream, and she pushed her husband forward.

Aduba moved swiftly up the walk, took a quick hold of his son's hand, and held him back so he and I were moving little boy and dog farther and farther away from each other. Neither one liked it.

"Baba! Baba! I want to pet the doggy," his son said beseechingly.

"Boys," I said sharply to Sam and Mike. "Take Molly into the backyard and leave her there, okay?"

"Yeah, okay," Mike said, and he got a grip on Molly's collar from me. Sam pushed on her rear end until she turned. She didn't want to go. She'd seen one of her favorite things in the world, a little boy. But they got her moving.

"Let's all go in the front room, shall we?" I asked, rather desperately.

Tom, now out of his trance, gestured to Kelly and Zeke, and they got out of the front hall and moved into the adjacent parlor.

Aduba, still hanging on to his reluctant son, waited for his wife to catch up, then took her arm and helped her into the house.

"Kristin, this is my wife, Zala, and our son, Jachike. Zala and Jachike, this is my colleague at the university, Professor Kristin Ginelli."

I shook hands with a still trembling Zala. I bent down a little to shake hands with six-year-old Jachike.

"Jack. I am called Jack," he said, and then he solemnly shook my hand. His father and mother frowned.

I didn't reply, I just turned to usher them into the front room as well.

"Juice, anyone?" I asked. Aduba took juice, and Zala just shook her head no. I left it to Tom, Kelly, and Zeke to serve themselves and went to get the tray with the plantain toast and the yam canapes. And down the hall came the Ginellis.

I grabbed the tray of hors d'oeuvres from the kitchen and hurried behind them into the front room.

I introduced Natalie and Vince and shoved some juice into their hands. Vince gave me a sidelong look, but I'd been really clear about what would be served this evening.

Then the boys came running back. Good, they'd left Molly in the yard.

"Sam, Mike, this is," I hesitated, oh well, "Jack. Why don't you guys and Jack go into the TV room? I set up some juice boxes in there for you and some chips."

I looked up at Aduba.

"That's okay? Juice, chips, and a Lego movie?"

Aduba was sitting down on a sofa next to his wife, his arm around her. He glanced at her, and she nodded.

"Certainly."

"Come on!" Sam said to Jack, and they all ran off toward the TV room.

The doorbell rang. It was either Adelaide or perhaps one of the minions of Moloch. I couldn't quite remember if I'd invited any minor demons as well. It was Adelaide. I let her in and tried to fill her in quietly on our new mix of guests while I took her red cape and hung it up in the front hall closet.

She raised her eyebrows at me, but she made no comment. Probably just as well. What was there to say?

When I ushered her in to the front room, the whole scene had shifted. Tom, Vince, and Aduba were standing by the fireplace, deep in a discussion about, it seemed, truck engines. Aduba had taken out a small piece of paper, and he was leaning on an end table drawing something while Tom and Vince looked on with, it seemed, great interest. Natalie had taken Aduba's place on the sofa, and it appeared she and Zala were discussing the decorative trim on their dresses. I hadn't even had time to remark on it, but Zala was wearing a stunning, long, white dress with wide stripes of embroidery around the neck, cuffs, and all the way down the front. Natalie had changed out of her asbestos house dress, and she was now wearing a dark blue dress with embroidery around the hem and the cuffs. Zala was fingering the embroidery on Natalie's cuffs, and I could hear her saying, "Really? And this you obtained here in the Chicago? Where is that?"

Kelly and Zeke, I noticed, had disappeared. Then I heard music coming from the library and realized they'd retreated there.

I looked at Adelaide, she looked at me, and we tip-toed back into the front hall. I filled her in on the video game chat room and the exchanges I'd had with Mel Billman, whom she'd not met. She frowned deeply while I speculated on the various interpretations of the messages.

"What the hell is wrong with these people, Kristin?" she asked, echoing Alice perfectly.

"They are seduced by the thrill of hate, I think, Adelaide."

Then I led her into the dining room, and we discussed John's situation a little more while I got out a place setting for Zeke and moved another chair up to the table. I was glad it was a big table.

I took Adelaide back to the front room, introduced her, and then ushered everyone into the dining room. I hadn't done place cards. I actually hadn't given it a thought, but everybody arranged themselves in the their preferred discussion groups. It really was like a breakout session for a class. The truck guys sat together, Natalie and Zala sat together and continued to finger the embroidery on their dresses, Kelly and Zeke sat together, the three kids sat down at the far end of the table, and Adelaide and I sat at the other end. Everybody served themselves, parents helped kids, and it all seemed to be working okay. Sub-cultures, I thought.

Everybody chose the lasagna. The vegan food will freeze, I thought.

After dinner, I passed around a carafe of decaf coffee to go with the fruit and ice cream dessert. The kids had begged to be excused, and I sent them into the kitchen to eat their ice cream. Kelly and Zeke had retreated back into the library.

The rest of us took some more coffee and went back to the front room.

It was now or never. I cut Aduba out of the pack and ushered him toward the front hall closet before he could go into the front room.

"I have something for you. I want you to take it for your talk at the rally tomorrow."

His smooth face usually held little expression, but I noticed that muscle starting to work in his jaw again. His go-to stress move.

I went to the closet and got out a large shopping bag. I'd placed some tissue in the top to hide what was in there.

I handed it to him unceremoniously.

"It's my old, bullet-proof vest. Wear it tomorrow. There are straps at the side so you can make it fit you. I'm not joking around with this. Wear it."

He stood stock still and for a moment I thought he would refuse. Then he reached out, took the straps of the bag, carried it over to the front door and placed it along the wall.

"Thank you," he said, his back still to me. "You are becoming a good friend to me. I hope I can return the favor some day."

I waited until he turned back to face me, and then I just nodded.

"I must collect my child, and we must go home. It is late," he said, like we hadn't just been contemplating the possibility he'd face bullets tomorrow.

"I'm glad you know so much about trucks," I said with a smile, not only to change the subject, but because I was so grateful he did know about trucks.

"My two older brothers re-build truck engines in Nigeria. There is little I do not know about the engine of a machine such as your father-in-law's. But," and here he paused while we were walking down the hall, and he gave me a quirky smile I'd never seen, "Your father-in-law, he keeps calling me 'Abbie.'"

I stopped dead in my tracks.

"Abbie?" I said horrified.

"Yes." He kept smiling. "It is useful for when I use the office of the Jewish professor for prayer, no? Then I introduce myself to the Jewish God as Abbie, and all will be well." And he broke into a deep rumbling chuckle.

Wow.

"Okay, Abbie," I said, "let's find your son." I walked toward the TV room still hearing the rumbling chuckles next to me.

Oh, oh. The TV room was empty when we looked in. We hurried to the kitchen and only three empty bowls of ice cream remained. Then we heard them and looked out the kitchen window.

Jack was happily throwing a ball for Molly who was catching it and bringing it back to him. His delighted laugh was wonderful. Mike and Sam were digging a hole, to what end I did not know.

"He does love dogs," Aduba said thoughtfully, gazing at his deliriously happy son. "Perhaps, in time, a small dog. A very small dog." And we went out and called the boys in. Molly had to stay out to her great disappointment. She whined a little. Jack rushed back out, gave her a hug, and then came back in. His father shrugged.

The Abubakars said good-night, and they offered Adelaide a ride home. She graciously accepted. Our department chair was having a rough semester, and I could see the toll it was taking on her tired face.

After they'd gone, Nonna took the boys up to bed, and the rest of us carried the full trays of vegan food and the empty lasagna dishes back into the kitchen. I covered the vegan food with foil and stacked the trays in our huge, extra freezer. I insisted everybody leave the dishes soaking in the sink, and we retreated back into the front parlor. Well, except for Zeke and Kelly. They had made a base camp in the library, using one cell phone for music and the other for streaming videos.

"I need a drink," Vince said. He turned to Tom. "Scotch?"

"Oh, yes," said Tom. "Oh, definitely yes." Tom sat down heavily in one of the big arm chairs in front of the fireplace and just stared into space. I wondered if he'd want to talk later about Kelly, Zeke, and the social ambush.

I went to the kitchen and got some glasses and some ice. Vince dug out the scotch where I kept it for him. And I got another bottle of that good red wine.

I heard Kelly laugh in the library, and I smiled too.

People. You have to love them.

Well, some of them.

Chapter 11

I cast you out, unclean spirit, along with every Satanic power of the enemy, every spectre from hell, and all your fell companions.

—THE CATHOLIC RITE OF EXORCISM

Later that evening

Vince cornered me in the kitchen as soon as Tom, Kelly, and Zeke had left. I didn't want to leave those dishes, so I was washing the ones that wouldn't fit in the old dishwasher.

"So what's up?" he said, grabbing a tea towel and starting to dry one of the lasagna pans. "You look like hell and so does that lady professor of yours and the Muslim guy." He finished drying the pan, put it on the kitchen table, and then sat down, squeezing his bulk into one of the benches. He'd apparently parked his half-empty glass of scotch there when he came in. He sat in front of it, but didn't take a drink. He just waited.

I shut off the water and came over and sat opposite him. Vince had been a cop in Chicago for decades, and it was clear he hadn't stopped being observant the way good cops are. He'd wait me out until I spilled the beans.

I realized I wanted his insight, and so I laid it all out, holding nothing back. I even took out my phone and showed him the photos of the chat room screen shots in the game "Revenge."

"What is with these snot-nosed little sons of bitches, Kristin?" he burst out when he handed back my phone. "Jesus H. Christ, they're after Aduba, what? Cause he's got an opinion? Aren't these so smart college kids supposed to wanna think stuff? And besides, this is America, for Christ's sake. Aduba, he can believe what he likes. What the hell has happened to this country?"

I smiled inwardly that Vince knew very well what Aduba's real name was. Abbie, my Aunt Fanny. But I sobered as I looked at him. Yeah, sure, so what that he was convinced that Jesus Christ would defend a Muslim professor so he could be American? And maybe his eyes were a little rheumy with cataracts, but right now they were glinting with rage. His wrinkled face was a map of outrage. This was the mix of values, Jesus and being American and believing what you like, that had sustained Vince all his life, had sustained the decent, hard-working men like him, and now, these values, contradictory as they might be, were being taken down from the inside by a firehose of lies and hate.

"I think some are the college kids, Vince, but I'm also beginning to think there are outside recruiters, pulling them in." I watched him as he struggled with what he was realizing must be the case, what Vampire had said about "blue" in the chat room. He took a sip of his whiskey, and then he saw it, and he put the glass down so hard a little of the amber liquid sloshed up on the sides.

"Blue. God damn it. Blue. That's what ya think that stupid, creepy bastard meant, right?" His cloudy eyes bored into mine.

I nodded, but I also promised myself I was going to tackle him about not driving at night until he got those cataracts fixed. But not now. Now, we had to find creepy bastards.

"So, ya want me to come with ya tomorrow to this thing, see what I can see?" He looked past me, and I thought he was seeing some dirty cop, some dirty cop like he and I both thought had caused Marco's death. He looked like a really old, sad Italian Buddha.

"I'm tempted, Vince, I really am, but the boys come first. I'm not sure what's going to happen at that rally. There could be violence. I'd feel better if you and Natalie would take them downtown and like, go to a kid movie or something. Besides, then Carol can come to the rally, if she wants. I know she's really, really worried about Giles organizing this thing and how that makes him a target."

He nodded his greying head.

"She ain't wrong about that."

I sighed.

"I know." And now I knew the source of the tension between them. Carol hadn't wanted Giles to become such a visible leader. But Giles, I was learning more and more, did what he thought was right.

Vince knocked back the rest of his whiskey and got heavily up from the bench seat. He briefly placed a hand on my shoulder, and then he went to the back stairs and climbed slowly up. I watched him go. The heaviness of his grief was like a yoke on his shoulders, bending him down.

I took out my phone. Alice had texted me earlier in the evening.

"7:30 west side of midway u r wf me & mel."

That was nearly six hours from now. I got up, adjusted my own yoke of grief, and trudged upstairs.

✳ ✳ ✳

It was a beautiful morning. I'd fixed myself a giant mug of French Roast, and I was morosely drinking it, watching Molly enjoy the rising sun in the backyard and thinking, "Rats, the nice weather will swell the crowds."

Carol came down the backstairs and her face was so pale, her freckles stood out like caramel sprinkles on vanilla ice cream.

I'd texted her early this morning that the Ginellis were taking the boys for the day. I'd assumed Giles would have been leaving very early, and Carol was alone when she came in. She smiled weakly at me and poured herself a cup of coffee. I was amazed. Carol hated coffee.

"Giles already gone?" I asked.

She nodded.

"At six." She sipped a little coffee and made a face, but then took another sip. I assumed it was the caffeine she was after. She looked like she was taking a bitter-tasting medicine.

"You coming to the rally?" I asked quietly.

"I don't know," she said slowly, bending her head over the cup so that her bowl of brown hair hid her face.

"I'll look for Giles, do my best to watch out for him," I said firmly.

"Thanks," she said shortly, re-filled the cup from the coffee pot and went back upstairs.

I hoped their relationship would survive this. Again I cursed our toxic times. I topped off my portable coffee mug and picked up a backpack I'd filled with I.D., a whistle, and some granola bars. After talking with Vince last night, I'd added some mace and a collapsible baton made of steel that I kept locked in a safe in my bedroom closet. I picked up my sunglasses and headed toward campus.

It really was a beautiful day. The sun was gilding the campus turrets and even the gargoyles looked a little happier than usual. Well, what did they know? They were just stone carvings that were supposed to frighten away evil spirits. Right now they were doing a pretty crappy job of that, and I frowned up at them as I passed by.

I approached the grassy mall that bisected the campus, and I could see a lot of campus police cars parked around the perimeter. There were some Chicago police cars as well, but not as many as I thought this occasion required. Maybe they were just late. I hoped.

I could see in the distance that demonstrators were already gathering. As I got closer, I saw signs leaning against the temporary stage that had been set up. There were some of the usual "Love Trumps Hate" or "Hate Not Welcome Here" as well as a lot of "Black Lives Matter to US." Then I saw a small knot of people moving toward that area carrying signs that said "Avenge Heather," referring, I knew, to Heather Heyer, the young woman who had been killed when a white supremacist drove a car into the crowd of nonviolent demonstrators in Charlottesville. Uh-oh. I thought the word "avenge" was ominous. Then, I spotted a more wordy, academic-type sign, "Fascism Not to be Debated, Needs to be Abolished."

As I got closer, I could see over to the sidewalk on the south side of the field. The counter demonstrators were also gathering. Their group was heavy on flags. I saw both Nazi and Confederate. I also spotted flags bearing the Valknot, the three interlocking black triangles that honored good old Odin. The Valknot meant Odin's followers were willing to die for him because he'd hurry them along to Valhalla, the sort of Viking heaven, so they could party even though they were dead. Crap. I remembered what I'd read about Odin and his capacity to do, effectively, mind control in today's terms and provoke what one historian had called "his gifts of battle-madness, intoxication, and inspiration." I squinted at the faces, though some had already pulled up bandanas to hide their identities. But their weedy bodies still said "university nerd" to me. I hoped they were incapable of real battle madness. But hate had a lot of power. I had to keep reminding myself of that.

I moved closer and spotted two guys wearing white, open tunics with a red-tipped cross and the words "Deus vult," or "God wills it" painted on them. These were Crusader symbols. Crusaders. Sure. The anti-Muslim trump card, so to speak. I was absolutely sure no god worthy of worship had willed that medieval debacle.

I spotted Mel over the heads of the crowd. I started walking toward him and from a distance I saw Alice come up to him, talking on her radio. Both were in full uniform. She looked really angry. I came up to them, but I didn't interrupt.

"So the city cops, they're just going to form a 'perimeter,' whatever the hell that is supposed to mean at this point," she said, clipping her radio back on her belt. "And there's fewer than Gutierrez thought, or so Steve says." I assumed she meant Steve White.

"What the hell?" Mel said, frowning.

"What the hell it means is 'You're on your own, suckers,'" Alice said between gritted teeth. "We gotta spread out."

"You," Alice turned to me. "You stick with me. Mel, where you gonna be?"

Mel surveyed the mall that was filling up rapidly with demonstrators. He narrowed his eyes and looked twice over the scene before he replied.

"There, I think, between the stage and the demonstrators. Weakest point. Those jerks," he nodded his head toward the counter-demonstrators, "need to see a lot of badges between them and the speakers." Now Mel was making himself a target.

I looked at Alice as she nodded at him. She knew. Her face was set, and she narrowed her eyes.

"You bet. Kristin and I will take the front of the stage, try to protect the speakers from that direction. Steve said that's where he'd be."

"Right," said Mel, and he strode off.

Steve, the handy, tall, white guy. No, I thought. He needed to be with Mel. How to suggest that?

"Ah, Alice?" I said, tentatively and then thought, 'What the hell, this is no time to dance around.'

"Yeah?" Alice said, her eyes not on me but on the counter-demonstrators across the street.

"Call Steve back. Tell him to stick with Mel."

Alice looked up at me. Then she nodded and took out her radio and spoke to Steve. She turned back to me, her mouth pursed like she was tasting something very bad.

"So, Mel and me, we each get our own white bodyguard?" She looked away so I couldn't see her face, but I could hear the bitterness in her voice.

I looked down at her and waited until she looked at me again. Then I held her eyes.

"I'll do what it takes, Alice, and to get to you they'll have to go through me." I spoke softly so only she could hear, but I emphasized every word.

"Yeah, I know," she said, resignedly, and then she looked away, adding, "You idiot."

Suddenly her shoulders tightened, and she abruptly turned back to me.

"You're not carrying, are you? I'd hate to have to arrest you right here." She had her "don't mess with me" face back on and her voice had a rough edge. She might arrest me at that.

"I have mace and a steel, retractable baton. Both legal. And I know how to use that baton to great effect, Alice, and in the right places."

"Yeah, I bet you do," she said and tried to snort but it came out as a jagged laugh. Then she turned and started marching toward the stage.

* * *

Alice and I walked around, looking for what might be trouble spots, but we stayed near the stage, covering about twenty-five yards in each direction. The number of people at the rally continued to grow. I kept watching the counter-demonstrators, too. There were still fewer of them, but their numbers were growing too. I started counting. Maybe close to a hundred, jostling on the sidewalk with their stupid costumes and flags. Most now had bandanas around the lower part of their face, and there were some of those long, black trench coats made so popular by mass shooters. I was seriously worried whether there were weapons under those coats.

Then the crowd began to stir and an older, African American man wearing a suit and a clerical collar came up the stairs on the right side of the stage. He walked directly to the mike and with no preamble began to pray. His deep, sonorous voice boomed out over the crowd.

"Oh, Lord, we ask for your blessing . . . "

The sudden start seemed to have taken the counter-demonstrators by surprise. They quickly pulled out bullhorns and started to try to drown him out with racist chants. I recognized the "We will not be erased!" in the blare of the bullhorns.

I looked up at the preacher, and he seemed to calmly go on praying, his greying head bowed.

Then I tensed and nudged Alice. We were now directly in front of the stage, and two groups, about a dozen each, were converging on the platform from each side. Then I spotted Jane and realized the people in the two groups were wearing choir stoles in the university colors. Okay, okay, I thought. Singing. Fine.

But my stomach dropped as a noise like a huge intake of air drew my, and, as I looked around, frankly everyone's attention away from the stage. With my height, I could see over many in the crowd and on the far west side of the mall, a balloon was beginning to inflate. I glanced at Alice, and she was just still scanning the crowd for trouble. This must be the balloon that Gutierrez had mentioned that would hold some kind of sign.

The sound of the air intake got louder, and the balloon started to rise. I got a huge shock as the form of the balloon took shape. It was a giant Mickey Mouse.

As it rose, the crowd began to cheer and clap. Mickey's white-gloved hands were holding a banner that read "Hate is Mickey Mouse."

As Mickey became almost fully inflated, the choir burst into song.

"M, I, C, K, E, Y, Hate is Mickey Mouse. Mickey Mouse, Donald Duck!"

As they sang "Donald Duck," from behind me I heard a really weird honking. No, not honking. Buzzing. I turned and saw that a huge number of people, perhaps as many as a hundred, had taken out plastic kazoos were starting to play along with the choir.

"Doo, doo doo, brrr brrr brr, doo doo doo doo doo" went the kazoos in time with the choir. I glanced at Alice, and she was continuing to scan the crowd, though a small smile had turned the corners of her mouth upward. By now the crowd was laughing and singing along.

I went to the left side of the stage to see how the counter-demonstrators were responding to Mickey and the music. I thought their numbers had shrunk some. I couldn't locate the Crusaders, and I thought a number of the flags had been carried away or at least furled up. A few faces now had their bandanas down, and I thought the right word to describe their faces was "nonplussed." I could see the back of Mel's head, and a guy I thought was Steve White, standing with their backs to the stage, facing the counter-demonstrators.

Then I spotted Giles, standing a little apart on that side of the stage. He had a small smile on his face. He wasn't exactly relaxed, however. He was looking down at a clipboard, and I could see every tendon on the backs of his hands as he clenched it.

Of course, I thought, he orchestrated this. He wasn't only a math Ph.D. candidate. I knew that he had been a peace activist in his native Senegal. I'd read a little about this use of humor to disarm an opponent and empower a protest. At the time, I'd kind of dismissed it as wishful thinking, but amazingly it seemed to be working. Yelling back at these white supremacists was what they wanted. Being compared to a cartoon character and then laughed at, not so much. And, of course, the choir's participation had Jane written all over it. I thought it was Saul Alinsky who had once said, "Never go up against people who sing together."

Speaking of the choir, I realized they had now stopped singing the Mickey Mouse song, and they had launched into what became a medley of protest songs. "We Shall Overcome" was followed by "Blowin' in the Wind," and then "We Shall Not Be Moved." The crowd was singing along. I moved back up next to Alice where she was positioned at the front of the stage. She was still scanning the crowd in sections. Just because most people were singing didn't mean there was no danger from that direction. I got down to business and scanned sections in the opposite direction.

Then there was movement on the stage behind me, and I turned.

The choir was stepping back, and a tall, young, African American woman was walking toward the microphone. She was wearing a long, plain white dress, her hair bound up in a white scarf. I turned back from the stage again and continued to scan the crowd with Alice.

Behind me I heard the first notes of Billie Holiday's haunting ballad about lynching, "Strange Fruit." I shivered as the woman's voice seemed eerily similar to Holiday's. I didn't think I was imagining that deep, even distilled passion and despair.

"Strange trees bear strange fruit. Blood on the leaves and blood at the root, black bodies swinging in the Southern breeze. Strange fruit hanging from the poplar trees."

The crowd had stilled, and many started to cry. I glanced over at Alice. She roughly grabbed her sunglasses that were hanging on her jacket pocket and put them on and continued her own systematic perusal of the crowd, though her round shoulders shook a little.

The woman finished, and the crowd erupted in applause.

I continued my own examination of the crowd, looking for anything that might pose a threat, when I heard a familiar voice start to intone with both British formality and Nigerian cadence. Aduba.

I took a quick glance around toward the stage. He was wearing what I thought was traditional West African clothing. Good. There was plenty of room for the bullet proof vest under those layers of outer robe and under tunic. He was right behind me at the microphone and as he glanced at the crowd, I saw him register my presence. He nodded. I hoped that meant he was wearing the protective vest.

His voice rang out, and the crowd stilled.

"As a young man growing up in my native Nigeria, I saw much violence between Muslims and Christians. I dreamed of America, where all religions were equal in your Constitution. Religious freedom, it is America's gift to the world and now, in this country, I see it is threatened. This must be protected."

He went on about how Africa and the United States have a history of both pain and promise. When he finished, the crowd gave him a thunderous ovation that went on for several minutes. He actually came back to the microphone and nodded at the crowd.

He was followed by several speakers, most of them students, though there was one political science professor I recognized. The crowd started to find places to sit down on the grass and several took out various picnic items.

I'd heard nothing from the counter-demonstrators for a while, and I went back to the left side of the stage and looked over at the sidewalk. They were almost all gone. There were some scattered leaflets on the ground. Wow, they really hadn't liked being laughed at.

The choir came back for another medley. I was watching the crowd leave and not paying much attention until I recognized one of the lines from Woody Guthrie's "Old Man Trump," in which Guthrie had made his views on his landlord, Fred Trump, very clear: "Old Man Trump knows just how much racial hate he stirred up in the blood-pot of human hearts when he drawed that color line here at his 1,800-family project." I shook my head.

Jane had some gumption to include that segment in the choir's selections. The choir moved on to "Ain't Gonna Let Nobody Turn Me Around," but the statement had been made.

What a day.

The mall was almost completely empty now. Mickey had been deflated and was being packed up and stowed in the truck that had carried him to the rally. He had done a good job for a mouse.

No, it was Giles and Jane, and Aduba too, and the other speakers who had done the good work here, I thought, as I walked to where Alice was conferring with Steve. I didn't see Mel.

"How many photos did he get?" Alice was asking, and her pad was out.

"Oh, hundreds," Steve replied.

"Where was the photographer?" I asked, not having seen anyone obviously taking pictures, that is, apart from the hundreds of cell phones that had been present.

"Top of the truck," Steve said, jerking his thumb to the truck that had brought Mickey.

"Telephoto," he went on. "Hope he got good angles on some of the faces that weren't covered."

"Campus cop?" I asked, not knowing anyone had those kinds of skills, but certainly there could be.

"No," Steve said shortly. "My husband."

"Tell him thanks," I replied.

"Sure," said Steve, and he turned and went toward the truck, his long legs carrying him rapidly away.

Alice let out a breath that came from the bottom of the soles of her feet.

"That Giles guy," Alice began. "He did some really good work here today. Tell him, will you? And the chapel lady, she did too. Gutsy."

Yeah. I hoped Jane wouldn't pay a price for the Trump daddy landlord song.

"They did, Alice. I wouldn't have believed it if I hadn't seen it with my own eyes."

Alice took off her police cap and shook out her brown curls. They sprung out like they'd been restrained too long.

"Me neither. I never would have thought it." And she walked away to the west, into the rising wind, her hair blowing free. I thought I could hear her humming "doo doo doo, doo doo doo, doo, doo, doo, doo, doo."

Chapter 12

You belong to your father, the devil, and you want to carry out your father's desires. He was a murderer from the beginning, not holding to the truth, for there is no truth in him.

—JOHN 8:44

Sunday afternoon

I walked away from the campus, humming under my breath too. What an extraordinary day. I glanced at my watch. And it was only just after one o'clock. Then my cell phone rang. The display said "Natalie." They must be home from the movie.

"Yes, Nonna," I answered, but it was Vince.

"You okay? That Carol, she's here, said people sang, and the jerks ran away. That true?" Vince sounded as disbelieving as I had felt.

"Well, sort of Vince. I'll tell you about it when I see you. Where are you all now?"

"Your house. Boys fed and in their room. Natalie thinks they will nap. Hah. Not those boys. Where are you?"

"I'm walking home."

"So listen, Kristin, Vince Junior on his way to pick us up. We were supposed to watch their kids for him. He's got business and Marilyn is off some place. I don know what's up with that." Vince sounded very disapproving.

Well, Vince Junior and Marilyn had four kids. I didn't exactly blame her for wanting a break.

"She's with girlfriends, Vince, he told you. In Las Vegas," I heard Natalie in the background.

Vegas?

"Yeah. Sure," said Vince. "Anyway, Vince Junior coming and pick us up, take us to Wisconsin. The guy, he says a few more days on the RV anyway."

"I told Vince Junior no necessary," Natalie spoke loudly in the background. "We could take one of those cars. You just put in the address, and they come."

What, an Uber to Wisconsin?

"No, Natalie. Vince Junior is coming," Vince said firmly, I assumed to her.

Then he spoke into the phone, I assumed to me.

"She took that course at the Y, and she's got all these things on her phone now. She wants to try that car one."

Apps?

The cell phone buzzed, I assumed with an incoming call for them. Vince spoke rapidly.

"That's Vince Junior. That Carol, she's here says she can stay with the boys so we're gonna take off. Talk to you soon. Keep your head down," Vince said, and he ended the call. I shook my head, trying to clear it. Talking to the Ginellis in stereo like that always threatened to give me a headache.

But before I could call Carol and confirm things with her, my text tone sounded. I looked at the screen and was astounded.

"Meet? Talk? Heard about rally. John Vandenberg."

I hesitated. How did John know my cell phone number? Well, I would find out when I talked to him. I'd meet with him, I decided. Maybe the rally was doing more good work. But first I needed to check with Carol.

She answered on the first ring and said the boys had actually fallen asleep on their beds. She confirmed she'd be home "studying." I thought it more likely she meant "waiting for Giles," but I didn't press it. I said I'd be back in an hour or so.

Then I texted John.

"Okay. Where?"

"Daily Grind. 50th & Wexel."

About eight blocks. No point in getting the car.

"15 min."

"Thanks."

*　*　*

I couldn't figure out what was going on. I had been sitting in the coffee shop for twenty minutes and still no John. I'd texted him I'd arrived, but no reply. I had just called his cell number that had displayed on the text screen. No answer. I contemplated ordering a second cup of coffee, but there were limits to how much coffee even I could drink, though the dark roast at this place wasn't bad.

Then my text tone sounded. It was from John's number. "No point nothing worth it." And that was it. Ominous.

I remembered I'd sent John's student information, including his address, to Mel after the copy shop incident. I looked it up in "sent mail" and realized he lived only a block away from the coffee shop. I could call the campus police for a wellness check, but with the rally cleanup going on, I didn't know how soon anyone could get there. I was close, and I had a bad feeling. I'd learned not to ignore that. I got up, paid for my coffee and walked quickly to the address of his apartment.

A young man pushing out the door of John's apartment building let me in without any question. Typical lack of concern for security in Hyde Park. So stupid, I thought, as I checked the mailboxes. Yes, John's name was there, along with another. Brant, I squinted in the dim light of the hallway, Higgens? I turned on my cell phone light and directed it on the scribbled names above the boxes. Hingston. Roommate I assumed. 405. I looked up the gloomy staircase and started to climb. I decided to try not to touch the handrail as the stains were layered on with some patches that actually glistened even in the shadows. I also decided not to speculate what made them glisten.

I arrived on the fourth floor without meeting anyone and went to knock on 405. Then I realized it was actually partly open. I pushed it open slightly more and called out once, my words sounding loud in the darkened room, but then I didn't call again. The smell of defecation had hit me.

I saw the feet dangling and an overturned chair. I forced myself to look up past the slack arms and stretched neck, all the way to the bloated face. It was grotesquely disfigured, pushed up by the choking rope. It was barely recognizable, but I knew it was John. I realized that in the back of my mind I'd been worried something like this would happen. And now it had.

No time to think. Seconds counted. I ran into the room and grabbed John's legs and pushed him up to take the weight off his neck. He wasn't that big a guy, probably 5'8" or so and 160 pounds, but he was, in fact, dead weight. I hoped not. Not forever. Not this young.

I put my shoulder under his hips to free one hand and tried to wrestle my phone out of my pocket to try to call 911. My hands were slippery from the involuntary voiding that stained John's pants, and I struggled to make the call.

"What the hell?" An angry voice yelled from the doorway.

I turned my head a little toward the angry voice that was now saying "Oh hell, oh hell no."

"Get over here," I commanded. "Help support his legs, I'm trying to call 911."

I felt other arms go around John's legs, and I sagged a little when I felt the body rise slightly off of my shoulder.

"Christ, he's covered in shit!" protested the voice.

I pressed send immediately on my phone and tried to speak slowly when I heard the operator come on. I gave my name, described the hanging and repeated the address twice.

"Hurry!" I said and ended the call.

"Take the full weight," I instructed the guy who had come in. I assumed it was Brant Hingston, the roommate, but this was not the time for introductions. He was now supporting John's weight with me. From what I could tell from the lift, he seemed taller than John, though not quite my height, and he had good upper body strength.

"What?" he breathed. "What?"

"Hold him yourself," I said, as clearly as I could, almost directly into his ear as we were so close, jointly supporting the weight.

"Why?" he breathed out.

"I'm going to find something to cut him down," I said curtly.

"Oh, okay. Yeah. Okay. Got him," he said, and I felt his arms tighten.

I let go and ran to a galley kitchen that was along the side wall. I jerked open drawers, hunting for a sharp knife. I grabbed one and ran back.

I stood the chair upright and climbed up.

"Ready?" I asked. "I'm going to cut the rope. He's coming down."

"Yeah. Okay. Yeah," he gasped.

I started to cut through the cheap rope, and it snapped almost immediately. Despite the efforts of my helper, John's body fell to the floor.

I dropped the knife and jumped down. My helper just stood there, looking down at John's body, lying flaccid on the floor.

I pushed past him, bent down and used a tissue from my pocket to cover my fingers while I loosened the rope from John's neck. The cop part of me was registering the need to preserve evidence as well as try to save a life. There was the typical V-shaped groove in the neck where the side knot had pulled up, choking off the airway and the carotid artery so no oxygen or blood had been able to get to the brain. For how long? I wondered. But the head wasn't lolling like the bones of the spine had snapped. There might be a chance.

I started pushing on the chest doing CPR.

"Go downstairs!" I sharply instructed the guy who was standing behind me, seemingly frozen. "Wait for the EMT's and direct them up here."

"Yeah," he said, and walked out the door on stiff legs, wiping his hands on his pants as he went.

I put one hand behind John's head to straighten it a little to better open the airways, and my hand came away with some blood on it. He's been hit on the back of his head.

"Oh, John," I thought as I put my filthy, bloody hand back on his chest to push again, willing his lungs to respond. "Who did this to you?"

This wasn't suicide, it was murder.

Chapter 13

Accordingly the act of self-defense [when] one's intention is to save one's own life, is not unlawful, seeing that it is natural to everything to keep itself in "being," as far as possible.

—THOMAS AQUINAS, *SUMMA THEOLOGICA*, 64.7

Sunday afternoon

I moved aside so an EMS technician could take over working on John, and then I stood up to answer questions as well as I could. A mask and bag had immediately been placed over John's nose and mouth. I told both the techs who'd rushed up the stairs I'd found him hanged and had tried immediately to hold him up, and when this guy had arrived, I nodded to helper guy, we'd worked together to cut him down. No, I answered the one on the bag, he'd never been conscious or breathing that I could tell.

The tech doing the CPR stopped and placed one of those portable defibrillators on his chest. He turned the device on. I thought he would shock John's heart, but he just looked at the small screen.

"Flat," he intoned.

"We should call it," the one on the bag said quietly. And they stopped working on John.

He was dead.

The other tech nodded at his partner and left, I assumed to go get something to transport John down the stairs. The one who'd called it on John went out into the hall and started talking on his phone. Helper guy, clearly Brant, the roommate, was sitting slumped in the living room area, his head down and his hands hanging down between his knees.

I knew one of the calls the EMS technicians were making was to see how soon the police would be here. I thought if I were going to look around, now was the time.

It didn't take much detection to see the huge Confederate flag hanging on the wall opposite the door. Below it was a desk that was a complete mess. I moved a little closer, trying not to draw attention to myself. Jumbled fabric was piled on one side of the desk. I could see a corner of the Valknot symbol crudely painted on it and hanging partly down one side of the desk was what looked like one of those makeshift Crusader tunics. "Oh, John," I thought. "What an idiot you were."

I glanced back. Brant was still morosely looking at the floor, and the one EMS tech in the hall was still turned away from me, talking on a cell phone. The other seemed not to have returned. I didn't want to touch anything on the desk, but I moved closer and looked down. Some computer printed pages looked like schoolwork. I didn't see a cell phone, but it could be buried in the mess or even in John's pocket. A couple of the original flyers protesting Abubakar's lecture were crumpled on the side opposite from the flag and tunic, and something was written over and over on one of them. I took another quick glance over my shoulder to make sure no one was watching me and took out my phone. I snapped a photo of the partly crumpled paper that had writing on it with the zoom function on. It looked like a number written over and over, scrawled so deeply it had cut through the flyer on the one corner I could see most clearly, with perhaps a couple of words. I'd try to decipher it later. Before I put my cell phone away, I snapped two quick pictures of helper guy.

I heard voices in the hall and turned as two uniformed Chicago police officers came up the stairs. They were both white and seemed quite young. Must be beat cops responding to the earlier call I'd made. I stepped away from the desk and stood in the kitchenette. I could see them conferring with the EMS technician, though glancing through the door toward where John's body lay on the floor, a coil of severed rope next to him, and on to me and Brant.

The shorter of the two remained in the hall, still conferring with the tech. The taller one, his close-cropped, blond hair nearly invisible over his ears before the rest was covered by his police cap, came in carefully, avoiding the area where John lay. He grimaced, probably from the smell. He walked toward Brant in the little living room, who stood up, and then he made a curt gesture for me to come over and join them. He took out a notebook.

I didn't like that curt gesture, or his silence. He should have first identified himself and asked who we were. I decided I needed to take the initiative. I walked briskly over to him, though taking care to move around the outside wall also to avoid the scene.

"Officer," I said clearly and firmly as I walked up to him. "Officer Fulbright, correct?" I asked, as I got close enough to see his name that was clearly printed on his name badge. He nodded. "I'm going to remove my I.D. from my back pocket." I waited for another nod, and then I slowly lifted my flip wallet from my jeans, using my left hand, the hand that had not touched John's bloody head. No sense waving a bloody hand at a young and seemingly surly young cop.

I handed it to him while I went on speaking.

"I am a former Chicago detective, and now I teach at the university and consult part-time for the campus police. You're out of District 5, right?" Since that was also on his badge, below his name, it was not a big leap, but Fulbright lasered very ice-blue eyes on to me, with just a hint of surprise turning up the unwrinkled corners. I just plowed ahead. "I used to work out of the 14th. You can see my campus I.D. there," I pointed to the wallet he was now holding open, "and you may certainly take one of my cards with all my contact information."

He frowned, and then painstakingly wrote my name on his pad and took one of my cards.

"What are you doing here? And who's he?" Fulbright asked, his words clipped while he lasered those glacial blue eyes back on to my face while handing back my wallet.

Still not identifying himself. Interesting. He should know procedure better than that.

"I have no idea who he is," I said, nodding my head at likely-Brant who was standing in front of the broken down sofa like he was auditioning to be one of the stones on Easter Island. He was about as tall as surly cop, and as I had deduced from his strength in helping to lift John, his upper body was muscled under his T-shirt.

"I came here because this person, John Vandenberg," and I turned and gestured with my left hand toward John's body on the floor, "was one of my students. He was recently suspended from the university, and he texted me he wanted to talk. We had agreed to meet at the Daily Grind, a coffee shop about a block away, and he didn't show. Then he sent a text I thought was concerning, and I decided to do a wellness check on him. I had his home address in my email. The door was ajar, and he was hanging by that cord," and again I turned to gesture, still only using my left hand, "and I rushed to push him up by the legs and call 911. This guy," another left-handed gesture, "came in and helped hold John while I cut him down. I tried CPR until these EMS techs arrived and took over."

Fulbright was writing away, and I thought I'd wait until he caught up.

"And you?" he said abruptly to likely-Brant, who seemed to startle awake.

"I'm Brant, Brant Hingston, I live here."

Man of few words.

"I.D.," snapped Fulbright, holding out his hand. Hingston dug around in a back pocket and brought out a billfold. Fulbright took it, flipped it open and started writing again. Brant studied the floor. He's trying not to be here, I thought.

"So, what's your story?" Fulbright asked him.

"Well, I came home, and I saw her," he pointed at me, "standing in the room and John was hanging from the ceiling." Inaccurate. How interesting. Roommate guy was trying to distance himself in more ways than one.

"I was holding John up by the legs when you came in," I corrected. "I asked you to hold him too, and you did."

"I don't remember that, it's all a blur," said Brant, not looking up from the floor.

Now I was seriously annoyed.

"Officer, check his pants. You can see there where he got fecal matter on him from when he was holding John up so I could cut him down."

We all looked down at Brant's khaki pants and sure enough the light tan material had brown stains all down one side. Hingston had his stone face on as he looked down, and I almost expected him to say "I've never seen these pants before in my life."

"Well," said Fulbright sternly, "what about that?"

"I dunno. Like I said, it's all a blur." He was literally stonewalling. My suspicion of Brant and his role in all of this went sky high. At the very least he had to be one of the white supremacist crowd, given the Confederate flag decoration and the stuff on the desk.

I was also beginning to get very tense about how this whole scenario had been set up. Somebody had murdered John Vandenberg, I was certain of it from that head wound. It was possible the texts that got me here weren't even from John.

Time to take the initiative again before more experienced cops could arrive.

"Officer," I said as firmly as I could. "I need to call this in to the university police. Then I'll come to District 5 and give a witness statement and sign it."

To my absolute amazement, and, in fact to Hingston's, who finally looked up and whose tanned, even-featured face registered absolute shock, Fulbright just nodded.

"Hey!" Brant blurted out, but Fulbright seemed to ignore him.

I nodded back like one cop to another and moved firmly around the crime scene area and down the stairs. The second cop, still on the phone, glanced at me as I walked by him. I made a quick note of his name from his badge, Michael Belcher, also District 5, but I didn't pause. I moved down the stairs trying to maintain my air of authority and not appear to be running.

When I was out of sight I really started to move and was out of breath by the time I got to the street. I veered left and cut down an alley so I'd be out of sight when actual cops who might detect things arrived. Just in time. I heard the squeal of brakes behind me as a car pulled rapidly up and screeched to a halt, double-parking in front of John's building. A dirty brown sedan. Had to be the detectives. I pulled back further into the shadow of the alley and watched who got out. Kaiser and Brown, and they were practically running. Or, in Carl's case, waddling as quickly as possible.

I turned and moved quickly down the alley, thinking. I was more and more convinced that I had been lured to the scene so I could be implicated in John's murder. The rank incompetence of these two young officers had been my only saving grace. So far. They should have held me there until a Scene of the Crime officer and the detectives had arrived. Given that Kaiser and Brown were the ones rushing to the scene, I could have been held for hours while the whole scene was examined, and perhaps, given who the responding detectives were, even taken into custody. The laxity of the beat cops might have been due to their assumption of suicide, and they wouldn't know about the head wound officially until the Cook County Medical Examiner had done the autopsy. That was mandatory for suspected suicide.

But I wouldn't want to be Fulbright and Belcher right now. Carl would be tearing into them in a rage that I'd been allowed to leave.

Yes, I'd head down to District 5, but only after I'd gotten in touch with my lawyer, Anna Feldman, and arranged to have her meet me there. And, against all protocol, I'd shower first and scrub myself with Oxy-clean, especially my hands. And wash and dry my clothes. We had plenty of that oxygen producing detergent, as it was the best at getting rid of the stains of all the gunk the boys managed to get on their clothes. It was also the type of detergent that did make blood and fecal stains undetectable. Still, they might be able to get some of my DNA from John's shirt, so the washing up would be just a delaying tactic. That really didn't matter since I'd already admitted to trying to save him.

I was a big believer in self-defense, and thank you Thomas Aquinas for that moral guidance, and I would do what I could to thwart any attempt to pin John's murder on me. And, meanwhile, I'd try my best to find the real murderer or murderers.

I got around the corner and quickly cut into the next alley. I could make it home going alley to alley just in case Carl took it into his head to look for me. In the next alley, though, I stopped and took some deep breaths. I took out my phone and realized I was putting stains on it as well and it would need cleaning. Rats. Should have used the tissue again. I didn't want to put the phone near my face, so I moved behind a large, overflowing trash dumpster and used the speaker phone function.

"Anna?" Thank heavens she picked right up. I told her I'd need her to go with me to District 5, but that I'd call back with details when I got home. And when I was sure I could not be overheard. "Certainly," she replied. I loved that about Anna. No muss, no fuss. Just the facts and the law.

I started walking briskly toward home. I needed to call Alice too, and read her in, but same deal. Not where I could be overheard.

＊　＊　＊

I called Carol as I ducked from alley to alley, and fortunately she and the boys, along with Molly, were down the street at the little pocket park there. Phew. I wasn't sure I had a good answer for why I was so messy. Mike would pick up on that in an instant. And Molly would give me away just from the smell. I told Carol I'd witnessed a crime and had to go make a statement at the police department. Carol knew me well enough not to ask any questions with the boys nearby. I did ask if Giles had come home, but she said, in a kind of flat voice, "No, but I know where he is." Still not going well there, I thought.

I went in our back door, using the tissue this time, and when I was in the kitchen I immediately called Anna. I explained as quickly as I could what had happened, and we arranged to meet at District 5 in an hour. I hung up and headed for the shower by way of the laundry room. I picked up the detergent and used it in the shower to scrub myself clean, especially my hands and under my nails. I still felt a little like Lady Macbeth. Then I threw my clothes into the washer with more of the detergent. I used tissues and the detergent to carefully clean the outside of my phone. I dried it and flushed the tissues down the toilet. Clean and dry, I fixed some espresso and called Alice.

I caught her at home, and she tried to put me off by saying she was fixing dinner.

"John Vandenberg is dead, and I think he was murdered," was my response.

"Aww, hell. A jerk but still a kid. How'd it happen?" Alice asked, and I could hear a few pots banging as she probably moved them off the stove. Dinner would be delayed at the Matthews house.

I gave it to her step by step, along with my growing suspicion I was being set up and how Kaiser and Brown had been rushing to the scene.

"So, you meeting that lawyer at District 5? Good idea. That Kaiser purely hates you. When?"

I looked at my watch.

"I better leave now," I said.

"Call me after, you hear?"

I heard.

* * *

It was dark outside when I walked wearily to the attended lot where I'd parked my car. District 5 was not in a neighborhood where you'd want to leave your car unattended for a minute. Anna's limo passed me and pulled up to the door to pick her up. The driver opened the door and she exited the police station. She walked firmly down the stairs on her stiletto heels, her black, fitted jacket and skirt completely unwrinkled, and she stood out like Coco Chanel had paid an unlikely visit to a concrete block prison.

I had not been allowed to just write up a statement and sign it. Anna and I had been forced to wait in an airless interrogation room for more than an hour until Kaiser and Brown had rushed in. When Kaiser abruptly pushed open the door, he was practically drooling, he was so happy to have me in a box. Then he saw Anna sitting cool and collected in her beautiful suit with about a pound of gold jewelry on, and I honestly think he swallowed some of the drool.

Anna and I had been down this road before, and I knew to let all the questions go through her, and I answered when she nodded. Kaiser, as was his charming way, had started right in on sexual innuendo and kept it up. He made snide remarks about "meeting for coffee" and "my teachers never did that for me" to try to get me to defend myself. It was a good thing Anna was there, as I would have been tempted to express astonishment that Kaiser had actually gone to school. But I didn't. Brown didn't say much in his second-banana role, but he asked one good question. "Where's Vandenburg's cell phone?"

That was bad. They hadn't found John's phone. That increased my suspicions both that he had been murdered, and that the murderer or murderers had tried to set me up. That cell phone would prove John's phone had texted mine. I had deliberately left my cell phone locked in my car's glove compartment, but before I'd gone in to the station, I'd taken a screen shot of the text page and sent it to Anna. She showed them the picture.

That really set Kaiser off. "We need your phone!" he snapped at me.

"Get a warrant," Anna calmly replied.

Then Kaiser moved on to fire rapid questions about Giles Diop and his role with BlackLivesMatter and the rally. I nodded at Anna and replied quite truthfully that I knew absolutely nothing about it. But, I thought, better be sure Giles has his own lawyer.

Finally, I was allowed to write out a witness statement. Anna checked it, and then I'd signed it.

As I sat down in the driver's seat of my car, I realized the back of my shirt was wet with sweat. The night was clear, and it wasn't really that cold, at least by Chicago standards, but I shivered and turned on the heat in the car. Then I took my phone out and engaged the hands-free mode.

I called Alice, and we talked while I drove.

Alice zeroed in on John's missing cell phone as well.

"Man, you dodged a bullet," she remarked. "They meant you to take the fall."

"Yeah, I see that Alice, but why was he killed? I don't get that."

"Must be somethin' he knew," she mused. "Maybe he was gonna to tell on the rest, give names and all that."

"Well," I replied, "I guess that could be it, but murder seems extreme for that."

"These guys are extremists, Kristin," Alice said dryly.

Well, that was the truth.

*   *   *

I let myself into the quiet, darkened house and felt huge waves of fatigue threaten to overwhelm me. I hadn't eaten since the morning, but I couldn't face food right now.

I dragged myself upstairs and called softly up to Carol to their apartment.

Giles answered that the boys were asleep, and Molly had been out. So Giles was home. I thought about cornering him about whether the police had been in touch with him and whether he had a lawyer, but midnight was not the time for that.

I was glad he was home. I peeked in on the boys and Molly, and they were all sound asleep.

I got into my bed and called Tom. I just needed to hear his voice. But the call went right to voicemail. He must be in surgery.

I turned off the light and thought about being lonely even in a relationship. And then I thought no more.

Chat Room of Video Game "Revenge"

Midnight Sunday

Vampire726: S*** S*** they got Moloch the N***** bastards got him need revenge man need revenge man what the hell

Demon196: don't freak u p**** casualty of war there will be blood for blood fight White Genocide slamming the C*** and the ISIS N*****

Incubus75: is it done?

Demon196: s*** yeah

Vampire726: what?????

Demon196: told u dont freak

Chapter 14

Not necessity, not desire—no, the love of power is the demon of men.

—FRIEDRICH NIETZSCHE, *DAYBREAK: BOOK IV, APHORISM #262*

Monday

I woke early, the watery light of early fall enough to rouse me from what had passed for sleep. I dimly remembered a night of broken images of bloated faces. I felt the twinge of a headache start as soon I opened my eyes.

I dragged myself up and headed to the kitchen. Molly got up and left the boys' room when she heard me. She padded behind me, her nails clicking on the hardwood floor. I let her out and fixed myself a triple espresso. When I'd gotten the first sip of scalding coffee over my tongue, I scooped a little kibble into her bowl and let her back in. Her tawny fur was mottled brown in patches. Great, it was raining. I just sat down cross-legged on the cool kitchen floor, sipping and trying hard not to think. I didn't succeed.

Molly finished her kibble and came over to me. Her soft brown eyes regarded me for a minute, and then she just sank down on the floor beside me and put her big, warm head on my thigh. Even with water off of wet dog fur, drool, and particles of kibble dripping on to my pajamas, it was very comforting. Dogs just know when solace is needed.

I finished my coffee, patted Molly and stood up. I can wallow just so long, and then I need to get going on something. I'd dress, eat with the boys and go into the office. I hadn't touched my email in three days, and while monotonous it would feel like doing something.

* * *

It was barely 7:30 a.m., and I was already at my desk. Even though I had flipped on the overhead lights, I turned on my desk lamp too. The dark grey of the rainy Chicago day blocked most natural light. My days continued to start at dawn, I thought, though I had seen a light under Adelaide's door when I'd come down the hall. Worse to be department chair, I guessed.

I booted up my computer, and then I froze. Literally. I couldn't move for a second from the shock.

My screen flooded with porn, and as image after image pounded on to the screen, I was horrified to see my own face pasted on some of the grotesquely sexualized pictures of women, most spread-eagled and in the sex act. Then words started to scroll down over the porn.

"You will be raped very soon."

"You killed John and you deserve to die!"

"You'll pay for f****** that rag head!"

Threats. I shook myself free of the initial shock. Well, okay, time to document. I took out my phone and started to videotape as much of the filth as I could capture as it scrolled by. I tried to use my keyboard function to scroll back up to get what had gone before, but I realized I had no control. Pretty sophisticated. Someone had taken control of my computer. I kept taping with one hand and hit speakerphone on my desk phone with the other. I punched in Adelaide's extension, and when she answered I just said, "Get to my office now. It's an emergency."

I actually heard her office door open within seconds. The woman could move, I'd give her that. She was shortly at my open door, and I gestured for her to come over and look at my screen.

She frowned, but then she briskly walked around my desk and looked over my shoulder. She gasped in shock. The feed was speeding up, with porn and threats coming rapid-fire, bursting on to the screen, one being covered by another. And then the screen went black. My computer had crashed.

"Well, hell," Adelaide said from behind me. Yeah, that pretty much summed it up.

She walked very slowly around my desk, her large, round shoulders hunched forward. Her body was curling up in self-protection. Adelaide had good reason from her past to fear sexual threat. I hated she'd had to see that hot mess on my computer, but I could not keep it from her. It was an attack on me, Aduba and by extension our department. Actually, I thought grimly, it was potentially an attack on the whole university computer network.

Adelaide sat down heavily in the chair opposite my desk and then shifted around ,registering the bumpy seat of the chair. I had one chair in my office section. It was really uncomfortable, and I liked it that way. I kept it for students so they wouldn't get too relaxed, and they'd get to the point when they came to see me.

Adelaide opened her mouth, whether to complain about the chair or comment on the cyberattack on me, when we were both startled.

"Excuse me," said Abubakar's deep voice. "Am I disturbing?"

Adelaide and I looked at each other blankly for a second, then Adelaide stood up and turned around in front of my desk. I stood also.

"No, of course, not," I said slowly. "This is your office too."

Abubakar looked from one to the other of us, the muscle in his cheek starting to work. I was sure he could tell something had happened. Best to just tell him right away.

"Aduba, actually we need to tell you something and then show it to you. It concerns you too."

I picked up my phone off of my desk and walked around until I was standing by the screen that divided our offices.

In as matter-a-fact voice as I could muster, I summarized what had just appeared on my screen. I passed over my cell phone and clicked the video. I heard his breathing speed up as the horrible images unfolded.

"This is truly terrible," he said, frowning and passing back the cell phone. "Who would do such a thing?"

I was about to reply, and then I looked over at Aduba's computer. Of course, I thought, he would most likely have been cyberattacked as well.

He saw me looking at his computer and started to walk over to it.

"No," I said abruptly. "Don't even open it."

He pulled up and then looked back at me, frowning deeply.

"No, really, don't do it," I said sharply. "It's likely your computer was attacked too. We need the administration's help with this issue, and we need someone with IT skills to take your computer, and mine, and see if they can track who perpetrated this hate crime." I realized I was talking a mile a minute and breathing hard. Slow down, I told myself, but I thought I could feel my heart pounding. It was an attack, and it wasn't something I could kick and punch in defense. I hated this online nonsense.

Adelaide hadn't said anything to this point, but she came up next to me and put her large hand on my arm. I felt a slight tremor and realized she was trembling slightly. Was she steadying me or was I steadying her? I put my hand over hers as it lay on my arm.

"Okay, let's take this one step at a time," she said slowly, withdrawing her hand from under mine. "I will go down to my office and call the Academic Dean. I'll tell him what's happened and get his advice. You two just sit tight, and let me take this now."

She stepped past me to look directly up at Abubakar where he was standing stock still, halfway to his computer. Adelaide had been slumping with the shock, but she squared her shoulders and looked directly at him. She was doing what she could to try to stay steady.

"Okay?" she asked him firmly. "You agree?" Her head swiveled toward me. "You too, Kristin?"

"I agree," said Abubakar, rather formally. I just nodded.

Adelaide abruptly turned, her dress billowing out slightly behind her as she strode out the door.

"I must think," Abubakar said, probably as much to himself as to me. He followed Adelaide out the door, and I heard him open the door to Dr. Abraham's office that he used for prayer. I don't know what prayers covered this kind of catastrophe, but I sincerely hoped Allah was up to giving Aduba advice, or at least comfort. Or maybe my colleague was calling his wife.

For myself, I headed down to the coffee machine.

*   *   *

Coffee in hand, I sat back down at my desk and pulled the Norse mythology book off the shelf again. That was a wonderful thing about printed books. They wouldn't suddenly just turn on you and spew out filth and threats. The words in printed books stayed steady, unmoving.

I actually managed to lose myself in descriptions of Norse shamans who were called "Berserkers." They would go on the battlefield naked except for an animal mask and pelts and then, effectively, go beserk, "howling, roaring, and running amok with godly or demonic courage." Beserk. This attack felt like someone going beserk, but in the Norse sense of appearing crazy to win a power struggle. Only now, the battlefield was my campus, and the beserkers were trying to take it over. I was so deep in thought, I was startled when I heard Adelaide enter my office, followed by Aduba.

I grabbed my consciousness and forced it to return to the present, and then I realized Adelaide looked ghastly. It looked like all color had been bleached out of her face.

"What?" I asked, horrified at how she looked. I glanced at Aduba, and the muscle in his jaw was working so hard he appeared to be chewing.

"Emails are circulating on campus with some of those disgusting photos of you. Some of Dr. Abubakar too. It's awful." She swallowed and took some deep breaths and then actually swayed a little. Yeah, this was awful, but I was more afraid for Adelaide in that moment.

Abuba saw it too and grabbed a chair from his side of the office and quickly put it behind her. Smart. She didn't as much sit down as fold.

I reached down under my desk. I always had water in a little frig there, and I grabbed a bottle, opened it and hurried it over to her. She held it for a minute, and I thought I was going to have to bring it to her lips, but she was recovering a little, and she drank.

Aduba and I looked at each other and then back at Adelaide. I know I was wondering about whether to call 911.

Adelaide drank again, and a little color came back into her face.

She looked up at us hovering over her and managed a small chuckle.

"Don't look like that kids. I'm okay. Just give me a minute." She drank again.

We waited.

"Sit down, will you?" she said, sharply. "I feel like I'm in a redwood forest with the two of you looming over me."

I grabbed my own uncomfortable student chair and brought it over near her, and Aduba rolled his desk chair over. We sat down.

"Here's the thing," she began. "This is an attack on the university, as well as an attack on the two of you, and that's a matter for the President's office. He's coordinating this and wants to see all three of us in about half an hour." She paused and took a sip of water. I thought her breathing wasn't yet quite right, and she went on, wheezing slightly.

"Kristin, you'll need to send that video. I told the Dean you had taken that. Here's a secure email address for that." She took out a small piece of paper with the address written on it and held it out to me, a slight tremor in her hand. Then she shook her head a little. "Apparently it's a big deal to take over computers like that. It's criminal." She took another sip of water. "They're talking about bringing in the FBI. Some task force."

She slumped and for a second I got really alarmed again. But then she sat up.

"So," she said, handing back the now empty water bottle. "We'll leave in about fifteen minutes, okay? It will take that long to walk over there."

"No," I said.

"No?" she asked.

"No. I'll call campus security and get someone to drive us over. Especially you," I said firmly.

"I don't need . . . "

I cut her off.

"No argument, Adelaide. Take the help."

She sighed deeply and got up.

"Alright. Whatever. Just let me know when the car's here," and she walked slowly out the door.

"That was a good thought," Aduba said to me as we sat and looked at each other. "I do not think she is well."

I just nodded. He was right.

I thought of the Beserkers on the battlefield. Yes, this was a battlefield, and John was already one casualty. I hoped Adelaide wouldn't be one more.

"I will meet you at the front of the building in 15 minutes," Aduba said abruptly. He carried his desk chair and student chair back to his side. He was moving very stiffly, like any sudden move would shred his control. He turned and walked out. This shared office thing was not working.

I picked up my desk phone and called Alice.

"Yeah. I know," she said flatly instead of a greeting. "You okay?"

Was I okay? I felt like there were two of me, one who was sickened and even embarrassed by this attack, and another me who was just on the job.

"Well, I've been better," I said dryly, and Alice did rumble a little laugh.

"Listen, Alice, here's why I called. Aduba Abubakar, Adelaide Winters, and I are going to a meeting at the President's Office in about half an hour. The thing is, Alice, I'm worried about Adelaide." I described her dizziness and the shortness of breath.

"Does she have the sugar?" Alice asked.

Sugar? What? Oh. I thought. Diabetes.

"I don't know, Alice. I'll get on her case later about what's the matter, but right now I wondered if someone from campus security could come in a car and take us to the main administration building. I don't want her to have to walk."

"Yeah, sure, I'll call downstairs. And you call me after, you hear? I'll bet the captain will be at that meeting, but he'll tell us just what he thinks we need to know. He's kinda close with info, you know?"

Yeah, I knew. My own verdict on Captain Gutierrez wasn't in yet.

"Of course. Yes."

"And Kristin?"

"Yes?"

"That's not you. None of it. Bastards made it up. And we'll get 'em."

"Thanks, Alice."

Not me. Not me. Not me.

Chapter 15

Everything is possible, from angels to demons to economists and politicians.

—PAULO COELHO, AUTHOR OF *THE ALCHEMIST*, INTERVIEW

Monday

As the campus police car rolled slowly across the quadrangle toward the central administration building, I tried to dredge up what I knew about the new university president, Roger Elliott Anderson. Anderson had only been formally hired in early summer as his nomination had been very controversial. He hadn't even been inaugurated yet.

The presidential search itself had been contentious, I recalled from what I'd read in the university newspaper, since it cost about $200,000. And the outside search firm had come up with this M.B.A. guy from Wharton with no academic experience and no administrative experience. Well, I hoped he had studied more than that other Wharton graduate who had become U.S. president.

This new university president was also supposed to be rich, I guess on the theory that somebody with money knew how to attract money. I wondered if that were true. Anderson had made his money in the Dot-com revolution, I thought, but then had done other business ventures that I could not recall.

There had been very well-written editorials in the school newspaper (they were by faculty in the liberal arts, so one would expect them to be well-written) denouncing this trend in higher education toward hiring business people to run academic institutions. The tone had been a combination of shock and disdain, but I could see why boards of trustees would pick someone from their own world. They thought they would get "control" and "success-oriented results" and so forth and have no more of these messy, conflicting ideas and demonstrations on campus. Hadn't worked out that way so far, but early days in his presidency. I profoundly doubted it would work out, however. One editorial, I recalled, quoted a business-type president who had said any instructor who goes into a classroom without a lesson plan "should be shot." Nice combination of NRA thinking along with the control mentality. Never mind that no class discussion worth the name went according to "plan."

Was this what Anderson was like, I wondered, as we got out of the car and headed for the lobby elevators. Important to reserve judgment, I mused, and then turned to wait for the colleagues. Aduba had given Adelaide his arm as we exited the car, and alarmingly, Adelaide did not disdain it. She'd taken the help. I moved ahead of them to press the elevator button, and I could hear her breathing rapidly behind me. Not good.

The elevator took us up smoothly and rapidly to the top floor. No worries about using the elevators in central administration. The presidential offices, I knew from the one time I'd been here before to negotiate with the previous president about what it would take for me not to sue them, took up the whole top floor. There was a kind of reception/guard desk right outside the elevator door. I walked up and gave the bored-looking guy sitting there our names and said we were expected. He glanced down at a sheet on his desk and just nodded. "604" he replied. Not a huge amount of security here. I knew where the office was, and that was good as the guard gave no directions.

I continued to walk ahead. The President's office occupied the turret at the end of the corridor. All these old, medieval-style buildings on the main quad had these turrets that ran up the corners, yielding semi-circular rooms on the inside. We had this in Myerson along with the fading stained glass in the windows.

The door to 604 was open, and as I approached I could see a young, Asian man sitting at a desk that was completely transparent. Plastic? Glass? A huge computer monitor took up most of the desk. Behind this clear, angular desk was a white, modular credenza that blended with the wall that had been painted the same flat white.

I crossed the room toward the nearly invisible desk and identified myself and indicated that Dr. Winters and Dr. Abubakar were right behind me.

"Hi, I'm Henry Chu," he said, standing up and speaking in a slight Chinese accent. "Go right in. President Anderson is expecting you." Probably good to have a Chinese speaker in the university offices these days with so many international students, and especially Chinese students, attending the university. To say nothing of the fund-raising possibilities. I wondered if Mr. Chu had come from one of Anderson's businesses.

I could hear Aduba and Adelaide still coming slowly down the corridor, so I moved to the side of Chu's desk, as much as I could discern where the transparent desk ended, and waited. But President Anderson saw me through his open door and called out.

"Come right in! Welcome!" His hail-fellow, well-met heartiness struck an off note for me. Well, perhaps he was nervous. This attack had to be a huge test of his very new presidency.

I moved a little more to stand in the doorway of his office so I could see him and was about tell him I was waiting for my colleagues when I saw his office. If Mr. Chu's office furniture was off-key for the stone-walled turret office suite, President Anderson's was jarring. There was a huge oriental rug centered in the middle and a desk that was a large, oval shape lying on its side. I could see through the oval to the expensive pants legs of the man standing behind it. You'd have to wear pants to sit at that desk. You could see right through the middle. I followed the expensive looking pants legs up to the smoothly tailored suit jacket, red tie (unfortunate), and the horned rim glasses and the brown hair that was lacquered and stood up in the center of his head.

"Come in. Come in," he repeated and walked out from behind the desk. I could hear Adelaide and Aduba were now in the outer office identifying themselves to Mr. Chu, so I took a few steps into the room and on to the rug that I though was a Bokhara. There were also some Mies Van Der Rohe Barcelona chairs scattered about, and they didn't seem to be reproductions. I hoped the university budget had not been hit up to pay for this décor.

"I'm President Anderson," said the man who had created this kind of setting for himself. It looked like an exhibit I had seen in Lisbon of a collection by this wealthy, immigrant guy named Gulbenkian who had just collected very expensive things and thrown them together and then donated the whole lot to Portugal. The style should be called "Acquisition."

"I see you are admiring the rug," said Anderson.

Well, no. I was gazing down and tensely waiting for Adelaide and Aduba to join me.

"I can only imagine your parents and grandparents have even more such lovely rugs in their homes."

My head snapped up. Wait a damn minute, I thought. You researched my wealthy family? Yes, the Hilger family was very wealthy. I suddenly realized, for the first time at this school, I was being regarded as potential donor and not a faculty member. Well, I thought grimly, my parents and grandparents have better taste than you do to throw expensive stuff together in a pseudo, post-modernist mishmash like this.

I just kept silent. He frowned slightly, his well-maintained skin drooping a little into some not quite invisible lines. After fifty, it's hard to hide those lines I thought.

Then Anderson was giving Adelaide and Aduba less hearty greetings than he had given me and leaving out references to their family's wealth or lack of it. I realized I was embarrassed and furious, and given how emotionally on edge I already felt from the cyberattack, I was going to have to watch myself or I would tell this red-tie wearing, hearty fund-raiser, business-type just what I thought of him.

I moved over to walk next to Adelaide as we were being ushered into a small conference room adjacent to the office, and I whispered, "How are you feeling?"

She took a look at me, and especially at my rigid posture and clenched fists and whispered back, "Better than you are, apparently."

We walked further in and there were two men seated at an extraordinary conference table. It was a highly polished oval (what was with all these ovals?) of wood, with a clear glass center through which you could see little red struts running in all directions. It was disorienting. Was this table by M.C. Escher?

I quit looking at it and focused on who was already seated at the table, and really, who was not. Kaiser and Brown were absent. Did this mean the university was staunchly committed to not connecting the dots on the murder and the cyberattack? I recognized Captain Gutierrez. He nodded as we appeared, his wrinkled face grave. A middle-aged, African American man who could have had FBI tattooed on his forehead, was sitting opposite Gutierrez, scrolling down his messages on his phone. He did not look up.

"So, so, take a seat, please," said President Anderson moving toward the head of the table. Behind him hung a painting so grimly blood red, black and swirling I thought it might be a portal to hell. Satan falling into the burning lake in John Milton's *Paradise Lost* came to mind.

Get a grip, I told myself. Just a lousy painting.

"Help yourself to some coffee if you wish," said Anderson. Gutierrez and silent FBI guy had shiny red cups and saucers in front of them, I realized.

Okay, words to which I could relate. I moved to the credenza along the side wall. At least I thought it was a credenza. It was a large, red lacquer oval lying on its long side. In the center was an art nouveau coffee pot with vines crawling up the sides, and some red lacquer cups on a tray. I moved rapidly toward the coffee.

"Adelaide, Aduba?" I asked.

Aduba said "No, thank you very much," and Adelaide just shook her head, whether at me or to decline coffee I wasn't sure. Probably both.

I reached for the coffee pot and realized the vines that made up the handle were actually snakes. Perfect. I hate snakes. I picked it up anyway and poured myself some coffee. Then I carried it to the opposite end of the table from President Anderson and sat down.

"Good. Good," said Anderson in the faux hearty voice I was beginning to detest. "Now let's get down to business, shall we? We have to deal with this prank someone has played on our colleagues here, and . . . "

Before I could even react to that outrageous statement, FBI guy cleared his throat and started speaking in a deep, sonorous voice that certainly commanded attention, his dark eyes still on his phone. Then he deliberately put the phone down on the idiotic table and looked Anderson right in the eye.

"If I may, President Anderson. Let me introduce myself to those of you who have just arrived." He turned his impressive shoulders and looked at Adelaide, Aduba, and me in turn. This guy didn't do anything in a rush, it seemed.

"I am Agent Paul Lindsay, head of the Chicago FBI Cybercrimes Division." He took out some cards from inside his suit coat and passed them around. I was sitting so far away, Aduba graciously got up and slid mine over to me on the slick table surface.

"We investigate criminal activity that is done on computers, but we also target criminal activity that is done to and through computer hacking and infiltration of computer systems. The latter is what we have here.

"With all due respect, Mr. President, this is not a prank. What has happened on your campus is a cybercrime. I have been checking," and he paused to tap his phone screen, "with our forensic detail who are working with your university IT people. Given the particulars of this invasion, and the inclusion of pornography, there are a number of crimes involved. In addition, we need to determine if a worm has been planted in your university system that could be used for gathering personal data, financial data and other forms of not only theft but manipulation."

I was watching Anderson's face as it paled in shock. His smooth skin seemed to slide down his face like thick syrup poured over ice cream. Hacking. Theft. Invasion. Not a prank.

"Once we determine the extent of the hacking, we can take countermeasures. This was a sophisticated attack. I have seen the video you provided, Professor Ginelli, and taking control of a computer as was done reveals a high degree of expertise. The emails with pornographic photos that also circulated were designed to lure people into opening the email, and that makes us believe the goal was to insert a worm." Another deliberate look around the table.

"Questions?"

"Yes," I said, in as calm a voice as I could manage. "The university computers are now shut down, correct?"

Agent Lindsay nodded.

"My colleague, Dr. Aduba, and I have been personally attacked and defamed by the content of these emails. Will they be eradicated before the system is back up?"

Another nod.

I turned to look directly at Anderson who was still staring at Lindsay.

"So, President Anderson, what will you do to inform the community of the utter and total falsehood of these photos, and what especially will you do to restore our reputations?"

"Well, I, well, I will need to consult with our university attorneys, frankly, and . . . ."

Come to think of it, why weren't there any university attorneys at this meeting, I wondered. Had Anderson thought he could handle this as a "prank" even though he'd known the FBI would have a representative at this meeting? It didn't make sense to me.

I just talked over Anderson.

"I will have my own attorney contact the university attorneys and make sure you and they do everything necessary to restore our good names and reputation." I realized I was speaking for Aduba, and that was not right. I stopped talking and looked over at him. Then, with a shaking hand, I took a drink of coffee, signaling I planned to shut up.

Aduba's face looked so rigid I thought if he spoke it would crack, but his voice was strong and clear. And he didn't directly address Anderson, he turned and spoke to Lindsay who was seated on the same side of the table as he was.

"I will need to be kept informed of what is found, and I will need to consider how this affects me and my family, and I will decide what I need to do about this." He paused, took out his own card and passed it over. Lindsay took it and Aduba went on, his eyes fixed on the agent.

"One thing I know about the Internet is that nothing ever actually goes away. This will follow me, my career and my family forever."

Oh. God. How true.

"I will keep you informed," said Lindsay, not dropping his own gaze. "What you say is entirely and terribly accurate."

Gutierrez broke in at this point, his barely accented voice stern and his salt and pepper mustache practically bristling. He was clearly holding in his annoyance at not being introduced or even acknowledged by the President.

"Let me also introduce myself," he said, also passing over cards. "Professor Ginelli I have met, since she consults for us," and he nodded in my direction, "but I have not met the other two professors. I am Captain Alfonzo Gutierrez, head of Campus Security."

While my colleagues each introduced themselves, I watched Anderson. In fact, I had been watching him since Gutierrez started speaking, and he had blanched at the words "she consults for us." How out of touch was Anderson, I wondered? Somebody had briefed him on the fact that I had a huge trust fund and was heir to a fortune, but not what I did at the university? Or, all of what I did at the university?

"We have a student suspended and murdered," Gutierrez said flatly when the short introductions had finished.

So they did know it was murder.

Anderson drew in his breath but said nothing.

Gutierrez looked at Lindsay, who had clearly taken charge of the meeting.

"Is the FBI the lead investigators on that now? What are the connections? If not, why no Chicago police at this meeting?"

"We are coordinating with the Chicago police, yes. If we uncover evidence of a connection between these cybercrimes and the murder, jurisdiction will be determined." Lindsay looked down at his phone as it lit up. An incoming text claimed his attention, and he rose.

"I need to meet with our people. Captain Gutierrez, will you accompany me?"

Gutierrez just nodded and got up as well.

Lindsay addressed Adelaide, Aduba, and me as he stood to leave.

"I don't think I need to remind you all to keep a low profile," he said ominously. He nodded to Anderson.

"Mr. President."

And they left. Just left.

So, Anderson, not a prank then, right? But I didn't say that aloud.

Aduba, Adelaide, and I just sat and watched Anderson as he seemed to struggle with what to say. I could suggest some things, but I decided, again, to be silent.

"Thank you for coming," he finally said in a monotone, and he rose as well.

I stood up and put both hands down on the table and spoke across the weird expanse of the conference table in as controlled a voice as I could manage.

"I will have my attorney contact your office later today to talk about specifics of what the university will do to reverse some of the damage done to the reputations of me and my colleague by this vicious attack."

Anderson just stood there. He was so plainly outside of his skill set that I wondered if he'd want to continue to do this job. Or if the board would want him to continue. It could be the attorneys would just take over, and they'd keep him just to raise money. Who knew?

Aduba, Adelaide, and I walked out silently and rode down in the elevator without speaking. When we got out to the main quadrangle, we stopped.

Adelaide spoke first.

"Listen. I think I need some time and really, I'm fine." I raised my eyebrows at her, and she just shook her head at me.

"No, really, don't hover. And remember, you two, 'keep a low profile means keep a low profile,'" but she was looking at me more than Aduba. Then she turned and walked slowly away from us.

"Do you want to talk to my attorney?" I asked Aduba who was watching her walk away.

"I too need time to think," he said slowly. He nodded at me and walked, not across the quad but in the other direction, toward the west where I thought he lived. I watched his rigid back until he went between two buildings and disappeared. "We're losing him," I thought sadly. This attack was a stealth kind of ICE, a way to get rid of somebody whom the white supremacists deemed an outsider.

I sat down on an empty bench in the middle of the quadrangle and called Anna's office. While I waited for her to come on the line, I watched the students crossing the quadrangle. I thought of John, who would never walk here again. Had he really been recruited through violent video games? And who was doing that? And how many of these other hurrying figures were also playing those games? How many were getting lured in?

I was so deep in these dire thoughts that I jumped when Anna's voice came on. I read her in on the meeting with the President. I had already sent her the video when I had sent it to the email address Adelaide had given me.

Anna said she was referring this to her partner, Alastair Ackerman, who specialized in defamation and slander. He would contact the university lawyers immediately and then contact me. I reminded Anna that the university computers were shut down, so to use my personal email or call my cell.

"I would do that in any case since we may have to sue them. Best for my firm not to use your university contact information." And then she hung up.

I really just should have gone to law school, I thought, as I dialed Alice. Would have been cheaper.

I got Alice's voicemail so I just sent her a text instead.

"Call me. Done with president."

And really, I was totally done with that president.

I got up and became one of the people crossing the campus.

Chat Room of Video Game "Revenge"

Monday afternoon

Vampire726: s*** man so great tits and tits ISIS N***** probably really doing it f*** him

Demon196: gotta keep hitting gotta bring it closer to the c*** shut down system damn damn u check usual place more do it fast she's gotta feel it for real

Incubus75: feebs on it

Demon196: u chill

Chapter 16

Never trust a demon. He has a hundred motives for anything he does ... Ninety-nine of them, at least, are malevolent.

—Neil Gaiman, *Preludes & Nocturnes (The Sandman #1)*

Monday afternoon

I walked slowly home. Obviously no point in heading to my office. I was sure my office computer had been taken by the investigators. I had a class to teach tomorrow and right now I couldn't even remember the topic. I had notes at home and could prep there.

My cell rang. I assumed it was Alice calling, but the display said it was Carol. When I answered, she was hysterically saying my name.

"Kristin??? Kristin???"

My heart nearly stopped. The boys. Something was the matter with the boys.

"Carol, what is it?" I choked out.

"ICE is trying to find Giles. I knew something like this would happen. I warned him. I warned him."

It was awful, but I still breathed a sigh of relief. Not my boys.

"Okay, slow down. Tell me what's happening," I said firmly.

"Mrs. Levinson, you know, our neighbor, she stopped me at the beginning of the block. I think she'd been waiting for me. She said she thinks there are two ICE agents parked across from the house. They have knocked on the front door several times, and when they get no answer they go back to their car."

Well, Mrs. Levinson should know ICE agents when she sees them, I thought. Regina Levinson was our next-door neighbor and a retired attorney who volunteered with the Chicago Immigrants Rights Project, a not-for-profit that provided legal services on immigration issues.

"So where are you and the boys now?" I asked as calmly as I could.

"We're in Mrs. Levinson's kitchen. She gave the boys kugel and fixed me some tea. I'm in the front room so the boys can't hear me. Oh, Kristin, I knew it. I knew it." And sweet, calm Carol sobbed.

"Where is Giles now?" I asked as I started to jog toward our house.

"In class, I think. I've tried calling him. He doesn't answer. Oh, oh, suppose he just walks home, and they get him?"

"Now Carol, think for a moment. Giles has legal immigration status. I know that and so do you. Does he carry his papers with him?" I puffed that out as I sped up from a jog to a run.

"Yes. Yes. He has started to since, you know, since Trump was elected." She hiccupped, but the sobbing seemed to have stopped.

"Carol, Carol, listen to me. Put Mrs. Levinson on the phone, would you?"

"Okay," she said, and I could hear her steps as she left the room.

"Kristin?" Regina's no-nonsense voice asked.

"Yes. Regina, what's the best thing to do right now?" I got that out even though now I was running flat out.

"Go get him, Kristin. Use your car. I think you can get to it from the alley without alerting these guys in front. I'll have Carol text Giles repeatedly until he answers and just tell him to meet you out front of the quad entrance. Bring him here, to my house, through the alley."

Regina and Alan's house was directly south of ours, and we shared a fence with a gate between the yards and an alley. Garages opened on to the alley.

"Okay," I puffed out. "Almost to the alley. Tell Carol to do that. And Regina, thanks."

"No problem. They're out of control, ICE agents these days. My parents escaped from the Nazis in Germany to this country, and now we have this? Not on my watch." Regina ended the call.

I skidded to a stop at the entrance to the alley and looked around the corner. Empty. I jogged over to our garage door and used the fob on my keychain to open the door. I jumped in the car, pulled out as quickly as I could and headed to campus.

About three blocks later I heard my text tone. I hit the hands-free, text voice app, and the metallic voice said, "Got him. He'll meet you. Carol."

I drove cautiously through the streets crowded with kids walking home from school, though I wanted to floor it. I turned down University Avenue and saw Giles waiting. I pulled up, and he got in.

"*Merci*, Mrs. Gin. I am so sorry to bring you in to this," he said quietly.

Well, hell. Before I pulled away from the curb, I turned to look at him.

"You're kidding, right? Don't you know me at all? Don't you know whatever you're up against is my fight too?" All the emotion of the day was ganging up on me, but for crap's sake, how could he apologize for this?

"I do know this. But I don't want to bring you more trouble. This is my problem."

"No, Giles. It's our problem," I said, and I turned on my signal, pulled out and drove back toward the alley.

$$* \quad * \quad *$$

I'd had the boys start on their homework in Regina's kitchen while she talked to Carol, Giles, and me in her study. She'd examined Giles's immigration documents and noted that while they were in perfect order, that didn't mean he couldn't be taken in and questioned. Carol gasped, but Giles just looked solemn. Regina went over Giles's rights several times with him.

To even question him, she said, they needed a warrant signed by a judge, and Regina was betting they didn't have one. If they did, Giles would in fact have to go with them, but she'd go with him as his attorney if he agreed. Giles nodded.

She told us her plan. And we all got up to put it into action.

Carol and Giles would take the boys out the Levinson's back door and through the gate that connected our yards. They'd get into our house that way and let Molly out.

Regina and I would watch out her back window and wait until we saw them safely in the house. She and I would then go out her front door and walk casually up to my front door and let ourselves in. If stopped on the way, Regina would do all the talking. If not, we'd enter my house by the front door.

The plan got underway, and quickly Giles, Carol and the boys crossed to our yard and let themselves in the back door. In a minute, the dog was out in the yard.

Regina and I left by her front door and walked up my front walk. As I unlocked the door, Regina said to me, "They're exiting the car, and I think they're heading this way. Let's go in and lock the door."

We did, and it seemed like ten seconds later there was a hard knock on the door. Giles quietly joined us in the front hall as we had planned.

My security camera had a record function, and I pressed the button for that and then nodded at Regina.

"Yes?" Regina answered in a polite but firm voice. She might be nearly seventy, but you couldn't tell it from the strength she put into that word. "Who is it?"

"Open up. We need to speak with Mr. Giles Dop."

Naturally they mispronounced Giles's last name. I wondered if it were deliberate contempt or just ignorance.

"I need to see your identification, please," Regina said firmly. "Hold it up to the camera by the door, please."

"I said, open up," an angry voice replied.

"I need to see your identification, please. Hold it up to the camera by the door, please," Regina repeated in the same polite, firm voice.

This went on twice more and finally we saw two billfolds flip open. ICE agents.

"Thank you. What do you want?"

"We need to speak with Dop. Right now," said angry voice guy.

"Do you have a warrant signed by a judge?" Regina asked. "If so, please slip it under the door."

"Open the door. Quit screwing around," angry voice guy said.

"If you don't have a warrant signed by a judge, then please leave," Regina said calmly.

We could hear them conferring, though not clearly enough to tell what they were saying.

"You're only making it worse on him," one of them said.

Regina said nothing.

We heard their retreating footsteps. I went to the front window and watched them drive away.

"Okay, Giles," Regina said. "Let's talk again some place private here, and we'll go over what you say when you're stopped and so forth. This isn't the end of this, I think."

"Of a certainty," Giles replied, and he called to Carol to join them. I showed Regina into the small library room, and they shut the door. I went to the freezer and took out one of the pans of African vegan food and put it in the oven. Then I went upstairs to check homework. It was progressing, though slowly.

I came back down, let Molly in and sat in the TV room. I didn't turn on the lights even as the fall afternoon darkened. Kaiser had called ICE on Giles. I was sure of it. My phone rang. Alice. Thank heavens. I answered and filled her in on all that had happened from the fed guy and the useless president to the whole staged ICE thing.

"Well, hell, Kristin," Alice said. I thought so too. This kind of evil was straight out of hell.

＊　　＊　　＊

Carol and Giles had taken their portion of the African vegan casserole up-stairs to their apartment, and I served out portions for the boys and me in the kitchen. Regina had declined to stay and join us, even though since the food was vegan it was also Kosher.

I took a little taste before putting their plates down on the table. It was very spicy, but delicious. I warned them not to share any with Molly as her stomach did not do well with spice. I opened a can of beef broth and dumped it all on her kibble.

As soon as I sat down, however, Mike started in with rapid-fire ques-tions about who was trying to get Giles and how could they and if Giles had papers how could they try to arrest him? Sam was looking solemn, and it was clear they had been paying close attention to what had happened at Mrs. Levinson's house.

I didn't want to brush them off. They could very well witness Giles being taken away given the tactics of ICE I had seen this evening.

I put down my fork and leaned forward, making eye contact with the big brown eyes that belonged to their father.

"Some people don't want great people like Giles to be in our country," I began.

Mike started to protest, but I said, "No, listen to me. They are wrong, and many other people want them to stay and be part of this country. Mrs. Levinson helps people like Giles all the time. We have to help. I'm trying to help."

"But he's got legal papers! It's not right!" Mike burst out. He did like the law, and I thought it was because it was reassuring to him in a world where his father had been killed by bad guys.

"It totally stinks!" Sam added and pounded his small fist on the table so that his plate fork rattled.

"It does stink, Sam, you're right, and you're right too, Mike. Giles has rights and we will all protect those rights. And we will do that using the law, and we will do it peacefully. I promise. Now, let's talk about how school went today."

While we ate, I heard about these two kids, Reggie and Paul, and they had gone on a cool trip to Italy with their parents and had gotten to miss school and couldn't we go on a trip? And Mike added, inspiration striking, "We could take Giles, and then those guys couldn't get him." They weren't going to give up on worrying about Giles. Me neither.

I told them about Italy and served another round of casserole.

*   *   *

The house was finally quiet, and I was working on pulling together some kind of class for tomorrow when the doorbell rang. My heartrate went sky high. Had ICE come back at 10 p.m.?

I hustled to the front door and looked at the security camera screen. It was Tom.

I started breathing again and let him in.

"I'm sorry to just come by so late," he said wearily as he walked slowly through the door. I hurriedly scanned the street, didn't seen any suspicious cars, and quickly closed and locked the door behind him.

"Kelly's sleeping over at a friend's house. Some big project due tomorrow and, well, from what I'd seen in a few of those emails, I thought you might like some company this evening." He looked down at me, his tired blue eyes filled with concern. Oh, Lord. How good did that concern feel. Tight feelings in my stomach relaxed just a little.

But I didn't answer, I just put my arms around him and put my head on his chest. His arms came around me, and we stood like that for a second.

"You don't know the half of it," I said into his damp raincoat. "And I am so, so glad to see you."

He swayed a little, and I stepped back, looking up at his lined face.

"Have you eaten?"

"Not today," was his reply.

I took his coat and hung it up on an inside door to dry.

"Come on. I have casserole I can warm up for you, and then I'll fill you in."

"Any more lasagna?" Tom asked hopefully as he followed me to the kitchen.

I was betting he'd eat the African vegan food since he hadn't eaten all day.

I put some of the casserole in the microwave and poured us two glasses of the good red wine. I also poured some water for Tom.

I was right. He just mechanically ate what was in front of him while I tried to bring him up to speed. I realized how long it had been since we'd been able to talk and how much had happened. I went over John's death, clearly a murder, the attempt to frame me, the cyberattacks, the inept president, the FBI involvement, and finished up with the visit from ICE this evening. Tom listened intently, clearly thinking as I spoke.

"Why was that student killed?" he asked, clearly going to the heart of the matter. He was right. Murder should always be considered first.

Tom went on.

"Could his involvement with these white supremacists have caused his death? You say there was a Confederate flag, garb from the white nationalist protest, and some flyers. Is it possible they killed him before he could talk to you about what was really going on?"

Tom took a sip of his water and waited.

With so much happening, I hadn't even given that murder scene much thought. Amazing. What kind of detective was I? Suddenly I remembered the pictures I had taken. I told Tom I had some photos of the scene, and I pulled my phone out of my pocket while he went on methodically eating the spicy casserole and drinking his water between each bite.

I scrolled to the photos I had taken, especially of the desk, and I enlarged the shots of the crumpled papers with the writing on them.

I frowned as the writing came into focus.

It was the number "23" over and over and over, including the hard scribble that had torn through the paper. And, as I enlarged it more, I saw that number twenty-three was followed by the words "doesn't lie."

I put the phone in front of Tom so he could see that frame.

"What do you make of that?" I asked. "'Twenty-three doesn't lie.' Twenty-three what? Twenty-three of what doesn't lie? Are there twenty-three people involved in this white supremacist conspiracy?" I asked, with dawning horror. That many?

"Well," Tom swallowed some casserole, took another big drink of water and then went on, "that '23' could mean the number of human chromosomes. Did he take a DNA test?"

I sat back, stunned. How I wish I had been able to search John's apartment.

"You know, Tom," I said slowly, "Suppose he had gotten one of those DNA kit tests and found out he wasn't really white, whatever that means. And suppose his white supremacist buddies found out?" I thought about the scene some more and good ole Brant showing up and trying to implicate me.

"My money would be on the roommate. He's clearly one of the conspirators, and if John had taken a test and found out, what, that he had African ancestors, for example, Brant would have blabbed to the others." I sat there looking down at the phone.

The torn paper with "23 doesn't lie" practically carved into it showed John had been very upset when he wrote it. Well, that is if he had been the one to do it.

I saw Tom's plate was empty, and I asked him if he'd like more. He nodded, clearly still thinking about what was in that photo. I got up and nuked some more casserole and brought it over.

"Still," I went on, "would they kill him for that? It seems so extreme."

Tom ate silently for a moment.

"They're extremists, Kristin," he said dryly.

He was the second person to say that to me. I thought I needed to know more about extremism. I voiced that thought aloud.

"I have a psychiatrist friend, Dr. Jannik Fisher, who is both an M.D. and a Ph.D., and he researches the psychology of extremism," Tom said, clearly thinking. "I could see if he could meet with you to give you some insight."

I nodded. It was a good idea. I had to stop thinking of them as crazy jerks and realize there was a logic to this, however repulsive.

We drank our wine in silence and then went to bed. I snuggled Tom's back and slept dreamlessly until morning. When I woke, he was already gone.

Chapter 17

The Demon: What an excellent day for an exorcism.

Father Damien Karras: You would like that?

The Demon: Intensely.

Father Damien Karras: But wouldn't that drive you out of Regan?

The Demon: It would bring us together.

Father Damien Karras: You and Regan?

The Demon: You and us.

—THE EXORCIST

Tuesday

Carol, Giles, and I met in the kitchen. It was barely 7 a.m. The feeling was that of a small, police tactical unit preparing for an action, except none of us were armed. The plan, and we had been over it several times now, was that Carol would walk with Giles to the math library, taking her cell phone with Regina's number on speed dial and the video screen prepped and ready to record. Giles had his ICE script memorized, or so he said.

"No, I do not need to repeat these same words to you again," he had said a little testily to Carol and me as we all stood in the watery morning light that managed to penetrate the leaden skies. We had not turned on the overhead lights. I nodded to Carol in as reassuring way as I could, and they both departed by the back door to head to campus through the alley. Molly whined a little as they went in the yard without her. I watched them lock the back gate again, and I let her out.

Just in time. The boys thundered down the back stairs.

I was ready with cold cereal and also a bribe of plenty of cut up mangoes, their favorite fruit. Sometimes you couldn't get the mango peeled and ready to serve before they had taken most of it out of the serving bowl and eaten it. Then I had walked them to school in a fog that had rolled in from the lake. Uneventful, however. No ICE agents jumped out at us, at least that I could see in the gloom. As I walked on to my office, people appeared and disappeared in the thick mist. I felt like I was in some old, black and white spy film. Except the spies were employed by my own government.

I got a small shock, however, when I'd opened the door to Aduba's and my office. His desk was bare, and his books were gone from the shelves. I looked more carefully. No, not all of his books were gone. Perhaps he hadn't just up and quit, but moved because Adelaide had gotten permission for him to use Hercules's office in his absence. Since all the offices opened with the same key, I walked down to that door, knocked, and when I got no response, I cautiously used my own office door key to open it. I peered in and breathed a sigh of relief. Aduba's books were stacked on the side of the desk and on a table, and a prayer rug was rolled up against the far wall.

I quickly closed and relocked the door, not that locking the doors was all that effective at keeping people out. Well, I thought, as long as I am already halfway down the hall, I could go all the way to the coffee machine. I did and made myself a double espresso. I deserved it. It was going to be a difficult morning in class.

✳ ✳ ✳

I looked at the class members as they shuffled into the seminar room, shaking water off of their anoraks or coats. The fog must have thickened into rain. They firmly avoided sitting anywhere near where John Vandenberg had sat the last time we had met as a class. No wonder. Now they were shuffling computers, phones, and the occasional book from backpacks on to the table, while also studiously avoiding looking at me. I assumed they had all seen the pornographic, photoshopped pictures that were supposed to be me. I couldn't afford to be embarrassed in front of them, both for myself and for them. That would give too much power to those yahoos who had attacked me, Aduba, and even our campus that way.

This was a class and I needed to direct it, but also let them engage. It wasn't that hard to do, since this was a class on events in American religious history that were still playing a big role today, fueling this crisis. Our syllabus for this week covered the early 20th century, and the white, Protestant nationalism, moral purity, and virulent xenophobia of that time. That time, it was clear, had not gone away, but had been growing under the surface and was now poisoning the present. My lesson plan, such as I had one, was to try to help them see that these events, from John's death, to the rally, to the cyberattacks, were fed by that past that wasn't, frankly, past.

I cleared my throat and suddenly every eye in class was on me. Well, except for Jordan who was scrolling down on his phone. I wondered if he was trolling me by looking at those pornographic emails. He was sitting at the farthest end of the table so I couldn't see. Or was I being paranoid?

"Jordan," I said firmly, "put down your phone." He turned it over and looked up with an almost smirk. He'd just done that to be a jerk, I thought irritably. But it gave me a second to realize how tense I was and to breathe before I spoke.

"First," I said, "I need to acknowledge the death of our former classmate, John Vandenberg, and I'd like us to take a moment in silence to remember his life in whatever way is best for you."

Emma already had a tissue out and tears appeared. Mei, who was sitting next to her, put a small hand on Emma's arm. They both bowed their heads, I noticed, as did most of the class as I scanned them. Jordan's eyes wandered to his phone, but he didn't pick it up.

I waited thirty seconds and then said, simply, "Thank you."

Mei raised her hand.

"Yes, Mei."

"Professor, let us also say how sorry we are that those terrible emails came around about you and Professor Abubakar. That was truly horrible," she said firmly, her chin up so that her curtains of black hair framed her serious face.

Emma nodded tearfully and whispered "Yes, horrible."

"Thank you," I said sincerely and nodded to the class, not knowing how the rest of them felt, but including them.

"I keep reminding myself that was a trick," I said. "The photos, that is. Those photos are not actually of me and not of Dr. Abubakar. That stunt was meant in a very hurtful way, though, Mei, and that's how this current group we seem to have on campus operate. They are cruel, they lie, they fool people, they generate hate, and they mean to cause a lot of hurt. I don't see what it accomplishes, myself, except more hurt and thus more hate."

The class was silent, but then Jordan raised his hand. Really, Jordan, I thought, but I acknowledged him with a nod.

"So, what happened to John? The news has sh..," he stopped, "I mean, nothing, but that garbagey language about police investigating. Investigating what? You were there, right? Was he murdered? People say there was Nazi junk all over his apartment, and those activists got him."

How do they get to know this stuff? I wondered.

"I can't talk about an ongoing investigation, Jordan, and I would think you would realize that," I said in as suppressive tone as I could.

Jayden raised her hand but didn't even wait for an acknowledgment from me.

"Activists?" she ground out through her teeth. "What 'activists' do you mean, Jordan?" she continued, biting off each word. She had turned in her chair to look directly at him, and she clenched her hands into fists.

"Well," Jordan made his voice a hissing drawl, "I mean I don't know, but if you know I'm sure we'd all be charmed it hear it."

"You really are a jerk, Jordan," Jayden said dismissively and good on her.

I recognized the parody of the voice and the line Jordan had used. Voldemort. The boys had waged a concerted campaign of whining and pleading to get to watch those last two Harry Potter movies and I had insisted on watching with them. Scary movies. Oh, I thought tiredly, why does every class I teach seem to be allotted one smart ass?

"Nobody needs Lord Voldemort today, Jordan," I said coolly, "least of all this class when John, is, in fact, dead."

Jordon looked a little abashed but only a little.

I paused, took a breath, and plunged in.

"The turmoil on our campus these days did not fall from the sky. It has deep roots in American history and from exactly the period we are covering in this class. What forces from that period do you see driving current conflicts? Leave the technology out of it. That's an accelerant, like gasoline, it's true, but several of the underlying factors are the same."

Vihaan raised his hand and spoke briskly in his clipped British accent. Vihaan did not like conflict in class, and he liked to deal with the class material instead. Good on him.

"Well, it is those people who wore the white sheets, right? The Klan, yes?"

Most of the class nodded as did I.

"So those white people got together because they were scared of change. There were many immigrants like now, and that was an economic threat, or they thought so in any case. Women wanted to vote and the defeat of the Confederates and rights for the blacks made them want to dress up in white robes like to make their white skin their identity. In India, white is worn to signify purity, and I think that is the same here, correct?"

"Well, yes and no, Vihaan," said Nari softly, but firmly, daring to just jump in to the conversation. "We need to remember Christianity played a big role too. The picture here in this chapter we had to read," and she tapped our basic textbook that was on top of her computer, "is of those white people with those white robes and a burning cross. They take Christianity and make like their hateful ideas are Christian. The conservatives in Korea do the same. I mean, they don't burn crosses, but they use it like it makes their hate the will of God. It is dreadful."

Well, that was the most Nari had contributed to class all semester. And she was right on target.

Emma and Jayden nodded vigorously, and Jayden jumped in.

"Like those idiots who wanted to shut down the Rally Against Hate, you know? I saw some of them dressed up like Crusaders with those red crosses on the front and back. Crusaders! Can you believe it? Well, we shut them down good," she said, leaning back and crossing her arms, looking pointedly at Jordan.

"So, how many of you went to the rally?" I asked, and we filled the rest of the class time with discussions of how to deal with hate on campus and what the rally might have accomplished.

* * *

I looked out the window before I left to meet with Dr. Jannik Fisher, the psychiatrist friend of Tom's. Tom had gotten me a three o'clock appointment for today and I needed to get over there. As I peered through the wavy glass of my office, I could see that the rain and fog seemed to have blown back out over the lake. Dark clouds, loaded with moisture, scudded over that vast body of water to the east. The wind had picked up as the trees bent and shed the last of their leaves over the quad. They made little leaf tornados on the ground.

Fisher's office was not in the new biological sciences building, I had been surprised to learn. Tom had given me an office address that was in one of the older buildings like Myerson. It was directly opposite the quad from where I was, though it was ways across and would be at least a ten minute hike.

Really, I mused as I plunged into the wind, given what I've been seeing in these online chat rooms, maybe psychiatry was the wrong profession to help me understand people who called themselves Demon or Vampire. I might need an exorcist.

Too bad the Vatican's chief exorcist, Father Gabriele Amorth, has died, I thought as a big gust of wind took my hat and blew it into a puddle. I raced after it and picked it up. It was covered in mud. Yuck. I shook it and jammed it into my pocket.

Father Amorth might have thought the demons were trying to keep me from getting to Fisher. Amorth was the guy who had inspired the movie,

"The Exorcist," and he'd claimed to have cast out 70,000 demons over the course of his career.

That's a lot of demons, I mused, as I tried to stuff my long, blowing hair under the back of my raincoat. I bent my head into the wind and kept going, the article I'd read a while back on this real life exorcist coming back to me. The exorcist priest had often said that both Hitler and Stalin were evil. But, then, I chuckled to myself, he'd also thought yoga and Harry Potter were evil, so he was not exactly infallible on evil. Well, on the other hand, Jordan had just channeled the evil guy from Harry Potter, Voldemort. But, seriously, I thought, was all this about demons and the devil really fiction, especially the way our campus was being gripped by this? I remembered one quote from the exorcist priest that seemed on target. "The Devil is invisible. But in the people he possesses he can be seen through pain and blasphemies."

Well, that's about right, I thought, as I dashed up the stone steps and almost fell into the foyer. I was surprised my hair wasn't still out on the quad, blowing like mad. I shook like Molly and finger combed my damp, wind-ratted hair. I didn't want to look like a mad woman. Then I realized I was a little tense, meeting with a psychiatrist. I hoped I wouldn't blurt out various Freudian things about my parents.

"Get a grip," I told myself as I walked up the stairs to Jannik's office on the third floor. Better quit dodging this with exorcism fantasies and focus on what Tom had told me. Fisher was about fifty and he'd been born in East Germany. The reunification of Germany had happened in 1990 when he'd been a university student. Then he'd gone to Hopkins in the U.S. as an undergraduate and Harvard for his M.D. and Ph.D. Seriously smart guy, I thought as I reached his floor and walked down the dimly lit corridor, so reminiscent of Myerson.

The hallway was dark, but the door to 308 was open, and light illuminated it like it was the entrance to another world. I tried not to see it as an omen. I walked up to the doorway and peered in. No one was in a waiting room type area, and beyond, in front of a beautiful, two-story stained glass window, stood a tall figure, backlit so much he seemed only a shadow.

Must be the exorcist, I mean psychiatrist, I thought with a little frisson of fear.

"Please to come in," said the dark figure and gestured toward me.

Really, get a grip, I said to myself and I walked slowly forward.

Chapter 18

"I don't want to be a man," said Jace. "I want to be an angst-ridden teenager who can't confront his own inner demons and takes it out verbally on other people instead."

"Well," said Luke, "you're doing a fantastic job."

—CASSANDRA CLARE, *CITY OF ASHES*

Tuesday afternoon to evening

The dark figure turned out to be a very thin, very tall, and rather stooped man with a shock of greying hair falling over his forehead almost to his narrow, wirerimmed glasses. Lively blue eyes peered out at me from behind the lenses.

Fisher walked around the desk and formally shook my hand.

"Hello, please. I am Jannick Fisher. You are Professor Ginelli, correct?"

"Yes, yes, I am. Hello," I said, feeling terribly uncomfortable.

Fisher, on the contrary, seemed relaxed and happy to see me. Why? I wondered irritably.

He walked a little closer to me.

"Please, if you would, give me your raincoat. I will hang it by the door, and you could take a seat over there." He smiled again and gestured to a couch and chairs arrangement on the right side of his office.

I am not going to lie down on a couch, I thought, my little bit of anxiety growing.

He just watched as I shrugged out of my raincoat, however, and he took it calmly and hung it on a hook behind the door. Then he turned back, and I felt a little like I was being examined.

"A little tea, perhaps, to chase the cold away?" he asked while he made a courtly type of gesture, pointing to the nearest of two armchairs. Okay, fine. No couch, but ick, tea. I frowned. I hoped it wasn't that herb stuff Jane had.

"Or, better, some coffee?" he asked, with a little, wry chuckle. Oh, good gad, I was going to have to watch my face carefully. He must have seen me frown.

"Yes, coffee would be great," I said, sinking into a soft armchair with relief.

He turned toward the far wall and walked quickly across the room with a kind of gangly gate, almost like a giraffe. He really was tall, perhaps as much as six inches taller than my six- foot height. He opened a panel in a large wall unit, and I spotted a shining, stainless steel ECM coffee maker. Wow. It looked like something Tom might have in an ICU with all kinds of gadgets coming out at various angles.

He spoke over his shoulder as he flipped a switch on the machine.

"We Germans like what we call *Bijela Kava*, or what Americans call a latte, but this also makes excellent espresso."

He turned and looked at me inquiringly.

"Espresso, thanks," I said. Then I thought about the fact that this would be my fifth espresso today. Better not tell Alice, I mused. My coffee addiction was getting worse.

"I think I will have an espresso as well," he said and simply turned back and poured beans into the grinder and pressed about five different buttons. Small cups were taken off a top shelf. This guy was so tall he could practically have reached the shelves that went up to the ceiling. He gently put the little cups under the spouts. The smell of the intoxicating brew came across the room, and I started to relax.

He carried the small cups over, put them on the coffee table in the center of the seating area and took the other chair. He picked up his own cup and nodded to me. I picked up mine and we sipped. Oh, I thought, a little transported as a chocolatey, wine flavor covered my tongue, I have got to find out what kind of beans these are.

"So, how may I help you?" Dr. Fisher asked. I came back to reality and almost grudgingly put down the small cup and saucer.

"I don't know how much you know about what has been happening on campus," I began, "but there has been a hate crime, a student who was likely involved in that has been murdered, and now there have been cyberattacks. One of my colleagues and I have been the subject of those attacks."

He nodded.

"Yes, that horrific noose incident, and I have seen the other emails before the computer system was shut down. That was a very vicious and personal attack, I think. And those photos were created, yes? To foster a lie about you and your colleague?"

I nodded.

"The faking of those pictures is very telling," he said. He took another sip of his espresso and put it down.

"When I was growing up in East Germany, my father was a Protestant pastor and one of those who resisted the Soviet occupation. He was arrested several times, in fact. I was raised by him to just think of everything the government said, what was written in newspapers or said on the radio and television as just a fabrication and then to try to see through the fabrication to what they most feared and were trying to tear down and smear."

He paused and seemed to look inward for a moment.

"It was helpful, of course, to see how these lies were constructed, but also it made it hard for me to trust anything. It was very hard on my parents too. Such fabrications undermine people and societies. It is what totalitarians intend. They want you to feel you cannot know or trust anything. The only emotion allowed is fear."

He paused and looked at me with his penetrating blue eyes.

"Is this how you feel now, do you feel distrustful? Do you feel afraid?"

I registered how smooth and unlined his face was for someone who had to be at least fifty. Then I realized I was focusing on his face so I didn't have to think about what he was asking me. Okay, think, I told myself. Did I want to let this guy see how afraid I really felt? I hate feeling afraid, and I hate admitting I feel afraid.

He just waited, and I finally made up my mind.

"I am afraid to turn on my university computer. In fact, I haven't done it yet." There, I'd admitted that shameful fact.

"I really prefer a threat I can kick and punch or even shoot," I went on, not dropping his gaze. And to my surprise, he smiled a little and nodded.

"Yes, these kinds of computer threats are more insidious than a direct attack. That's a part of what made me want to study extremism." He stopped and then continued with sorrow in his voice, "But I never thought I would have so much to study here, in the United States. It is painful to realize how quickly a society can be made to degenerate into extremism."

He looked down at his hands for a second. They were resting on his knees, but his fingers were tense, gripping the fabric of his pants. I registered that his arms extended several inches beyond his jacket sleeves. Really tall guy. Then I almost smiled. I was dodging him again in my head, focusing on everything but what he was talking about.

Then he looked directly at me, and I couldn't dodge it.

"So, you like to confront things head on, yes?"

I nodded.

"But don't force it with this computer, and I believe, though I am no expert, they can program your computer to detect such threats and block them before they get to your screen. Make them do that. This is harmful to you."

Okay. Screening software. I could ask for that. I liked his practical approach. He didn't try to push and push at my feelings. He seemed to just accept them and deal.

I finished my espresso and thought what else I had wanted to ask. Well, one big one was how to identify the perps.

I put my cup on the small table and leaned forward, holding his eyes with mine.

"Here's the thing, Dr. Fisher. I need, along with our campus police, to find who is doing this. What is the kind of person I should be looking for?"

Fisher sat back and put the tips of his fingers together.

"Simply speaking, young white males. The rise of the Internet has been socially isolating for many, but especially young, white men. The community of white extremists is aggressively tight-knit, and that is very attractive. These ideologies are very appealing to young, white, heterosexual males who regard various women's groups, gay groups, black groups etc. with envy and then resentment."

"Resentment?" I asked, surprised and then angry. "The young, white guys who go to this school have so much. I mean, I want to say, 'how dare they feel resentful,' really."

"Yes," Fisher said calmly, tapping his index fingers together, "but that doesn't matter because these feelings are deeply irrational. Remember, not every young, white man feels this way. The ones who do have what I have come to call a 'need structure,' a weaker construction of the personality. Joining white supremacist, neo-Nazi or Alt-right groups appears to fill that need."

He paused.

"But again, not all are like that. There are also some stronger ones who see a way to dominate, and they exploit these weaker personalities, so you need to look for that kind of personality as well. They can often mask their desire for dominance very effectively with charm, jokes, and a façade of sociability. They are, in fact, the most dangerous. "

Well, speaking of danger, murder always qualified.

"Dr. Fisher, we do have a murder. And one thing I found in the murdered, young man's apartment was a scribbled '23' over and over and '23 doesn't lie' in one frantically written line. Tom suggested this could mean twenty-three chromosomes and that the young victim had taken a DNA test. Would his group have killed him, if, let's say, he found out he wasn't what they consider 'white'?"

"Certainly. They could definitely want to, in effect, purge this young man as he would be polluting the group race identity. And, if possible, try to shift blame to one of the groups or individuals they despise."

I thought of Giles and ICE. Sure. That fit. And, really, I thought suddenly, the effort to get me to John's apartment so his murder could be pinned on me. Yes, that fit as well.

Then he sat up straighter and looked intently at me, holding my gaze like his words would penetrate better that way.

"Given this event, you personally need to be very careful. These are men who are highly threatened by women, and this fuels their misogyny. They are dangerous because they equate activism with violence, and they think if they are not being violent then they are not active, but passive, and passivity is feminine."

He paused and then went on.

"Who do you think is doing these things?" He reached out for his coffee cup, took a last sip, put down the empty cup and waited.

"I have some ideas," I said slowly, "but no proof as yet. What you have said has been very helpful, but I have to get proof."

"Be very, very careful. The closer you get to proof the more danger you are in."

I knew that.

*　*　*

I called Tom as I walked slowly home. It was not as late as I had thought. Dr. Fisher had been able to pack a lot into a short time.

Astonishingly, Tom picked up.

I started to fill him in on what Fisher had said, but he interrupted.

"I've only got a few minutes before my next surgery starts, but it's a short one. What do you say we meet for dinner at Toscanini's at 8? Kelly is going over to Zeke's house to study, and your boys go to bed about then, right?"

Study? I thought wryly.

"Well, if you think so, that would be good," I said dryly.

"I called his parents. They will be home," Tom replied, a little defensively, given my tone.

I remembered "studying" with boys, but didn't take it further.

"Okay. Meet you there," I said, and he hung up.

* * *

I was in the front hall, putting on a jacket and thinking what a nice, peaceful evening it had been with the boys. While they'd eaten, they'd talked about friends at school and how easy math was and the ever-present scourge of spelling. Mike always argued that the existence of spellcheck made spelling obsolete. He'd actually used that word. I almost asked him to spell it but refrained. Sam just insisted spelling was stupid because yeah, computers. They'd gone to bed with no trouble.

Molly had come down to the front hall to watch me as I got ready to go, probably wondering if this excursion would involve a dog, when suddenly she started barking and even growling. This was not her normal way to act. She jumped up against the front door, scratching. Then, with my less acute human hearing, I heard someone on the front porch.

I looked at the security camera and saw the back of a figure running down our front walk.

I grabbed for Molly's collar and yanked open the door. Red paint was dripping off our light blue door. That figure had painted a huge, red swastika on the door.

"Stop!" I yelled, and Molly pulled away from my hold. She took off, chasing the figure that was running away. I shut the front door, automatically locking it, and then took off after them, taking the stairs at a jump.

About half a block away, I could hear yelling and a grunt. The figure had stopped abruptly under a streetlight. I could see Molly had hold of his sleeve. He was struggling to pull away from her. I put on as much speed as I could and saw him kicking out at her.

"Stop that!" I yelled. "She won't hurt you. Just stop!"

Then, as I was about ten feet away, I heard a yelp of pain, and Molly was down on the sidewalk. The bastard had kicked her hard in her side. He, and I could see now it was a he, started to turn to run, and I dove for his legs bringing him down on the hard concrete.

"Hey! Ouch. What the hell?" He started to push himself up, and I subdued him easily by sitting on the back of his legs. He probably weighed about 130 pounds. Then, as he continued to struggle, I grabbed his right wrist and twisted it backwards.

"Shit, shit. Stop that. You're hurting me!"

Molly was lying her side whimpering, and I was so incensed I really wanted to break his wrist.

"Shut up. Just shut up," I said and let up the pressure a little. He tried to get his cell phone out of his pocket with his free hand, and I chopped down on that wrist, and he dropped it.

"Ouch! What the hell do you think you're doing?" he said in a whiny voice. "Give me that." He was trying to turn over.

I just increased the pressure slightly on the wrist I was holding, and he stopped. He was short and thin and his wrist felt like a chicken wing. I did so much want to snap it my teeth were clenched with the effort not to push the wrist back any further.

"I told you to shut up," I said, putting my fury into words instead.

Molly was still whimpering.

He squirmed, trying to turn over.

"Stay still or I will break your wrist," I said between clenched teeth.

I got off his legs and allowed him to turn on his side, though keeping a firm grip on the right wrist. I knelt down between him and Molly. I petted her head, and she gave a feeble wag of her tail, but she was clearly hurt.

The dweeby guy now unbelievably started to cry.

"I'm sorry, I'm sorry. I didn't mean to hurt the dog. I really like dogs. I always wanted a dog." He had pushed himself into a sitting position and put out his free hand to pet her as well.

I almost shoved his hand off of her, but I stopped, thinking about what Fisher had said. I had hold of one of the minions, a needy white kid. What could I get out of him if I let him just snivel about himself?

"Just stay there, okay?" I said sternly, letting up on the pressure and just holding the wrist. I got my own cell phone out of my jacket pocket and dialed the campus emergency number. I identified myself and asked if Officers Billman and Matthews were on duty and found, to my relief, they were out on patrol. I asked to be patched through to them, and Alice's blessed voice came on.

I gave her my location and a brief description of what had happened. She said they were about four blocks away.

I called Carol's cell and told her what had happened. She gave the phone to Giles, saying she would go check on the boys. Good idea. I didn't know if the noise might have waked them.

"You are not injured?" Giles asked.

"No, I'm fine, Giles. Just take pictures of the front door, and then do what you can to cover it up after Mel and Alice see it. They're on the way." I thought for a minute. "We still have some of that blue paint in the garage, right?"

"Yes, I believe so," he said. "We will do that." He paused. "Are you sure you do not want me to come out there to be with you?"

I wanted to keep him away from all of this, at least as much as I could.

"No, Giles, Alice and Mel will be here in a minute. Protect the kids, okay?"

"Yes, of a certainty," he replied firmly and hung up.

I quickly called Tom, gave him a brief summary and asked him to come.

"Of course," was his solid reply. Surgery does teach people to respond quickly and efficiently in a crisis.

I had been watching dweeby, white guy as I made the calls. He had gone from crying to sniveling, and he continued to softly pat Molly. She wasn't moving now, and I was so furious.

"It was just some paint, crap, crap, no big deal. Just some paint," he blustered a little.

Dr. Fisher spoke in my head. "Weak structure of the personality." I swallowed my rage. Identify with the little creep, I told myself.

"So, you like dogs?" I asked.

"Yeah." Sniff. "But my grandmother wouldn't let me have one. Dirty, she said." He hiccupped.

"So, what's your name?" I asked conversationally. "Mine is Kristin."

His thin, ferret-like face switched into a smirk. God. That was eerie. Like a screen change.

"Yeah, well, like you'd like to know that."

Back to dogs.

"Your friends, do they like dogs too?" I asked. Even if he wouldn't tell me who he was, perhaps I could still get some names.

He tensed, smirk gone.

"Friends?"

"You know, whoever you hang with."

His face did another screen change, and I could see a flicker of hate there.

"Well, they like German Shepherds," he said nastily, but with a little laugh. The little shit was laughing about the dogs trained to attack civil rights demonstrators.

Oh the hell with identifying with him. I grabbed his phone from the sidewalk where it had fallen and quickly pressed the thumb of the hand I was holding to it.

"Hey! You can't do that!" he yelled and grabbed for the phone. I put just a little more pressure back on that wrist, and he stopped trying to move. I hoped it hurt a lot.

I looked at the phone screen. Two texts popped up. The first one had been sent half an hour ago.

Damn u Vampire dont go until after 11 u idiot

And the second had been sent ten minutes ago.

Where the hell r u?

Before the screen faded, I put the phone on the sidewalk and took my own phone from my pocket and snapped a picture of the screen.

"So, Vampire, why'd you vandalize my house so early?" I asked conversationally.

"Chem test tomorrow," he mumbled.

I kind of pitied whoever had put him up to this. Hard to get reliable vandalism from geeks.

Just then, Mel and Alice pulled up, lights flashing, and got out of the car.

"N******," said this pathetic specimen of the so-called Master Race as he saw them under the streetlight. "Figures."

Oh, how I wanted to snap that twig of a wrist, but I just pulled him to his feet.

Mel took charge of the little, racist sniveler and put him in the back of the campus police car.

I took Alice aside and gave her the kid's cell phone that I had knocked out of his hand. The screen had gone to locked again, but I showed her my screenshot, and then I showed Mel as he walked up.

"So, that's 'Vampire'?" Mel said, looking at the weedy specimen he'd just locked in the backseat. The twerp now had both hands over his face, his shoulders heaving.

"Apparently so." I tapped on my phone. "Here, I just sent the shot of those two texts to you both."

"That's what he did." I pointed to our front door, a block away. There was enough light from our front porch light for them to see the dripping red of the swastika still on it. Alice conferred with Mel, and then she walked down toward our house to take some pictures, I assumed.

I stayed behind. I didn't want to leave Molly. I took off my jacket, knelt down and put it over her and then held her head. Her eyes were closed, but there was a very small tail wag. I so wanted Tom to get here so we could get her to the emergency vet.

Alice came back and joined Mel standing over me and Molly. Racist sniveler was still hunched in the back seat of the police car, feeling oh so sorry for himself.

They both got out their notebooks. Holding Molly's head on my lap, I sat there on the ground and told them about Molly barking, us giving chase and the kid kicking Molly. Still, I said, I had tried to get names of his cronies, but failed. I gave a one minute summary of Fisher's idea of the deficient "need structure" of these white, male, racist recruits.

"The psychiatrist guy says they feel isolated. So try to identify with him, okay?" I said, the words sounding ridiculous even as I said them. And I'd become so pissed off I hadn't been able to carry out that advice myself.

Alice rolled her eyes, but Mel frowned deeply.

"How?" he asked.

"Well, Mel, you might be able to talk to him about video games," I said, the only thing I could think of. Dogs had not worked.

"So," Alice said, bending down to pat Molly, "this creep hurt the dog? You pressing charges right, for the door and hurting the poor dog?"

"Yeah, Alice. You bet. I'll text you after we get back from the vet." I paused. "Or better yet, let's use the threat of that to see what we can get out of him." I said the last in a rush as I had seen Tom's car coming rapidly up the street. Thank heavens.

"Good dog," Alice said softly, giving Molly another, very gentle pet, and then she stood up.

Tom came over, nodded to Alice and Mel, and bent immediately over Molly. They said a quick goodnight and drove away.

"I think we can move her carefully into the back seat," he said after looking at her gums and feeling lightly around her torso. "I don't think there's any internal bleeding, and she's not in shock."

Bleeding? Bleeding? I shivered with fear for her.

I opened the back door of the car, and Tom bent and gently lifted Molly, now wrapped in my jacket and placed her on the back seat. She whimpered twice but then settled. I climbed in next to her.

"You did right to keep her warm," Tom said, taking off his own jacket as well. "Cover her with this as well. It will reduce the chance of shock."

I gently tucked Tom's jacket over mine and held her head again.

Tom drove quickly to the emergency vet.

Chat Room of Video Game "Active Shooter"

Midnight

Asteroth76: done?

Demon196: the little s*** screwed up got picked up by c*** & n******

Asteroth76: the f***!!! he mouth off?

Demon196: dont panic under control

Asteroth76: no way the s*** is weak weak weak

Demon196: dont panic u idiot others got it

Asteroth76: they better

Demon196: who the f*** u think u are?

Chapter 19

"Run from the Furies . . ."

—Leonard, "Meeting at Winkel," *The New York Times*
(6 September 1982)

Wednesday

Molly was now sound asleep on a pile of quilts on the floor by my side of the bed, wearing a Bulls T-shirt pinned up along her back. A friend of mine had clued me in to this way of avoiding the dreaded cone.

The emergency vet had said the x-rays showed Molly had a cracked rib, but that her lungs were okay. She was in no danger. He had given her a shot of pain medication, and she'd shortly stopped whimpering. He hadn't wrapped her chest, but warned she might lick the area where she could feel the discomfort. I rejected his offer of a cone, and he'd given me some additional pain pills and told me to "keep her quiet for a few days." Good luck with that.

Tom had carried her up to my bedroom from the car and offered to stay.

"What about Kelly?" I'd asked, wanting to refuse without refusing. I thought his staying over again would confuse the boys, and, honestly, confuse me too.

"I can call Kelly. This is about the time I said I'd pick her up, so she can just come too."

Well, okay, that would stop that plan, I thought, but to my surprise, in listening to Tom's end of the conversation, Kelly was all for staying over once she'd heard Molly had been hurt. He'd left to go get her.

I sat down on the floor next to Molly and just put my hand lightly on her soft head in a kind of benediction. As I stroked her, I felt like I wanted to exorcize the petting the dweeb racist had done. What a mess that kid was.

I wondered how Molly had known to go after him and hold him? And, I thought with a sigh as I got up to go put clean towels in the guest room for Kelly, how am I going to explain to the boys I let Molly get hurt?

*   *   *

Thursday

I looked at the clock again. It was 4 a.m. and I'd been awake for an hour. Tom was deeply asleep next to me. He didn't as much snore as blow out little puffs of air. I got up, trying not to disturb him, though I thought nothing short of gunfire in the bedroom would do that as he was so exhausted.

I bent down to where Molly lay. She still seemed to be out cold. I listened to her soft, even breathing and felt her nose. The vet had told us that if she were in physical distress from the injury she would pant. A warm dry nose could indicate shock. I breathed a sigh of relief. Cold nose and even breathing. I lifted her jowl a little. Her gums were pink. Another good sign.

I stood up. Coffee for me. I got my ratty old robe.

As I started down the stairs to the kitchen, I heard footsteps behind me. I turned so abruptly on the stairs, I almost missed a step. Then I saw the shadow of Kelly following me down.

"Hey," she whispered.

"Hey, yourself," I whispered back and hurried down the rest of the stairs to the kitchen and flipped on the lights.

Kelly had on the same yoga pants and sweatshirt she'd been wearing when Tom had brought her to the house last night.

"I couldn't sleep," she said, a little nervously. "I hope it's okay I came down."

"Yeah, sure," I said, a little puzzled at how shy she was being. Well, maybe I'd figure it out, but not without coffee.

"Want some coffee or tea?" I said, turning to the cabinets.

"Coffee, please," she said, and she tucked herself on to one of the breakfast nook benches, pulling her legs up and wrapping her arms around them. Oh, God. She was a tight ball of teenager.

"I've got Jamaican Blue," I said, pulling the sealed container of the precious beans off of a top shelf.

"Yeah, that's good," she said absently, her head bent over her knees.

When enough of the chocolate brown blend had dripped into the pot, I poured it into two mugs, carried them over and sat down opposite her. I took a few sips and contemplated her over the rim. She lifted her head, took a drink and grimaced. Not really a coffee drinker. I got up and brought cream and sugar over with a spoon. She put three tablespoons of sugar in it and poured in enough cream to make coffee ice cream. Then she drank again.

"So what's up?" I asked.

Her tousled, brown hair fell forward as she frowned into the mug.

"It's Zeke," she said so softly I could hardly hear her.

I made a non-committal "mmmm" sound and took another drink of coffee. I'd been a teenaged girl, but not for a while. Best to just let her get it out, whatever the relationship angst was about.

"I'm afraid for him," she choked, and a tear appeared on her pale, round cheek. "He's like black, you know, and I'm just so, I don't know, panicked like that some cop will shoot him or one of these crazy guys who say the country is only for white people will hit him with a car, or I don't know, it's just awful." Tears fell freely now, and she bent her head again, face in her hands. I got up and tore off a couple of paper towels from the roll and handed them to her. She lifted her head and mopped her face.

Well, cripes. Not what I was expecting.

"Have you talked to Zeke about this, about how you feel?"

"I did once, you know, after the Rally Against Hate on campus. We went together and it was like so great, but there were those idiots in their costumes with flags and crap and as we were walking home I told him I was afraid for him." She took a drink of her sugary brew and then hiccupped. I was afraid for a second she was going to spit the coffee back up.

"And what did he say?" I asked when there were no more hiccups.

"He laughed and said 'don't be an idiot.'" She gave a sideways smile that was almost a grimace, then blew her nose and looked down at the wad of paper towels in her hands.

I sat and thought for a minute. She was being painfully honest, and I could only do the same.

"I don't think you're being an idiot, Kelly, but I'm not Zeke," I said slowly. I waited until she looked back up and I held her eyes. "You and I cannot possibly know what it is to be a young, black male today. But I do know what that kind of fear is, fear that someone you like will be hurt or killed."

I paused, gulped some of the coffee and went where I rarely was willing to go.

"You know my husband, Marco, was shot and killed, right?"

She nodded, her big brown eyes wide and her mottled face tense.

"I would always be afraid when he went out on a case, and I think he was also afraid for me when I did. We learned to live with the fear, and when the worst happened, and he was killed, it almost destroyed me."

I stopped, not seeing her anymore, just looking inward.

"But it didn't, and I started to live again." I paused and thought again what she needed to hear.

"I need to tell you, though, this new stuff, what's happening now in our country, on the campus, it scares me again."

I looked directly at her young face, red from crying and strained with worry.

"I think you're right to be afraid, but you also have to trust Zeke. And you can't let the fear take you over. You and I, your Dad, Zeke, Giles, Carol and eventually even the boys and lots of others will have to fix this, and when we work on making things better, that helps with the fear. You know, like Giles did in helping to organize the rally. We can't let the haters win."

She sat up straighter and brushed her hair back from her face.

"Yeah. Yeah. That's right. You know, Zeke and I we were talking to one of those Antifa guys at the rally. He was so cool. He said they were ready to protect people and like stop those jerks with the flags and stuff if they rushed the stage."

Now I was the one who sat up straighter.

Antifascists on campus? Of course there were. Why hadn't I thought of it? I wondered how much they knew about who was in the white suprema-cist network. I needed to check that out. But I also thought Zeke and Kelly could get in a bunch of trouble if they took their cues from them.

"Do you know the guy's name?" I asked. "The one you spoke to at the rally?"

"Weird kind of name. I don't really remember. Zeke might know."

"Ask him, will you?"

"Sure." She took out her phone from a pocket and texted him. Of course she did. At five in the morning.

But I also needed to steer them away from Antifa.

"And hey, you know what might be a good idea? You and Zeke could talk to Giles. He really knows a lot, and he could tell you guys where to plug in. How to help."

Kelly sat up even straighter and her eyes brightened.

"Yeah, totally, that's right. He knows a ton. I'll tell Zeke. We can volun-teer to do stuff. Talking to Giles, that's like brilliant. Thanks."

She started texting again. I was hoping she wasn't texting Giles and waking him up.

She finished tapping the screen and put the phone down.

"Really, thanks. Thanks for not treating me like a kid." She took a sip of her cream and sugar coffee.

"Well, you're not a kid, are you?" I said, realizing it myself. "And let me know the Antifa guy's name when you get it, will you?"

Just then her phone buzzed. She picked it up.

"Braydon Tanner," she read off the screen. "And Zeke sent a cell number too. I'll forward it to your cell." She tapped some more.

Zeke had an Antifa guy's cell number? Worrisome.

"Thanks. Great." Time to switch gears. "Want something to eat?"

"Yeah. Thanks."

I got up and brought over some bowls, cereal, and milk. She wasn't a kid anymore, but she was hungry. She fixed herself a bowl and dug right in.

I poured myself some more coffee and listened to her crunch through the cereal.

✳   ✳   ✳

After Kelly finished her cereal, we both went back upstairs.

Tom had already showered and dressed. He gave me a quick kiss on the cheek and started to head downstairs.

"Coffee made, cereal on the table," I called after him, hoping he'd eat something.

"Right. Thanks," he said, loping down the stairs.

I would keep the Kelly conversation to myself. She hadn't asked me to, but I thought she deserved privacy.

✳   ✳   ✳

"Whatdayoumean Molly's hurt? How'd that happen? When?" Mike asked angrily, getting out of his bed and standing in front of me, quivering. His dark brown hair, tousled from sleep, seemed to bristle with his anger.

I had showered and gotten dressed myself, and then gone into the boys' room to wake them up. I didn't want them to see Molly was not sleeping with them and go try to find her.

After they had sat up and seemed awake, I just told them Molly was sleeping in my room because she'd gotten hurt, and they had to leave her alone for a while.

"Yeah, like is it bad? She gonna die?" Sam jumped out of bed, stood next to his brother and almost shouted his fearful question at me.

"No, she's not going to die, Sam. She's just got a little ouch on one rib. Nothing else."

"An ouch? That's like baby talk. You mean it's broken, right? " Mike challenged me.

"No, guys, the rib is not broken. It is cracked a little, and it hurts her so she got some pain medicine, and that's why she's sleeping. The vet said to let her be quiet for a few days, and it would heal right up. She's a healthy dog."

I looked at the angry little faces turned up at me. They were using their anger to try to hide their fear about anyone they loved getting hurt.

"I wanna see her!" Mike insisted. "Me too!" Sam chimed in.

"Okay. Yeah, fine. But she's sleeping so don't wake her up."

I led the way down to my bedroom, and we all stood around the quilts. Molly was clearly still sleeping deeply.

"Why's she wearing a Bulls shirt?" Sam said in what he seemed to think was a whisper.

I gestured for them to follow me out into the hall and then answered him.

"That keeps her from licking where it hurts. Come on, let's go back to your room," I said.

When they were seated on their beds, I stood between them and gave a short version of what had happened last night. I stuck to the truth. I had chased a bad guy who was spray painting on our house, and Molly had chased him too. The bad guy had kicked her, and the vet had taken an X-ray and found she had that crack in her rib. He'd given her a shot for the pain, and I had some pills to give her later today.

"Is that guy in jail?" Mike demanded to know.

"Yeah, right! He belongs in the slammer, big time!" Sam made a fist and hit his own open hand.

"No, he's not in jail right now, but that could happen. Alice, Mel, and I are going to talk to him this morning. He needs to tell us the truth about why he did that. He's in big trouble. If he doesn't tell the truth, he'll be in even more trouble."

"Why'd you let Molly chase the bad guy?" Sam wanted to know, his dark eyes angry and also a little bright from unshed tears.

"I had hold of her collar, and she pulled away from me," I told them. "I am really sorry about that."

Mike sighed an enormous sigh.

"Yeah, well, she's kind of strong," he said slowly.

Absolution.

* * *

I had walked the boys to school and then come back and awakened Molly. She was able to walk downstairs and go outside without much discomfort. I pushed one of her pain pills into a cheese stick. She ate it up and then ate about half her kibble. Much relieved, I left her with Carol down in our library. Carol had said this was a study day for her and she'd keep Molly company.

It was just 8:30 a.m.

I needed to get over to over to the campus police station to meet Alice and Mel and interrogate "Vampire," AKA "Vampire726," whose real name was Jacob Mayer. Alice had left me a detailed text message last night. Jacob had been a little more forthcoming from the back of a campus police car, and, after they'd verified his real name, they had dropped him off at his dorm with stern instructions to come to the campus police station this morning at nine. They were holding the threat of my making a police complaint over his head and the kind of university discipline that would happen if I did that, up to and including expulsion.

The wind was intensifying in force from the west as I headed out again, a chilling, wet cold that now blew directly in my face. The wind whipped leaves and trash at me. I thought grimly it was like the lies and hate crimes trashing our campus.

I pushed through the gale and the trash, feeling my fury rise at all that had happened. I let the rage fill me as I struggled through the swirl, getting angrier and angrier. The noose, the murder, the threat to Giles, Zeke, Aduba and others, Carol's angst, the suffering of Molly, and my kids' fear. I was working myself up into a fine state to interrogate a lying, sniveling, white supremacist dweeb. I wished I were a Fury myself, I thought with a certain literary irony. I was so damn mad I felt like I had been summoned from the underworld to take vengeance on liars, and thank you for that, Homer.

I yanked open the door of the campus police station and stormed inside. Alice was standing in the lobby, conferring with the guy at the desk. She turned when the door slammed open, and when she saw me, she raised her eyebrows. With my tangled hair flying everywhere and my windblown coat half off my shoulders, I probably did look like something summoned from the underworld.

"Hey," she said dryly, and then then turned and said to the guy at the desk, "Room 309."

She came up beside me. I was trying to get my hair and coat under some semblance of control.

"Come on," she said and headed for the stairs. "You got a comb in your bag, I hope," she went on as I trudged beside her. "We want to scare the kid into talking, but if he sees you like that he might faint first." Then she chuckled a little and headed briskly up the two flights of stairs.

*   *   *

"Come in and sit down, Mayer," Mel said sternly as Jacob Mayer timidly opened the door to 309. His shoulders practically met in the center of his chest he was hunching so much. His shoulder-length, brown hair was unwashed, and he peered at the three of us sitting at the table in the barren room through the dirty lenses of his wire-rimmed glasses. He looked so much like a rabbit, I expected his nose to twitch.

Before Jacob had arrived, Mel had suggested he would take the lead and be "the big, aggressive, black guy this kid would fear the most." We were going to do a classic good cop, bad cop on the kid, playing on the kid's racism. Okay by me, though it had been a little jarring to hear Mel say those words in his usual calm, measured tones. Most of the time, he reminded me of that guy who did the insurance commercials telling you "you're in good hands." And with Mel, you actually were.

"You're late!" Mel accused sternly before Jacob had even settled in the one vacant chair we'd left for him.

"Yeah. Yeah. Well, I didn't exactly know where to go, you know?" Jacob whined.

"Don't make excuses. You're in enough trouble here as it is," Mel ground out, and he consulted a tablet in front of him.

Jacob fidgeted, wiggling his skinny butt around in the hard wooden chair.

"So, you call yourself 'Vampire726' online. Right? Vampire like it said in that text? Who else is doing this kind of crap? Who was texting you?"

"Man, you know she shouldn't have like taken my phone like that. That's private," Jacob countered, pointing a shaking finger at me.

"That's Professor Ginelli to you," Mel said, raising his voice.

Jacob jumped a little on his hard chair.

"And let me tell you, Jacob," Mel went on, keeping his voice stern, "there's no such thing as privacy when you're committing a crime. You are in a mess of trouble here and you better start coming across with some information or Professor Ginelli here is going to file a police complaint against you, and you'll be out of this school so fast your head will spin."

Mel glared at Jacob, tapping a finger on the tablet.

Jacob was silent.

"Mel," I said in as calm a voice as I could muster. "Don't yell at him. Can't you tell he's confused? I bet it wasn't even his idea to do that spray painting, right, Jacob?"

I was trying out my good, white woman role as well as I could, playing off the psychiatrist's advice. So, would Jacob here crave the approval of the longed-for goddess figure? I was giving it a shot, though suppressing a desire to gag. I saw Alice's fingers grip her ever-present notebook so hard her knuckles stood out, but she made no sound.

Jacob turned to me.

"Yeah, well, I mean, no, it wasn't my idea exactly but well, you know, I mean they thought you should like be quiet and not go against your race like that. Got people upset, and, well, I mean, that's why." Jacob trailed off.

"What people?" Alice said, turning her head and giving him what I called "the look," the look she gave that made students on campus toe the line.

"I'm no stooge," Jacob said, his voice much stronger. The whine was gone and his face had done that weird shift I'd seen last night when he'd gone from sniveling about dogs to bragging about how German Shepherds were his "friends" favorite kinds of dogs. His loathing for Alice was terrible to see.

"Yeah, well, but are you a murderer?" Mel broke in sharply. "Were you there when they hit John and strung him up to die? You're the one we've got, Jacob, and we can turn you over to the cops like that," Mel reached out with his long arm and snapped his fingers nearly under Jacob's nose, "and you'll go away for life."

"He killed himself!" Jacob nearly screamed, all his bravado gone. "He wasn't one of us, and he knew it, and he killed himself. The cops know that. You can't fool me. The cops know that, and you're all a bunch of liars."

"How do you know what the police know, Jacob?" I asked in what I hoped was a vestige of my goddess voice.

"Oh, no. I'm not saying anything about anything to you. You're not even cops. Get away from me!"

He stood up and the chair tipped over backwards. He looked so scared I could see the whites of his eyes behind the dirty lenses of his glasses. Sweat dotted his forehead.

He turned jerkily, ignoring the fallen chair, nearly ran to the door, yanked it open and disappeared down the hall.

"Well, that went well," Mel said sarcastically.

"You'll need to file that complaint, Kristin," he continued. He opened the tablet screen, entered a few words and pressed enter. He passed it over and there was an online complaint CPD form.

"Yeah, okay." I said, scanning the form.

But then I looked up at each of them.

"The student leader or leaders of them, I think, are in touch with a cop or cops, right?"

Mel and Alice looked at each other, and then both nodded to me.

I went on, looking at the "Chicago Police Department" logo on the online form in front of me.

"This is more than a bunch of needy, young, white guys acting out their insecurity by targeting minorities. This is a conspiracy, and there is some kind of police involvement."

"Could be," Mel said, looking over at his tablet where it sat in front of me. "I've gotten on to this WhiteLivesMatter website using an alias. A lot of people on it use screen names, and some, I think, are cops. Rhetoric seems like it. And they are very, very fond of the N-word."

"White lives matter?" Alice snorted. "White lives always matter. What the hell are they yakking about?"

"White genocide," said Mel with a straight face.

"Mel," I asked as Alice muttered several choice words under her breath, "how can they get away with that these days with the scrutiny of hate speech on social media?"

"The Russians."

"What? Those damn Russians?" Alice asked angrily.

"Yeah," Mel said calmly. "They use a Russian social networking site called vk.com." He gave a wry smile. "All the white supremacists love it. No censorship."

"I want to take a look," I said, looking down at his tablet.

"No," Mel said, reaching over and taking it back. "You need to be really careful about this kind of stuff. I have identity-masking software on a different device, and I use it to get on, and even so I use wifi at coffee shops."

He looked steadily at me.

"These are dangerous people, Kristin. Don't think you can just waltz on to their website. They'll track you."

They're tracking me anyway, I thought, but I kept my mouth shut.

"So, really, not a big surprise there are cops in this mess," Alice said. "Talkin' about cops is what set that idiot kid off." She paused. "So what do we tell Gutierrez?"

Mel and I didn't answer. Did we trust Gutierrez?

Chapter 20

[A] demon can work on man's imagination.

—Thomas Aquinas, "The Assaults of the Demons,"
Summa Theologicae, Question 114

Thursday

I walked out the door of the campus police station and was astonished to find that the weather had cleared. It was almost pleasant.

Instead of heading on over my office, I sat down on a bench on the main quadrangle. Students passed, mostly staring at their cell phones. Were some of them neo-Nazis checking for instructions on what hate crime to perpetrate next? Somebody was directing all this. Jacob was not only a whiner, he was clearly a follower. I thought maybe John had been a follower too. Who were the leaders? Was it a racist cop or cops, or did it really just originate here? Who was Jacob afraid of? It was clear, without all the stupid numbers, that Jacob was Vampire, and John must have been Moloch, but who was Demon? Who was Asteroth? I didn't know enough to hack them and find the names behind it. It was so frustrating trying to sort out who was doing what when they were playing around in video games with fake names. And on websites hosted by Russians. What a world.

Antifa, I thought suddenly. Don't they hack the hackers as well as confront them at rallies?

I took out my phone and found the text from Zeke with Braydon Tanner's cell. I copied it and composed a text to him.

"You don't know me, but would you meet me at my office, Myerson 301 some time today? Hope you can help me figure out what's happening on campus. Professor Ginelli"

I read that over to myself, and it seemed lame. If I were an anarchist, I wouldn't meet with me, an authority figure, in an office. I deleted office, Myerson and so forth and substituted "some place." Then I deleted the whole next sentence. Too controlling. Then I took out "Professor" too. I re-read my shredded text. "Meet me some place today?"

Not enough. What else? What would make him want to talk to me? Well, Antifa was known for its direct action. I thought of the pigeons and added, with a wry smile, "Sick of this garbage, Ginelli."

I pressed "send" before I could revise it again. Either they'd bite or they wouldn't.

As I approached Myerson, my phone buzzed.

"Cool Beans. 1."

Gotcha.

* * *

I was sitting in the coffee shop called Cool Beans at a back table. I'd gotten there a few minutes early. I assumed Braydon would know me. I certainly wouldn't know him.

I used the time to check my school email on my phone. The university computer system had been cleansed and was back up. I'd had a text on my phone sent last night from our new security program, the one designed to tell us to "shelter in place" if we had an active shooter on campus. Great. That did not make me feel secure either. The text had said simply the system had been "fixed." This morning, I'd braved opening my computer when I'd gotten back to the office, and no porn had jumped out at me from my screen. Good. That blocking software I'd requested when I'd gotten the new computer seemed to be working. For now, at least. Until somebody figured out how to bypass it.

When I'd checked my email at the office, I'd seen that there was a statement from the University President about the computer hacking and the "false and defamatory" photos that had been circulated. It contained a stern statement about how that was a federal crime, and the FBI had been called in. It was a pretty good statement. It sounded scary. The denunciation of the "false and defamatory" photos that had been created and circulated about Professors Ginelli and Abubakar had a threat attached as well. Anyone downloading or circulating those photos could also be subject to federal charges. Then there was some boilerplate about the "values of the university" blah blah. All in all, not bad. I should send Alastair Ackerman a note thanking him. Though, of course, Aduba had been right. Whatever was out there on the Internet was there forever. Those fake photos had probably already been beamed out in to space, and Martians were looking at them.

After reading the President's statement a few more times and then saving it, I'd gone into the student database to find a photo of Braydon and some information on him. Astonishingly, his profile had been scrubbed. In the line for "High School," it read "an average school," he was from "a place" in "a boring state," his parents were "alive," and his emergency contact phone information was what I thought I recognized as the White House phone number. And, of course, there was no photo.

Well, I thought as I closed my computer, no face Braydon from a place in a boring state was exactly the person I thought could help me. If he would. I wondered if Braydon Tanner was even his name. But then I wondered if he could hack his student info, had he done the porn hack?

But, I'd decided to meet him anyway and now, in the coffee shop, I kept watching the door. A little after 1, two guys wearing bandanas around their necks as well as ballcaps and sunglasses entered and scanned the room. Wow. Way to advertise you don't want the security cameras in the coffee shop to photograph your face.

I had opened the camera app on my cell phone, as well as my email, when I had sat down. I zoomed in on them and quickly took a picture of the side of the head of each of them. Nobody seemed to have told them what a huge identifier ears were. Their ears were right there, not at all covered by their choice of hats. I scrolled a little more, but mostly watched them in the camera box.

They took their time, looking at each coffee drinker in turn, and then at each of the baristas. Seemingly satisfied the FBI hadn't infiltrated Cool Beans, they headed directly for my table. I hit another app and then put my cell phone in my pocket.

The guy in the lead was probably a little under six feet and wore wire-rimmed glasses. He had on a khaki jacket, T-shirt, and jeans that were torn at the knees. Of course he did. The second guy was taller and thinner. He wore thick, black-rimmed glasses, a pea coat, and the obligatory T-shirt and jeans. Both of them had pasty white skin. Figured. Either they were inside hacking or their faces were covered by those scarves at outdoor rallies.

"You Ginelli? asked the first guy as he reached the table. I could see some dirty blonde hair sticking out below the cap.

"Yes," I said. "Braydon?"

"No, that's me," said the taller guy. I could see thick, dark hair around his ears, and a distinct, dark, widow's peak coming down over his forehead under the brim of the hat. "He's Richie," he said with a slight chuckle, indicating the dirty blonde hair guy. "You know, for Richie Rich?"

They both took chairs and sat down, grinning at me.

"Braydon, I loved your online student profile," I said. "So informative. Your own work?"

"I have no idea what you are referring to," said Braydon, continuing to smile.

"Of course not," I continued. "Listen, you guys, you both know what happened to Professor Abubakar and me, correct?"

They nodded.

"I am assuming that was not your work."

Both their pasty, white faces flushed a little.

"We're antifascists, not morons," said Richie indignantly.

"Besides," said Braydon, "we're feminists and anti-racists. That kind of corporate exploitation of female bodies and racist hate is such crap. Typical of the fascists."

Okay, we needed to get beyond slogans.

"So do you know who did it?" I asked, looking at each outraged face in turn.

"Look," Richie said, "that's not how we operate, okay? We'll take action if and when we find them."

"And suppose you find out who killed John Vandenberg? Will you take action then, or might you need a little help from someone like me?" I was getting a little flushed in the face myself, I assumed.

"You're tied in with the campus cops, right?" Braydon asked.

I nodded.

"And they are tied to the Chicago cops?"

I nodded again.

"You don't get it, do you?" Braydon hissed. "You're as blind as the rest of them." He slapped a hand on the rickety wooden table so it rocked on its uneven legs. "The cops don't want to know who killed Vandenberg, they want to find a way to blame BlackLivesMatter, and us as well, and from what we've heard, they want to blame you too. Why the hell would we tell you what we know so you can tip them off? And why would you want to?"

I didn't reply, just looked at Braydon and then at Richie, thinking.

"You don't really know Antifa, do you?" Richie asked into the silence.

"No," I said, "I don't think I do."

"Well, we're anonymous," he said dryly.

Smartass, I thought. My distain must have shown on my face because Richie bristled a little.

"Look," he said, adopting a kind of lecturing tone, "we keep our mouths shut, we do what needs to be done, and that's that. We learned from what happened in the past. You know, like to White Rose?"

I nodded. He was referring to a university student group who had called for active, though non-violent, resistance to the Third Reich. Hitler had had them all killed.

"Well, we don't want that to happen to us."

"Yeah, well I get that," I said slowly, though I thought they had a very romanticized view of whatever it was they did.

So, that didn't mean they didn't know exactly what was going on. I looked at each of them in turn.

"I know you actively confront the white supremacists and try to disrupt their attempts to pass off their hate speech as free speech, but aren't you all hackers as well?"

"Not us, no. That would be illegal," said Braydon in a mock serious tone. Richie Rich barked a laugh.

"Okay, I get that too," I said, nodding. "But some members of the Antifa network do hacking. I mean, Wikipedia says so."

I could do sarcasm too.

They both laughed.

"But what does that entail?" I asked in a more serious tone.

Richie looked a little shocked at my abysmal ignorance, but he spoke patiently, though he tapped the long, thin fingers of his right hand on the table. Tension? Boredom?

"See, racist sites, for example, have weaknesses in their code. Some Antifa members look for those weaknesses, re-write the code, and take control of the site. A site that calls itself 'Race Realism' was made into a site devoted to arguments about cycling." Richie snorted. For a minute, he sounded like Alice.

"Here," Braydon pulled out his cell phone. "You know 'Stormfront,' right, the neo-Nazi site?"

"Yes," I said, glad to be able to say I knew something.

"Well, now it's all about weather."

He passed the phone over and I saw the "Stormfront" logo had been replaced with billowing dark clouds that filled the screen. A new logo appeared from the mist. "Eyes on the Skies" it said in bright, red letters.

"That's good," I said, smiling at them. "But the white supremacists catch on, right, and change it back?"

"No, they can't. They're such complete idiots they can't figure out how to search the code and eliminate the hack. So they think they can create a new website, but they import graphics and so forth into the new site, and that's already been re-written. By Antifa."

"It's almost too easy," Braydon said a little sadly. Then he caught himself. "I mean, for those who do that kind of thing."

"So could somebody, I mean, not you guys, but other people, hack these dangerous jerks who are messing with our campus and find out who they are? They're using video games to plan, and now, I've learned, Russian hosted websites to communicate. They've gotten somebody killed."

Messing with white supremacists was all very well, but John had been murdered. Instead of focusing on that, they were having fun with me, dancing around and disclaiming knowledge while these white supremacists did what they wanted and were getting away with it.

"Why don't your precious cops get a court order and find out who they are?" Richie asked, disdain in every world.

"They don't seem to be doing that," I said. "You may be right that they are looking everywhere but at the real culprits. That's why I need your help. I need to know if you have any information I can use to find them, stop them."

"We're anarchists," Braydon replied, smirking. 'We don't do 'information.'"

They started to get up to leave.

"Listen," I said sharply, "if you find out who killed Vandenberg, tell me anonymously. I'll take it from there."

They were shaking their heads silently, but they sat back down.

"You must have looked into who I am before you came, right?" I asked, looking from one pasty white face to the other.

Nods.

"So you know I don't stop until I find out who hurt someone, and I get them prosecuted and jailed."

"You've never gotten whoever killed your husband prosecuted and jailed," Braydon said nastily.

A direct hit. He saw it and liked it. Richie, not so much. He frowned at Braydon.

Well, when I'm hit, I hit back.

"If I ever find out you knew who killed John, and you didn't tell me, I'll see you're prosecuted for a lot more than some hacking. You could be named accessories to murder after the fact." I paused and glared at both of them, and then I held Braydon's eyes.

"And, Braydon, though it is none of your business, I haven't gotten my husband's killer, and the guy who set him up, prosecuted and jailed. Yet. But I never, ever give up. Keep that in mind as well." I paused, and again looked hard at each of them in turn. "Remember, I captured and killed the first murderer I chased on this campus. Don't mess with me. You'll regret it."

I slapped two of my cards down on the table.

"If you find out who did the murder, tell me."

They took the cards, though they knew, and I knew, it was a power play on my part. They knew dozens of ways to contact me, many of which were likely illegal.

But I had managed to wipe the smirks off their faces and, I noted with grim satisfaction, scare them a little.

I watched them leave and then took my cell phone out of my pocket and turned off the audio record function.

* * *

I called Alice as I was walking back to campus. She picked up. She was in the office for another hour. I told her I had a tape to play for her.

I was now sitting at the table in her office, my phone between us.

"So, what? You think these jerks did the hacking?" Alice asked after she'd heard the recorded conversation.

"No, I don't think so," I said slowly, "but I think they know who did. Or they suspect. I would bet hackers on the campus of that sophistication know each other."

"Humph," Alice said. "Probably right. But they won't tell you. Too full of themselves."

"I don't know, Alice. About the hacking, probably not. But murder is a whole different ball game."

She frowned, clearly thinking.

"What worries me, Alice, is that too many people, not only these kids, but that exchange about red lines and 'r u blue' and then what Mel said about WhiteLivesMatter are telling us one way or another a cop or cops are involved."

I paused, considering.

"What did Gutierrez say about Jacob and what's happening there?"

Alice didn't answer. She got up, opened the window and then got out her little metal box from her jacket hanging on her desk chair. She sat next to the window, lit a cigarette, took two puffs, blew the smoke out the window and then ground the partially smoked cigarette out in her sand. She put it carefully away and then sat back down opposite me.

"That kid, Jacob Mayer, has been suspended. The Dean is treating it like a prank, Gutierrez said. He's pissed, but not saying much. Me and Mel, we met with him, and it was like he was shut down. Just gave us that info and said he had to go."

So Vampire had missed his chem test, I thought. And that's all?

"It's got to be outside pressure, Alice."

"Ya think?" Alice said tersely, looking out the window. The medieval arches and turrets of the buildings on the main quadrangle were just visible in the distance, darkened and stained by the grime on the glass. It was stained in reality too, I thought.

"So how do we break through that?" I said, wanting to take a sledge hammer to the tall piles of stone out there, looking so sure of themselves and hiding so much hypocrisy.

"Damned if I know," Alice said grimly, still looking out the window.

Well, she had the damned part right.

Chapter 21

I'm always annoyed about why black people have to bear the brunt of everybody else's contempt. If we are not totally understanding and smiling, suddenly we're demons.

—TONI MORRISON

Thursday

I t was almost pitch dark when I exited the campus police station, and it was only about three in the afternoon. I looked up at the sky and an enormous cluster of black clouds was coming in from the west, blotting out all colors. The whole scene looked like one of those black and white photographs of the campus that used to hang in the old coffee shop before it had been made over to look like South Beach.

I thought I'd better put a move on or I'd get soaked before I reached home.

As I jogged along, threading my way along the sidewalk, I thought I should get one of those watches that measured your steps. I was really putting in the miles these days, crossing and re-crossing this patch of the city.

Just as a drop of freezing water hit my collar, my cell phone rang. I wrestled in out of my pocket. I looked at the screen. Regina Levinson.

"Yes, Regina?" I answered, while still hustling along. It was now sleeting.

"Kristin? Yes, this is Regina. Carol just called me a moment ago. She's at your house, but she said two men who identified themselves as Chicago detectives accosted her as she was coming up the front walkway just a few minutes ago.

"She's very upset. She said she asked for identification, they refused, and the shorter one actually shoved her back toward the front door, and yelled 'quit stalling, we came for your boyfriend.' I wasn't home at the time. If I'd seen this, I tell you Kristin I'd have been out there in a New York minute."

Of course she would have. I thought of the five-foot tall, nearly seventy-year-old lawyer confronting the two bully cops and shuddered.

Regina paused, a little out of breath. Then she went on.

"Carol told me she asked for a warrant repeatedly. They never produced one and just stood on either side of her, the tall one leaning over her, and the short, fat one leaning right on her arm, I would bet to intimidate her. But the child has guts. She stood her ground, I guess you'd say, and they finally went away."

Short and tall. Fat and skinny. Kaiser and Brown. Had to be. I was so furious I was having trouble breathing myself.

"When they left, she called me. She said Giles is at the math library."

I ducked into an archway to escape the worst of the sleet that was now pelting down, though I was so furious I actually felt hot for a second.

"Regina," I asked quickly, "what's the best thing to do?"

"Well," she said, in her matter-of-fact voice, "I'm not a criminal lawyer. You need to get him a criminal lawyer right away, right now really, and, Kristin, he should go nowhere near the police without an experienced criminal attorney with him."

Okay, I thought, barely registering the freezing water seeping down my back.

"Thanks, Regina, I said. "You've the best."

"No, I'm not the best," she said, managing a small chuckle. "You get him the best, *du hörst mich?*"

German for "you hear me?" I heard her. But first I'd call Carol.

"Yes, Kristin?" Carol answered, her voice barely above a whisper.

I told her about Regina calling me, and I asked her if she was okay.

"Yeah, sort of okay. I'm just so cold, you know? And I can't reach Giles," she said with a tiny sob.

"Listen, Carol," I said firmly. "You need to get warm. You might be a little bit in shock. Fix some hot tea with sugar, get under the fake fur throw from the library and cuddle the real fur dog on the couch in there. Turn on the gas fire. And don't worry. I'm on it. Regina said to get Giles a first-class criminal lawyer, and I will."

"Yes, okay, yes," she said with a sniff. "Molly is leaning against me like she knows I need her. And she was barking the whole time those police were hassling me outside. I could hear her through the door."

Molly was clearly feeling better and ready for another round with neo-Nazis.

Suddenly, as I thought about Molly barking inside the door, I realized the video security camera controls would have been above her.

"Carol, the front video cam is on all the time now. Can you grab your computer and while you're warming up download that footage, and send me the section where the cops are hassling you?"

"Yes, yes. I know how to work that. I will."

"Very good. Now I'll call Anna, and then just go to the math library and get Giles. We'll protect him, Carol. Really we will. Try not to worry."

"Okay," she breathed. "Okay." And we hung up.

I huddled further back into the arch and called Anna. Remarkably, she did not pick up. Instead of leaving a message, I called her executive assistant, Eleanor Abernathy, who told me to hold on. Anna was just finishing with a client, and she'd tell her I was waiting.

I shivered, feeling the wet cold now and my anxiety. I huddled back against the stone wall of the arch, and thought grumpily that for what I was paying Anna and her firm, I should be her only client. Like the mob.

"Yes, Kristin," Anna's voice said into my cold, wet ear.

I filled her in on what had happened with Carol, and what Regina had recommended.

"Yes, Ms. Levinson is exactly correct," she said, sounding like the New England Brahman that she was, and not at all like I imagined a mob lawyer would sound.

"I will find my colleague Bennett Washington and make the referral. He is excellent. I will text you his number."

I immediately heard my text tone. Anna was as quick at texting as Adelaide was leaving a room.

"Thanks, Anna," I said, my teeth starting to chatter.

"And Kristin? You say you have a security camera video of these police pushing Ms. Diop?"

"I think we do, Anna. Yes. I haven't seen it yet."

"Be sure to get that to Washington right away. That is outrageous, and he can use that very effectively to protect Mr. Diop." A pause. "I am sending you his email."

"I will." And I heard my text tone again.

I realized I was shaking from the wet cold. I needed to get inside a building before I got hypothermia. I pushed further into the arch and opened a door on my right. It was an entryway, the stone floor wet and muddy. But it was warmer.

I scrolled to Giles's cell phone number and called it.

"'Allo? Mrs. Gin?" he said quietly. "I will need to walk out into the hall." I heard his footsteps and a door opening. Thank heavens he'd picked up.

I decided, as I waited, not to waste time on explanations until we were face to face.

"Yes, I am here," Giles said.

"Are you at the math library?" I asked shortly.

"Indeed, yes."

"There's a coffee shop there in the basement, right? Meet me there in ten minutes."

I didn't even wait for him to reply. I hung up, put up my coat collar and left the warm little entryway that smelled like a stew of wet student and mud.

When I got out to the sidewalk, the sleet had stopped, though the concrete still glistened with icy patches. I walked as fast as I dared.

* * *

"Giles, you need to let me in," I said as I gripped a hot, cardboard coffee cup with both hands, trying to warm them while also holding on to my temper.

From across the little, rickety table, Giles looked at me with his serious brown eyes, giving nothing away.

When I'd met him at the basement coffee shop, I filled him in on what Carol had told Regina Levinson, what Regina had said and then on my lawyer and friend, Anna Feldman, recommending Bennett Washington.

So far he had only frowned and then said merely, "It is not for you to worry about."

That had really pissed me off.

I checked my phone to see if Carol had gotten that security camera clip and emailed it to me. It was there.

"Look, Giles," I said sharply, "I am worried. And if I were you, I'd be really worried right now too. Just watch this, will you?"

I turned my phone around and pressed play.

I could see the small screen upside down, and I could hear Kaiser yelling at Carol, including several choice swear words, and Brown backing him up. Carol was between them, and she looked terrified. I looked up at Giles's face. It was rigid with shock, and, I thought, some suppressed anger.

The video had been sent in two files. When the first one ran out, Carol was still asking through trembling lips if they had a warrant. I reached over and pressed play on the second one.

This one was worse. Kaiser was offensively bumping her, pushing her arm into her breast, and Brown was leaning over her from the other side. When she stepped back, they followed. Then it seemed like some pedestrians came by on the sidewalk behind them, and I heard a voice call out "everything okay, Carol?" Kaiser and Brown stepped away from her, probably afraid of being seen by witnesses, and then Kaiser said, "You quit stalling you are probably in this too!" He and Brown disappeared from the screen. Carol had cut the tape off there.

Giles had tears in his eyes.

I waited for a minute and then spoke.

"Look, Giles. This is not just about you, okay? This is about her as well. And me, and the boys. And, really, those cops," and I tapped my finger on the screen, "have to be stopped. They think they can do pretty much what they want to people."

Pain flickered briefly across his face. I jumped on it.

"The law is nonviolence too, you know. When we stand up for the rule of law against bullies, that helps make a more decent society."

He dropped his eyes and looked down at the scarred table top.

I knew I was laying it on a little thick, but I didn't let up.

"Use the law, Giles. Protect your wife, protect yourself. And, really, protect me and the boys too."

I reached a hand across the table and tapped the screen of the phone with my index finger, punctuating every word.

"Talk. To. The. Lawyer."

He sat perfectly still, and I waited. Then his shoulders sagged a little, but his chin came up.

"Whatever this costs, I will pay you back. We must write it up, and I will sign."

"Certainly, Giles. I will give you a copy of the invoice from Anna's firm, and we can do that," I said firmly, though in my own mind I was considering how to get Washington to give me two bills. Well, cross that bridge when I came to it. Besides, Giles didn't have to know about the retainer I had started paying Anna's firm last year. That was my business.

I took a big drink of the now lukewarm coffee and shivered a little, probably more from suppressed tension.

"Now," I went on, "here is the lawyer's name and contact information. I am sending that to your phone." I did, probably not as quickly as Anna but still pretty fast.

"And here's the two video files." I forwarded those to his phone as well.

"You need to call Washington now. He's expecting to hear from you. Once you have agreed he is your lawyer, he will act on your behalf. Send him those videos. It gives him a lot to work with."

I stood up, taking my coffee.

"I'll wait in the hall."

"No," Giles said firmly, getting up himself. "I will go down the hall. There are study rooms for use. I can speak there in private."

He left abruptly, and I sat back down and sipped my cool coffee.

Maybe I felt a little guilty about pushing all those buttons to make him get help, but I knew what the police were capable of, at least some of them. And, I wondered, was Giles really at risk from immigration as well? Could he be locked up for a month even with legal papers? I realized I needed to know more about ICE. The whole, sudden attention Giles had gotten from ICE didn't make sense to me unless it was part of a larger pattern.

*   *   *

"So, then what happened?" I asked Sam as we sat around the kitchen table having African vegan casserole. It had certainly come in handy to have these nutritious, frozen meals. I was thinking about just ordering another round to freeze when we finished these.

Molly was sniffing around under the table still wearing her Bulls shirt. But she was clearly feeling much better. It had probably given her a boost to have defended Carol and then comforted her.

"So, this kid, he like says to the other kid, why doncha talk right and the other kid says some words I think in another language and then he says can you talk like that and the first kid he gets all mad and stuff, but then we had to go in and do some reading."

Sam stuffed a big bite of casserole in his mouth, and Mike took over.

"Mister Meyers he like was watching and he spoke to the kid who was ragging on the other kid so they came in after. I didn't hear but Mister Meyers looked really pissed off," Mike finished with satisfaction.

"Angry. He looked angry. Pissed off is not polite," I corrected a little absently, focused more on what the boys were saying. If I had decoded it correctly, they were telling me about schoolyard anti-immigrant sentiment. In lower school. Oh, lord.

"So, where are Carol and Giles?" Mike asked suddenly. "Why're they gone so much?"

Mike missed nothing.

"They have a meeting at an office downtown. I don't think Carol has left yet, and I don't know when they'll be back." I just blew past the rest of why they were gone so much.

"How about some ice cream?" I asked quickly. The distraction that always works.

Giles had let me know, when he came back to the coffee shop, that Bennett Washington said he would call the station and try to talk to Kaiser and Brown and find out why they wanted to speak to Giles. He had wanted Giles to stay put at the math library.

I'd left to go home then, asking Giles to keep me informed. I had already texted Carol that I would pick up the boys. She needed to stay home where she could feel safe. What an awful thing to experience, I thought.

While the boys were upstairs doing some math homework, Giles had called again.

Washington wanted him to come directly to his office, as soon as possible, so Carol was going to meet him at the math library, and they'd take an Uber downtown. There was no warrant for Giles's arrest, but he was wanted for "questioning."

"Mr. Washington," Giles said, "thinks it best if it is a conversation at his office. I said certainly. Those police, he said, agreed to come there, to his office, this evening." And he hung up.

Just then Carol came down the backstairs with her coat on, looking pale and tense.

"You sure you want to do this?" I asked softly. She looked awful, but she also had a kind of New England winter look on her face. They're not wimps, the people who grow up with Maine weather.

She was about to speak when Sam came thundering down behind her with a question about his homework. She just whispered, "Yes," and I gave her a pat on the arm and followed Sam back upstairs. I wanted to go with her and Giles so much, and I knew that was a bad, bad idea.

I'd settled the math question. Then I read to the boys and tucked them in.

✳ ✳ ✳

The boys had fallen asleep with Molly back in her bed between them. I was down in the library with a glass of wine and a book I was not reading. I'd tried calling Tom, but his phone went right to voicemail. He was probably in surgery.

My cell phone rang, startling me. I looked at the screen. Not Tom, Anna.

She didn't waste time. I liked that in a person who billed in eight minute segments.

"I sat in on the meeting just as an observer," she said. "They have nothing."

"John Vandenberg," she continued, "was part of a list-serve for Black-LivesMatter that Giles administers. John got emails from Giles about BLM meetings and so forth along with hundreds of others. Your Detective Kaiser claims there are "other emails," but he could produce nothing. There are no charges, but it is clear Kaiser really wants to find a way to connect Giles to the murder especially through you. Both he and Brown made a lot of insult-ing insinuations about Giles as your "live-in boy" and Carol as a three-some, and I must say Giles did not let them make him angry as they had hoped."

She paused.

"Washington is so smart. He let those guys run that line out for a while, and then he played the videos you'd sent on the big flat-screen in the conference room where they were. Kaiser and Brown nearly swallowed their tongues. Bennett told them he had already filed a formal complaint with the Chicago Police Department asking for their suspension. Kaiser looked like he was going to explode, but Brown just put a hand on his arm, and they got up and left.

"Is Carol okay?" I asked her. I still didn't think she should have gone with Giles.

"I had her sit in my office. I saw those videos too, Kristin, and that would traumatize anybody." She paused. "She probably needs some counsel-ing because of this."

Jane, I thought. Maybe Carol could talk to Jane.

"Well, Anna, I'm glad I had that tape."

"Yes. I am too. Those two, and particularly that Kaiser, are a disgrace," she replied seriously. "Bennett Washington is African American, and Kaiser kept calling him 'you' rather than use his name. It was outrageous. Bennett, like Giles, remained calm. I did too, of course. I was just an observer, but I truly wanted to punch Kaiser several times."

She then chuckled a little and said, "But I imagined you were there and wanted to punch Kaiser, and what I would say to you to stop you, and that helped a lot. And then, we might say, they did get punched with those videos." She paused.

"Giles met privately with Washington after that, and of course that's privileged, but Bennett said it went well." Then Anna said good-night and hung up.

That Carl. He'd managed to piss Anna off, and I'd never seen that hap-pen. At least that she'd let on.

And I was proud of Giles for not taking the bait. Of course, I had an impression that he had at least been questioned by the Senegalese police for his peacemaking work in his home country, so I suspected he had been through worse interrogations than this one. But I also knew well if Giles had just been picked up by Kaiser and Brown on his own and taken to a Chicago police station for "questioning," things could have gone very dif-ferently. I mean, look at what had happened to Carol out in public. The City of Chicago had gone into tremendous debt paying off lawsuits because certain Chicago cops had been found guilty of torturing confessions out of innocent suspects. I would not put that past Kaiser and Brown at all. I bet Bennett Washington knew that as well. It sounded like he had done a great job for Giles, and with any luck Washington could get Kaiser and Brown investigated and perhaps suspended. Even fired. I hoped.

Just then I heard the front door, and Giles and Carol came in. They were speaking softly and headed directly up the stairs to their apartment. I didn't come out of the library and let them have their privacy.

I knew what I needed to do. I got my computer out and opened up the identity-masking software. I went about the task of creating a fake, white male identity for myself. I'd use it on the WhiteLivesMatter website.

I took a sip of wine and considered what name I should use.

Bob Ewell. The name of the despicable, lying, white racist in *To Kill a Mockingbird* would be perfect.

None of these creeps would have read that book. Well, none of them except the one I was targeting, I thought, and I got to work creating the fake profile. I hoped he'd take the bait.

WhiteLivesMatter Website Chat

Thursday midnight

The Ghost: cant believe this s***** Mudslime & c**** think they
   run the world gotta clean house gotta clean house u wf
   me?

Blue Leopard: we must restore order. What the enemy destroys
   we take back ten-fold and make our home and streets pure
   again.

Bob Ewell: they look at us like we're dirt

Blue Leopard: Damn straight

The Ghost: who the hell r u?

Bob Ewell: a believer

The Ghost: Yeah? What the f*** do u believe, Bob?

Bob Ewell: I believe white is right

Blue Leopard: f****** A

Chapter 22

*The golden moments in the stream of life rush past us, and we
see nothing but sand; the angels come to visit us, and we only
know them when they are gone.*

—George Eliot (Marian Evans), *Janet's Repentance*

Friday

I'd stayed up until 3 a.m., scanning the posts and chat rooms of White-
LivesMatter and contributing an occasional racist remark as Bob
Ewell, but no one else engaged except "The Ghost" and "Blue Leopard."
As I closed my computer and turned off the light, I wondered if I could
find either of those two also posting in the video game chat rooms, but
under other names. It would take some textual criticism to figure that
out, I thought wryly, and thought no more.

I awoke to the sound of banging and realized the boys were already up
and using the bathroom. They could not seem to manage to simply close
a door. With the next slam, I sat up with a groan and realized there was
banging in my head as well. I got up slowly, pulled on some sweats, stuck my
phone in my pocket and stumbled downstairs.

Carol was in the kitchen, dishing out oatmeal to the boys. Her family's
wonderful maple syrup was already on the table, and the boys didn't seem
to be complaining about oatmeal. I headed straight for the coffee pot, filled
a giant mug and then slumped down in a seat at the table. The boys were
arguing about some Lego creation they had made, and I zoned out.

Then Carol called to the boys from the front hall, and I registered she'd
left the room to get ready to walk them and herself to school. They both
jumped up, gave me oatmeal tinged kisses and ran out. Suddenly Molly and
I were alone in the silence. She cocked her head at me, and I realized there
was left-over oatmeal in the boys' bowls. I scraped that into her dog dish and

put the bowls in the sink. That was almost too much effort, and I collapsed again at the breakfast table.

My text tone sounded, and I took my phone out of my pocket. Alice.

"*POLICE REPORT IN. MEET COFFEE SHOP HALF AN HOUR?*"

The all caps hit my eyes like she was shouting. I looked at the time on the screen. It was only eight.

"Make it an hour, okay?" I typed slowly.

"OK" came back immediately.

I need aspirin and a shower. At least.

* * *

"So he was murdered," I said quietly, as I handed back the hardcopy of the police report to Alice. I'd known it already, but still awful.

"Yeah. It's pretty clear," she said, twirling an unlit cigarette between her fingers. We were sitting on damp, metal chairs on the coffee shop's outside patio. She could have lit the cigarette, but she was just holding it. Probably for the same reason I had a big cup of water in front of me. Our chosen coping mechanisms can sometimes make us feel worse.

The autopsy had shown Vandenberg had been hit hard on the back of his head. The blow had cracked his skull. I thought he might even have been unconscious before he was hanged. I hoped so. And I doubted he was the one who had sent those last texts to me.

"So what you been up to?" Alice asked, putting her unsmoked cigarette away in an inside pocket of her black uniform jacket. The jacket had a sheen of moisture on it. She had probably been out on patrol from early morning when it was still raining.

I grimaced and dug my phone out of my pocket. I started to scroll to the screen shots I had taken of the WhiteLivesMatter chat room.

"Oh, crap," Alice said, reading my face correctly. "This isn't going to be good."

"No, Alice. It's the very opposite of good," I said bleakly.

I passed over the phone.

"This is a shot of an exchange on the WhiteLivesMatter webpage chat room from last night. I'm Ewell."

She took the phone and frowned so deeply at the screen I thought it might crack.

Then she looked up, mask in place.

"Blue again. So cops right? And a ghost? Jesus these guys are weirdos. But why you call yourself Bob Ewell? That's not a weird, jerk name, right?"

"Well, it's an idea I had," I said slowly.

"Naturally you had an idea," Alice said and reached for her inside jacket pocket. Then she stopped and just patted the outside. She was actually making me want to smoke with her visible struggle to cut down.

I quit stalling, took a breath, and plunged in.

"Bob Ewell is a racist character from that book *To Kill a Mockingbird*. I'm betting our friend Vampire726, or Demon196, and some of the others with those kind of weirdo names on the video game, are mostly students, but there's got to be crossover with this WhiteLivesMatter site. I just get the feeling, from watching the chats, that the website people might be outside recruiters, older types, some of whom could be cops. Like that 'Blue Leopard.'"

She nodded.

I let out a long breath and then rushed on.

"So I think a student will recognize the Ewell character from the book and know it's me and, well, come after me."

The damp wind blew Alice's hair into a froth of curls as she stared at the screen. Then she looked up at me and handed the phone back.

"You are so damn crazy."

I knew that. I silently put my phone in my pocket.

"I need coffee," I said, and I got up and headed to the coffee shop to get some. A small one. As I reached the door to go in, I smelled cigarette smoke coming from behind me.

*   *   *

Alice's "don't be stupid" farewell played over again in my mind as I sat in our faculty conference room waiting for what Adelaide had billed, in a mid-morning email, as a "short," underlined, emergency faculty meeting. None of the colleagues had yet arrived.

Before leaving the coffee shop patio, I'd argued back to Alice that, in my own defense, I didn't think rattling their cages to stir up these creeps was being stupid.

"Yeah, sure," Alice had replied grimly. "That's what you always think."

Maybe she's right, I pondered as I sat there in the empty meeting room. I always do think that, that is until all hell breaks loose.

Then I was startled out of this unproductive line of thought as the door opened, and Adelaide came in with Aduba. Donald followed on their heels.

Adelaide sat down heavily in the chair at the head of the seminar table. Her lined face was pale, and she looked exhausted. The large chair seemed to dwarf her. Her frizzy, grey hair lay flat against her skull like it was too fatigued to stand up around her head. I felt guilty that I had not taken time to go see her and find out how she was after she'd seemed so ill when we'd gone to the President's office. I told myself I'd follow her to her office after this meeting and not let her give me the slip.

Aduba sat down next to me, and he didn't look much better. His jaw muscle was working again, and I thought his face was thinner.

Donald sat alone on the opposite side of the table, and he had the nerve to have a healthy-looking, light tan. There was no sunshine in Chicago. How had that happened, I wondered? Then I realized he must use a tanning salon. I didn't think my opinion of him could get lower, but it did. He also had a self-satisfied look on his face. I felt myself getting angry.

"So, thank you all for coming," Adelaide began, making a visible effort to speak firmly. She looked down at some papers in front of her, then up at each of us, and she went on.

"I have had a request from the President's office that you cancel your lecture, Dr. Abubakar. The President is concerned that the school will not be able to provide adequate security."

"Well, finally this university has come to its senses," Donald blew out from under his mustache. He really needed to avoid sibilants.

"Shut up, Willie," I said and then realized I had spoken aloud. I was so tired I was actually speaking my mind. I'd have to watch that, but then I saw the look of pure rage on Donald's face, and I didn't regret it.

"May I remind you, Professor Ginelli," he hissed across the table at me, "you are a junior faculty member and will need my vote to retain your position?"

I leaned forward on my arms and made as though I would going to rise from my chair. I had the pleasure of seeing Willie shrink back, looking scared and ready to run if I actually did stand up. I settled back down and smiled at him.

"That's enough!" Adeliade said, breathing hard. "This is not about the two of you, so just keep it in check, will you, and try to act like professionals?"

"Sorry," I said to Adelaide, meaning it. I was just making this harder for her and that was bad form on my part.

Willie said nothing.

"Dr. Abubakar," Adelaide went on in a serious tone, her tired eyes fixed on him. "This isn't really a request, I think." She paused. "I sincerely hope we can reschedule your inaugural lecture for spring semester, but I can't promise that, of course."

Aduba was silent for more than a minute, looking not exactly at Adelaide, but at the stained glass window behind her.

"Thank you for that courtesy," he said, still looking out the window. "I am sure a lot of thought went into the President's decision."

I didn't know him well enough to judge whether he was being sarcastic. Then he stood up.

"I will cancel the lecture. Excuse me, please." And he left the room.

Adelaide slowly got up too and gathered her papers. I stood up as well and waited as she started to walk toward the door. Gone was her ability to sprint from a room, though I hoped not forever. I followed her out. Willie was still sitting at the table looking at some papers in front of him, so I turned off the light as I left.

"Follow, me, would you Kristin?" Adelaide said quietly as we got out into the hall.

"Sure," I replied, nonplussed. We walked silently down the corridor toward her office. I felt a little pang as I passed her excellent coffee machine, but I stoically just walked behind her into her office and shut the door behind me.

Adelaide made it as far as her couch, then just sat down and leaned on a pillow.

Now I was getting alarmed.

"Sit," she said a little breathily. "I can't talk with you looming up there." I sat.

"Okay. A couple of things," she said, her face pale and drawn, and her voice even more wheezy than it had been in the meeting.

"First, I've been talking to your friend Tom, and he has recommended a good cardiologist for me. I've seen him, the cardiologist I mean, and I'm scheduled to have a procedure this coming Monday. They're going to put in a stent, a kind of tube thing to keep an artery open, going to my heart. I'll be out of the office for a week to ten days."

Wow. Not good. Adelaide, mother-substitute, friend, and all-around anchor in my life, was seriously ill.

"Don't look like that," she said. "I'll probably only be in the hospital overnight, and then I can work from home."

"Seriously, Adelaide?" I protested. "I'd think you could take a little more time than that."

"Well, you're not my doctor, are you?" she said sharply, a little more herself. "And don't blame your friend Tom. I asked him to keep it confidential until I figured out what was wrong."

Oh, yeah? I thought.

"Anyway, here's the other thing I wanted to tell you." The breathiness was back, and she paused.

"The administration has accepted the offer of an anonymous donation for the Kim, Ay-seong Meditation and Prayer Room, and I need you to meet with the designer next week while I'm out."

"Of course," I said, "I'll do that," touched that she had pushed forward my offer even when she wasn't feeling well. I teared up. Fatigue, stress, and now worry for Adelaide were getting to me.

"Come on, come on," Adelaide said, with a touch of her old briskness. "Be glad we have something positive going on."

"Yes," I sniffed, "you're right." I paused and thought.

"I'll ask Aduba to consult, and Jane Miller-Gershman and her wife, the Rabbi, as well. I'll ask all of them if they can be here when the designer comes."

Adelaide nodded.

"Good. Here's the designer's phone number and email address."

She took a paper off of her coffee table and handed it to me.

"Shandra Lax, Sustainable Designs," was written at the top with the contact information below.

Okay. I didn't know how the university had come up with this firm or designer, but it was a start. I realized I did feel positive about this.

"And then we can have a dedication ceremony," I said with more energy, getting into the spirit of it. "I'll let her family in Korea know and see if Edwin Porterman could come back from London for that." Edwin had been very close to Ay-seong and had been devastated by her death.

"That's all good, Kristin," Adelaide said tiredly.

I came back down to reality and just went over to her desk where a carafe of water stood. I silently poured her a glass and brought it back.

She drank it slowly.

"Adelaide, I'm going to go get my car and drive you home," I said firmly, expecting an argument.

"Thanks," she said.

Oh. No argument. Not good. It was beginning to dawn on me how sick Adelaide really must be.

I hustled home, got the car and was back in less than twenty minutes. I parked in the loading zone behind Myerson. Adelaide had fallen asleep on her couch by the time I got back. I roused her and risked taking her down in the rickety elevator.

"Adelaide," I said after I had settled her in my car and was driving toward her apartment, "maybe you should stay at my house until Monday. I don't think it's a good idea for you to stay in your apartment alone this weekend."

"My sister Elaine's here," she said tiredly. "She came last night." She closed her eyes, and I thought she'd fallen asleep again.

"Besides," she said with a chuckle, not opening her eyes, "I don't think I'd survive the weekend with the constant energy levels of your darling boys, and, of course, the dog. And, really, especially you." And she fell asleep.

Well, she had a point.

* * *

I set my alarm for midnight and crawled into bed. A nap was essential if I was going to do any effective white supremacist trolling tonight.

As I leaned back on the pillows, I belched slightly from Giles's Senegalese peanut and chicken stew. It had been delicious, but the combination of garlic with ginger and cloves was now working on my already acid-filled stomach. I reached over to my nightstand and grabbed a handful of antacids. Too many late nights, too much coffee, and too much stomach-churning stress had caused me to buy an extra-large bottle of antacids and keep it handy.

The boys had gobbled up the stew and gone to bed without much grumbling. Carol and Giles had taken their portions upstairs, though they had both seemed less tense to me as we had exchanged a few words in the kitchen. I pondered their relationship as I crunched up my antacids. I hoped they were talking, working things out. I reached over to turn off my light and thought, as I lay back in the dark, about why I hadn't called Tom after hearing about Adelaide.

"I'm too tired for that" was my last coherent thought.

Chapter 23

do not just
slay your demons
dissect them
and find
what they've been feeding on

—ANONYMOUS

Saturday 1 a.m.

I had my tablet open to the video game "Revenge" and a pad on the kitchen table next to it. I had the WhiteLivesMatter website open on my computer and I had my cell phone connected to the Internet to do research.

My idea was to cross-reference the various pseudonyms and look for textual clues to see if I could spot commonalities in word patterns in the posts on the video game versus the website. It was possible we were dealing with a small group of actors only using different names in different places. I made a list of the actual names of persons who had come up in the investigation, or of those whom I thought might be involved, and then lists of all of what Alice called the "weird" names from any place I had looked. Now to do some critical analysis. I was finally finding something useful from my academic training in this investigation.

The most common weird names in the video game chat room that seemed relevant had been Vampire726, Moloch111, and Demon196. The annoying numbers made it that much harder. Over 700 Vampires, for heaven's sake. I just had to make sure the numbers matched. Moloch, we had determined, had been John and I drew a line on my pad from his name to Moloch. Vampire had clearly been Jacob Mayer. I drew another line. Those names no longer appeared, but Demon did. I scanned through the chats.

Demon196 was distinctive. He was very directive, lecturing and even cursing out others, but he had chat-speak down pat. A younger person, then? Who was Demon196? I could not draw a line for that name yet, though I had my suspicions.

Even though Moloch and Vampire were no longer on the chats, Demon196 was still messaging with Asteroth76. Looking at those chats, I suspected Asteroth was John's roommate, Brant Hingston, but I had no proof of that. I went back as far as I could in the "Revenge" chat rooms, using Asteroth76 instead of Demon196 to search. It was producing some new information. Asteroth76 interacted with Crawler, Volt, Daemonknight, and Traeyghrin.

I made some notes on those chats. The same kind of obscene patterns of racism and sexism appeared, but there were few specifics other than, "gotta get 'em" and so forth. Crawler and Daemonknight were not numbered. They used more complete sentences and even the occasional period, and I had spotted one comma. These demons were far less familiar with grammar-free chat-speak. Older generation? I marked those names on my list.

I wrote up some more notes and then shut down the tablet, logged off the game and just looked at my pad. What makes someone pick a particular online name? I'd picked Odin for his gender-bending characteristics, or, I thought suddenly, was that the only reason? To be honest, I also liked Odin's aggression and the fact that it was Odin who made the rules and followed no rules himself.

I'm not going to catch these guys unless I get inside their heads, I realized, and that means getting inside my own head. Uncomfortable thought. I had been looking at these white supremacists like the big snakes in the zoo the kids liked so much, but that wouldn't get me closer to figuring out who they actually were. I had to come closer and figure out what we had in common. Well, I did equate physical aggression with "doing something," like the shrink had said. I wrote that down at the bottom of the pad. That surely was Odin.

Then I sat back in my chair, almost physically jolted. What about the choice of Bob Ewell as my fake persona on WhiteLivesMatter? Yeah, I'd told myself I'd picked that vicious racist for literary trolling, had even laughed about it to myself. Ewell as a character typified the worst of white America, and that had nothing to do with me, the child of Scandinavian immigrants, right? Well, no. That wasn't right, really.

I tapped my pen on the pad. What is it about whiteness that these guys and I had in common? Crap. I so did not want to go there. But I wrote down the question. Then I thought about it.

Basically, being white meant I always assumed I was in charge. That's one, for sure. Yeah, like telling Giles what he needed to do instead of letting him decide, or my deciding what he should pay the lawyer. And worse, my late night conscience asked, would you really be willing to walk around in Alice's brown skin or had that just been your default bravado? Probably the latter, I acknowledged and bent back over my pad, making notes, looking down at the names I'd written, trying to see through them to the people who had chosen the names.

See through them? That made me think about the one who called himself "The Ghost" on the WhiteLivesMatter website. Ghosts were white but sort of invisible, right? Who was white among these names who wanted to be invisible, working behind the scenes?

Well, I thought, I'd better read up more on these demon names, and then research the biographies of my list of suspects.

Crawler, I discovered after looking at various websites devoted to demonology, was the demon name for a huge blob of flesh spotted all over with eyes and mouths. True to his name, he could crawl anywhere. Volts, I discovered, were flying, demonic eels.

Ick.

Daemonknight seemed pretty straightforward. That was the name of a demon that was a knight with red eyes. Traeghrins, I read, were massive demons with serpent-like bodies and a skull shaped like a woman. The drawings on the demonology websites showed the woman grossly sexualized. Well, nothing new there, I thought, as I went back to my pad and made more notes and drew more lines. Who hated women? Unfortunately, it seemed all of them did.

But then I started a biographical search. It was helpful and fairly horrible how much you could find out about people's history just from a regular, online search.

I went on with this, going back and forth, until I realized I was starting to do the same research over again. Too tired. I packed everything up and took it up to my bedroom. I put on my pajamas and then decided I'd check on the boys and Molly.

All seemed peaceful, but Mike had kicked off his covers so I went over to his bed and tucked them around his feet.

I stubbed my toe on something hard under the edge of Mike's bed. I massaged my toe and then bent and picked up the hard object off the floor.

Oh, no. It was Mike's tablet. The tablets were supposed to be kept in the family room on a shelf and used only when Carol, Giles, or I were around to supervise.

I had also installed parental controls on both Mike's and Sam's tablets. With a bad feeling, I carried the tablet to my bedroom, sat down and tapped the screen, put in my parental passcode and clicked on the browsing history. Mike had managed to get around the parental controls, it seemed, by going to an approved website and then surfing from there. With my heart in my throat, I looked at the places he'd gone. He'd checked out various games and had spent time with one car racing game. No single shooter games, at least.

I went back to their bedroom and used my cell phone light to look for Sam's tablet. I found it under a cushion on a chair in the corner. They had both clearly hidden the tablets.

I unlocked it and tapped the screen. He had the same browsing history as Mike.

I put the tablets on my dresser, turned off the light, and then just sat in the dark.

This is how they recruit them, I thought, and shivered.

* * *

When the sun came up, I went downstairs to fix coffee. I drank the first gulp of scalding liquid down so fast I didn't even feel it until I registered my throat hurt.

I needed to talk with Giles and Carol before the boys got up. We'd need a united front. I went upstairs to the second floor and listened at the bottom of the staircase that led to their third floor apartment. I could hear movement, so I texted both of them that I'd like to meet in the kitchen now if they had the time. A text came back immediately from Carol. "Be right there."

When they came down the stairs, I just asked them to follow me to the library, and I headed there, carrying the tablets. I shut the door behind us.

I wasted no time. The boys would be up very soon.

"I found these hidden in the boys' room late last night." I turned on the tablets and handed one to each of them, open to the browsing history.

Carol looked at the screen, gave a sharp intake of breath and looked up at me, her freckled face pale. Giles uttered what I knew to be a French expletive.

"Yeah," I said to both of them. "My reaction too."

"Well," said Carol, her voice low, "we certainly need a better place to keep these than on a shelf in the family room."

I nodded.

"No, it is not just that," Giles said, his eyes narrowed behind his glasses. "They will get around that somehow, sometime. At a friend's house, perhaps. They must be warned. And rewarded."

"Rewarded!" I burst out. "For what?" My fatigue and my anxiety made my voice very sharp, but Giles did not take offense.

"Punishment, and there must be some privileges denied for a while, will alone only make these forbidden places even more enticing. They have been very smart about this." Giles tapped the screen of the tablet. "They should be given a coding game and some lessons to show how to be creative without getting into danger."

Well, crap. Giles and his pacifism sometimes really ticked me off, especially since he often seemed to be right. Forbidden fruit is the tastiest. At least that's what St. Augustine thought when he was a kid, and he stole some fruit.

"Yeah, okay, Giles." I looked at both of them. Then I paused, hating to show weakness, knowing that was a flaw in me. I sighed.

"I'm just so scared."

Giles nodded. Carol's eyes glistened.

"You are not wrong to be scared," Giles said in a low tone.

I heard the boys in the kitchen calling our names.

"Let's talk to them here, after breakfast. All of us."

*　*　*

Three sets of brown eyes stared at us. Then Molly lay down and closed her eyes, so it was just the two, Mike and Sam, with Marco's eyes, looking apprehensively at me, Giles, and Carol.

I held the tablets on my lap and as soon as they had come in they had seen them. Standard interrogation technique. Let the suspects realize they are caught.

"Explain this," I said sternly, tapping the screens of the tablets.

Sam looked over at his brother and his upper lip quivered a little, but he was silent.

"I mean, like, what? Those are our tablets," Mike said, and I realized he was going to try to brazen it out.

I stayed quiet.

"Yeah, well, we took 'em to our rooms. Sorry," Sam said in a rush, not able to hold on to his anxiety completely and mimic Mike's stonewalling.

Mike nodded, but I could actually see in his assessing look he was trying to judge how much I knew.

I just looked at them, waiting.

"And we did stuff, too. Sorry." Sam was cracking. His upper lip was really quivering now.

Mike stayed silent, so I opened one of the tablets, the one with Mike's name on the top, and held it to the side so they could both see it. I entered the parent passcode and scrolled to the browsing history.

"Yeah, well, that's the stuff we did," Mike said. At seven, it's hard to stonewall for too long.

"Tell me the stuff," I said sternly. "All of it. Starting with you, Mike."

"Well, I went there," Mike pointed to the bottom of the page at the beginning of the browsing history, "and then I saw I could get there because it's like called a mirror. It's the same but not blocked," he pointed again, "and then I figured I could search from there, and then I opened that," he pointed farther up the screen, "and well, then we played that." He looked up at me and a brief look of satisfaction crossed his face.

Good grief. He knew about mirror sites, sites that are proxies for other sites, and he knew that the blocking software apparently doesn't register them.

Meanwhile, Sam was nodding away.

Christ. Giles was right. They were proud of it, especially Mike who was admitting he had been the one to figure it out.

"Here's the thing," I said, and stopped, trying to keep my anger within bounds that would scare them some, but not blow them out of the water. Hard to do, when I just wanted to scream.

"The thing is," I started again, "when you do this, when you go on the Internet to places that grown-ups don't think are safe, there are bad guys looking for you. Trying to get you. Trying to trap you. Trying to lead you to maybe message with them. Be their friends. But meanwhile they want to hurt you. Hurt you bad. Who do you think makes these mirror sites that aren't blocked by parent software? People who want to hurt kids."

Sam was now openly crying. Mike looked shocked, but I could see part of him was also weighing my words.

"This is the truth," Giles said. "Your mother is telling the truth. I have seen this, know this." Carol nodded.

"So here's what's going to happen," I said sternly. I outlined a complete ban on all tablet use and TV time for a month. There were actual gasps of outrage.

"It could be longer if you try to push me," I said, letting the anger show a little more.

"But then," and I glanced at Giles, who nodded. "You also have been very smart. Just not in the right way. So we'll look into getting you a coding program and teaching you how to do that. Then you can write your own games and not have to go looking for them."

"All right!" Sam said, tears drying on his cheeks.

"Thanks," Mike said quietly.

"I hate parenting in the age of the Internet," I thought to myself.

Chapter 24

Anger is easy. Forgiveness is hard.

—SUSAN THISTLETHWAITE

Sunday

I sat at the kitchen table, listening to the sound of the boys yelling in the backyard and Molly barking. As far as I could tell, the boys were pirate captains, and Molly was the crew. It was so peaceful, these sounds of play. But it didn't make me feel peaceful. I was still angry and deep down totally frightened.

I knew I should call Tom, but I was not in a good place to have a civil discussion about why he had kept Adelaide's condition from me and especially not willing to hear that he'd been right to do that. And I was scared for Adelaide undergoing that surgery tomorrow.

My cell phone rang. Tom calling me. I hesitated, but then pressed "accept." Did I accept, I wondered, as I said a cool "Hello, Tom."

"Do you have time to take a walk along the lake?" Tom asked quietly.

Did I? And did I want to?

Carol was studying in the library. I could ask her to relocate to the kitchen for an hour, keep an eye on the pirates outside.

"Let me check," I said, and put down the phone. Carol, when I asked her, said she was fine with watching the boys for an hour.

"Okay," I said, not able to get past the frigid tone in my voice. "Where?"

"What about we meet up where the lakefront path crosses in front of the museum?" Tom said, clearly having thought this plan out.

"Yeah, fine. Half an hour." And I hung up.

＊　＊　＊

I saw Tom's back from a distance. He was on the path where it curved oppo-site the museum, looking at the lake. The air was so clear, I felt like I should be able to see across to Michigan. I stopped and looked at his tall figure, waiting for me, and I felt my anger give way, like an ice dam breaking up along the shore in winter, taking some of the fear with it.

But not all. I started walking again and soon came up behind him.

"Hi," I said quietly.

"Hi, yourself," Tom said and, as he turned, he just put his arm around me. More ice in the dam gave way.

We stood silently looking at the play of sun and clouds on the immense expanse of this body of water, so beautiful and so quickly treacherous. It had almost killed me once.

"Adelaide asked me to keep her condition confidential," Tom said matter-of-factly.

"I don't like it, but I get it," I said, realizing that I did.

We turned and started walking slowly north, into the light breeze, at first in silence.

But I had to know.

"What are they going to do to her? You can tell me that, right?" I asked.

Tom gestured to a bench on a little hill ahead of us. We sat, and he turned to me.

"What did she tell you herself?"

"Well, just that she's having this surgery tomorrow to open an artery, and it really sounds serious." I clasped my hands in front of me and gazed at the unforgiving expanse of water.

"It's actually not that serious," Tom said in his doctor voice. "They will make a small cut in a blood vessel, either her groin, or her arm or neck. Then they thread a small line up through that to the blocked artery. That tube has a little balloon at the end of it, and they'll inflate that, opening the artery. Then they put the little mesh stent in there to keep it open. The mesh stays there, but the balloon and tube come out. She'll be a little sore where they make the incision to insert the tube and somewhat tired, but she can likely go home on Tuesday. Most of the time, people are actually awake during the procedure, just with some light anesthesia."

"Awake? Really?" I imagined the tube snaking through a blood vessel and shivered.

"Sometimes. And it only takes about an hour. You'll probably be able to see her shortly afterwards. There's very little risk to this, though obviously always some."

I focused on some birds out over the lake, dipping and gliding on the air currents.

"I just want her to be okay," I said slowly, realizing how much Adelaide meant to me. She was not only a mentor, but also a parent-substitute, like the Ginellis. My own parents were kind of the anti-Ginellis, stone cold and unloving.

"Don't worry so much," Tom said, putting his arm around me as we sat on the bench. "I know the doctor doing this. She's excellent."

"Well," I said slowly, "speaking of worry, that's not the half of it." I went on to tell Tom about the boys and their bypassing the parental controls and how that had scared me given what I was seeing in my late night trolling of these vicious video games.

"At seven?" Tom said, turning to look at me, his face registering his shock.

"Yeah, exactly," I said grimly.

"I worry about this with Kelly, of course, and we've talked about the danger online. I have her computer password, and I've checked her browsing history occasionally, but what you're saying is she could go to one of these mirror sites, and I'd not know what it was. Is that right?" His voice was thick with tension.

"Yeah. I think that's right." I turned to him and put my hand on one of his that was gripping his knees. "It's like there is this filth right below the surface of our lives, waiting to suck young people down into the depths, getting into their being, corrupting and threatening it. It's been a horrible thing to look at, let me tell you." I paused, holding on tighter to his hand. "But I'm glad I have. I would hate not to know that horror is there and what it can do. Has done."

We sat for a while in silence, the wind coming up to make jagged waves that burst on to the shore.

*   *   *

I gave up trying to sleep. It was after midnight, but my anxieties just kept feeding on each other. Might as well troll the idiots online.

I checked the chat rooms of the "Revenge" video game as Odin, but I didn't see any of the cast of characters I was following. I logged out of that, and went over to WhiteLivesMatter in my Bob Ewell persona. I searched around for any chats that seemed relevant, not posting anything myself, but I didn't see anything either.

I was starting to get drowsy and thinking of logging off when a Direct Message popped up on my screen, startling me.

Ewell u there?

It was from a JRiver. Not a name I knew. I typed back.

Yeah

JRiver Direct Messaged back and we chatted.

theres a meet Mon nite u in?

maybe who r u?

a white soldier

what meet?

White Pride uni group

yeah sure can get wf that

midnight stay sharp 4 place

ok

I waited, but there were no more messages. I took a screen shot and texted it to both Alice and Mel with a suggestion we meet Monday after-noon at the campus police station and make a plan.

I shut down my computer and turned off the light. The next thing I knew it was morning, and Adelaide was about to have surgery.

Cell Phone Text

Monday 2 a.m.

Is it done?

Man use the burner this is stupid

Shut up about that. Is it done?

Yeah yeah done keep yr shirt on & use burner

Just do what I say u little s***

Chapter 25

A silly idea is current that good people do not know what temptation means. This is an obvious lie.

—C. S. Lewis, *Mere Christianity*

Monday

"Don't hover," Adelaide said sharply, though there was still a little more breathiness to her voice than normal.

She was lying on a bed in the recovery room, and I thought she actually looked pretty good for someone who'd had a tube go through a blood vessel and stick something in an artery. She had some more color in her face than she'd had recently, and her eyes were focused and clear as she ordered me to step back from the bed where I was, indeed, leaning over her. The chilly, little, white-on-white room had two chairs, and I took one. Her sister was already sitting in the other one.

I had waited with her sister Elaine while the procedure took place. It had seemed like an eternity, but my watch said it was only a little over an hour until the nurse had come to fetch us.

Tom had actually texted me that he'd stopped by during the procedure, and all was going well. I'd shared that information with Elaine who'd just nodded. She looked eerily like Adelaide, same hair color, height, and weight down to the same flowing dresses. She was a slightly younger version is all, and she was not a chatty person, to say the least.

Then the same nurse came, asked us to step out of the little cubicle, and she'd pulled the curtain across.

Apparently Adelaide had passed the "you can go to a room now" test as we were informed when the curtain was pulled back.

Elaine followed the nurse into the corridor, however, and I took the chance to speak directly to Adelaide.

"Are you really okay?" I asked, hovering again.

"Yes," she said firmly, "and you need to get to the office. Philosophy and Religion is getting a little thin in the ranks, and we don't want Willie to take it into his head he's in charge."

Oh, God no.

"Yeah, well, you're right. I'll head over there and lock him in his office if necessary."

"Atta girl," Adelaide said, and then she closed her eyes.

I said good-bye to Elaine in the hall and headed to the office. I looked at my watch. It was only 9:30 in the morning.

*　*　*

It was very quiet in our corridor as I approached my office. No sign anyone was in yet. Our previous faculty secretary, Mary Frost, had retired, and she'd not been replaced with a full-time person. A work/study student came in three days a week, for what purpose I didn't even know. I'd seen her once, checking her cell phone while sitting behind Mary's old desk. Naturally.

I spent some time composing an email to Aduba and Jane about meeting with the designer for the Ay-seong Kim prayer room. I also added, in the Jane email, that I'd appreciate it if she'd ask her wife to join us. I was careful to indicate to both of them just that Dr. Winters had asked me to follow up on this while she was out of the office. I proposed Friday for that meeting, pending confirmation from the designer, and I'd attached her online resume.

Then I sat back and started to think about the Direct Message I'd received last night in my persona as Bob Ewell. Alice had texted earlier this morning that she and Mel would be in her office at one, and she'd added "what do you think you're playing at?" But we both knew it wasn't play.

I needed coffee in order to be able to think, I realized, so I went down the hall and filled the well of the De'Longhi with water. I also wet a cloth, cleaned the stainless steel machine until it shone, and I straightened up the table. Adelaide must do this every morning, I realized, as I'd not found the coffeemaker empty of water before. I pressed "brew" before I could get too maudlin about missing her.

I took the steaming cup of dark coffee back to my office and took out my pad of notes on the cast of characters we were dealing with. I sipped and thought.

*　*　*

"They know who you are," Mel said, tapping the copy of the DM he'd transferred to his tablet, "and they're just trying to draw you out." He, Alice, and I were sitting around the small table in her office.

"Yeah, I know they know it's me. But we don't know them. Not yet," I said flatly.

"What the hell is the matter with you?" Alice said, shaking an accusing finger at me. "You're makin' yourself a target again. And how'd that work out last time, huh? Huh?" More finger wags.

"Well, we got him, didn't we?" I said. I knew where Alice's anger was coming from. She was scared for me. The finger she was wagging at me was attached to a hand that was shaking a little.

"So," Mel said, and his dark face had all the expression of a statue on Easter Island, "for the sake of argument, what are you thinking?"

Alice snorted and said another "huh," but didn't add anything else.

"Well, presuming JRiver lets me know a location, I will go there. I thought you both could be on patrol, so to speak, near the location. I don't think there's a meeting, really, I think it's a set-up, probably to kill me."

"Now wait a damn minute," Alice blew up. "'Kill me', she says, like it's no big deal. Really, how are you still alive bein' so damn crazy?"

"I'll wear my vest," I said, going on, "and as soon as I can make an I.D., I'll call you in your car on my cell. Then I'll try to take cover, and you both can just do the rest."

"Bah," Alice said. "You forgot what happened the last time you oh so smart, and you gonna draw the guy out, and it blew up in your face? Come on."

I didn't answer. She was right.

"Why do you think whoever this is wants to kill you?" Mel asked quietly.

"Because I'm pretty sure I know who they are, some of them at least."

I turned to Alice. She had that look on her face that stopped students in their tracks. I swallowed and spoke.

"I told you I'd chosen the name Bob Ewell to hook a student who would know that character from literature. It's working, clearly." And I tapped the tablet too.

"Look, it's clear the police are not investigating the way they should. What does that tell us? We have to make them show themselves, and I can't think of another way."

We all sat silently.

"Tell Gutierrez, or not?" Mel asked abruptly.

Hmm. The subtext of his question was whether Gutierrez was so tied into the police he'd tip somebody off, accidentally or even on purpose.

"Not," Alice said in a low voice.

"So, let me outline this," Mel said, and he reached for a pad and pen. He made a timeline and indicated assignments.

"Where are the weak spots?" Mel asked when he had an outline.

"The whole damn thing is a weak spot," Alice said grimly, drawing the pad over to her and starting to make changes.

She was right.

But we had to try.

Chapter 26

Dionysius says (Div. Nom. iv) that "the multitude of demons is the cause of all evils, both to themselves and to others."

—Thomas Aquinas, "The Assaults of the Demons," *Summa Theologiae*, Question 114

Monday evening

It was 11:45 p.m. and I was walking down the main street that led to campus. At 8 p.m. "Bob Ewell" had gotten a DM from "JRiver" on the WhiteLivesMatter website. "*White Pride midnight basement Chapin.*" Midnight in a basement? What romantics these jerks were turning out to be.

If JRiver was who I thought he was, I believed he thought he was playing with me, trying to spook me. I messaged back "*got it*" to JRiver and logged off. I had immediately let Alice and Mel know, and they'd acknowledged they'd be in place, per Alice's final plan.

Earlier in the evening, I'd read the boys (and Molly) the next chapter of *White Fang*, the adventure story I was reading aloud to them. I thought tonight the title was more than a little ironic. When I'd finished, I kissed them and turned out the light.

Now I stood in the doorway of their room, listening to their even breathing. Was I risking too much? I wondered as I looked at their little bodies snuggled under the covers. Their lives would never be the same if something happened to me, their last remaining parent. But what kind of a world did I want for them growing up? Not this one. Not one where neo-Nazis were on the rise.

I went to my bedroom and got out my bulletproof vest. Aduba had returned it to my office the previous week, but the side straps were still extended. I shortened them and tried it on. The feel of the vest always gave me a little adrenaline charge from remembered ops.

I let Carol and Giles know I was leaving. I had read them in on Alice's plan earlier in the day. I checked my watch. It was 11:30 p.m. Time to go. I had on black jeans, black, long-sleeved T-shirt, and running shoes. I put on a loose jacket on over the vest and pulled on a dark knit hat. I put my cell phone within easy reach in my pocket, Alice's cell phone number already on the screen.

The plan was I'd just get close enough to old JRiver to positively identify him, then I'd call Alice and Mel, and, optimally, have time to take his picture before I ran for cover. Then Mel and Alice would pick him up. That is, if JRiver was the only one who was coming. I had my suspicions who else would be showing up to greet me well before I reached Chapin.

It had rained earlier in the evening and rolls of bleak, dark clouds raced overhead toward the lake. The roiling clouds obscured the moon, and the only light was from the occasional streetlight that had not been broken. There weren't many.

I heard footfalls behind me. I was being followed and very poorly. I walked on toward the cross street where I knew Alice and Mel were parked a block north. I reached that spot and stopped. My follower stopped too.

I turned and called out.

"Hello, Demon196, or should I just call you Jordan? And really, Jordan. You called yourself JRiver? Jordan River? Very trite.

"What the hell do you think you're playing at?" I continued as I took out my cell phone to call Mel and Alice.

"You c***!" Jordan started yelling, and then there was a ping and a bunch of brick off a low wall near where Jordan was standing exploded. He screamed.

Damn it. Someone was shooting at us using a silencer, and from the angle it looked like they were aiming at Jordon. It also seemed like the silenced shot had come from the north, the same direction as where Alice and Mel were located.

"You're trying to kill me like you killed John!" Jordan yelled, startled.

"No, you idiot," I yelled back as a stone cap on the corner of the same wall next to him exploded, "I'm not armed. We have to duck and run, Jordan. We have to get away! I think it's you he's aiming at. Follow me."

I ran south down an alley opposite the low wall toward the big, grassy mall that bisected the campus where the new, giant art installations had been placed. I just needed to get behind the building at the corner to call Alice and Mel.

I heard footfalls behind me but farther and farther back. I was outpacing Jordan. At least I hoped it was Jordan and not the shooter. I risked a look back and yes, it was he, scurrying along, gasping for breath. Geeks are so out of shape.

I reached the corner and turned, digging out my cell phone. I pressed the number on the screen and nothing happened.

"I hacked your phone," Jordan wheezed as he came up to the end of the alley. "You have no service now. He's gonna arrest you, you murderer."

I grabbed his arm and pulled him around the corner.

"What are you gibbering about, Jordan? I didn't kill anybody. And If you're so sure I'm a murderer, why are you running away from the shooter?"

"You killed John!" he shrieked, pulling away from me to run towards the big statues that loomed up out of the gloom on the mall.

"Who told you that lie?" I yelled after him.

"We know it's you and that weirdo N***** you live with, you did it. Probably with that Mudslime too. You did it," Jordan sobbed as he ran into the open.

I shook my head, just amazed. It was like these guys were in a cult, and they'd drink the Kool-Aid even when part of their mind knew it would kill them. What had that Trump guy said, he could shoot somebody in public, and his followers would still support him? That was how deeply Jordan was sunk in this mindset. He could run away from someone shooting at him, run toward me, in fact, and still be convinced I was a murderer. It was so bizarre.

I checked my cell again. Still no service. I couldn't just stay here. I'd better risk running out into the open after Jordan. I hoped he had his own cell phone, and I could convince him to call Alice and Mel.

I sprinted out from behind the building across the open space of grass toward the huge, weird shapes looming ahead. I heard another ping, and I quickly ducked behind the first statue. It must have been fifteen feet high, and it appeared to be made of metal. Good. I thought I could see Jordan's shadow as he crouched behind a statue about thirty feet away. I called out.

"Who is 'we,' Jordan?"

"You don't know, do you, c***? Blue lives matter more than black ones. He's gonna catch up with you. You'll go to jail!" Jordan's voice was quavering, but he sounded like he was close, now just twenty feet away from me, behind another statue.

Just then three more pings caused the metal on the installation where he was hiding to ring like gongs.

"Watch out!" Jordan yelled loudly. "You're missing her! You're missing her! You almost hit me!"

"He's aiming at you, Jordan," I said in the calmest voice I could manage. "You have to know who it is. It's a cop, right?"

"You don't know anything, do you, you N*****-loving whore!!" Jordan screamed as more pings caused more metal to fly off the statue where his voice was coming from. "We run deeper than you jerks will ever know."

"It's Al Brown, right Jordan? He's 'The Ghost,' but what you need to realize is that he's the one who killed John Vandenberg, and now he's trying to kill you. Listen to me. He's not here to arrest me. He's here to kill you because you know who he is right? You figured that out, and he can't risk that. Then he's going to kill me. He's not even a cop now. Did he tell you? I heard from a lawyer who filed a complaint against him that he's been suspended.

"Look, Jordan! Your life depends on this. Call this number and tell the person who answers where we are." I repeated Alice's cell number several times.

"You're lying!" Jordan said, but I could tell from his voice he was weakening.

I'd begun to suspect Brown when I researched his work history and realized he had formerly worked for ICE. It made the ICE connection and their focus on Giles come into focus. And Al had spent so much time being second banana to Kaiser. That had to have been humiliating. The shrink's insights had been helpful. I hated Kaiser so much I had fixated on him, wanting him to be the murderer until I realized what a powerful motivator resentment was for these white supremacists. Brown was a tower of resentment.

I moved laterally toward the statue to the right of where I thought Jordan was hiding and decided to try to test my suspicion. I pressed "record" on my phone. Even if I couldn't make calls, I might still get a confession recorded.

"I'm right, aren't I, Jordan? Al Brown is your cop mole?" I called out.

I could hear Jordan sobbing, but he didn't confirm one way or another. And I bet he'd not called Alice's cell number. I was just about to risk running toward where I thought he was hiding when a shadow came around a tall statue to the left that had large struts and what looked like a windmill on top.

The clouds parted for a second, and I could see the long, bony outline of Brown.

"Be quiet, Jordan. Al Brown is stalking you," I called to Jordan.

"Yeah, right!" Jordan yells. "Sure, blame the cops you race traitor."

I checked my phone. Still no service. Rats.

Now I could see Brown in the watery moonlight. His thin, long face was twisted in a horrible smile. He was holding a gun with a long silencer in two hands, walking purposefully toward the statue where Jordan was hiding. One more statue was in his way, and then he'd have a clear shot.

"Jordan," he said almost conversationally, "I'm going to be glad to kill you, you stupid, arrogant jerk. I bet you've got tainted blood just like that half-breed Vandenberg. We need to wipe you mongrels from the face of the earth. Then I'll kill her and make it seem like she blew you away. And I'll never have to listen to you again, you miserable snot."

His gun flashed twice and I heard Jordan scream "No, no, not me, her!" Jordan was so indoctrinated even when Brown admitted he was trying to kill him, he didn't believe it.

"Brown!" I called as loudly as I could, trying to draw his attention away from Jordon. "Did you get tired of being Kaiser's gopher? You know just being white doesn't actually make up for your licking his boots for years."

"You can shut up now," Brown said in the same conversational tone. "I'll get to you in a minute after I finish off this idiot."

"Hey!" Jordan exclaimed in outrage. Well, Brown was right about one thing, Jordan was an idiot.

I was thinking about how to take Brown down without getting shot myself when my phone text tone dinged. I must have regained service. I looked at the screen and the incoming text said, "*Yr welcome*" with the Antifa symbol below. I looked up and under a distant streetlight I thought I could see a figure with a hood and scarf over its mouth. Then it disappeared.

I pressed send immediately, and Alice came on. I let her know where we were and that Al Brown was armed with a gun and silencer. He was trying to kill Jordan.

"Keep your head down," Alice said and hung up.

I couldn't do that.

I could see Brown's shadow moving past the big windmill statue, and then he would be behind the next one. It looked a little less sturdy. It was now or never. I couldn't let him just kill Jordan.

I put my phone in my pocket, record still on, and ran full tilt at the statue. I jumped at it with both feet. It wobbled but didn't go down. Brown got off a shot at me but only through the material of the statue itself. I felt a little burn on my arm, although the bullet had spent some of its force. I moved to the side of the statue as Brown tried to scramble around it to get off a clean shot at me. I put my back against the statue and pushed as hard as I could. The whole thing fell over and landed on Brown's legs. He screamed in pain.

Jordan came out of his hiding place, but I could see Brown was still holding his gun, despite his legs being smashed under the weight of the statue. He yelled a string of curses and pointed the gun at Jordan.

"Get back behind that thing, you idiot," I yelled at Jordan. He jumped back. Not soon enough. Brown got off a shot, and it seemed to catch Jordan in the shoulder. He wailed and fell down.

Then Brown fell silent, and his hand opened, releasing the gun. He seemed to have lost consciousness. I raced around the twisted pile of metal and what looked like broken balsa wood framing and kicked the gun away.

Jordan was lying on the grass, holding his shoulder and yelling a blue streak.

"S*** it hurts. S*** it hurts," he kept saying.

I walked over, and he looked up at me and said piteously, "Help me."

I looked down at him.

"You'll live," I replied coldly. The "unlike John" thought I kept to myself.

"Hey!" he yelled, outraged, as I walked away.

I went over to where I had kicked the gun and peeled off my jacket one-handed to use it to pick it up. Then I sat down on the grass myself and called Alice's cell phone and gave her a quick update so they'd know what they were walking into.

Mel answered.

"We're only about a hundred yards from you now."

I could now see their headlights and their flashing lights as they drove across the grass. I took out some tissues from my jeans pocket and put pressure on my own arm. Brown's spent bullet had still been able to tear a gash in my forearm, and it was bleeding.

Before the car had hardly stopped, Alice jumped out and ran toward me. She crouched down next to me.

"You okay?" she asked, looking down at the wad of bloody tissues.

"Yeah," I said. "Just a gash."

"Who are those two?" she asked as she took off her own jacket and put it on my shoulders.

"The guy under the statue is Detective Al Brown, currently suspended from the Chicago Police force. The kid," I nodded my head toward crying Jordan, "is a student, Jordan Jameson. He's Demon196."

"We called the Chicago cops while we were racing over here. I'll call the EMT's now," Alice said as she pulled out her phone.

I listened as she efficiently described our location and the injuries. It wouldn't take long. From where we were, I could actually see the corner of the university hospital emergency room.

In fact, the wail of sirens could now be heard in the distance.

Mel was bending over Jordan, putting pressure on his shoulder. Jordan was babbling.

"He shot me. That cop shot me. He tried to kill me. Why'd he try to kill me?"

Alice and I looked at each other in disgust, and I got up to walk over to Mel and Jordan, keeping the pressure on my own arm. I had only a few seconds to try to wise Jordan up before the Chicago cops got here, and, when Brown regained consciousness, I was sure he'd start lying his head off.

I crouched down next to Jordan.

"Look Jordan, Brown told you he was going to kill you, make it look like I had done it, and then kill me while he pretended to try to 'save you.' He wanted to silence you. You knew who he was, didn't you? He couldn't risk that."

"He used his regular cell phone to text me, can you believe it?" Jordan whined. "I mean I knew right away what his real name was. I made him get a burner, but he still used his own phone sometimes." Jordan shook his head in disbelief. That seemed to jar his shoulder, and he took some shuddering breaths.

"What did he tell you to do?" I asked, and I hoped my record function was still on.

"He told me to just draw you out of your house and follow you. That was the plan." Jordan sniveled. "Then he'd arrest you. That's what he texted. That's all. Check his phone. I didn't know he'd be here shooting. Jesus, he shot me." He moaned and lay back on the grass. I hoped he'd remember it was Brown who'd shot him before his white supremacist ideology shut him down. At least I hoped I had a phone recording to back it up.

I took my phone out of my jeans pocket and looked at it. Yes, the red record button was still lit. I hit save and then moved away from Jordan and sat back down on the grass.

Alice crouched down next to me again and took over putting pressure on my arm.

"Same arm?" she asked.

She was talking about how she and I had met. Alice and Mel had been the responding officers when a mugger had put a long gash in my forearm with a knife.

"Nope," I said, smiling over at her. "Other arm."

"Still. Seems like old times," she said, deadpan.

We both laughed.

Chapter 27

The demon is a liar. He will lie to confuse us; but he will also mix lies with the truth to attack us.

—WILLIAM PETER BLATTY, *THE EXORCIST*

Tuesday

The two injured jerks had been taken away in ambulances. Mel and Alice had explained to the two Chicago police officers who had arrived that Al Brown was a suspended Chicago detective and the shooter. Mel had produced the gun, still wrapped in my jacket. We'd all seen that Brown hadn't worn gloves, he'd been so arrogantly sure he'd kill his targets. His prints should be all over the gun. Mel had gone on to explain that Jordan Jameson was suspected of being a student in league with Brown.

One of them, a tall, white cop with a close cropped military haircut, grimly produced an evidence bag the second time Mel asked for it, and Mel had dropped the gun into it. Mel prudently asked for a receipt, citing chain of evidence. The cop, Alan Hanson per his name tag, looked pissed off, but took out a pad and wrote out the receipt.

I admired Mel for a lot of reasons and especially then. He was so savvy. The gun could have gotten "lost," it's true. The blues tend to protect their own.

That same cop then started to question me aggressively. I was glad I'd taken off my bullet-proof vest, and Alice had thrown it into the trunk of their car. No point in aggravating this angry cop any further.

I knew better than to talk to an angry cop without my attorney, but I just used my bloody arm as an excuse to go to the ER to get treated. I said I would come in later today and make a full statement if he'd tell me where and when. We'd argued about that for a couple of minutes, Alice and Mel backing me up, citing my role as a campus police consultant. Finally, after taking my information, and giving me a time and location for the interview, they let Alice and Mel drive me to the ER. But a Chicago police car followed us.

In the car, I called Tom and woke him. It was 3 a.m., I was shocked to find. I have to say this for Tom, he goes to being totally asleep to totally alert in about five seconds. He said he'd meet me at the ER in about fifteen minutes. I didn't doubt it.

As we walked into the ER, Mel and Alice said they'd wait until Tom came. I checked in at the front desk and told the nurse sitting there I'd wait for Dr. Grayson. It was wonderful how fast the ER personnel worked when you brought your own surgeon. I was quickly ushered into a freezing cold cubicle (why do they keep these ER rooms so cold?), offered a chair and given a nice, warm blanket. Shortly thereafter Tom opened the door.

"Seems like old times," Tom said, his tired blue eyes revealing his concern even as he joked. That's how I'd gotten to know Tom. He had fixed the gash from a knife wound the night Alice and Mel had brought me in after the mugging.

"That's what Alice said," I joked back, and I smiled vaguely at him, suddenly feeling a little woozy. I must have lost more blood than I'd realized and shortly Tom was helping me to get up on to the examining table and lie down.

I felt a cold swab and then a pin prick that I thought must be the anesthetic. I let my eyes close, just to rest them, I said to myself, and I must have fallen asleep.

I awoke to Tom taking my blood pressure. Whatever it was, it must have seemed okay as he helped me sit up. There was a nice, neat pad on my forearm and some gauze holding it in place.

"Not too bad," Tom commented, seeing me look at the bandage. "Just seven stitches."

"Wow. Seven. I didn't think it was that bad," I said, a little shocked.

"Well, the bullet tore at the skin some," Tom replied as he helped me stand up. "That's why it was bleeding like it was."

He took my arm.

"Come on. I'll drive you home and get you to bed."

As he pushed open the door, he said, "I can't stay because I need to get home to Kelly, but you'll be fine. Just stay at home and rest today."

Rest today, I thought groggily as we walked across the street to the doctors' parking area. I couldn't rest. I had a class.

By the time Tom walked me up the stairs to my bedroom, I realized teaching was not in the cards. It was after 4 a.m., and I was exhausted.

Besides, I'd need to tell them their classmate had been arrested. I just wasn't up to it.

Tom helped me undress and get into bed, then he gave me a quick kiss on the forehead and was gone.

I had smuggled my cell phone into bed with me. I opened my university email account and sent a group message cancelling Tuesday morning's class. Then I texted Carol and Giles, telling them briefly I'd gotten in at 4 a.m. and would sleep in a little having cancelled my class. We had managed to get two of the perpetrators arrested, I added. Then I sent a brief email to Anna, indicating I'd need her later today because I had to give a statement to the police about some suspects I'd help catch. I added time and location.

Then I shut off the light, and knew no more.

* * *

I jerked awake because my hand felt cold and wet. I opened my eyes and saw Molly had nosed up my hand at the side of the bed so it was on her snout. The boys were kneeling on the opposite side, staring at me. I registered they were dressed for school.

"Hey, everybody," I said in a fake cheery voice. I patted Molly on the head and retrieved my wet hand.

"So what happened?" Mike asked, in very much the same tone I imagined the police would use questioning me later today. His dark eyes and serious face reminded me so much of Marco I swallowed.

I sat up against the headboard but was careful to keep my bandaged forearm under the covers.

"Well, good news. Alice, Mel, and I got two of the bad guys. They've been arrested. I think one of them was the guy trying to get people to hassle Giles. And one was a student who was doing all sorts of hateful things online."

"That great," Sam said, bouncing a little on the bed. I tried not to wince.

"Are there any more of them?" Mike wanted to know.

I thought for a minute about lying, but I decided against it. It would comfort them for a while that "we got all the bad guys," but then there would be more arrests. At least I hoped there would be more arrests.

"No, I don't think that's all of them," I said, looking both of them squarely in the eyes in turn. "I hope we'll get some names from the two we've captured, but I think there's more." In fact, I was sure of it.

"When I get big, I'm going to be a cop like Dad," Sam said seriously. "Then I can help you get lots of bad people, and we'll put them all in jail."

"Sounds like a plan," I said. Sam jumped down off the bed and ran down the hall. Molly ran after him.

"You get hurt?" Mike asked, looking with suspicion at the arm still under the covers.

"A little," I said. "I had to get some stitches." I raised the bandaged arm and placed it on the coverlet.

"How many?" Mike asked. He was going to be a fine lawyer.

After I'd answered Mike's questions about the gash and the stitches to his satisfaction, we heard Carol call they'd be late for school, and he got down off the bed and left. I could actually imagine him with a small brief-case heading to another interrogation.

I thought I'd better call my other lawyer, Anna, and plan for today's interview.

* * *

Anna and I were back in a crummy interrogation room in District 5. She looked great in a red, fitted suit jacket and black slacks. In fact, she looked a little like Elizabeth Warren. I had to glance down to remember what I was wearing. Oh, yes. Brown slacks and a three-quarter length cream-colored blouse that ended at my elbows. The cops would clearly be able to see my bandaged arm, and Anna had insisted I use a scarf as a sling to really show I was the injured party.

We sat, not speaking, while we waited for Officer Hanson to arrive. Since Kaiser and Brown had been suspended, and Brown I hoped was under arrest in some hospital, I wanted to know who had taken over investigating John Vandenberg's murder.

I had talked at length to Anna, first on the phone this morning and then in her limo as she gave me a ride. My arm was hurting, and I really didn't feel like driving. She had cautioned me to let her ask the questions about both Brown and Jameson.

Finally the door opened and Hanson came in with his scowl in place on his chiseled, "I'm a super-cop" face. He was followed by a medium-height, medium-aged, and medium complexioned guy in a tan suit. If this guy stood in front of a beige wall, he might literally disappear.

Hanson introduced himself to Anna but did not speak to me. Beige guy took out two cards and put them in front of us.

"William Somerset," he said in an even voice. And that was it.

I looked down at the card as did Anna. His rank was detective.

Hanson immediately leaned forward toward me and started firing questions.

Anna held up a manicured hand and he ground to a halt.

"My client is prepared to read a statement and then she will sign it. Any questions you have will go through me."

"All right," Somerset said mildly.

"Before my client begins, however," Anna continued, getting out a pad and pen from her briefcase beside her chair, "Please tell me your full names, your rank, and your relationship to this investigation." She clicked the pen and waited.

Hanson got very red in the face and made a sputtering sound. Somerset, on the other hand, just complied.

"I am a Detective out of District 6, and I have replaced Detectives Kaiser and Brown in the Vandenberg investigation. I am also lead detective on this case." All this was said in such a smooth monotone I nearly nodded off.

Hanson grudgingly gave his rank as sergeant and added, "Responding officer to incident." He spat these words out like each one gave him a pain in a tooth. Why was he so angry, I wondered?

Anna nodded to me, and I got out the statement I had typed up one-handed this morning at her instruction.

I could do monotones too. I read it at a moderate pace, and I went over my actions the previous night, from walking to a meeting to which I had been invited, to realizing one of my students, Jordan Jameson, was following me, to realizing Jordan and I were being shot at by a gun with a silencer, to running away, to hiding behind the art installations on the mall, to recognizing Detective Al Brown, currently suspended, holding a gun with a silencer and shooting at Jordan, to getting shot myself (and I pointed to my bandaged arm in case they hadn't noticed it) by Brown, to kicking over the statue on to Brown to keep him from killing Jordan and myself, a threat he had made verbally and that I had caught on tape, to calling the campus police number and summoning help. At no time had I been armed, I added at the end.

"Do you have this recording with you?" Somerset asked mildly when I had finished.

"I will email it to you," Anna replied coolly.

"Now, listen up," Hanson burst out. "Why were you even . . . "

Anna talked right over him.

"Has Albert Brown been arrested? And what charges are being brought against Jordan Jameson?"

"Now wait a damn minute," Hanson sputtered. "You waltz in here, won't let us question your so-called client, and now you want us to answer questions? Dream on, lady."

"It will be in the public record," Anna replied in her law professor voice, totally dismissing him.

Somerset said nothing.

"Sign that, Professor Ginelli, and we will leave," she said, gesturing with her beautifully ringed hand to the printed document on the table and then handing me her pen. I signed and dated the document and left it on the table.

"Thank you," Somerset said in his soporific voice. "Your information will help with charging both Brown and Jameson." He pulled my document toward him.

Anna and I both nodded and headed for the door.

"What the hell?" I could hear Hanson asking Somerset.

Anna's limo was waiting, and we both got in.

She immediately started reading emails on her cell, and I called Alice.

"You arrested?" Alice asked as a greeting.

"Nope," I said. "Just gave them a written statement, and we left."

"Huh," Alice said.

"What about Gutierrez?" I asked.

"Now he pissed off," she said. "But mostly with you, I guess. We're all supposed to meet him in his office at three today."

"Let's meet in your office at two," I suggested.

"That'll work," she said, "I'll tell Mel."

And she ended the call.

* * *

Alice, Mel, and I had agreed we'd stick to our story. After all, I mused as we walked down the hall together toward Gutierrez's office, we'd better hold the line on that as otherwise I would have given false information to the police. Not a good idea.

Mel knocked, and we heard a barked "Come in!" We walked through the empty reception area and through the door to Gutierrez's private office.

Captain Alfonso Gutierrez stood behind his desk, and one look at the rigidity of the deeply carved wrinkles on his face told me he was furious. Even his huge, black mustache was rigid.

"Sit," he said, indicating three chairs in front of his desk, but he didn't sit down himself. He wasn't a tall man, but I thought for a second he might have grown a few inches from the steam that was filling him up.

He looked at me for a full minute. I was familiar with this technique, and I resisted squirming and I held his eyes. That seemed to help some, and he sat down in his chair.

"Give it to me, Ginelli," he said with no preamble. "What the hell happened?"

I didn't even glance at Alice or Mel.

He already knew about the chat rooms of the violent video games and how Mel had scoped out the code that led us to catching Jacob. I didn't think it would hurt to remind him of that, and he gave one sharp nod. Then I tacked on extending my own online trolling to the WhiteLivesMatter website and finding some crossover, as well as some indication that there were potentially Chicago police involved.

I didn't think Gutierrez's frown could get any deeper, but it did. Some of those wrinkles began to look like cracks in the Chicago streets after a long winter.

I kept going. I ran through the fake invitation to the "White Pride" meeting on campus, and then I went through nearly verbatim what I had said in the written statement I'd given to the police this morning. And I included the names of the officer and the detective to whom I'd given these statements.

Then it was Alice's turn and then Mel's. They stuck to our story that they had been on patrol, and I'd called them from the mall where the art installation was located.

Gutierrez didn't comment as each of them spoke, but his black eyes drilled in to each of them. When they finished, he sat silently, clearly thinking.

I hazarded a question.

"Captain Gutierrez, do you know if Albert Brown and Jordan Jameson have been arrested?"

He focused on me, and his anger showed in his deeply craggy face again. I actually began to think it wasn't the three of us he was angry at.

"What I know of Brown is not from the official channels of communication. There I have been shut out. Have been for some time."

He sighed deeply.

"But I know some people. I called. Brown is in the University Hospital with two broken legs and is being treated as a 'person of interest.' He has been saying you tried to kill Jameson, Ginelli, and he was merely trying to protect the young man. Since you are not arrested, I think he is not believed. There is that little matter of the gun you secured, Officer Billman, with his fingerprints all over it, and with this tape you tell me you made, it will be difficult for him to deny."

He paused.

Difficult, but not impossible. Other police have been on tape and still are not sent to prison.

"This Hanson, my friend says, has very shall we say 'conservative' views?" Gutierrez looked like the word 'conservative' was not his first choice for an adjective. Ah, another cop white supremacist. Great. Gutierrez's anger was becoming more understandable, and we were getting to the part that had really pissed him off apparently.

He went on, "And the detective, Somerset, is a *culo besador*, you understand me?"

"Ass-kisser," Mel translated, deadpan. I was glad he did. I'd taken French in school.

"Quite so, and possibly brought in after the suspension of those other two *cabezas de mierda*."

"Shit heads," Mel contributed. Well that was pretty close to the French, so I'd gotten it.

Gutierrez was on a roll, and he continued. These were more words than I thought he had spoken in the months I'd known him.

"Now on the student, Jameson, I know more because the Dean's office has told me this much. His parents have hired him a lawyer, a good one, the Dean thinks, and Jameson will likely not be arrested. Not if he cooperates."

"What do you think we should be doing now, sir?" Alice asked.

"I am 'not-in-the-loop' you might say," Gutierrez said bitterly. "I think we must focus on our own campus. These students, Mayer and then Jameson, it is likely they are not the only ones drawn in to this garbage. We must root it out on our own campus."

"And if the ones recruiting them are police?" I asked.

"We root them out too," Gutierrez said, and I was sure from how his mustache was bristling that boded no good for crooked cops.

∗   ∗   ∗

I was walking slowly back across campus toward home when my text tone sounded.

I looked at the screen.

"What the hell? You cancelled your class? Why? Winters."

Oh, good. Adelaide was feeling better.

Chapter 28

With artificial intelligence, we are summoning the demon. You know all those stories where there's the guy with the pentagram and the holy water, and he's like, yeah, he's sure he can control the demon? Doesn't work out.

—ELON MUSK

The following week

A lice and I were sitting at an outside table at her favorite coffee shop. It was my opinion it was getting too cold to be meeting outside, but yet here we were. Alice had out a cigarette, though she hadn't lit it. Yet. She had taken to holding cigarettes and twirling them between her fingers. She was getting quite good at it though her fingers must be freezing.

The piercing west wind was driving across the midwestern plains, and it seemed it was aiming directly at our table. I shivered and took another sip of hot coffee. We were the only ones sitting out here. That was good because what we were discussing should not be overheard.

"So, yeah," I said, continuing. "I met with Somerset again, though this time at Anna's office. He keeps asking me 'am I sure,' and 'don't you think Brown actually meant . . . ', trying to catch me in a contradiction." I sighed. "I just let Anna answer. It's ridiculous how obvious he is. It's clear that audio-tape I made is a big problem for them, and they can't just let Brown off the hook for attempted murder." But how big a problem, I wondered? Cops had gotten off scot free even with videotape of them choking unarmed people. Gutierrez was right.

"You just be careful, you hear?" Alice said sharply, pointing her unlit cigarette at me.

"Yes, I hear. What do you hear?"

"Well, cause there's students involved, Gutierrez has gotten some info from that Somerset. Some good, some not so good."

She paused. Fiddled with her cigarette.

"Well, what?" I asked impatiently. I was going to have icicles hanging off my nose in a minute because it was running from the cold, and the snot was going to freeze. I swiped at it with a tissue and took a big swig of coffee. The coffee was cooling.

Alice finally went on, consulting her little notebook.

"So, Gutierrez has been told that the Jameson kid's computer has been confiscated. And the kid's told Somerset, apparently through his lawyer, that they should check Brown's cell phone. If you can believe it, the kid says he warned Brown not to use his own cell, use a burner. Brown blew him off. Seems like the kid is pissed off at that, not just about getting shot. And yeah, he's said he's Demon196 and JRiver."

"Well, to add to that," I said, "here's something Anna told me. She's been pressuring the D.A. to convene a Grand Jury and indict Brown. Just go around Somerset, actually."

Alice nodded, looking pleased.

"Yeah, but the D.A. told Anna about those texts between Brown and Jameson, and he told Anna they don't exactly show it was Brown who killed John. They think they need more to tie him to that. But they'll probably indict him for shooting Jordan and me. Brown was keeping Jordan in the dark about who really killed Vandenberg, trying to keep him believing it was me and Giles."

Alice took a few notes, and then she took out her matches to actually light the cigarette.

Oh, crap. I thought I was about to hear the "not so good."

She took one puff and then started reading from another page in her notebook.

"So the kid also told the police that John's roommate 'knows plenty' about John's murder and that they need to 'grill him.' Can you believe it?"

Then she took a giant drag on her cigarette and flipped some pages. She was stalling, I thought. Then she grimaced and read off her notes.

"Kid said 'Brant told me how pissed they all were at John. He's a N*****, can you believe it? And some R****** too, hard to believe.' That's supposed to be direct what he said."

She looked up with a face carefully wiped of expression, and she took a short drag.

So, Tom was right, I thought. "Twenty-three doesn't lie" meant John's despair at his DNA test results.

I shared that with Alice, who put down her cigarette and took a few notes.

I waited until she stopped writing.

"Here's another thing, Alice, that I think you should pass on to Gutierrez, see if they can get the Brant kid to admit it, that is if they investigate him. Did Gutierrez say Somerset had said they would?"

"I don't know if he knows," Alice said dully. An investigation conducted by someone like Somerset who was trying his best not to investigate was beyond frustrating.

"Well, the thing is, you know I saw that shrink, and what I'm thinking is that killing John and setting me and Giles up for it wasn't the main point. The main point was that they had to purge John from their group because it was a massive betrayal, and he needed to be killed to keep the group 'pure.'"

"Huh," Alice said, her head bent over her notebook as she wrote.

"Gimme that shrink's name and contact info," she said without looking up. "I'll pass that on to Gutierrez. Maybe he can get a consult."

"Yeah, exactly," I said, and scrolled on my phone contacts, read Dr. Fisher's information off to her, and she wrote it down. When she finished, she looked at her half smoked cigarette lying on the metal table, and she took it over to the smoker's trash can.

"Couple more things," she said after she had sat back down. "That other kid, Mayer?"

I nodded.

"Jameson's emails with him show he was kind of a pawn. Didn't help hang the noose, but he did try to make those posters. Now, worst thing for that Jameson kid is that some files in his computer show he's the one who hacked the university system, spread that filth about you and the Muslim prof. So he, and his fancy lawyer, and his parents, are having to deal with the Feds. No chance he'll get off from that."

Oh, God, I thought, really shocked. Funny, smart Jordan would have to do time. He had given himself the right online name. Demon. The world's religions often warn that demons can destroy you when you summon them. It's inevitable. His life was wrecked. That attack on Abubakar and me had been horrible, and it would follow us probably forever. But it would basically destroy Jordan and really hurt his parents. You can't just play around with evil and not have it affect you as well as others. Lives get ripped apart. My hatred for this white supremacist ideology just boiled in me. How the hell had they gotten him in so deep, I wondered? But then, I thought, don't think he's an innocent child. He had done what he'd done. For what, though? To feel powerful? Special? Part of a giant social scam?

I really felt sick.

Alice and I parted, she promising to fill Mel in and follow up with Gutierrez. I promised to keep her in the loop about what Anna found out and anything I learned.

But no more outdoor meetings until spring, I promised myself. I went into the warm coffee shop, threw away my cold coffee, and bought a big, hot cup. And sat down to thaw out and to mourn.

*　　*　　*

It was a Tae Kwon Do night, but with my arm I thought I shouldn't take the class, or even drive. I called Kelly. I asked if she'd walk over to our house and drive my car. Since she'd just gotten her learner's permit at fifteen, she was thrilled to be asked to drive. I'd have to drive the short distance back after I dropped her off, but I thought I could manage that.

The boys were equally thrilled when I said we'd be going to class, and they raced upstairs to get into their uniforms even before they'd had their dinner.

I'm neglecting them for this investigation, I thought as I listened to the bumping and slamming coming from upstairs.

Neglected kids try to find parent substitutes online.

I won't let that happen, I promised the ceiling as I heard them ragging on each other.

Chapter 29

I never thought of it as God. I didn't know what to call it. I don't believe in devils, but demons I do because everyone at one time or another has some kind of a demon, even if you call it by another name, that drives them.

—GENE WILDER

Monday of the following week

I was still tired from not sleeping well, and I slowly trudged up the stairs to our office floor. When I reached the landing, however, I got a little energized. The work on the Kim, Ay-seong Meditation and Prayer room had started. We were using the correct Korean order for her name on the plaque that had been ordered.

I just stood there in the hall for a while to watch the two workmen as they stripped the room of its ugly, stained, paneled walls, and dragged out the awful fluorescent light fixture with the dead flies in it.

Despite all the campus upheaval, our committee had met several times with the designer, Shandra Lax, largely due to the efforts of Jane and her wife, Rabbi Gershman, to get us together. Before we'd convened for the first time, however, the Rabbi had asked if she could invite a local Buddhist leader, Azan Nakshatra, to join us. I'd emailed briefly with Adelaide to check with her, and she'd replied, shortly, "It's your party." I gratefully contacted Azan, as he immediately asked me to call him, and he had joined us. He was terrific. I was thinking of recommending to Adelaide that she ask him to teach an adjunct class on Buddhism. It was a scandal, really, that Philosophy and Religion no longer had a Buddhist teaching classes. We'd lost the guy who taught Buddhism to the computer sciences.

Aduba had made all of the meetings and was engaged. I so hoped this prayer room signaled to him that he was welcome, that he was one of us. As white supremacist attacks in this country and around the world got more horrific by the minute, that was a signal we couldn't send too strongly.

Sustainable Designs and Shandra in particular had proved very easy to work with. We had a simple and yet, I thought, both serene and flexible concept. The room had to accommodate prayer and meditation by many faiths and persuasions, and it was small so it was tough not to load stuff in and make it feel cramped. But, in fact, the worst part had been how to let people know when the room would be in use. After our committee had argued about it for a while, a small metal "In Use" or "Not in Use" device, kind of like on airplane bathrooms, would be permanently installed on the door, and certain reserved times, as for Muslim prayer, would be listed on a sheet in a frame next to the door. Aduba had agreed to take charge of that one, since we had no permanent faculty secretary.

Adelaide had started coming back to the office late last week, though she wasn't arriving as early as in the past, and the coffee-prep had fallen to me. Adelaide's doctor had told her she had to give up caffeine, and she was stubbornly refusing decaf. Well, who wouldn't? I felt terrible for her. I headed down to the coffee machine, straightened up, added the water, checked the supply of coffee and emptied the donation jar. The rest of the stock was in my office.

* * *

I finished with the coffee set up and headed over to Jane's office. She and I had had a couple of conversations after the design meetings about what to do regarding the continued turmoil on campus. There was bad feeling all around, a kind of rancid, oil slick on the surface of community life made up of equal parts of suspicion, anger, and fear. You could practically smell it. It was polluting and hard to get rid of.

Jane's idea was that we think about prevention, and I was good with that, though I didn't see how it could work. I was heading over to meet with a pastor from Michigan she'd invited, the Rev. Dunn she'd mentioned before , the person who knew about video game chat rooms. He'd developed workshops for parents and separate ones for young white guys to help these groups identify the issues that made these guys vulnerable to white supremacist online recruiting.

We met in Jane's office, and I politely refused the herb tea she made that tasted like stewed leaves and twigs. She gave me a wry smile when I declined. Rev. Dunn had brought his own coffee in a to-go cup from the excellent coffee shop on campus. I recalled he was a graduate, and he knew his way around. I warmed to him immediately.

Rev. Dunn was younger than I had imagined. He seemed to be in his early thirties with a pale face, and dark, stick-straight hair that spilled over on to his forehead and brushed his deep, brown eyes. He was wearing jeans, boots and a faded, blue, crew-necked sweater. No clerical collar for Rev. Dunn, at least not for this meeting.

He didn't waste time on pleasantries.

"You have to use a multi-faceted strategy," he began. "It's not only parents, it's faculty members and administrators who need training for the warning signs of early recruitment."

He took out some material and handed it to me and Jane.

"Here, use these. I wrote this stuff based on the work I've been doing, and what I've learned works and doesn't work."

Jane glanced at the pages and then spoke.

"I think this will be helpful, Ethan," she said in her quiet voice, "but we need to get people talking about the idea of prevention." She paused, looking at his intense face.

"Do you think you could come back, give a talk in the chapel that we'd advertise heavily, and then do a follow up interview with 'The Register'? We could make what you've got here available and people might actually look at it if there was a campus-wide effort."

It was a good idea. "The Register" went out electronically and not only to the campus, but also to alums, parents, and donors. It could create some buzz and then there'd be demand. I nodded but didn't speak.

"Yeah, sure," Dunn said briskly, "I'll do it. Give me some dates. But look," and he leaned forward in his chair. "You have to be prepared to go further."

Drawn by his energy, I leaned forward too.

"How?" I asked.

"There is a need for undercover work to figure out who are really the instigators of this recruitment online then get their information and ultimately expose them to the administration for discipline or expulsion in the worst cases. This is called 'bash the fash,'" he said, without a trace of irony.

"Of course," he went on, "the worst of the instigators will be outside agitators, so you'll need to have a legal strategy to pursue them."

Whoa. I liked this guy. Then I glanced at Jane, and she was frowning. Dunn picked up on that frown.

"Look, Jane, think about the power you have as a university chaplain and how you can deploy it."

"Well, let's start with the lecture, shall we?" Jane said noncommittally and went over to her desk to get a huge day-planner. I didn't know people still used those.

They conferred together about dates while I sat and thought about "bash the fash," i.e. "bash the fascists." I wondered what my acquaintances in Antifa thought of that. Perhaps they'd even invented the phrase, I mused.

Suddenly I realized Jane and Dunn were both standing up, and they seemed to be finished with date planning. He said he had to be going. I shook his proffered hand, and he hustled out. Really focused guy. I liked him a lot. He wasn't just going to tut, tut from his pulpit and let young people get recruited into hate.

I looked at Jane.

"We can't ask students to spy on other students," Jane said firmly.

"No, I agree with that, Jane," though I wondered about Antifa and what they'd be willing to do. I'd learned that Anarchists were very hard to direct, however.

"I do think I can bring that up with the campus police and see what we could and could not do," I said as I reached down for my backpack.

"Well, be that as it may," Jane went on, tapping the cover of her day planner, "we'll get this lecture going right after winter break."

She gave me the date. I dug out my phone and entered the info into my electronic calendar.

It was clear that a lecture and educational events were the limit of what Jane thought she could do from the chaplain's office. I didn't think she was wrong about that, in principle, but I agreed with Rev. Dunn that it wasn't enough.

As I walked back toward my office, I thought more about the idea of online, undercover work. I thought it needed to be done by the campus police because of the high risks involved and not by students. There had been a murder, my colleague and I had been threatened, Giles had been harassed, Jordan and I had been shot, Jacob expelled, plus it looked like Jordan was going to jail. Really, the whole campus had been harassed with the hanging of the noose and the leaflets. I thought horribly, this is not the end. It was likely just the beginning if we didn't work to disrupt it.

I reached the office floor and was pleased to see that the bigger debris from the demolition had already been removed. I could hear scraping sounds from inside the future meditation and prayer room, but I didn't go check.

Just as I sat down in my office, my cell phone rang. It was Alice. Good. I had been planning to call her.

"I was just going to call you," I answered, thinking about what Rev. Dunn had said.

Alice broke in.

"Brown has died from a heart attack."

"Oh, my God," I burst out.

"Yeah, well, I don't know if God did it or not, but apparently Brown had a bad heart. Was being treated for that for a while. He had made bail, gone home from the hospital and had a part-time caregiver because of the broken legs. The caregiver found him dead in his bed. He'd been dead several hours."

I digested that.

"Meet in your office?" I asked.

"Coffee shop," she said and hung up.

Well, she needed the nicotine.

* * *

"So," Alice said, twirling her unlit cigarette. "That's all I got from Gutierrez. Mel was there too."

"So Somerset let Gutierrez know?" I asked, hands clasped around my hot coffee. It actually wasn't as windy today, so I was not completely frozen.

"Didn't say. Gutierrez is so pissed off, hard for him to speak for the words he's keep'in in his mouth," Alice said, now using the unlit cigarette to punctuate her words.

"Yes, well, that's not hard to understand. He knows or suspects a lot he's not saying."

"Yeah," Alice said, and she patted her jacket, feeling her lighter but not using it. I had never heard of this way of cutting down on smoking, just going through the motions of smoking but not actually smoking, but just like Alice it was unique. And maybe even working.

My caffeine habit had not improved at all, I thought, as I gazed down at the huge to-go cup I had. Maybe I could get small cups.

"So you said you wanted to talk, what about?" Alice asked, interrupting my self-flagellation.

I summarized the meeting with Jane and Dunn.

"Huh," Alice said and twirled her little cigarette baton, thinking.

"It's gonna be a no go," she said finally, her face set in the bleak lines that were appearing more and more frequently. I so hated these white supremacists it could choke me if I let it.

"Well, maybe, maybe not," I said, pushing on. "Let's get Mel involved and then go see Gutierrez and maybe even ask that guy Steve White to come too," I said talking it through with her and myself. "As campus cops and a consultant, we will be looking for incitement to violence, not spying on students. We'll have to make that clear. It isn't 'free speech' when it is hate speech that provokes harassment and ultimately violence."

"I'll let you make that argument, Perry Mason," Alice said dryly.

Then she switched back to Brown's death. She thought Brown's death would "seal the deal" for the investigation into John's murder to go nowhere.

I didn't think she was wrong, but part of my mind was on Dunn's point about outside recruiters. Some of those, maybe all of those in this mess, were cops. Could Hanson and/or Somerset be among them?

How to get at that?

Alice got out her phone and checked it.

"I gotta go," she said, tucking the unsmoked cigarette away in her little box.

"So, listen, I'll talk to Mel and if he agrees, then I'll tackle Gutierrez first if you want," I said.

"I want," Alice said.

"Then you'll ask Steve?"

"Sure, since it will never happen anyway," she said in a dull voice, and she turned away to try to do her job.

"Dirty cops" I thought as I followed Alice's example with the non-smoking smoking and threw away most of my coffee. How much had white supremacists infiltrated the Chicago police force? Small wonder Alice's shoulders were hunched forward as she walked away. Her body was closing in for self-protection.

I needed to get back online, probably to the WhiteLivesMatter site as that seemed to be where we suspected the cops hung out. I'd stopped going to the chat rooms or the website, but there was no other way forward that I could see but to resume doing that.

I'd need a new white guy identity and screen name, I thought, and I pondered new names as I walked back to the office. Bob Ewell was completely blown.

WhiteKnight, I thought. Simple, like these idiots. I'd probably have to be WhiteKnight2000 as there would be lots of other WhiteKnights.

Good. Safety in numbers.

*   *   *

Wednesday

"Good idea, I'm in," Mel had said in his deep voice when I'd called him about pitching the idea of several of us keeping an electronic eye on students and looking for signs of white supremacist recruitment. Mel was a man of few words.

So we were back in Gutierrez's office, and Steve White had joined us at Alice's request.

I had expected a little push back from the Captain, but he too had given a short, affirmative answer by email when I'd asked him for a meeting and had given a brief description of what we might do.

"Run that by me again," Gutierrez said when I'd pitched the idea at greater length, and he focused his gaze on me. Not a gaze to be taken lightly.

"So the idea this pastor, Rev. Dunn, shared is that the online communications of students need to be monitored for signs of white supremacist recruitment or plans to engage in acts of harassment or even physical violence," I said, not even pausing for breath. Gutierrez was frowning so deeply at me, I felt like a perp.

He was silent, and the four of us shut up too.

"Going to be tricky," he finally said, tapping a pen on a blank pad he had in front of him. "Probably needs to go through the President. Only he could authorize this."

"Tell him to think about what will happen if we don't do this, and there is more harassment and violence," I said sharply, and Alice turned her head slightly to give me "the look," the one that paralyzed students. Yeah, probably not a good idea to lecture the captain like that.

Gutierrez didn't even seem to notice, though.

"You know all the campus groups will have to be scrutinized. They won't go for just checking on the white supremacists." Tap, tap, tap on the blank pad.

"Yeah," I thought to myself, "more than likely. But that doesn't mean that's what I have to do."

"We can do that," Mel said firmly. I was startled and thought for a second he was responding to my unspoken thought. But he wasn't. He was just stepping up as he always did.

WhiteLivesMatter Website

Blue Leopard: White Genocide is coming I tell you we have to get rid of all the breeds trying to pass as white trying to pollute our purity gotta get 'em all

Direct Message WhiteKnight903 reply to Blue Leopard: Yeah get 'em but how?

Reply DM Blue Leopard to WhiteKnight903: they used to know how to do this in the old west get a rope and you'll know what to do

Reply DM WhiteKnight903 to Blue Leopard: I get you I get you

Chapter 30

In the realm of hatred and anger, and other negative emotions, demons are the masters.

—ALEXEI MAXIM RUSSELL, *FORGOTTEN LORE: VOLUME 1*

Wednesday

I was sitting in my office at work, pondering what I had so far in figuring out this whole conspiracy and especially who had killed John. I had been on the WhiteLivesMatter website for the last two nights, direct messaging with "Blue Leopard." He checked a lot of the boxes the psychiatrist had mentioned. He was a furious misogynist, ranting about what a "white c***" had done to "The Ghost" who was "really a man" and "a patriot," and he resented the way he was forced to "give a s***" about those "N******" who should be sent back to the jungle, not given a job and on and on. And he loved talking about the "old West" and ropes.

I took my notes on "Blue Leopard" and used my personal tablet, not my university computer, to go over to the video game "Revenge" and search back again for chat room messages by Crawler. I suspected Blue Leopard was also Crawler. Then I went to a new screen and re-read the description of "Crawler" in the "Demonicpedia." Yes, there was an online encyclopedia of demon names. Why not? Crawler, as I recalled from my earlier search, was the demon spotted with eyes and mouths all over it. Leopards had spots all over them.

I was narrowing the search. I thought I now knew who this was. I had done a background search of the person I suspected, and there were lots of tells. He had been at ICE with Brown, and now he also worked out of the same district as Brown had. He'd also been suspended twice based on citizen complaints of misconduct, reinstated both times. Both complainants had been African American women.

I had taken screen shots of all these interactions and sent them to Mel and Alice, but I'd also started copying Gutierrez. He hadn't emailed me not to, so I kept doing it.

I thought I had enough to bring him my idea. I used my cell phone and called him.

Astonishingly he picked up his own phone.

"I need to see you," I said without preamble. "I think I know who our murderer is."

"4 p.m.," he said and hung up.

I texted Alice and Mel that I was meeting with Gutierrez at 4:00 p.m. about what I thought I had. Could they join me?

Mel didn't reply, but Alice just replied "*Ok*," and let it go at that.

I met Alice in the hall outside Gutierrez's office, and I said I was surprised I hadn't heard back from Mel.

"Family crisis. He's in South Carolina," she said curtly. Her constant, low level burn was very much in evidence. And again, I thought, why not? It was surely warranted.

I had a batch of print-outs of the screen shots I had taken of what I thought were the relevant posts of both "Blue Leopard" and "Crawler." I had also downloaded a photo from the Chicago Police Department website of the person I thought used those online names, as well as a bio page for the person I suspected.

"What are you proposing?" Gutierrez said slowly, having looked at all the material and listened to me.

"I need an appointment with that FBI agent, Paul Lindsay, that we met in the University President's office."

"Why him?" Gutierrez asked, tapping again on a blank pad.

"Well, because frankly I don't have any idea whom to trust in the Chicago Police Department. I think Lindsay at least will take this material and use it himself because it is a conspiracy being conducted online, and I think that's cybercrime, or he'll know who should get it." I paused and looked at Gutierrez's increasingly pained face. "Otherwise I think it will get buried."

Tap, tap, tap.

I glanced over at Alice, but she was giving nothing away. Her face was a mask of non-expression.

"Yeah," Gutierrez finally said. "I'll do it."

He turned to Alice.

"Officer Matthews, if we get the appointment, I'd like you to go too as a representative of this department. I'll let you know if I do, and when and where."

"Yes, sir," Alice said quietly. But then she glared at me for a second. Alice was not happy. I used my strategy of shutting up and just nodded to the Captain.

*   *   *

The next morning Alice and I were sitting in an anteroom in the downtown FBI offices, waiting for Lindsay. I'd offered to drive, but she said she'd take the train and meet me there.

Lindsay arrived with what was clearly another agent, a tall, grey-haired, Arab American with one of those beards that framed his jaw, wearing an "I'm an FBI Agent" dark suit. Introductions were made, and we learned the new agent was "Kamal Nadar," and he was with the "Counterterrorism Unit." Great.

The two men ushered Alice and me into a spacious office with a conference table. Lindsay gestured us to seats and offered coffee or tea. I bravely declined coffee. Alice glanced at me, raising her eyebrows. I was already caffeinated enough with finding out we were meeting with a counterterrorism agent.

"So, Professor Ginelli, I have heard from Captain Gutierrez that you have collected some material for us," Lindsay began.

I cleared my throat, and I reached down to a large purse that I was using as a substitute for my backpack. Somehow carrying a backpack into FBI offices didn't seem like quite the thing.

"Yes, yes, I do." I had fortunately made multiple copies of the screen shots, the bio data, and the photographs. In addition, I had a new screen shot Alice had not seen from late last night. It was a threat.

"Blue Leopard to WhiteKnight903: Bitch needs to die. Avenge The Ghost."

When I passed that one to Alice, she looked up, horrified. Well, I'd been pretty horrified too. It was a death threat. Against me, apparently.

"So, I said," trying to control my trembling, "I think this pattern of screen names of both Blue Leopard and a demon called the Crawler is the same person." I took a minute to describe Crawler and its spots, noting also that leopards have spots. "And 'Blue' tends to be online code for police. There is a Detective named Horace Williams whom I have previously met. You have his photo there." I pointed to the copies. "And that's his bio. He has had a lengthy relationship with Albert Brown.

"Williams has moles all over his face and hands and likely over all of his body. When I was interviewed by him one time, I got a very clear sense of someone who has probably been treated cruelly because of what he looks like, and he has learned cruelty. I think he has gotten drawn in to this white supremacist network because of what he looks like, and he is harboring barely concealed rage at how he thinks he is treated because of that. He's turning that into rage against minorities, as ironically the black spots of his moles could seem like his skin is trying not to be completely white, and he has to ruthlessly suppress that."

Was I sounding too much like the psychiatrist? I ground to a halt.

Lindsay was reading the papers with the screen shots, but Nadar was looking at me with a steady gaze. I tried not to squirm.

"You could be a profiler," Nadar said finally.

I felt I really should give credit to Fisher, but Nadar was continuing.

He turned to Lindsay.

"I think we need to investigate Williams, get confirmation that he is indeed the one called 'Blue Leopard' and also 'Crawler.' Then we can get a warrant. This last one, the threat, is ominous." He tapped the page with the last screenshot with a long finger. "He's accelerating."

Alice nodded, looking at me.

"Agreed." Lindsay stood up, gathering the papers I'd given him.

"Professor, keep a low profile. We'll get on this."

He glanced at Nadar and seemed to get a wordless confirmation.

"Agent Nadar's task force is looking at white supremacist infiltration in the Chicago Police Force. He has been brought here to do that. Trust me when I say we'll get on this."

Nadar gathered the papers in front of him, nodded at Alice and me, and they both left the room, I thought a little rapidly. Good gad. Did they always walk that fast, or was this really an emergency?

Alice came up next to me, and we walked out of the office, over to the elevator and out to the street in complete silence.

Once out on the street, Alice took my arm.

"You okay?" she asked, looking up at my face.

"Not really," I said, still trembling a little. I knew she could feel it.

"Well, you need an emergency coffee." And she dragged me to a corner coffee shop that had outdoor seating. Yes, and Alice needed an emergency cigarette.

What I really needed was wine and chocolate. I kept that to myself. "I'll get that when I get home," I thought and followed her to the corner.

When we'd had our drugs of choice, I drove her back to Hyde Park. After she exited the car, she leaned back in.

"You even know what 'keep a low profile' means?" she asked in her stern "don't mess with me" voice.

I nodded.

"I do, Alice."

"Huh," she replied and walked briskly on to the campus.

* * *

I was home by noon, and I rattled around the house. Everyone was gone. Molly was glad to see me at least. I thought I should try to pull together an actual lecture for next week. I had been reduced to showing documentaries to my class that covered aspects of the periods we were discussing, but I didn't feel good about that. That was not exactly teaching.

I called Tom on his cell, though I knew I wouldn't get him. I got to at least hear his voice for two seconds. I just left a message. "Call me."

Then I went in search of wine and chocolate. For lunch. That combination of alcohol and sugar made me feel a lot better, but it didn't actually help me write a lecture.

At 3 p.m., my text tone sounded, and it made me nearly jump out of my skin. Lindsay. "*Call this number*" it said, and the number followed. I pressed it, and it rang once and he answered.

He started right in with no preamble.

"Nadar has determined that Williams is indeed both Crawler and Blue Leopard. Under his task force authority, he has gotten us a warrant to search Williams' apartment, confiscate relevant items and take him into custody. Warrant just came through."

Wow, I thought, that was fast. But then again Williams was a threat and wasn't that the whole FBI thing, stopping threats?

"That will go down about ten tonight, so stay home, lock your doors, and I'll call you when we've got him."

"Okay," I gulped.

"Head down, you hear me?" Lindsay said in a really FBI guy kind of a voice.

"I hear, but listen," I said, urgently. "I think you should also alert Dr. Abubakar to stay home with his wife and child this evening, perhaps even ask him if he feels he needs additional protection. These guys have targeted him several times."

"On my list," Lindsay said briefly and hung up.

Just then I heard Molly's joyous "the kids are home!" bark, and I went to the front hall to hug them. I'd need to tell Carol and Giles, and of course Tom, what was going to happen tonight, but not now. Now I'd eat vegetables and hummus with my kids and hear about their day.

As the kids ran toward the kitchen, I took a second to text Tom. "*Call me absolutely as soon as you can.*" And then I also texted Alice. Just one word. "*Tonight.*"

Chapter 31

Do what you gotta do so you can do what you wanna do.

—DENZEL WASHINGTON

Thursday night

I'd explained what the FBI agent had said was going down to Tom when he called around dinnertime.

"Kelly and I will sleep over tonight," he'd said immediately.

I was glad.

I'd asked Tom, Carol, Giles, and yes, Kelly, who had arrived in time for dinner, to come in to the library while the kids were upstairs doing their homework and just indicated the bare bones. The FBI was executing a warrant tonight, and it was someone I'd identified. I emphasized there was likely no threat at all to me, but each one of them needed to promise to keep this absolutely secret, not that any promise was necessary for the others. Kelly, I wasn't sure, and I over-emphasized to her what the FBI agent had said about secrecy. I almost asked her to give me her phone, but I didn't. I did tell her flat out she couldn't tell Zeke until it was all over.

"Well, yeah," she'd replied, a little huffy. "Like duh."

Giles had just looked at me, and I knew he was taking in the dark circles under my eyes and my pale, drawn face. I could have told him he didn't look much better, but I didn't. We all just went in to the kitchen and ate his signature recipe called *Thiebou jen*. It was the national dish of Senegal, a stuffed fish simmered with vegetables in tomato paste, some very tasty spices and served over rice. When he'd first made it a couple of years ago, he'd said it was for celebrations. I hoped that would be the case tonight. I ate some of the stew and then went upstairs and gulped a handful of my antacids. I noticed the big bottle was now only half full.

* * *

Tom was sound asleep next to me, but I was sitting up in bed waiting. Lindsay had said he'd text me when the warrant had been executed and Williams was in custody, but my phone screen was stubbornly blank. I knew this because I was staring at it. It was nearly 11:00 p.m.

Molly suddenly stood up with her head cocked, listening. She had come in to stay by me after the kids had fallen asleep. And then, my less acute human ears also heard a noise.

It was breaking glass. Someone was trying to break in.

I shook Tom, and he was characteristically alert within seconds.

"Someone is trying to break in. Call the campus police, not, I repeat, not the Chicago police." I gave him the correct number. "I will go draw whoever it is away from the house. Get Kelly, Carol, and Giles up, and everybody needs to stay on alert. Let the boys sleep if you can. Stay here on the second floor. Don't go downstairs."

Tom started to argue, and I didn't even respond. I hurried to my closet and got out my gun and some ammunition from my safe. I loaded the gun, put it in my waistband, happy I had remained dressed in jeans and a sweatshirt. I took out my old handcuffs, and, what the hell, I also grabbed the retractable baton. I buckled on my bullet-proof vest.

I came back out of the closet, and Tom just looked at me. I think he realized I wouldn't waste time on talking.

"I called them," he said flatly.

"Good," I said and hurried down the stairs. Molly followed, growling in a low tone.

Now I could hear the noise was coming from the back of the house. I grabbed some keys from my purse, unlocked the security devices on a side window and slid up the frame. One thing I had spent money on in this old house was security.

I climbed over the sill and dropped to the ground. It was only four feet down. Molly put her paws on the sill to follow me. I pushed her back and slid down the window. She woofed in shock at being excluded. She'd had a taste of perps and clearly wanted more. But I didn't want her to get hurt again.

I crept along the wall of the house toward the back. I could now hear banging and scraping and furious swearing.

"Kill your brats, kill that N*****, kill you, you race traitor white woman, kill you your s*** mutt and then go over a kill the Mudslime and wife and brat. You're all dead you're all dead."

It was Williams, and he had literally become a berserker now, especially since he had encountered my steel core door, high grade locks, and key-locked windows. I could see broken glass on one window next to the door, but he'd been unable to unlock it, and he was too grossly fat to fit though where he'd broken the glass. He had failed at jimmying the lock, so he was trying to batter down the steel door.

Molly's barking got louder and that seemed to further infuriate Williams.

"I'll gut you, you filthy mutt," he yelled, swinging a crowbar wildly at the door.

I crept up behind him. He was in such a state, he wouldn't have heard the Mormon Tabernacle Choir if it had marched up behind him singing "Amazing Grace."

"Just shut up," I said as I got behind him. "You're not getting anywhere near my dog or anyone else." He didn't even have time to turn before I hit him over the head with the baton. He went down like a bag of wet cement.

Even though he was stunned for the moment, I grabbed the crowbar and an ugly Luger pistol he had placed on the top step next to him and tossed them into the yard. Then I cuffed him to be sure he'd stay under control, and I sat down on one of his legs to keep him from jumping up if he regained consciousness.

I took out my phone, and Lindsay took that moment to text me. "*Got in Williams apartment. He's not here. Collecting evidence. Some agents out looking for him.*"

I texted back, "*Got him. He was trying to break into my house. I knocked him out and cuffed him.*"

My phone rang.

"Cops on the way?" Lindsay asked, breathing hard.

"Campus cops only," I said. "I'm not nuts."

"Almost to car. Heading to you. Hang on to Williams."

"I will," I said, and he hung up.

Just then Steve White came around the north side of my house, his gun drawn.

"Hi, Steve," I said.

He assessed the scene and holstered his gun.

"Hi, Kristin. Want me to let Alice know?"

"Yes, thanks." Better him than me.

I called Tom and gave him a quick summary.

"I'll come to the back door," he said.

"No dice," I replied, looking at the battered door. "I bet it won't open. It's badly damaged. Campus cop here, FBI on the way. Just come out the front and walk around the back will you?"

"Sure," Tom said, and I could hear he was moving. "Down, Molly," he said.

My cell phone rang again. Alice.

"You okay?" she asked.

Was I?

"Yes," I said, and I thought I actually was. For the first time in weeks. I filled Alice in.

As I hung up with Alice, somebody flipped on our backyard flood-lights and pretty soon the yard was fairly crowded. Carol had stayed with the boys, who fortunately had not awakened, but Tom, Giles, Kelly, Molly, Steve, and I were standing around looking at the unconscious Williams. Tom had thought to put Molly on a lead. That was good as she was glaring at Williams and had bared her fangs. I'd had Tom check Williams's vital signs when he'd arrived, and Tom said he was okay, just still out.

Then Lindsay, Nadar, and a team of agents came rushing around the side of the house.

I showed Lindsay Williams's crowbar and gun on the ground and then told them they could come meet us in the kitchen when they were done out here. They'd need to use the front door.

My team and I went in and had hot chocolate.

Except for Molly, who had warm milk.

Chapter 32

Dr. Barringer: There is one outside chance for a cure. I think of it as shock treatment - as I said, it's a very outside chance... Have you ever heard of exorcism? Well, it's a stylized ritual in which the rabbi or the priest try to drive out the so-called invading spirit.

—WILLIAM PETER BLATTY, *THE EXORCIST*

Friday

"Kristin, could you tell us what you can about where the investigation into John Vandenberg's death and related issues stands?" Adelaide asked from her position once again at the head of the seminar table. She actually looked okay, especially considering what was going down here. She had good color in her face, and she was no longer sinking into the big armchair.

This was billed as a faculty meeting, but we had a lot on our plate this afternoon, and apparently first up was debriefing the colleagues on the capture and arrest of Horace Williams. Unusual as academic meetings go, but not so much with this department.

"I can't give you details on the ongoing investigation, largely because I don't know them, but I can tell you that Detective Horace Williams has been arrested for the murder of John Vandenberg, as well as for related charges." Including the attempted break-in at my house, but I kept that to myself. Lindsay had given me some updates earlier in the day, especially Williams's arrest, and how he fit in to the online white supremacist group. Lindsay had said he had already fully briefed Captain Gutierrez and together they would see the university president later in the day. I'd bet the president would not be thrilled with that.

Adelaide did not visibly react, but I'd already talked with her at around noon. I'd also briefed Aduba not an hour ago in this very room. He currently was stone-faced, but he had been clearly shocked earlier to hear that this conspiracy had involved law enforcement. "Here? Even here?" he'd said a couple of times. The U.S. was apparently still viewed in some places around the world as a country where law was respected and enforced. It was jarring to many immigrants to find out what was actually the case. And to citizens, I'd thought bitterly.

Donald Willie was hearing this for the first time, however, and his face was increasingly pale under his faux tan.

I cleared my throat.

"As I understand it, Williams and another detective, Albert Brown, who knew each other and had worked together before, joined a website called WhiteLivesMatter and found a focus for their own feelings of inadequacy and resentment. They seem to have encountered one of our students, Jordan Jameson, on that same website, and they all began to message each other in different ways."

I paused and took a sip of cold coffee.

"Anyway, when Dr. Abubakar was appointed, they were all outraged. When his inaugural lecture title was announced, they perceived it as an attack. Jordan had been recruiting other students into an informal, on campus, white supremacist network by using the chat rooms of violent video games. John Vandenberg was one of them, as was his roommate, Brant Hingston. They planned the noose incident, and Jordan was the one who hung the noose. Brant made the flyers."

Brant was in this up to his neck, I'd learned.

"Then John Vandenberg received results of a DNA testing kit he'd done to showcase his pure whiteness, and he'd been shocked and appalled to find out he had both African American and Native American ancestry. He fatally shared that information with his roommate, Brant, who had then told the key conspirators. They seem to have determined to kill John to, as it were, kill two birds with one stone. They could purge this mixed-race guy from their group and frame me as the hated woman, and Giles Diop as the African immigrant threat, at the same time. I believe, though this will need to be proved in a court of law, that Williams and Brown did the actual murder, but I believe Brant had known. I don't know that for certain."

I stopped and sipped a little coffee again. I had already decided to leave out my online trolling, especially since I planned to continue it. But as a faculty group, we had to think about the future. And I had to channel what I'd learned this fall from Giles about conflict reduction. It was going to be an effort.

"Chaplain Jane Miller-Gershman has identified a pastor from Michigan, Rev. Dunn, who works to keep young, white men from being recruited by these white supremacists, or to get them out of it if they've been pulled in. He will give a lecture here on that right at the beginning of winter term. But, we need more."

I took a card from in front of me and held it.

"Donald," I said in as friendly a tone as I could manage, "here's a place where you could really be of help."

Willie jumped slightly, and then sat forward in his chair. His face flushed. He looked very angry.

"What? What do you mean? What are you accusing me of now?"

I suspected this would be his first reaction. "Do not meet anger with anger" I heard Giles say in my head. Yeah, yeah, Giles.

I took a breath and let it out slowly.

"I mean your expertise is what we need on this campus to prevent more recruitment by these white supremacists, and we must think about those young men who have already been drawn in. How to get them out?"

I held out Rev. Dunn's card.

"Chaplain Jane and I would be very grateful if you would connect with Rev. Dunn and see about how you both think that could happen."

I took another calming breath. It was time to quote what the psychiatrist had said.

"Apparently there is a need structure that makes some young, white males vulnerable to this. Surely with your training, you know about that."

A grudging nod. I was getting to him.

"May I give you this?" I asked, waiting apparently patiently while thinking to myself "come on, let's get on with this." But I didn't say anything.

Donald got up slightly from his chair. I did the same, and he took the card from my outstretched hand.

He looked at it for a second and then began to talk about Jung. I confess I tuned that out a little, but I tried to look interested.

He was finishing. " . . . in a positive way."

"So right," I said.

Adelaide looked at me like I'd grown two heads. Well, Adelaide, I said silently, this is the new me. Positive communication. Some of the time at least.

She visibly shifted gears.

"Thank you, Kristin, and thank you Donald." She nodded at both of us.

"Now, Aduba, will you fill us in on the progress on our next faculty search?"

Aduba put his glasses on and opened a neat file folder on the table in front of him.

"Certainly. I have drafts here of the position description and, when we are all agreed on this, I understand there are standard procedures for advertising open positions."

We all nodded.

Nothing like the regular process of academia to numb the mind.

✳   ✳   ✳

The discussion was finally winding down when I heard noise from the hall. It was the caterers.

The Kim, Ay-seong Prayer and Meditation Room dedication ceremony was going to be held at 3:30 p.m., before the Jewish sabbath started. We needed to get on with it. There would be a small reception in the hall following the dedication.

Adelaide quickly ended the meeting.

I jumped up to go check on the arrangements. I had ordered from my new friends, the African vegan folks, and they were, as I expected, all set. I checked my watch. People should be arriving shortly.

I looked into the little room, and it looked so wonderful. The lighting was recessed and had several different dimmer settings. There were half a dozen lovely Muslim prayer rugs as well as a little fountain dribbling water over some polished stones. A small, wooden credenza held prayer books and scripture from a dozen faiths. Jane, her wife, Rabbi Emily Gershman, Aduba and our new Buddhist friend, Azan Nakshatra, would preside over the dedication itself.

The first person to arrive was Edwin Porterman. I could see his close-cropped, black hair and his dark eyes first as his tall frame ascended the last stairs. Then I saw a magnificent hat and under it a white-haired, African American woman. That must be Aunt Melda, I thought, touched. Edwin's Aunt had raised him and done a superb job. He had started to fall in love with Ay-seong not long before her murder. Edwin had flown in from England where he had a scholarship to the London School of Economics. I rushed down the hall to greet him and meet Aunt Melda of whom I'd heard so much.

Just below them, I saw Zala Abubakar and Jachike, who liked to be called Jack, coming up the stairs. Jack immediately let go of his mother's hand when he saw me and ran up the last few steps. "Where are Sam and Mike?" he asked me excitedly.

"They'll be here, don't worry." I patted his shoulder, and, as he raced toward his Dad, I greeted Zala more formally.

True to my word, Carol, Giles, Sam, and Mike were coming up the stairs, and my two did the same as Jack and raced up the final stairs. I got a brief hug, and then they saw Jack and sped down the hall to him, pulling some cards from their pockets. Pokémon cards had replaced screen time as their new passion, and the three boys went to the end of the hall, sat down on the floor, and began to spread out the cards. Mrs. Abubakar looked pained as Jack's white pants and embroidered tunic started to accumulate the grime of our floors, but she did not say anything.

Then the elevator door opened and Dr. Hercules Abraham, Holocaust survivor and Professor Emeritus of Judaism, came out. I knew him to be a brave man, witness his willingness to take our elevator. He came directly to me, arms already open to give me a hug. He had flown back from France for this occasion, and I was so glad to see him.

Alice and Mel arrived, and I was really touched to see they were both in spic and span uniforms.

I was still looking for Tom. There was always that "will he have an emergency" disquiet when expecting Tom, but, there he was now, coming up the stairs and with both Kelly and Zeke. I said hi to them, and then Tom stood next to me, taking my hand.

I squeezed his hand, and then I left him to check on the dedication leaders. They were in my office that I had left open for them. I peeked in, and Jane nodded to me.

"I think we're set."

They came out together and stood at the door of the little room, a pale gold light from its beautiful sconces spilling out on to the floor of the hall.

Prayers were said and objects donated and blessed. The Abubakars presented a small and exquisitely carved statue of Jesus sitting on a rock, clearly preaching the Sermon on the Mount. Hercules had brought a beautiful Korean language bible for the room. Buddhist chants, Christian prayers, readings from the Koran and a blessing in Hebrew flowed into the room.

Then Edwin stepped up and read a poem he had written for Ay-seong.

I hadn't cried until then, but I couldn't help it. His grief was still so raw.

I will ask him for a copy, I thought, have it framed, and it will hang on the wall.

Sadly, Ay-seong's family had never responded to my invitation.

We all milled around in the hall, munching on the tasty spread of hors d'oeuvres and drinking juice. I was so glad to see Donald had stayed, and he was talking a mile a minute to Adelaide, who looked very polite about it.

Probably outlining more about how Jung would deal with white supremacist recruitment.

Hercules came up to me and gently nudged me down the hall so we
could talk in private. He said he had been following the events on campus
and was deeply concerned.

He was right to be, I thought.

"These are the same ones who herded my people into boxcars, Kristin.
They must be stopped."

"I know, Hercules, and I'm doing my best," I replied.

"Your best it is true is always more than enough," he said, a little of his
usual twinkle in his eyes. He left me and went over to talk to Aunt Melda.

I went over to where Aduba was standing, looking down at the three
boys messing around with the cards.

As I came up, I heard Jack say, "and I'm going to name my new dog
Hulk."

I glanced up at Aduba.

"Yes," he said, resignedly, "we will have a small poodle named Hulk."

"Well, he'll be a big dog inside," I said smiling. "The good news is I can
give you lots of pointers on house-training."

Aduba looked back at me, his smiling face turning serious.

"Then you should call me 'Abu,' it is my name with friends."

"Okay, thanks. I will." I paused. "And some of my friends call me Odin."

Abu looked startled for a minute, and then we both laughed.

Oh, good, I thought. He's staying.

Chapter 33

Hate cannot drive out hate; only love can do that.

—Dr. Martin Luther King, Jr.

Saturday

Tom had asked me to go for a walk along the lake again. I realized, astonished, I was free to do it. Carol had told me the boys had a last minute birthday party invite, so she'd take them to that, and then she and Giles were going to go to a friend's house. I'd wanted to visit with Edwin, but he'd said he wanted to visit some Chicago friends before he returned to England.

It was a lovely fall day. Chicago has normally lousy weather, but fall is the best season. It was warm and sunny and there was hardly any wind, even by the lakeshore. Probably one of the last days like this before winter sets in I was thinking as we walked along. We were approaching a boathouse a little north of Hyde Park.

Tom cleared his throat and stopped. I stopped too and looked at him and the look of utter terror on his face almost stopped my heart. His sparkling blue eyes were nearly grey, as, I noted in alarm, was his face.

"Tom!" I said, facing him.

"Wait. Wait." He said. "Let me just get this out." He cleared his throat again.

"I love you Kristin. I love you so much I can't stand us to be apart any more than we have to. I want to marry you."

"Oh, oh, Tom." I was just robbed of speech for a minute. Then I saw his open face, and I knew I needed to speak.

"I love you too, more than I can say."

A little color came back into his cheeks, and I thought he started breathing again.

"And yes, Tom, I would love to marry you, but I have to talk to the boys, and . . . "

What? Tom was waving his arm in the air. And then I heard them behind me.

Around the corner of the boathouse came Sam, Mike, Kelly, Carol, Giles, Zeke and even Edwin running toward us carrying balloons. Giles had Molly on a leash, and she had a balloon tied to her collar. Alice and Mel were coming too. And holy, moly, coming more slowly behind them were Natalie and Vince Ginelli. Kelly reached us first and handed the balloon she was carrying to her Dad. I saw a sparkle. It had a ring tied to it.

"I thought I'd better not let the dorks carry this balloon, or it would be floating over to Michigan by now," she said. But her eyes were full of tears.

Mike and Sam ran up. Sam had a balloon, and Mike was carrying a big box of what looked like chocolate truffles.

"Come on, you three," Tom said as he untied the ring from the string of the balloon. "Let's get this ring on her finger so we can go eat!"

Trembling, I held out my left hand, and four sets of hands, big, medium, and small, pushed the ring on to my finger. I kissed them all, and then I held the boys close to me, one on each side. I could feel how tense Mike was. I looked down at him and little tears were rolling down his face, dropping on to his T-shirt. Tom had one arm around Kelly, and then he bent and his other arm went around me and the boys.

I looked up and met the eyes of Natalie and Vince. They were crying too, but bravely also trying to smile.

Marco, I thought, you will always be with me.

"You know," Sam burst out, "there's cake back at the house. And stuff to drink. And we can eat these chocolates! He picked up the box and shook it." Yes, probably now more as chocolate mousse, but they'd still taste good.

"Sam's right," Tom said, smiling down at him.

I turned and kissed Tom.

"Come on!" Sam said, impatiently. "You can kiss later!"

How true.

And there would be chocolate truffles.

Till death do us part.

Chat Room of Video Game "Predator"

Beelzebub821: man my mom is on me all the time she read some stuff about how bad this white pride is keeps visiting parent websites wants me to get out more its so S***** she tried to look at my computer browsing for F***'s sake

Incubus75: gotta stay strong gotta stay white your DNA has u set for success don't blow it just don't listen and can show you how to hide where u go

Beelzebub821: sure sure white is right yeah but makes me want to split take off she's on me all the time show me how to hide it

Incubus75: theres a lot you need to do right here talk more soon we have to save this country so u gotta lie tell her she is so right and hide your stuff this is a war

Beelzebub821: I hear you

Discussion Questions for
When Demons Float

1. The author uses the image of demons to show how tempting violent extremism can be. Is this an image or idea you find helpful or unhelpful in understanding how white supremacy is spreading in the United States?

2. College and university campuses around the country are struggling with the difference between free speech and hate speech. How do you define each of those concepts? Can free speech be protected while hate speech is regulated?

3. The events on campus are stressing Kristin's relationship with her friend Alice Matthews, the campus policewoman, and also with Giles Diop, part of the graduate student couple that helps take care of Kristin's children. What does she change in her own behavior to try to improve communication with each of them? Is she doing enough? Too much?

4. Kristin is trying to find a way to relate to her Muslim colleague, Dr. Aduba Abubakar. What do you think Dr. Abubakar thinks of her efforts? Do you think he will stay at the university or leave?

5. Sam and Mike, Kristin's young sons, figure out how to get around the parental controls on their tablets. What should parents be doing these days to protect their kids and teenagers when they go online? Is it even possible?

6. The plot of *When Demons Float* is based on the rise of white supremacy in the United States and the book explores why this kind of extremism is attractive to some people. The psychiatrist Kristin consults to try to understand this phenomenon tells her that online extremism fulfills a need for some people who feel alienated and resentful. For others, it is a way to get power over others. Why do you think people are attracted to extremism today?

7. Even as Kristin and her family and friends are celebrating at the end of the book, more recruitment of young, white males into white supremacy goes on. Can we really eliminate this in the age of the Internet? Or, is the Internet not to blame, and if so, what is the primary problem?

Made in the USA
Columbia, SC
07 July 2020